IN THE RAFTERS OF PARIS

IN THE RAFTERS OF PARIS

Jeff Senatra

EMPTY HANDS ETC. PRESS

Preface

Having an affiliate close at hand is crucial, someone you can alert and trust in time of need. When a large continental landmass *and* an ocean lay between you and your property, reliable resources must be gathered. The man I turn to for this is one Patrice Bujon. I call him Patrick, and he's been looking after my place for years.

It's an old servant quarters on the top floor of a renovated building in the Mouffetard district of Paris, Latin Quarter, 5th Arrondissement. Somehow or other, you'll forgive my glossing the details (after all what follows is not about me and my real estate, but rather is a recount from one who briefly lodged there), back in the 80s I caught wind of its vacancy while in Paris doing some graduate studies work, and moved in for six months or so. When it was time to return to New York, being in position to handle rent both in Brooklyn and in Paris, I kept the lease, recognizing what I had on my hands. I've used the apartment often over the years, but after I moved to California I found myself using it less and less. I began renting it out to friends when they traveled abroad, and then to friends of friends, and so on. Before I knew I was filling it regularly just by word of mouth, and this small Paris apartment became a splinter cottage industry unto itself.

Naturally, it being a very old building, with the frequent change of occupants wear and tear on the place is a concern. I hired Patrick to keep things in order. He makes small repairs as needed and checks in on the place at my request. Lapse of time between guests is usually minimal, but sometimes a number of weeks do pass when the apartment stands empty. In these times I ask Patrick to stop by before the next scheduled renting, just to make sure things are kosher.

During one of these periods Patrick entered the apartment and discovered something unusual. There, I was told, piled on the table in a neat stack were notebooks, a total of six in all. Five were the standard composition variety, but one was bound in beautiful, soft brown leather. It looked of excellent grade. That one came first in succession. A scrawling and seemingly hurried hand had filled the first five books cover to cover, but only partially made its way into the sixth; a large portion of that one remained silently empty.

Scrawling is hardly apt description for the handwriting. The penmanship throughout was awful, irreverently sloppy with arrowed lines frequently snaking from bunched-up words squeezed along margins and riding over scratch-outs. It was quite difficult to read in parts. Patrick doesn't speak English so couldn't read it at all, and didn't know what to make of his find. He notified me by telephone and then sent the notebooks to my home in Redwood City. It was obvious who they belonged to, and the last I'd heard from him was when the apartment key came back to me in the mail the way I'd sent it—taped to the same thin piece of brown cardboard I'd taped it to, with no note. When weeks passed and still my messages remained unanswered, curiosity got the better of me and I began reading. At first the handwriting was a struggle. It was mostly in black ink but broke into blue two/thirds the way into the forth notebook, and by then I was well enough acquainted with the script that decipherability came more easily. The work was so intensely personal I felt a sense of shameful violation in reading it (there were little blur splotches sprinkled throughout the pages, and I knew instantly what those blur stains were when I saw them), but the raw realness moved and fascinated me.

More time passed and I made another round of attempts. The

phone number I'd been calling was no longer in service, and my emails were met with the same void-like silence. I searched the internet and there were past mentions of him but nothing current, and he didn't seem to belong to any online social community. The writing had clearly been abandoned. I thought of sending it on to the address where I'd sent the apartment key, but having no proof he still resided there I was reluctant to do that. A strange guardianship developed in me for these notebooks, and the idea of them becoming lost was not one I could easily accept. I was drawn to read them again, this time jotting down notes and copying out lines as I went in order to see the words in more legible form, just for my own pleasure, which evolved into typing out the manuscript altogether. During that process I'd made some adjustments to the text. I then shared the manuscript with a friend, a Stanford man who for his own reasons asks to be excused from any credited mention, but who also expressed similar, though more restrained nods toward the raw beauty of the work. A series of events was set into motion from that viewing like trees slowly falling one after another, each knocking the next down, eventually facilitating here the presentation of Patrick's discovery.

Of course, due to the personal nature of the notebooks, pains have been taken toward identity preservation. New names have been found for those appearing most predominantly in the writing, prominent among them the author himself. Roman Parish is the name I've invented for him. I never met Roman face to face though I did have a few phone conversations with him, and recalling those conversations after having read what he wrote the name Roman Parish seemed evocatively appropriate. Other disguising efforts have been employed as well to ensure protection, both by the author and by myself, but I won't go into them here. The story the author tells, however, has been left intact for better or worse and has not been altered or elaborated upon in any way, except one.

Near the beginning of the fourth notebook a passage is boxed-in with pen strokes, setting it apart from the rest of the text. Verb tense shifts from past to present here and that stymied the transcription process temporarily, until it dawned on me. Because the scene depicted is later repeated with slightly different wording but once again in past tense, the passage seemed to be isolated for a reason, and after some consideration I believed it contained significance to the author in a way I didn't quite understand. In the end, to eradicate the issue for myself primarily, but also as a way to salvage the material whole without any loss, right down to the opening quote bannered ominously across the top margin of the first page of the first notebook, the leather-bound one, I chose to begin the manuscript with this orphan passage as a kind of disembodied introduction. And that, aside from the title (which was cobbled from the recurring moniker the author seemed fond of using for the apartment) and for the correction of obvious technical errors, as well as guessing at an unreadable word here and there (I thought that better than elliptical or bracketed blanks), *that* is the only radical liberty I have taken with the work. And I can only hope, if the author is indeed still among us and should become aware of what I've done here, having released his story this way to the world, I can only hope he will not be too displeased with the outcome, and that in leaving his story behind, some vehicle, some peaceful craft, however small, has been found to carry him forward.

Richard Fields
Redwood City, California

If you bring forth what is within you, what you bring forth will save you.
If you do not bring forth what is within you, what you do not bring forth
Will destroy you.

Gospel of St. Thomas

Matice lies beside me. It's pronounced *Mateechay*, not like *Matisse*. I'd made that mistake the first night we met and was immediately scolded. I hear her, Matice, breathe heavily beside me in the blue evening dimness that's filling the apartment like smoke and rising up to us in my bed. She's turned away from me on her right side. Sounds like she's breathing through her mouth but because her face is hidden I can't tell. This is the first time she's slept next to me. She says she doesn't sleep with people. This is the third time we've had sex and she's never stayed the night. She won't stay tonight either this is only a nap, though it's almost 10 o'clock.

I study the slanted beams above us. The hallway light suddenly goes on and illuminates the round window in the wall to my left. It's like a porthole in a ship. To open it you tip it forward from the top. It is open, and a cool cross-breeze pulls over us coming up from the open window below and streaming through the halfmoon-shaped gap in the slanted wall between the center beams where they meet the platform of the loft. Yellowish light now fills the porthole. I hear a door close and a lock turn, then the click of heels, sounds like a woman's, descending the wooden stairs. I'm on the top floor, the fourth, reached by a wide winding stairway. I listen to the footsteps grow fainter until they reach the bottom. After a moment the hallway light goes out, it's on a timer, and the bluish hue returns. I'm in Paris…I say it in a whisper to myself as I stare at the beams. I have to keep reminding myself of this because I can hardly feel it, the reality of it. I'm in Paris…I pull my left leg out from beneath the thin white comforter and lift it naked to touch a beam above. Pointing my toes I feel the rough hewn surface of the dark wood with the tip of the big one. This is all the space there is between the single mattress and the uppermost slant of the ceiling overhead. On the side where Matice lies there's maybe a foot above her. And here is where I like it best, in this lean-to of rafters.

This is not a movie, Matice said earlier. We'd spent the afternoon exploring a different arrondissement of the city, the 19th. First it was Butte Chaumont, then the surrounding neighborhood. On our walk back to my place we had stopped for a drink during Happy Hour in the Bastille, on St. Antoine.

I feel sorry for you, she said, looking at me over her pint of Heineken.

What she meant was that our little romance is short-lived, a passing of time nothing more, a temporary delusion and distraction for both of us. And she's right of course. I'll leave in a week and a half and she'll resume looking for men here in Paris. But I felt something burst in me when she said it.

This is not a movie. I feel sorry for you.

*****

It was raining when I left San Francisco. As I made my way to the airport raindrops slashed at the windows of the train when it emerged between stations and crawled up the glass like jittery spermatozoa. It was a soft spring rain, just heavy enough to get your attention and create the appropriate mood, but not problematic. The kind of rain I imagine on the day of my funeral. I opened the door to my apartment ready to leave, saw the rain showering down upon the sloping street and newly deflowered trees of my neighborhood, the wet luster of the fresh green foliage quivering through the needled gray, and said to myself: Perfect. Because it was. Because I was going to Paris as if I were going to my own funeral.

As I finished packing that morning my entire being shook, body and soul. I wept, as I'm weeping now as I write, weeping because I am afraid...afraid I'll never complete this, whatever it is...My pen just hovered over that last word for a good 20 seconds, that should tell you something...I'm weeping and afraid because this is all I have to keep me together, and if I fail here... If I fail...

That morning I kept stopping in the middle of doing things as I prepared for the trip, to sob, to take deep breaths, to ask myself what I was doing. I didn't know what I was doing. I must be out of my mind I told myself. Of course I was, had been for days. What the fuck are you doing? Over and over that question came. Who goes to Paris heartbroken and unemployed, alone, for three weeks? Plus, you were just there six months ago, with her. You've seen it, and to see it again knowing that you've already seen it, with her by your side, will haunt you. She'll *haunt* you!

At one point I stopped loading my bag, overwhelmed with in-decision on what to add next while trying to decide how much

I actually needed to bring, when suddenly I fell at the foot of my bed and prayed, to *some*thing, *anything* that might listen, prayed for help. I don't do that—pray—but everything in me screamed this was wrong, that it was irrational and foolish. But it was too late. Tickets had been purchased, arrangements made, friends, *people* knew I was scheduled to leave. If I didn't how would I look to them? Yet it was too much for me and I knew it. My nerves were unspooling and my mind was a thick cloud, my actions confused and circling. It was in my eyes. I saw it as I looked at myself in the mirror. I saw it in the eyes of others when they looked at me on the street. It was in my voice. Words, the few that came, came as if weighted in my throat dragged with the anchor of a heavy heart in ruin.

For days I'd been trying to figure out a way to gracefully halt the process. I saw no way out. And as I write this now, seated at the small red table in my tiny Paris hovel I've rented in the Mouffetard, looking through the raw-wood framed windows swung open to the cool morning air, looking out onto the rooftops and southern high-rises of Paris, a large pigeon like a grouse fluttering in the trees of the courtyard below and one roosting peacefully on the fish skeleton antennae of a neighboring apartment building, from somewhere I hear the lazy grunt of a raven, as I sit here writing this, I wish only to leave.

A t the airport I joined the long intestinal line coiled before the Air France check-in counter and stood there looking at those about me. They were mostly French. I spotted one obvious American couple, pale longhaired hippy nerds. The rest were French I could tell. And those were only the ones in line. There was also a group beyond the tape standing off to the left bidding bon voyage to family and friends. As I listened to them speak in French—joking, conversing animatedly, waving and gesturing, smiling, laughing, all seemingly so happy, happy people with happy lives—I found myself almost sneering. They made my stomach leap and tighten. In them I recognized my first bitter taste of the isolation that I was sure lay ahead.

I wanted to turn and run but stood my ground, invisibly crumbling, begging silently for someone to save me. I hoped to hell the flight would be cancelled due to that Icelandic ash cloud hanging over the Atlantic, wreaking havoc for so many, interrupting flights in the UK and elsewhere in Europe. No such luck. My flight was determinedly on schedule.

A woman behind me in line began talking on her cell, loudly saying her goodbyes to a friend, explaining how she'd been offered an apartment while in Paris through François but due to one thing or another it was not going to work out and she was staying instead at the hotel where her parents always stayed and although she was going to arrive before her parents this time the concierge, whom she'd spoken with when she'd called ahead and who of course remembered her, he'd of course set aside a room especially for her until her parents arrived, and the conference which she was going to Paris to attend was on Wednesday and she'd only be there a few days after that and on and on and on she went...

God I envied her. God how I envied that annoying woman.

She had a reason to go to Paris and knew people there, if only her parents—that's how squashed I am, envious of that woman for her parents—and best of all she was only going for a few days. I had none of that. I was going for absolutely no reason at all other than I presently was at liberty to. That, and the fact that I had promised myself this trip two years ago when my contract expired.

For nine years I had been at that job, installing exhibits at that museum, and over the last few years it'd begun taking me over. I was growing tired of taking care of other people's art, making them and the museum look good while my own artistic impulses dried up. I felt myself getting older with each passing year. My body had all kinds of aches and pains. The joints of my elbows and knees frequently burned. My feet hurt. I wouldn't be able to sustain that kind of work much longer. And what was worse my own art, my writing, was suffering, slipping further away from me with time and each new installation as my attitude ever darkened. I needed a break.

I was under full-time contract for two years while the museum underwent renovation and redesign, de-installation and then reinstallation in the newly remodeled facility. Prior to that I'd been primarily part-time with no benefits, so this was a big deal. First time I had medical insurance in a decade. At the end of that two year process my contract would be up and my future then to be determined. Would the museum offer to extend the contract or a permanent position? Would I go back on-call, coming in to install exhibits as needed as I'd done the first six years or so I'd worked there? No one knew. Personally I hoped for the latter, to allow time and energy for my own work again, but right up to the end I just never knew. True, I did express at one point, and loud enough those who mattered could overhear, that if I didn't get back to my own work soon I was going to *die*, but I didn't mean I wanted to leave altogether. I just wanted some time off.

So until the end I never knew what was going to happen, but I did know one thing: I needed to find it again, my creative voice, my desire and inspiration to write again. It had all gone from me and I needed it back. I thought the stimulation and new experiences of travel would help. Turns out my employers were very astute, very generous. After nine years they decided in the end to give me all the freedom in the world to chase my pursuits. It quickly became clear that when my contract was up I would not be asked back—ever. I lost my job one month after I lost her.

At the time I'd made that promise to myself, about the trip, at the beginning of the last two years, I had conceived of something very different. I dreamed of a broader European experience encompassing three or more countries perhaps, by train, for two to three months maybe. I had never done that kind of traveling. Prior to that time I had only been to Europe once before, for 10 days—Paris, Barcelona, Madrid—but that was the start of it. Those 10 days put Europe in the blood.

That trip was with a former girlfriend, the one before this last, seven years ago, the one who felled me first, the one who this last was responsible for finally getting me over. No one until her was able to provide this miracle. Five years in between and dozens of women came and went, but it was her finally who made me fall in love again.

After those 10 days, and the subsequent decimating end to that relationship (we'd been together five years), I had been dying to get back to Europe, especially Paris.

Like San Francisco, I fell in love with Paris upon sight. I felt so at ease with the culture, and, although I couldn't speak French, I seemed to fit in. Or so I imagined. At least my personal aesthetic and demeanor seemed to.

Anyway, I had promised myself this trip, but in between things happened. I met her, who changed my life, reawakened me to love, and gave me everything I could want, even more than I could've dreamed for. In between a second trip to Paris was arranged, a two week stay this time, and in those two weeks my love for Paris was confirmed. We had rented an apartment on rue St. Julien le Pauvre, off Quai Montebello, directly across the Seine from Notre Dame. I had only to open one of the long rectangular swinging windows in the living room that looked out onto rue St. Julien from the top fourth floor, lean forward slightly looking to the left, and there it was—Notre Dame in all her splendor. My God. And she had done that, provided that. I contributed only nominally. Even the airfare was free because of her. When we met she had just spent eight months traveling around the world for her employer, a software company; racked up a lot of free mileage. She was VP of customer service, or something like that. Went to India three times during that period to work with her outsourced team there, jetting over to Thailand or down to Australia each time from India for a little R and R, then maybe over to London, then New York, then Chicago (where she actually lived) before coming back to California where it would start all over again. Hers was a life utterly foreign to me or anyone I've ever known, and the success she had professionally allowed her to afford this beautiful French apartment on rue St. Julien.

And there were other things that happened too, many more things, including the loss of her love finally, and the trip as I originally conceived it did not manifest but mutate into an impetuous flight back to Paris, where I just was, with her, who left me almost two months ago now, left me shattered, and I no longer knew why I was about to board a plane to return where I was so happy for two weeks with her…well, just over a week with her really, she joined me five days into the trip, but happy nonetheless, barring the few fights that erupted. To me it was an amazing experience; I thought it was for both of us. I've learned recently though it was apparently otherwise.

My birthday was eleven days after our return to San Francisco, my first and only birthday with her. For a present she put together a collection of photos from the hundreds we had taken during our trip and made a bound hardcover book out of them, coffee table style. I loved it. A spectacular gift. I looked through it over and over and absolutely couldn't get enough of the photos in that book. I wanted to kiss them, eat them right off the page. There was even a dust jacket to the book, and on the inner flap of the jacket was printed:

Roman,
I will always be filled with warmth

when I think of our time in Paris.
Thank you for creating these
beautiful memories with me.
All my love,

Four months later when the end came it was not among the things she'd dumped on the stoop of my apartment building. When I had asked for it (evidently an oversight in my cleansing from her life—she gave it to me a few days later) explaining what it meant to me, how important it was to me, she kindly informed me that the photos in that book only masked just how bad she felt that trip had been. I thanked her for that, of course.

How quickly an object of pleasure and love—there were some really beautiful and artistically taken shots in that book, a pleasure to view disengaged from nostalgia altogether—how quickly and sadly that object turns to abject nausea. Just the thought of that book now makes me want to chuck my pathetic guts out.

So why was I going? Why was I about to fly thousands of miles away to a foreign-speaking country to a city that will only remind me of her, half out of my mind with a heart in shreds?

To save face, that's why. To retain respect in others' eyes, that's why I was going. The other reason, ostensibly the deeper, nobler one, the one I told myself was the *real* reason, that of going in the hope of finding my words again, that one only hung in the air now as overly romantic snotdrivel and delusion. But a man broken has only delusion to cling to, and I was clinging.

And so I stepped forward to the pretty but aging woman behind the Air France counter. She was brunette, with translucent skin wearing too much makeup, and her smile was large and happy, another one happy with her life, although this woman was American not French. I saw the enormous wedding ring she bore and thought of her husband, wondered how he could afford such a magnificent ring. They must have a wonderful life, I thought, she and her husband. Big house on the Peninsula probably, fine dining, regular wonderful Mediterranean exotic trips with other rich friends, tennis in the Tunisian sun. Her employment with an airline was inconsequential, an economic superfluousness just to keep her busy, with the added bonus of free travel for her and her husband, not that they needed it, but why refuse a little icing on the cake? How could her husband refuse that? And how did he enjoy his wife's enormous breasts? She had enormous breasts, this woman, but not in what I'd call a good way. I am not a large breast man myself. My taste runs small to medium. But nice breasts are nice breasts and that all depends upon the shape. This woman's hung in a massive pillowy drooproll beneath the dark blue uniform. I know they had absolutely nothing whatsoever in the world to do with me but they made me cringe all the same. Overall she frightened me a little, this woman. Those breasts, that smile, and the wide unfocused quality of her eyes that betrayed that smile, as if chemically induced. And I was jealous of her, of that ring and the happy security it suggested. And I just knew, even though I didn't like the look of her breasts I knew her husband did, and that they were happy and made love regularly, happily, and I was not happy. I was not I was not I was not, but I had been...Oh God, I was, for over a year, with her, and oh so recently...She was smiling at me now, this woman, eyes bulging and shifting, extending her left hand toward me weighted with that sparkling beast squatting there on her finger, waiting to receive my passport. And so, unhappily, I stepped forward.

One of the best things so far about being here in Paris, or one I've come to enjoy the most these first few days anyway, is sitting here at this little red table and looking out the window as I'm doing now. The table is the color of thinned blood, round, but one half of it is collapsed down against the wall beneath the window to conserve space. The apartment is so small that if the table were folded out completely it would take up most the floor.

I've just returned from another all-day journey around the city. It's now about 9 PM. I've thrown the window wide to let in the cool evening air. The sky is pale blue with a haze of clouds softening the horizon beyond the tall rectangular high-rises surrounding the city at its outer rim, as if standing sentry. They catch the declining sun's pale goldenpink light and dribble it down onto the rooftops of the smaller buildings nested on a slope before them. Black swallows weave through the portion of sky framed like a picture by my window. They sail through the air above the trees of the courtyard and way out over further rooftops like playful dive bombers, chasing each other in twisting circles and swoops. The moon is eggshell white and half full hanging exactly in the center of the window, near the top of the frame. Birds are singing, and I can hear accordion music wafting up from rue du Pot de Fer, on the other side of the building. A man plays to the restaurants that line the street there. It's a very peaceful scene, almost bucolic. Stark contrast to what I encountered down there in the Paris streets. It's Saturday, and hoards upon mobs are swarming. Love and sex abound. Incredibly sexy women were everywhere I turned. The torture of that was killing me.

During the five years I wandered in the wasteland between relationships I developed skills I'd never quite had before. Somehow during that period I'd learned techniques and acquired interactive abilities that attracted women. I'd never dated so much in my life or had so many fleeting sexual encounters as I did then. Sometimes they'd come without even trying. Suddenly someone would just be there presenting herself, as the situation presented itself, sitting down next to me at a bar, looking at me across a restaurant floor, whatever, and we'd be off. It was intoxicating, the exhilaration of those encounters, like the greatest drug, and I felt myself becoming addicted though resisting that dependency. The only other thing I've felt that came even close to it was performing on stage with my band.

A woman once followed me into the men's room at the Lone Palm. This was probably year 4 in the wasteland, by then I'd gotten pretty good. We had chatted briefly as she stood next to me at the bar while she waited for her drink order. Somehow we got talking about films. I had recently seen one she had seen and we'd both liked it. That led to the discussion of another film, and so on. It was an intelligent, sober interaction glazed with a thin sheen of flirtation, but that was it. She took her drinks and returned to her friend waiting at a table along the wall behind me. I kept turning around periodically to see if I could catch her eye again but there seemed to be nothing, so I forgot about it. Moments later I went to the restroom. There was a single urinal in there and a toilet in a closet. I was in the closet with the door locked behind me. I heard the outside music swell louder and then go muffled again and I knew someone had entered. There was a knock on my door. Yeah! I said over the sound of gurgling urination. Pause. Then there was another knock. YEAH! *Shit!* I said this time, annoyed now at the persistence. It was obvious the thing was occupied. I mean the door was locked and it was quiet in there, I was sure the guy could hear someone was pissing. I shook my head at the idiot, finished, and flushed. When I opened the door and walked out, ready to shoot whoever it was out there hell with my eyes, I saw that it was the girl from the bar and my heart jumped.

Blonde and pretty, she stood just inside the restroom door leaning against the wall perpendicular to the urinal, her arms behind her back distending her generous chest forward. There was the slightest, suppressed smile on her face. I stepped up to the sink just across from the closet door and washed my hands. I wanted her to see that I was clean. I was playing it cool but inside I was fire. Adrenalin pumped through me. The instant I came out and saw her, and saw nor sensed no surprise in her at seeing *me*, I knew why she was there. And the warm rush gushing through me at that moment was what is was all about.

She was very attractive—short pale-yellow hair swept loosely behind her ears, voluptuous full figure. She stood there sucking in her cheek to smudge away her smile, looking at me, waiting.

You in the wrong place? I said, never taking my eyes off of her as I quickly washed my hands, heart pounding.

I don't think so, she said.

Without looking I grabbed a stack of paper towels from the ledge to my right, wadding them in my hands and tossing them aside in one motion as I moved in my hurry to get to her. I cupped the back of her willowy dancer's neck, it was like a ballerina's, I cupped it in my right hand as my left arm encircled her curvy waist, gluing my body to hers, and kissed her. We stood there a moment that way, kissing against the wall by the urinal, until I felt sure someone would be walking in any second to mess things up. I danced her then from the wall into the closet.

The best thing about this door, I said, is that it locks, and I slid the thin bolt into place.

Now she stood against the wall inside the closet like she did by the urinal, and she looked so good I didn't know where to begin. I embraced her, deciding on that long, fine neck of hers, kissing it up and then down to those nice full breasts. She was wearing a thin sweater top with a lowcut V neck. I raised the bottom of her top and started kissing her belly, starting high up between the wings of her ribcage and fluttering downward, over the fleshy wink of her navel and further, down to the rim of her belt stretched low across her pelvis. Caressing the worn brown leather with my fingertips I slid them along to the wide brass buckle, considered a moment going lower still but felt it was too soon, then lifted my head again and went back upstairs, leaving her midriff exposed. Her breasts were the size of grapefruits and I held the weight of one in my palm. I began here now, and as I did out of the corner of my eye I saw her roll her top back down and knew she felt self-conscious, though I didn't know why. It was a perfectly nice belly, creamy and flat and pretty, and its skin was warm and wonderfully smooth—but women were like that, I thought. I distinctly remember thinking that. Women were often like that for some reason about their bellies, I'd seen it before, and I remember shrugging within myself then wondering about it as I carried on. We kissed some more and my hands continued to roam and they met no resistance, but then something came over me. Suddenly I couldn't do it. I wanted to terribly, but I wanted to do it properly, in this girl's bed or my bed or somewhere else but not there, not then, not in that bathroom. I remembered our conversation earlier. I longed for something so much more than this. I had been lost in this wasteland for so long and was so full of emptiness, so void of love, so weary of being so alone, that it just came out. My mouth lifted from her neck and, taking her face in my hand, I looked into her eyes. I was almost blind. My vision was seared golden with passion. It took a few seconds to focus, but her face emerged. A question hung silently upon it as she looked back at me.

See a movie with me, I said in a throaty whisper. Tomorrow night.

And as soon as I said it I knew. Her body shifted, slackened in my arms and sank back against the wall.

You want to see a movie with me?

Yes, I said, I do, and kissed her again, and she kissed me back but it was different now. It was the sluggish kiss of someone thinking.

Well if we're gonna see a movie, she said, then you have to leave. I need to pee, and you need to leave.

She pushed me out.

Fine, I knew what I'd done, suddenly shifted the whole dynamic and was now allowed no further liberties. Fine. I had changed spontaneous anonymous passion into a potential date, transmutation, humanized decorum restored. And if we were going to go on a date then I certainly couldn't see her pee now. Fine. Good. I was fine with that. That's what I want, I think—I thought—to wait, to do this the proper way so that a glimmer of hope can exist for...something, maybe...more.

I stepped outside the bathroom altogether. As I waited outside in the hall two guys walked past into the men's room. I imagined them getting quite a nice surprise to see her walk out of there. But wait. Now that I'd flipped things on her, I began thinking, maybe she'd take them on instead. Take them both on.

I waited. Seemed to be taking a while. My mind began to race. I started to walk back in there but stopped myself. No, couldn't do that. I waited some more. On the wall was an old black and white photo in a black frame. I occupied myself with it while I waited, examining it. An amazing shot capturing the Golden Gate Bridge during construction, taken from right on top of one of the towers looking down the long dipping cables. Christ, the balls of that, I thought, to stand up there...Finally the door swung open and the blonde came out.

Do you have a good memory? she asked.

Memory, the writer's honed tool...I've prided myself on my strong ability of recall, though it's proved a blessing and curse.

Yeah, I think so, I said to her. I'm gonna use it later tonight, I said to myself.

I don't want my friend to see us coming out of here together so I'm gonna tell you my number now, and then you walk out.

She told me her number, and as she stepped behind the curtain to the right into the ladies room she said with a smile: Nice bathrooming with you.

I repeated the number to myself until I could get back to my seat and punch it into my phone, which was in my jacket pocket draped over my bar stool. I called the next day, and a couple times after that, but I never saw this woman again. And so it frequently went in the wasteland.

It's an extreme example of course, and I don't mean to give the impression that this type of thing happened regularly by any means, I'm not saying I was anything special, but these things *did* happen.

Other times, most times, like anyone, I had to work for it. And developing strategy for dialogue on the spot, tailoring it to the moment and fitting it to the woman you're talking with while at the same time being genuine—I wanted to be genuine—developing timing, rhythm, anticipation, all of it, everything that went into it was part of a new art form I was continually learning then. And when it worked it was often more gratifying than the other because you knew it was you who created it, not just dumb luck or a gift from the gods, though there's always an element of luck in anything successful. But you knew you were largely to thank for your success and it was like taking pride in a job well done. And when she was in your arms, and your hands were loosening her clothing and touching her skin for the first time, exploring her body, like you knew you would, only a matter of time, and now here it was in your hands, the realization of your success could even be sweeter than what your hands held.

On a few occasions I'd said goodbye to one woman in the morning and that very night was undressing another.

Incredible and delicious to think of it now. Delicious and incredible. But as delicious as it all was at times it also became blandly empty. It was a stupid game, an empty repetitious and stupid game I was growing so weary of, as that moment with the blonde in the bathroom proved.

Of course at the time I'd regretted opening my big pussy mouth—she was fucking *hot* you idiot!—but at the same time, I didn't. Because what I was really looking for and needed I could not find, and didn't know if I ever would again.

Then, finally, jackpot.

Suddenly there she was, and my arrested heart resuscitated.

To be completely honest, it took a couple months to get rid of feeling single, to shed the notion that I could continue as I had been living, free to do as I pleased with whomever I pleased when the spark of the moment was ignited—I'd lived my life that way for so long up until then. But as our relationship grew and developed with time that feeling finally left and I was glad to see it go, and those skills I'd acquired while in the wasteland slowly atrophied. Gradually, happily now, I gave over to something I believed was greater. I gave over to her, to love, to the hope for a life with someone again.

And now...

Now she is gone, and at 44 I am once again in the wasteland, but with the rot of those skills withered, and I feel so vulnerably lost—emotionally, sexually helpless in the world. I'm afraid those skills are not the only wither I've been left with.

For weeks now, and God how it frightens me to admit this, but for weeks I have been unable to achieve a hands-free erection. And the ones I have been able to raise I've really had to work hard for, and are modest replicas at that. Lying there pulling nothing but putty...Can't even jerk off satisfactorily. Deflated will and ego = deflated dick. That's what she's left me with.

Stir that anxiety in with emotional annihilation, a heart that foolishly still believes it belongs to someone else, and the inability to communicate in the native tongue, and you've got a real winner here. Real fucking winner...

That's why I gave up finally and just came home at the start of the night tonight, home to my little red table and my window. Just couldn't take anymore...

I realize now that being here in Paris is my penance for losing her.

My God, how did I manage to lose her?

The swallows are very agitated now. They're zipping around in small packs of 3 or 5 or more, squealing as they sail across my square of sky. They remind me of the parrots on Telegraph Hill in North Beach last summer.

She had taken a vacation rental on Telegraph Hill for a month, last June. She was still doing that at the time, renting furnished apartments around the city because she still technically lived in Chicago, although her employer was in San Jose. When she wasn't elsewhere in the country, New York Baltimore DC LA for example, either for business or pleasure, she split her time between Chicago and San Francisco. At first when I met her she was staying in hotels, high-end hotels—Weston St. Francis on Union Square, the Palace, the W (I'd never even heard of W Hotel until I met her). When she needed to be present in her office in San Jose (the rest of the time she'd either work from her home in Chicago or was traveling) she'd take a room in one of these places. Usually she'd be in town a week to ten days, then off to wherever for about the same amount of time, then back again. That was the cycle. Eventually she realized it would be more cost-effective to her company, who was picking up the tab for travel and living expenses, to simply take short-term apartment rentals. It was also more comfortable for her, because she liked to cook and that made her feel more at home. And now, because I provided more incentive to extend her stays in San Francisco, it was more comfortable for us when we were together.

She always went through the same rental company. They had a number of apartments scattered about the city. If the same apartment she'd been renting wasn't available for her scheduled return she'd go online and choose another while away. She'd begun calling when she was out of town to ask me to check out the new place she was considering. I couldn't get inside the property but I'd go to the location and scout it out, get a feel for the building and the neighborhood and let her know my impresssions. We'd been together six months when she took the Telegraph apartment. It was probably the third or fourth place she'd rented at that point, and definitely the most expensive. I didn't need to this time, but I scouted it just the same, mostly out of my own curiosity. What's an apartment on Telegraph Hill going to be like? I was dying to know.

It was a beautiful late spring day when I went to check it out, a Saturday, I remember. Dragonflies helicoptered about, their wings glistening iridescent in the sunshine. I'd never seen such a heavy concentration of big, fat dragonflies in one spot. They hovered over a small garden that was just to the right of the building. Beyond the garden I could see the blue of the bay squirming. All I could tell was that the apartment was going to have an amazing view, and that's what I told her.

I was not mistaken. One glass wall opened out onto a patio with a sliding door overlooking the entire bay. Alcatraz and Angel Island floated just off the railing. You could see Sausalito and Tiburon and Treasure Island. You could see both the Golden Gate and the Bay Bridge. There was a high powered telescope resting on a tripod in the window that I amused myself with now and then, zooming in on people sailing on boats out there on the blue blue water, or taking a closer look at the surrounding terrain. It was a utterly breathtaking view. The apartment itself, however, was nothing special—long narrow awkward kitchen, cluttered living room. The bedroom was nice, but too bright. It also had a sliding glass door that opened onto the balcony adjacent the other sliding door in the living room, but there was no shade on the glass. Morning light filled the room and made it impossible to sleep late on the weekends, which we liked to do. Still, it was luscious to lie in that bed with her in the morning enveloped by light, looking through that glass at the blue out there just beyond our bare toes. That place was all about the view. Anyway, the parrots...

Telegraph Hill's famous Amazon parrots live in the trees of the neighborhood, by Coit Tower, which was just down the street from the apartment, and the apartment was directly in their flight pattern. They'd come streaking by in squawking green and red flocks just off the left corner of the balcony. You'd hear their crackling chatter first invisibly off in the distance, sharp and ricocheting behind neighboring buildings, and it quickly grew louder. When I heard it I knew to look immediately toward the balcony or I'd miss them. Suddenly there they'd be, a vibrant green and red streak blurring past diagonal to the balcony between the gap of buildings, yapping away as they headed home to their trees.

I loved it.

We put pieces of fruit out on the balcony table hoping to entice them so we could have a better, more sedate look, but the parrots weren't at all interested in that. They only streaked right by heading for home.

The swallows, which are now long gone—night's come in a kind of dark lavender and the moon shines high and bright in the right corner of the window—the swallows aren't nearly as dramatic as the Telegraph Hill parrots, but they have their own magic. Why am I suddenly reminded of Baudelaire? Maybe I'll visit his grave in Montparnasse this trip.

I've just noticed something. Resting on a thin ledge beneath the window along with some tea candles, a long splinter of wood (I see now that it has been broken off from the window frame, there's a gash ripped out at the bottom), an orange Bic lighter, and three small teal-colored ceramic bowls (holders for the tea candles), among these things is a box of matches. And on the cover of this box of matches is the image of a black swallow, wings sailed outward flying diagonally in the center of the box.

Someone else, some previous lodger here has enjoyed the magic of the swallows as well, and left a message in homage to them.

Maybe it's the magic of those swallows working on me, I don't know, but I can't get the moments of that Telegraph apartment out of my head now. I am just as present there, in my memories, as I am seated at this red table before my window in Paris. I see us as she drove us to work in the morning in her rented car. She always had a rental, most always a Prius, and most often a dusky blue Prius. Sometimes it was silver and sometimes pewter gray, dull as an old nickel, once in a while it was charcoal or taupe and a couple of times red, but most often it was that dusky blue color. Each time she came back into town she'd pick a new one up at the airport, preferred customer status. It's become symbolic of her to me, the Prius, and every time I come across one now in San Francisco, where they're ubiquitous it seems, everywhere you turn there's another fucking Prius, I can't help but flinch as if a fist was swiping wild at me from the street—especially if it's that dusky blue. I see us now, in this bullterrier-head-shaped hybrid, as we'd ascend into the cool morning air out of the parking garage beneath the Telegraph building, make the steep narrow climb out of there, turn right, loop around, and then drive up the other side of Telegraph. That street is divided by a wall and a median with trees, so we'd have to loop back up the other side, turning at the base of the trees where the parrots live, where the street hairpins, and drive up Telegraph one block to Union Street, make a right down the hill of Union a few blocks, then left onto Columbus, and here...here is where it'd start, the sensation that cameras were now rolling, that this was a film we were somehow starring in, that this was all some fantastic altered reality I'd slipped into with her—it was too perfect, too beautiful to be real...

From that turn onto Columbus what we'd see looming ahead, towering and growing larger like a genie rising from a spilled bottle as we approached, like a mottled pinheaded colossus guarding the downtown financial district, which its presence signifies—towering there at the end of the road where Columbus meets Montgomery was the tall pyramid of the Transamerica Building pricking the sky and almost daring us to enter puny from our quaint North Beach route. It was both imposing and gorgeous to behold, and every workweek morning I woke with her then this is what we'd see, and we'd laugh softly to ourselves as we drove along amazed at the magnificence of it, at the absurd beauty we'd experience as we began our days. From the view we woke to outside the apartment to the view of this manmade grandeur lording before us, I was filled with wonder at it all. How was this happening?

She'd drive us past the wide base of the Transamerica pyramid down Montgomery to Market Street, where I'd get out smiling after kissing her goodbye behind the wheel and catch the BART over to the East Bay where I worked, while she continued to San Jose 45 minutes south.

For the entire month of June we lived this way. When time in the apartment was up and she was leaving to go back to Chicago, she was always leaving to go back to Chicago, on that day we had spent all morning making love in the white sheets, holding each other and gazing from the bed through the patio door at the water out there. Later, after I'd showered and dressed, I was standing in the living room at the window when through the glass to the right I saw her. She was standing at the balcony door in the bedroom with her eyes closed, leaning against the open door frame. Naked except for red boyshort panties, she stood there with her arms folded loosely over her breasts letting the sun lap her entire body, smiling smiling out onto the beautiful splendor of the bay.

It was a perfect day, clear and sunny, and the view was stunning, but it was her I couldn't take my eyes from.

Seeing her standing there like that, skin liongold with a fading tan and long sandy blonde hair (it was still this color then) she took my breath away. Who was this beautiful creature and how did she come to enter my life?

She took her time getting dressed. Eventually she got into jeans and a tshirt and packed her bags. She called a cab (the Prius had already been returned at the airport after a short business trip she'd taken earlier in the week) but she was reluctant to leave.

I don't want to leave you, she said, and with the cab on its way we went back into the bedroom and took off our clothes.

It was hard and fast from behind, I knew she didn't have much time. The bed was on castors and rolled three feet away from the wall as if it were a raft set adrift, coming to dock against the dresser behind us. The door buzzed. It was the cab driver. He couldn't enter the building unless we let him in so we ignored it.

There was another buzz, a longer angrier buzzzzzzzzzzzzzzzz, but that was all. And when the buzzing finally stopped we fucked again in peace.

Sated finally, and dressed again, she called another cab. But now she was running late, in danger of missing her flight, and this time the cab took longer to show.

She got anxious, called yet again, a different company, and this cab arrived promptly.

Gathering her bags quickly she gave me a short kiss at the door and was off, but I on the other hand was in no rush to leave.

I walked back over to the big window and lingered alone at the telescope. I was never again going to experience a place like this in San Francisco and I knew it. I was breathing in my last deep breath of it, of that spectacular view, of my spectacular turn of fortune with this amazing woman. I looked around the living room one last time. There on a side table was a stuffed felt dragonfly someone had made. Emblem of the neighborhood, I thought, remembering the big dragonflies I'd seen the day I came to scout the location. Like the swallows outside my window here in Paris, the parrots and the dragonflies are the mascots of Telegraph Hill, and someone had left a message there too with their little stuffed dragonfly.

Finally, I'd had enough. I picked up my shoulder bag and flung the strap across my chest and walked through the apartment door, making sure it locked behind me.

The apartment was on the ground floor just off the lobby entrance and as I turned from its door toward the door to the building I saw a man through the glass pressing a button outside. I heard the faint buzz inside the apartment behind me. I walked through the small lobby and opened the outside door.

You call a cab? the man asked.

Nope, I said, and moved past him and the red white and green car parked idling on the driveway, feeling a little guilty. That *was* two ditches after all.

On my walk through North Beach I'd decided to stop at my favorite café, Caffé Greco, and as I sat at an outside table on the sidewalk in front, enjoying my usual cappuccino, I received a text, words I'll never again receive from her.

Made it. I love you.

T he woman at the Air France counter seemed a bit distracted as we went through the check-in process, frazzled even, regardless of the big smiles she offered.

I hope we still have the seat you wanted, I heard her say, speaking more to herself than to me.

It's an aisle seat, I said. Or a voice vaguely resembling mine did anyway. These were my first words directed to another human being that morning, and they were feeble to my ears.

She sliced at the keyboard with her long fingernails. Her eyes were wide and glazed-looking and they swiveled in her head, constantly flicking up and looking behind me as if expecting someone in particular to pass. All the while the smile was there.

Let me go check on something, she said, and suddenly walked away down the long counter to the left and consulted a moment with another woman checking in premium status passengers, then returned.

Oh she gave you a good one, she said. Upstairs. 11L.

I nodded.

I'll trust you, I said. Silently though I begged: Could you please stop this?

We gave your seat away already, she said, but this is a good one.

Her slender fingers continued to click at the keyboard. I watched them dance now, kicking a rapid Can Can across the keys. Then she asked for my bag and I collapsed the handle and handed it over and she wrapped the information sticker around the hand strap and tossed the bag onto the belt behind her. She handed me a boarding pass that looked strange. There was a small flap of paper attached to it that had a bar code, covering the bar code printed on the pass itself. Looking dubiously down at it in my hand as she directed me to my gate (despite what I said I did not trust this woman) I took it and walked off in the direction she pointed, but not to the gate.

I needed to change money, and on my way to check-in from exiting the train I passed a booth. I went back there. I walked by once, then back again, looking into the window each time as I passed. I stood in the corridor a long moment off to the right, just standing there looking into the glass at the two people inside. I knew I had to, but I wasn't eager to hand over this lump of cash in my wallet. Tentatively then, ever so slowly, I approached.

Finally I'd sidled close enough up to the window for the young man inside to notice.

Yes sir? Can I help you?

There was a young woman seated in there beside him to his left with her head down flipping through some papers. I looked at the two of them, these two young people.

I may be hypersensitive, in fact I know I am, but it seems the majority of people I see in the world now are younger than me. How did this happen? I see everything in my mind so clearly going all the way back to a toddler's stage. I remember youth in all its phases. Inside I feel young still. I look in the mirror and in my mind's eye at least I see a male of say 25 or 30 within the actual eyes of the 44 year old man looking back at me in the glass. I see the 19 year old with his first love, the one who taught him, or at least allowed practice enough to develop techniques of lovemaking which have endured and strengthened with time. I see the 13 year old big-eyed adolescent, hair parted in the middle and feathered glossy back covering the ears, soiling his white undies gray with mysterious uncontrollable nocturnal explosions and hiding them deep in the bathroom hamper. I see the four year old with the smile of heaven on his pale face, wearing a robin-egg blue wide-collared shirt as he poses in his first ever school photo. I see the wooden potty training stool with the red-rimmed white tin pot and the infant contentedly perched as he hums and kicks his tiny feet waiting to be aided in his finish. I see through the crystal onion of Time and its layers that continue to grow imperceptibly over one another but cannot fathom the osmotic accumulation and the frighteningly quick arrival and dispersion of each present moment.

Sir? Can I help you?

I need to change some cash, my voice strained.

To what currency, sir?

Euros. Sorry.

You want to buy some Euros, sir?

No I don't want any of this I said to myself. Yes, I said to him.

How much would you like to purchase, sir?

The day before I had attempted to get Euros at the exchange office downtown on Geary Street, just off of Grant. I had forgotten that you can use a card for the purchase; I thought the transaction had to be in cash. So just prior to going to the office I went to a nearby ATM, but the limit I could withdraw was only $300. I wanted 600. That would translate to enough Euros to arrive with, I felt. I took the 300 over to the money exchange on Geary. I knew it wasn't enough but I wanted to follow through anyway, at least check on the exchange rate. 1.47 to the dollar, I learned, the lowest it'd been since 2002, the man behind the glass told me. It's a good time to buy, he'd said. He was considerably older than me, which was comforting. As soon as I walked in I saw the sign on the glass indicating credit cards accepted. How much do you want? the man asked. I explained that I thought the transaction had to be in cash and had taken out my limit of funds for the day, which wasn't enough, and shaking his head he gave me a pitiful look over his eyeglasses. Along with the other information he provided, if I didn't want to come back downtown before my flight, he said, there was another outlet of the company at the SFO International terminal where I could change funds, which was where I was standing now.

Six hundred, I said. That's four hundred and twenty euro, right?

That was the price I was quoted the previous day on Geary Street.

The young man's fingers did a quick calculation on the computer.

That's right sir, he said. Sir, if you buy a thousand dollars' worth you get a better rate. You can put it on our credit card here sir, which acts just like an ATM card.

He lifted up a blue plastic card for me to see.

You will be charged a fee, but it will be about the same as your bank would charge if you use your ATM card. Very convenient, sir. And sir, you'll get two cards. In case one is lost or stolen you'll have a back up.

I knew about this card. The man the day before told me about it. But there were other fees too, or percentages attached to it, and this young man now was trying to explain them. My mind swam in his words and I was lost in their stream. I didn't trust it for some reason, trust him. I was going to be taken if I accepted I just knew it. On one hand it sounded good, but somehow...And a thousand dollars? I couldn't bear parting with that kind of money all at once. I hated the thought of parting with any of it. You're unemployed, why are you spending this money? You can't afford this. What are you doing what are you doing what are you doing...It rang in my head.

I stood there shaking inside, trying to decide.

Sir? What would you like to do, sir? How much would you like?

I don't know, I said, and stood there.

He looked at me. He shifted his eyes to his coworker. She looked up at me then too and they exchanged glances, then slowly she turned her attention back to whatever it was she was doing beside him. They both seemed to be Filipino. They were young and understood money and technology and these systems of banking and percentages and what's best. He probably had a girlfriend and she a boyfriend. I bet they were happy and uncomplicated. He began to shuffle papers and looked down away from me. They can tell, I thought. They can tell there's something wrong with me. Why don't they call security? Why don't they stop me?

I'll just take the six-hundred, I said. Half in cash and half on my card.

I took my wallet out fat with bills and removed the 300. The stack of money felt thick in my fingers. I watched my hands pass it reluctantly through the slot in the glass. He took it and quickly counted the bills before me on the other side. Then I passed my bank card through and he ran it. In a moment he was counting euro notes on the counter, again very quickly. This was really happening. I was going to Europe alone and out of my mind. The

Euros were all 50s, and two 10s.

I need some twenties! I said, panic floating just under the surface. Can you give me some twenties?

No. No twenties sir. Sorry sir.

He passed the Euros through the glass along with thc receipt.

Have a good trip sir, he said as I watched my hands gather the wide blue bills and tuck them into my wallet. This wallet, I thought. She gave me this wallet. Black pebbled leather with white stitching. I slipped the receipt into the outer pouch of my shaved suede chocolatebrown shoulder back, just under the flap. The bag (which she'd also given me—so much I'm surrounded with now, that's become integrated into my meager life, came from her) the bag was very heavy, and the weight of it dug the strap into my left deltoid. I gave a shrug and lifted the strap and spun the bag to the back of my hip, relieving briefly the pressure around my neck as I lurched toward security.

A fter my second game of pool with Pike, I won the first and he won the next, we went over to the bar to get another drink. Pike was drinking big 24oz cans of Pabst with Fernet, and for a change I was having a Belgian beer, Duvel Green. Usually it's Corona and tequila for me, but I felt like mixing it up. In the morning I'd be leaving for Paris. I came out to calm my nerves over some drinks.

Because I live in the Castro, San Francisco's gay district, I leave my neighborhood when I want to do this. There are two options readily available to me: Lucky 13, or the 500 Club. From where I live they're about equal distance away, but about 5 blocks from each other. These are the two closest straight bars, and for years have been the two bars I've frequented most in San

Francisco. Tonight I chose Lucky 13. It's a long dark narrow red and black place, with the longest bar in the city—175 feet. Something like that, anyway...Pike and I sat at the center of it. It was a quiet Sunday night, just me and Pike and Stereo and a few others in there, that was it. A lot of open, dark space and colored lights and those red and black walls. Pike and Stereo were shooting pool when I walked in and when Pike saw me he wrote my name on the chalkboard. I didn't give a shit but what the hell, I'd play. It'd been a while since I shot a game.

Pike was blasted I could tell, had that wide and piercing look to his eyes when he's that way. Still though he shot the eight hard across the red felt into the left corner to win. Stereo was hard to beat, but he was shithoused too, I could also see that, and when he lost he skulked off to the far end of the bar. Toward the end of our second game I told Pike.

Paris, he said. France...

Yeah. But thing is, I don't wanna go.

You don't wanna go. Parish, look at me.

He said that a lot, particularly when he was drunk, always wanted you to look right in his eyes. But they were too intense for me, had to keep my gaze elsewhere when we talked like this, until he'd say *look at me*, then I would, but only for a few seconds.

Look at me, he said again now, sitting with our drinks at the bar.

Parish. You're a creator. Creator of words, and music. Right? You still write songs?

Yeah, but not like I used to.

OK. But Parish, you're a creator. Don't forget that. Remember that. That's important.

Doesn't seem to mean much anymore.

Parish. Stop it. It does. It means a lot. Remember that. I know you're hurting right now, but do not fuck this up. Do not waste this opportunity. Go to Paris. Have fun. Write. But most of all have fun. Forget that bitch. Parish...Look at me...

I looked at him. His eyes bored right into me.

Parish, if you waste this...

His eyes were cold steelblue barrels and they blasted through me, and by not finishing his words they were made even more powerful because his eyes finished them for him.

I looked back down at my beer in its special glass, suddenly self-conscious of the uterus-shaped vessel before me. I nodded, but I knew what was going to happen. I was not like him. I wasn't like most people in fact as far as I could tell, and now I was not the same anymore. I was not who I was even just two months earlier. I was different now, I knew it, knew to my core I was not the same and felt I never again would be.

Have fun...What did that mean? How was I going to have fun feeling this way? I'll leave myself open to all possibilities, for anything that may come, I told myself, but to go with the predetermination to have fun was impossible. Inside me was nothing but slaughter. I simply wanted to disappear.

She's with someone else, in another relationship, and it only took a week, days even as far as I know. Or maybe there was an overlap and took no time at all. I wasn't sure. She'd told me this news just a few days prior to my leaving, that she was seeing someone, and I was carrying it with me to Paris. I'd be there with her ghost and she'd be in San Francisco with her new lover in her bed, in her new apartment, which we were to share. We'd gone apartment hunting together. I'd seen numerous two-bedroom places with her. All way out of my price range but comfortably within hers. I was going to contribute what I could but she didn't need it. She could handle the 2,600 a month herself no problem. Two thousand six hundred dollars a month, and no sweat. In the end she chose one I didn't see. That should've told me something. But I was going to have my own separate room, to work in, to write in. She said she wanted to help me with my writing, to help me get my book published, the one I'd written so long ago, and with her business acumen and charm I believed she could. And if not, her encouragement still meant the world to me, and I wanted to try again. She made me want to try again. I was going to get back to my writing, with her by my side and me by hers. But my place was taken now by someone else. *How!* My mind couldn't absorb it. Just a few months before, one month before she ended it, she'd sent this text message from Chicago: I am so very lonely without you. Being away from you just makes me realize how my life is no longer whole without you next to me.

Parish, Pike said. Go. Have fun.

We started shooting pool again. Pike took Stereo on in a rematch and lost. Then it was me and Stereo. He turned his black Giants cap around so that the orange, entwined SF was in the back and plowed the cue ball home. *UH!* he went, and the racked balls exploded. He creamed me.

After our game, Stereo and I sat at a table. They're all fastened in a row along the wall and we sat at the one nearest the pool table. Stereo's a hardcore regular. They call him Stereo but I have no idea why. Odd name for a friendly neighborhood dealer, though…Stereo told me he'd just gotten out of jail earlier that day. I assumed he got busted selling, but when I asked why he'd been in jail he said: My bitch called the cops on me. Pissed me off and I tol'er I was gonna kill'er over the phone one night. *Over the phone.* Bitch called the cops and said I threatened'er. Ain't that a bitch? My own lady…I didn't *threaten'er.* I just said I was gonna kill'er. Not like, I was gonna *kill* her. Ya know? Threw my ass in jail five days.

Pike came to the table with three shots of tequila. He's goin' to Paris tomorrow, he said.

Who's goin' to Paris? *You?*

I nodded.

Why you goin' to Paris? Stereo asked.

I don't know.

Good answer, he said. Whatcha gonna do there?

I don't know.

Good answer *agin*, he said, and we all knocked glasses and downed our tequila.

I don't know how I'd manage to do it, but before her I somehow got through life without having read Antoine de Saint-Exupery's *The Little Prince*. She'd said it was her favorite book, and on one of our first few dates she'd given me a copy. She came down from her room at the Weston St. Francis (that's where she was staying when we first met) with that big beautiful toothy smile of hers. I was waiting in the lobby (so rich, so opulent, and made even more so with the gold and glitter of the Christmas decorations dressing it) watching for her to emerge from the elevator hallway beyond the concierge desk. And then there she was, smiling the entire way. That whole rich room brightened, became even richer when she came into it, and when she saw me she smiled bigger, my God how she shined, walking toward me, smiling directly at me now, carrying this little gift, this slender paperback of wonder. She handed it to me immediately. On the inside cover she'd written:

Roman—
Only good friends get a copy of The Little Prince from me.
Thanks for being a good friend.

A couple days later after she'd returned to Chicago I read the book. It was so beautiful I cried chubby little tears. When I told her that, she didn't believe me.

One of the most beautiful parts of the book to me was when

the Little Prince came upon a fox he wanted to play with, but the fox said he couldn't because the fox wasn't tamed. The Prince didn't know what that word meant, and the fox explained it meant to create ties. The fox said if you tame me we'll need each other. You'll be the only boy in the world for me, the fox said, and I'll be the only fox in the world for you. So the fox, insisting that the Prince tame it, teaches the Prince how to go about it. And so the Little Prince tamed the fox.

But when it was time for the Prince to leave, the fox, now tamed, was very sad. When they said goodbye the fox told the Prince a secret.

One sees clearly only with the heart, the fox said. Anything essential is invisible to the eyes.

And then the fox said that you become responsible forever for what you've tamed. The fox said that people have forgotten this truth, but the Little Prince must not forget.

A couple months into our beginning she sent this text: I think you are slowly taming me.

That made me smile, and maybe for a while she actually did believe she felt this happening in her. But in the end I knew who it was who was being tamed.

T he line at security was long but it moved rather quickly. I thought I had allowed enough time when I left my apartment but the wait to check-in took longer than expected, and now there was only about 30 minutes to boarding. And I was starving. I'd have to do something about that too before I got on the plane.

The line moved and I reached the first agent checking passports and boarding passes. I handed him mine. He opened my passport with one hand and held the boarding pass up to it with the other. He fingered that flap, lifting it up to look underneath. I could tell he thought it odd. He looked closer and said something.

What? I said.

His accent was thick and of indistinct origin, beefy with a language and ethnicity I couldn't identify.

Wrong name, he said, and I caught it this time.

On pass. Wrong name.

That's what I was given at the desk, I said. They gave my seat away so they assigned me that one instead.

Wrong name, he insisted, and turned it around so I could see. There was a woman's name printed on the pass where mine should have been.

Hafta go back to desk, he said, and tucked the boarding pass into my passport like a hyperbolic book marker and handed it back.

Oh *fuck*, was my first reaction. Then, wait. Yes! Oh *yes*. Maybe this is it...

When you come back go to other side, he said, indicating with a gesture another stanchioned entrance to the far right of the winding line I had waited in.

I really hate airports. The crowds. The procedures. The scrutiny. The confusion. The waiting. The sadness of coming and going. All the stress they create and represent and the vast spaces they contain. All of it. I hate it.

I headed back to the check-in counter not sure why he said that, about going to the other side when I returned, then realized it was probably an expediting line.

At the check-in counter things were much calmer now. There were a few people waiting to be helped, but maybe it was the worry on my face that brought prompt attention.

Can I help you? I was asked. It was a plump woman with short sparkly blonde hair wearing gold-rimmed glasses. I looked for pillow-chest but she was nowhere to be seen. I stepped up to the counter handing out the boarding pass.

I was sent back here, I said. That's not my name on the pass.

I could feel the words scrape over my throat as they came out.

She looked at the pass. She lifted the flap. It was like a child's toy discovery door you couldn't help but peek inside.

Oh no, what did she do? the woman said in a grave tone and looked worried now herself, which was encouraging. I recognized her then as the woman Chesty had consulted with when she'd walked away and left me standing there at the counter.

Now I was hopeful. Was this the intervention I was praying for? Maybe it would be too complicated or take too long to rectify. I'd miss my flight and it wouldn't be my fault. Then I'd cancel or postpone the whole thing like I wanted to do in the first place and go home to suffer this meltdown in the privacy of my own world.

But in a moment it was all over. The woman simply typed a few things on the keyboard, printed another pass, and I was on my way back to security, this time entering to the right as I was told. I handed this new burgundy-jacketed agent my documents and she handed them right back, and I joined the screening process. I still had time to grab a sandwich on the other side.

I needn't look back over these pages to realize they're a conspicuous muddle. Out of practice as I am and particularly in my frame of mind I need to warm up, and I'm doing that as I go, following thought and memory where they take my pen. It's helping some, I think, focusing this way—calming me a bit. But if this is to be anything more than therapeutic activity, if this is to be a true yet *artful* endeavor, as I desire it to be, I must try harder at substantive form, build a more solid framework. Getting closer to it though, I believe. A rhythm's coming...

I've lost weight. Down to the last notch on my belt and it pulls there with ease. Lost maybe ten pounds, I guess. There's no scale here and I don't care anyway, but I'd guess about that, give or take. Ten pounds in five days. I look at myself in the mirror and it seems obvious to me but I wonder if she'd notice. Just haven't felt much like eating. Two boiled eggs in the morning and I'm good through the day. Plus, and I was aware of this, but it's expensive here. I didn't feel it as much last time because I had income then, was on paid vacation then, and there was a job to return to. This, and because of her of course. Mostly because of her.

She would hardly let me pay for anything, here in Paris or at home. Always a wrestle with her to let me pick up any tab. I explained I needed to, whether she cared or not I needed to. I succumb too readily to generosity and am too easily spoiled, I told her. Having been the youngest of six I'd gotten it easier than the others, I knew that. The baby. Carried over into my relationships, caused problems, and I did not want it to ever enter ours. I did not want any of my shit to corrode and smother this one. I'd worked too hard I felt excising it from myself during those five years I was alone and please, please I'd beg. And she'd relent, once in a great while. At first everything, dinners drinks cab rides, everything was on her employer, or so she said. Expense account. Alright, that didn't bother me. If her office was so fat they could shoulder it all, all her travel and lodging and living expenses too including entertainment, without affecting her in anyway, then, gravy. Let them. But once it became her own money it was different. Not to her, no. She still couldn't care less. She'd peel off 20s like they were dead skin. But I did, *I* cared.

For once in my life I could easily contribute and I wanted to. I was making the most money I'd ever made at the time. I'm sure a lot of people would say different, but to me $50,000 was doing alright. I got by on that just fine. I couldn't afford my own apartment like I preferred, still had to live with roommates, and I was dying to change that part of my life, but by my standards I was finally doing OK. Her income, on the other hand, was so fantastically ridiculous she seemed to leap at the chance to share it, habitually snatching up the check the second it hit the table. Many times, to avoid any argument, she'd adapt a preemptive approach and take care of it before it even reached the table and I had a chance to say or do anything about it. It was a constant battle with her, and she was adamant in her position, so after a while I just let it happen her way.

I spent such little money during our trip to Paris together that when I said I wanted to buy her a gift on our last day here I was prepared to pay almost any price. I let her pick it out. We wandered into a cutlery store across from Place des Vosges in the Marais. She decided she wanted a handcrafted sommelier. She chose a handsome one with a speckled, blonde wood handle. €175, about $300—for a bottle opener.

Ordinarily of course way too decadent and out of the question. Under the circumstances, however, it didn't seem quite enough.

I did not take anything for granted; I knew how extraordinary that trip had been because of her. But being here now by myself I realize to what great extent she'd made it so, just how special it actually was.

The refrigerator was kept loaded with delicious food, and we always bought more to bring back home with us while walking the city. Or we'd stop and eat well at a restaurant, as we wished, without much consideration of price. Just depended upon our mood and taste.

Again on our last day, approaching the apartment, we stopped at a charcuterie we'd been frequenting at Boulevard St. Germain and rue Monge. There's a little square there with a lot of shops where we bought cheese and wine and roast chicken. The chicken is sold at a white counter out front of one of those shops. I got un demi poulet the other day from there, I eat a lot of roast chicken because it's economical as well as tasty, but it wasn't as good as I remembered it being. Nothing is. I pass this square now many times each day. It's on route to and from this garret I've rented, which I'm growing so tired of already. The same routes, same streets I've wandered endlessly now, same people even, working in the shops and restaurants and cafés I see as I pass, the tourists constantly wandering in packs. My place is very near the house where Hemingway lived and the house where Verlaine lived in his later years and the building with its swirling blue iron gate where Joyce lived while finishing Ulysses, all on the same street, rue du Cardinal Lemoine, all within doors of each other. They all walked the same routes I'm walking every day now to and from this neighborhood. Did they eventually tire of them as well? Different time of course and different city too, not the dead museum it is now. That makes a difference. And when you actually have a life here, family, friends, and can communicate and participate in the culture and are working well in your craft and art...well, all that makes a world of difference to my experience now. Still...I don't know what this neighborhood was like in their day, but today it is filled with food, restaurant upon restaurant, shop upon shop, and it is where I am nearly starving out of shot nerves and lack of appetite, awash in emotion and fear and a dwindling bank account. My spot, 7 rue du Pot de Fer, will not be remembered. This is truly the last romantic book ever to be written.

On our last day, on our way back to the apartment as I was saying, she decided she wanted to buy some salami to bring back with us to San Francisco. We stopped at the charcuterie where she simply went down the long row of meats with the clerk in his white, bloodstained smock, dark pink splotches spattered across his belly, pointing as she went, indicating she'd like one of each.

There were about five and were probably €25 a piece. The clerk smiled happily and did her bidding. And this on top of the two she'd bought moments earlier at another shop up the hill in the Mouffetard, which were bigger and more expensive. Then she tasted a slice of freshly cut country ham and decided we needed to bring some of that back to the apartment with us too, for a snack later. Late that night we went out for a farewell steak dinner, again in the Mouffetard, at that tiny place near St. Etienne. Didn't think I'd have an appetite it was so late but she insisted, and in the glow of the candle at our darkened table in the restaurant's only window we both ate hardy, though I felt the sadness for leaving Paris already settling deep within me. The ham was abandoned the next morning in the fridge along with some other things, untouched. The salami, vacuum sealed, rode in our luggage nestled in our clothing.

That apartment was a dream. Spacious living room with low, dark wood exposed beamed ceiling and white walls. It was separated from the kitchen by a bar, the top of which was made from a smooth raw slice of wood that looked taken right out of a tree trunk, with all its organic irregularity of shape left intact. Two stools stood in the living room before it. The kitchen was small but equipped with all modern appliances and amenities, full-sized refrigerator, stove, dishwasher, even a laundry machine in there too the size of a trash compactor.

Immediately behind the kitchen was the bathroom. A small, deep bathtub, three quarters the size of one in America but one and a half times deeper, was entombed in a boxy white textured-tile frame, and it sat at the base of the wall of separation. Above it, making up the rest of the wall, was a sliding wooden screen. A nice feature to the apartment, this screen. Slid closed you had the privacy you needed. But open it lent such an airy quality to the space, looking through the kitchen into the living room with the light streaming in from the windows overlooking rue St. Julien below. A beautiful design, all the more beautiful for its country-like simplicity. Before she arrived and I was alone in the apartment for the first five days I kept the screen open the entire time.

The bathroom had a separate shower stall in addition to the bathtub, on the opposite side of the room toward the back. Here there was another door, to the left of the shower that lcd to the small bedroom. There was one window in there above the right side of the bed, covered by a thin red satin cloth. We woke in the morning to a sexy red light filtering in.

Outside the bedroom, through another door in the opposite wall, was the entrance hallway. To the right, the door leading down the winding stairs. To the left, up the short hall, and you were in the living room again, kitchen on the left. Et voila.

In the hallway was a glass cabinet filled with old French books, no titles I recognized. Besides, it was locked and we had no way to open it. Next to the cabinet was a large wood table with spiral legs. Antique, solid and heavy and dark. We never used it but to set our things on when we entered—the keys, the camera, books and bags.

On Sunday mornings the bells of Notre Dame boomed in one long clanging symphony through our windows across Quai Montebello and the river. The first time I heard them I leapt out of bed with her lying next to me and ran naked to the living room and threw open the windows. She came out and joined me and we stood there both naked listening and smiling and holding each other as that sacred sound filled the room. It lasted at least ten minutes.

One night we came home and opened a bottle of wine. Again I threw the windows wide, and stood there, glass of wine in hand, leaning on the metal railing just outside the left window looking out into the night at Notre Dame. Though the moon was bright and partially full, just begun to wane, the sky was dull black, with strands of long gray severed wool fingers floating softly through it. I was wearing the brown herring-bone hat I'd bought earlier in the day. It was a floppy brimmed hat, a David

Niven kind of country-estate hat, with a brass buckle in the band, and I was wearing it with a tilt and a rake over my right brow. I stood there leaning out the left window that way and she stood leaning out the right window with the camera and took shots of me down the outside of the building with my glass of wine and rakish hat and Notre Dame glowing behind me. I looked at her with sex and wine in my eyes. I curled my tongue into a tube and slid it out at her. I gave my best come hither and bedroom seduction stares into the lens. All with that glorious church watching illuminated over my shoulder.

Then I took the camera and her place at the window and began taking pictures of Notre Dame itself. I noticed the moon descending, coming closer and closer to the church, and I started taking a series of shots. The best one, in close-up, caught the moon crossing just behind the church's pinnacle, the thin metal cross of the spire visible and black within the white, softly blurred orb, like the crosshairs in a smudged, lopsided rifle scope.

Magical. It was absolutely magical.

I didn't think I would, but I walked down rue St. Julien for the first time yesterday and stood in the gray granite-slab street looking up at the top floor windows of building 12. The day she first arrived she stood in the same spot where I was now while I took a picture of her from the window high above, yellow October leaves scattered like starfish on the granite about her feet. She smiled big white teeth up at me, wearing big black sun-glasses, like a movie star, her dark hair (she'd colored it brunette now) streaming over her shoulders, over the wide round lapels of her pretty, cream-colored speckled wool coat that I'd never seen before (was it newly purchased for the trip? I never asked), torso slightly twisted half-spun around looking up at me, and how beautiful she looked, how happy she looked. Why did I never tell her how beautiful I thought she was in that moment?

The plane was a 747, with an upper deck, which was where my seat 11L was. Business class. Not only did my flight not get cancelled, I got upgraded. And although I'd requested an aisle seat (I always prefer aisle seats, even in movie theaters, or there's a sense of being trapped) this was at the window in a row of three. At first, as I approached from the stairs, I was still under the impression that my seat was on the aisle. I found the row, but there was a young woman seated on the end. She was cute. A spark of hope sputtered.

Sorry, I said. I think that's my seat.

We checked our passes. We looked at the signage above. She was right, it was her seat. Next to her was a man. Mine was at the window. She read it on my face.

It's not that bad, really, she said. These are nice big seats.

My expressions give me so easily away now it's disturbing. They seem uncontrollable.

Turned out she was right. This was the best window seat I'd ever had. There was a compartment between the seat and the window that my shoulder bag fit into, and with the lid closed it acted as an end table. And there was plenty of lateral and leg room. I really couldn't complain. Except—it was hot. There was something wrong with the air conditioning. They were working on it, but we were all sweating. I fanned myself with the safety instruction card I pulled from the pouch in front of me. And we weren't moving. There was a delay. The pilot's voice came over the speakers, first in French then in English, explaining something about not having the appropriate paper work, which needed to be completed before we could take off. They were waiting for it to be sent to them. Then another voice took over from directly behind me. It was the same woman who stood behind me in the check-in line. On her cell again, more goodbyes. This time she was talking to her daughter, who I gathered was rather young. She was explaining the plane, that it had two levels. Like that bus in England we rode, remember? And guess where mommy's sitting? That's *right!* Upstairs on *top!* She lingered and her voice grated on and on. The man to my left rolled his eyes and sighed in his seat. The voice continued. The man craned his neck backward to glimpse the face he could attribute to such inconsiderateness. Something told me he was French. He hadn't spoken yet so I wasn't sure. He had salt and pepper hair shorn close to his head, pale skin, and very thin lips stretching across a round owl face. Seemed French anyway. My anxiety was rising with the heat and the sound of this woman's voice and the obvious agitation it was causing. Numbing energy surged through my body. The muscle fiber in my legs burned and knotted. I flapped my knees back and forth and gently stamped my feet trying in vain to alleviate the surge of energy flowing down and trapping in them. How was I ever going to survive this flight? Ten and a half hours with this electricity in me. If I were on the aisle I could at least get up when I wanted to walk it off.

After about twenty minutes the heat began to subside and the cabin eventually cooled to a more comfortable level, but I was still imploding. I had to do something. I began talking to the man next to me. He seemed shocked when I first spoke. He jumped a little in his seat and his eyes popped. He appeared confused. Turned out he *was* French, and he explained French people don't just start talking to someone they don't know. Oh, sorry, I said. That was OK, he'd had to adjust to that during his visit in America. This had been his first time to the States. He went to New York, Chicago (I flinched internally when he said that, and blinked my eyes very very slowly) and then San Francisco, which he liked very much. His name was François. François, just like that friend of the woman blabbing behind us, the one who wanted to set her up with an apartment in Paris. What a coincidence. I didn't say this to him but I remarked to myself about it. What a coincidence, but not that unusual for me. That kind of thing happened to me all the time. We talked on, in fact all through the flight. Once I got him started hc got used to it, I guess. And I of course needed it. I told him my story, why I was going to Paris and all that. Oh, terrible. I'm sorry, he said, and made a sympathetic face. While we were talking a handsome French flight attendant knelt beside the girl on the end, smiling. They started talking. Bastard! I spat at him in my head. You and your accent and dreamy brown eyes. Fuck you. So easy for you isn't it, French flight attendant on a plane to Paris. Bet you do pretty well for yourself don'tcha pal. All these American women on their way over there, swooning for some French lover to take them, and here you are getting a head start on the competition. Fucker. And this girl spoke French. They were conversing easily in the language. Fuck you too. Smiling and giggling. Seems to be all working out. Here's a little bottle of champagne, for later, after we take off, he offered. I couldn't tell what he said but I saw him slip her the bottle on the sly. She blushed. Fucker. My new friend François and I went on. Did he live in Paris? Well, no. He worked there, and had a little place he'd stay in during the week, but on the weekends he went to his home in the suburbs. Oh, really, that's interesting. No, not very, he said. He worked in accounting, nothing very interesting about that, he assured me.

The plane finally began to move and we were all quiet now, even the woman with the cell phone was quiet, and slowly we rolled toward inevitable take off.

Then, and it seemed to happen all at once without hesitation or transition from the slow roll that lulled us along the tarmac, suddenly the plane roared and took us up into the sky and I sank into the cavern pit hell of my stomach.

We had loved that place on rue St. Julien le Pauve so much that we bought a bottle of wine in appreciation to leave for the young man who rented it to us, Christophe. He lived in the apartment across the landing, and the morning we were leaving I wrote a note to him expressing our gratitude. If he should ever come to San Francisco, I'd said, we'd love to host his stay, show him around. I tore the note out of my notebook and set it on the kitchen bar weighted beneath the bottle of wine. While we were getting ready to leave for the airport there was a knock at the door. It was Christophe. I asked him in saying I'd just written him, and showed him the bottle of wine and note on the bar. He read what I wrote with little reaction then picked up the bottle and looked at it curiously.

Eese zeess good wine? he asked.

He was the Frenchman, I thought, he should know shouldn't he?

I said that I didn't know, we hadn't tried that brand, but it seemed like it was. The price certainly suggested it was, anyway. I didn't say that to him.

Christophe had a tall, lean frame, a short blonde ponytail and goatee. He spoke English, but coated with a heavy accent. When I first arrived and he met me downstairs at the anteroom door to the building I was surprised at how young he was. I expected a middle-aged man for some reason. Someone renting an apartment in Paris via internet to people on the other side of the globe seemed to me would be an older businessman. Christophe, however, was probably 30, if that.

During the first week I was alone in Paris I had meant to ask Christophe out for a drink, to get to know him better. I ran into him a few times going to or from the apartment. He was with a different girl each time. I recognized he was probably someone good to get to know, a good contact in Paris. Now we'd found this apartment I intended to return, one way or another, and for a much longer stay if I had anything to say about it. I had mentioned this to her after she arrived, about asking Christophe out for a drink, and she thought it was a good idea, but we were so involved with ourselves that we never carried through with it. I'd regretted that. On our last night we'd picked up that bottle, along with the other goodies we bought, specifically to give to Christophe. It was the least we could do.

When the idea to return to Europe began to take shape, Christophe came to mind. After first an extended stay in Paris, I thought, I'd hop a train to other sites. Through email I asked Christophe about the apartment's availability, and, although I couldn't go anywhere near the price we'd paid last time, since I was a return renter and he could trust me, would he possibly accept $900, for say, three weeks?

I waited but never heard from him, so I figured that was a no.

I was still employed at this time, with about a month to go to the end of my contract, though there was still no word whether or not it would be extended. Although I was looking forward to having some time off, I still believed I'd be coming back for the first installation after the museum reopened, in a couple months or so. She had just ended it, and I was devastated to say the least, but still operating through the shock of it with a flush of anger while clutching to a thin veil of hope for reconciliation. After contact with Christophe seemed to fail I wrote the whole thing off; I wasn't sure it was such a good idea now, considering. And then something happened.

My boss was having a show of his artwork. We were all invited, me along with the crew I worked with, and where ordinarily I would have gone, as I'd gone to his previous shows, this one I couldn't make. It happened to be on the Saturday afternoon that I had scheduled a dentist appointment, and I had to keep that appointment.

I hadn't been to a dentist in years. I'd had no health insurance, and couldn't afford or was unwilling to pay the amount it would've cost without it. Over the last two years though I did have insurance, but never used it. Now that insurance was due to expire with my contract, and I wanted to get a visit in while it was still free.

Oh sorry you can't make it, my boss said. I'd've introduced you to Richard. He's gonna be there.

Over the years I'd heard of this Richard. He owned a little apartment in Paris. My boss had stayed there some years earlier, during his 50th birthday, and I'd listened to him talk about it many times. Tiny place, he'd said. In the Mouffetard. It's great.

We'd talked about Paris a lot, my boss and I. He knew how I felt about it.

So that was the spark of this trip, Richard. Through my boss I got in touch with him. I sent Richard an email, but again like with Christophe no response. My boss sent an email on my behalf recommending me as a renter. No response. So once more I began to forget about the whole thing.

Time quickly went on, and now it was becoming clear I was not going to return to the museum, and then the date for my contract to expire came, and I was gone altogether. And she was gone. It was *all* gone, everything my life was, the happiness of the previous year and the projected happiness for the future, the structure of my days, my plans, my love, gone, all *gone*. And it all happened so quickly and all at once, my life, it just came down like sheets of paper around me…

I didn't know what to do with myself at first, do with my time. I still lived in hope for her, and waded in misery through my days. Eventually I set to work finishing the task I'd started two months earlier retyping an old manuscript. My heart was no longer in it, but I was nearly halfway through when I left off and I couldn't leave it that way. Besides, it was on her old laptop and

I needed to get it finished and out of there so I could get that machine back to her and out of my life.

Months ago, when she offered to help with my writing, to help try to get my book published, she suggested letting her send the manuscript out to get retyped. The work was written so long ago I'd used an electric typewriter to do it, and if it was going to be resubmitted now it needed to be updated. I said I wanted to do it myself, because I was sure I was going to rework the thing as I went along. I began in February.

She had changed jobs and no longer worked for the same software company in San Jose. Now she was in a position created just for her by an old CEO she'd worked for at the Human Resource company he now ran in San Leandro. It was closer and accessible by train, so she no longer had to drive that long commute each day, which was a bonus. And, though there was still travel involved, there was considerably less travel than with her job before, which was the best part. And she was living in a longer-termed-leased apartment, still a furnished rental, but this one rented for four month intervals, and it was only a few blocks away from my place. I practically moved in. We were getting closer and closer to being together. The laptop was a remnant from her previous employer that she'd retained but no longer used, so I began using it. I had a laptop too, but hers had Office Word and mine didn't. Plus it was smaller than mine and more convenient to tote around, which I did, bringing it with me to Caffé Greco at times to work. Mostly though, I worked at her place while she was away visiting her family in Chicago, which she still frequently did—every other week. I occupied myself while she was gone by working on the manuscript. That work halted at the end of March, when we did, but I still had her machine. It was all I had now when my job ended so I threw myself into it, working at the table in my kitchen during the day while still trying to convince her how much I loved and needed her. Then, finally, there was a response.

Through email Richard said the apartment was available. Oh great, I wrote back, what would he want for say a three week stay? (More extensive travel was now out of the question.) He didn't know, he said, what would I offer? Well, how about 900? A day passed before I heard from him again, and I figured I'd lost him with that. Then there was another email. He said he'd probably prefer a thousand, but would take my 900. Oh great, thanks. I'll take it.

The next thing I knew I was buying a plane ticket and sending a check down to Richard in Redwood City. A strange-looking key came in the mail, I'd never seen any key like it, taped to a piece of thin cardboard. Great, I was going to Paris.

Oh no. I was going to Paris...

It came together so fast I didn't stop to think at the time, just jumped at the opportunity to get away, to see the city I loved again. It wasn't until a week later when it dawned on me what I was doing. And then she told me she'd been seeing someone, and I fell apart.

Five days before I was scheduled to leave I took her over to the museum. I thought it was important to me for her to see what my life had been involved in for the past year while we were together. I wanted her to see the gallery I helped install. It took a whole year to install that gallery, and I wanted to personally show her my handy work, the things I'd helped build, hang, mount, light, paint. I was particularly proud of the faux finish painting I'd done on some mounting brackets, painting them so that they disappeared into the sculptures themselves they secured. It was the first time I'd done that kind of work and I was very proud of the results. I received all kinds of compliments from the crew and other museum staff. I wanted her to see that most of all.

She agreed to meet me. We met at the Lake Merritt BART station. I came from the city and she from work, in San Leandro. She'd left early in order to meet. We ascended the steps of the platform together but from opposite stairs facing each other. Though I wanted to, we did not embrace. She was wearing a red dress and a long, thin, purple jacket. It was new. As we walked from the station to the museum, it was just one block, I looked at her and said: You look particularly vibrant today.

She looked over at me and gave a weak smile behind her big sunglasses, and the gulf between us clearly yawned. It felt creepy now to be with her, as it felt creepy to be there at the museum again, in that gallery where I'd spent so much time day in day out, where I'd done so much work, knowing I was no longer working there—that I was not wanted to work there ever again... What was I doing?

She seemed distracted and we more or less breezed through the gallery. When I showed her my faux painting work she smiled and said oh look at that, great, pausing only long enough to give the impression she was taking it in, then kept moving. It was a stupid idea going there, bringing *her* there, like a kid showing an uncaring mother his crayon drawing.

We rode the train back to the city together. She slid into the seat first and I moved in next to her. Close.

You need to back up. Seriously, she said.

I scooched over a bit, but kept my focus squarely on her as we rode. From her leather satchel she extracted a thick paperback, something about the political origins of Mexico City, and attempted to start reading.

What's that? Why you reading that?

I don't know, she said. Just saw it in a bookstore and it grabbed me.

As soon as I saw that book I got suspicious, but held those thoughts at bay.

She turned her attention to begin reading now in earnest, but I couldn't allow that. I had things to say, and I was not going to let this moment escape without at least trying to say them. She closed the book reluctantly and offered her blank, expectant gaze, and I saw the difference in it, the difference in how her eyes once looked at me and how they looked at me now; I saw that enormous and excruciating difference as I began to speak, and the response pooled quickly in me, leaking down my face with the slow and wasted words that came.

When we reached the other side of the bay and were standing in front of the 16th Street station, she told me then. My blood dropped into my boots.

Who is it? I asked, voice a trembling waver. Someone I know?

Not Jari.

I never thought it'd be him. But who, someone I know? It'll kill me if it's someone I know.

No, not really, she said, and smiled. She *smiled!* Big!

Not *really?* I suspected then who it was but at the time that weasel thought could not get by the much larger one, the one which would not fit inside my brain. How could this be happening! How could she be with someone else! She crossed the street now and I pursued. On the diagonal corner, in front of the Walgreens there, we stopped and I tried again.

Baby…I said, starting to say something, not knowing what.

Don't call me baby anymore, she said, and I'd heard those words before, my last girlfriend used those same words five years earlier. And just as I was trying to scoop my jaw back into place a man came swooping by out of nowhere, sensing the situation I guess, the energy between us, and leaned in close as he passed for both of us to hear.

You oughta *marry* that woman! he said. She's *beautiful!*

Only a portion of the storm was unleashed then, what had suddenly whirled up within me and could not be released toward her, the tornado swirling in my chest, I let at least some of it go at this man's words and was glad for the immediate intrusive excuse to do so, glad for the excuse for her to hear it, roaring *I WANTED TO!*

Shhhh stop it, she said, and ducked into the open Walgreens doorway. I dragged my scowl slowly away from the man's direction where my eyes had spun after him and followed.

You took advantage of me, she said.

What! I did NOT take advantage of you. I TOLD you. I TOLD you not to pay for everything, but you wouldn't—

No. Not financially. You took advantage of me emotionally.

What! I said again. You KNEW I loved you! You KNEW it! You KNOW it!

But she would not hear it. She stepped back out onto sunny Mission Street where we'd just stood, and before she turned and walked away she said: Have a good time in Paris, really. And with eyes streaming I watched her go, watched her walk from me up Mission toward her new home just two blocks further, which was to be our home to share.

At first I couldn't move, but then realized as she grew smaller down the street I had to, had to get in motion. In the opposite direction I wandered in a daze for blocks and blocks with tears falling behind my sunglasses. Every morning since that day I wake with tears. From the moment consciousness is regained and my eyes flutter again upon this world they start. I lie up there in the rafters staring at the beams overhead and bawl my eyes out. Then, when I think it's subsided enough, I climb the ladder down from the loft to slowly begin the day, take a shower. While dressing it hits once more and I collapse onto the couch, sit and rock on the edge of the thin futon and bawl some more. There's always a puddle at my feet when I get up from there finally, big wet ponds on the red tile. I simply cannot get her out of my mind or heart and the fact that I lost her does not cease to consume me with guilt. I wail at myself until I'm out of breath, gasp, and wail some more. The tears are endless rivers.

This describes my morning routine. Not one has passed since arriving to Paris where it's deviated.

As the plane descended and tipped banking over the ground, through the window in the bright morning light I saw a patchwork of green and the most brilliant yellow. Fields and fields of this green and yellow quilting out there. It was very beautiful and I'd never seen it before. I asked François what that yellow was and he told me but I don't remember, other than it was a kind of flower used in France for spices. The name of the flower I don't recall, unfortunately. But from hundreds of feet in the air and to fatigued eyes this yellow was the brightest yellow I think I've ever seen.

After we landed and disembarked I joined the rest of the plane's passengers at the baggage carousel. In the crowd I saw François standing across the room wearing a bright blue baseball cap with a red C on it. I quickly spun my eyes off him and never looked again.

Fuck the Cubs forevermore.

I wasn't accustomed to being with someone who traveled so incessantly, who was gone nearly half the time we were together. In common experience, when you're in a relationship that person's company is generally there to turn to and enjoy regularly; it's the rare times that person is absent. In our case, it was like a part-time long distance relationship with full-time commitment, and over the months that began to wear heavily upon me. Having just spent so much time alone, when she was gone it was like being right back in that place. And now that I'd found her I never wanted to experience that kind of aloneness ever again. So many weekends so many holidays when other lovers were together there I was alone, though I did have a lover. And as I'd walk the city by myself, all the couples hand in hand I constantly passed only magnified my loneliness. I tried to stay occupied I'd do things, but this feeling was inescapable.

Once I went to the Museum of Modern Art to see the William Kentridge exhibit, a South African artist I was unfamiliar with until then. There was a charcoal drawing of a man wandering alone on the curve of a hill beneath a broad, turbulent sky, and within the sky was written in blue bold chalk: HER ABSENCE FILLS THE WORLD.

It struck me like an arrow in the chest. I took a photo of it with my phone and sent it to her. Immediately through text she wanted to know what the image was from, where I was, and I told her. Told her that's how I felt. We were in constant touch that way, through text message mostly, but that couldn't fill her absence or relieve my loneliness.

To put her at ease in the beginning I told her I was used to being alone, and on one hand that was true. Is true. I'm quite adept at being on my own. But being comfortable with solitude is different than adjusting to loneliness, and that's where I never wanted to go again, back to that desolation. The balance had been tipped now though, and each time she went away I was lonely. Toward the end it grew to be nearly unbearable.

There were complications beyond her travel schedule as well. I saw the ring the night we met. I chose to ignore it.

I'll pursue this where it leads, I thought. And yes the swagger reeking in that sentence was present in me, I admit it.

I saw a pretty young woman and sat down next to her at the party. I kept glancing at her out of the corner of my eye, at the shape of her profile, her large and slightly protruding teeth that only made her seem more alluring, the toned yet nicely fleshy arms and shoulders rolling out tan from her sleeveless blouse. Then I noticed the ring on her left hand, tasteful medium-sized jewel clearly visible. We started talking.

How was she enjoying the party, how did she know Jari, our host? We work together. I helped him set up for the party. Oh really? Nice job. Smiles. Where are you from? I live in Chicago. Oh really? I'm from Illinois as well. Is that right? What part? I told her and asked if she knew it. Of course, sure, she said. You work with Jari but you live in Chicago? It's crazy, I know. I actually just spent the last eight months traveling all over the world, literally living out of a suitcase for eight months. Wow. And how does your husband deal with that? I noticed your ring. She touched the ring lightly with the fingertips of her right hand, adjusting the band absentmindedly. Oh, she said, it's interesting...

...I left that one there...

There was live music at the party and a guy with his acoustic was about to start. It was a large loft apartment and we were sitting upstairs, which was the bedroom. Overlooking the ledge of the railing we had a bird's-eye view of the living room, which was doubling as the performance space. We were quiet then and listened. When he was done we talked some more.

Where are you staying? The St. Francis, Union Square. Ah, fancy. It's on the company, they treat me well. I see...

As the night passed, we managed to keep sitting next to each other, talking, although there were breaks in between when I went downstairs for another beer or to use the bathroom and she did the same. Still we each always came back upstairs to our seats and our conversation. Then I was struck by brilliance.

Do you like German food? (By this time I already knew she was Polish. Wasn't that far off, I thought. I didn't know any Polish restaurants.) German food? Yum yeah, there's this place in Chicago I love. Well there's this place here I go to a lot that's excellent. Maybe if you have time you'd like to go one night. Yeah, sounds great. I'm here through this next week. (It was Sunday night.) Let me take your number.

I gave it to her and watched her punch it into her phone. A minute later I felt a vibration along my left thigh. I took my phone out of my pants pocket and flipped it open.

That's my email, she said. How about Wednesday night?

Great, I said.

And that was it. Shortly after that I left. It was getting to be around eleven and I figured my night was now complete. Besides, I had work in the morning and had to get up early. And I thought I'd stop for one more on the walk home, a quiet one by myself, to think about what just happened, this girl I'd met and enjoyed talking with all night, who was married...Shit...

I started putting on my jacket getting ready to leave and she said: Oh, taking off?

Yeah it's getting late, hafta get up early tomorrow. Unless...? I was thinking of stopping for one more on the way home, wanna join me?

Oh...better not.

OK. Sure.

I mean, I'm gonna help Jari clean up when this is done, and probably crash here tonight.

Struck out there, I thought. But that was alright. There was Wednesday night...

A pleasure meeting you, I said, and I'm looking forward to Wednesday.

Yeah me too. Bye.

Later the next night I was at home when my phone buzzed. A text. It was her.

I responded.

Another one came.

I responded again.

After the third message I wrote back: Why don't you just call me?

Five seconds later my phone rang.

We talked for two hours.

B oy this is taking a long time, isn't it? a woman's voice asked.

Indeed. The entire plane was gathered about baggage claim carousel 6 at Charles de Gaulle airport. We watched one red bag circle endlessly the belt unclaimed, the rest refused to appear, going on 30 minutes now. I had finally lowered my shoulder bag to the floor and was squatting over it as I watched with burning exhausted eyes the maddening and redundant trek of that red bag when I heard it, the voice. Maybe it was the obviousness of the question. Maybe it was because it was an American voice that posed the question, and an elderly one at that. Most likely it was the combination of all these. But somehow I managed a smile and looked up over my right shoulder.

Yes, I replied. It is.

Her head jerked down at me, angled like a bird's, then jerked away again. She wasn't expecting a response; the question within her had simply slipped audibly into the outside world. She was a small woman of about 65, with straight shoulder-length gray-streaked hair. Her black eyebrows were angular and knit with concern and impatience, but she seemed kind. Right away she reminded me of an old girlfriend's mother, who hadn't liked me very much, but the resemblance was like a warm embrace. There was something else about her too, though…

Is it always like this? she asked. Have you been here before? Maybe we should ask someone.

I didn't know who it would be we'd ask. The only people in sight were fellow passengers waiting uninformed like us. The only thing to do was to wait. I stood up to speak next.

Yeah I've been here before but I've never experienced this.

She nodded nervously and watched unsmiling the baggage carousel.

I spoke again. I was already hungry for English and companionship and we'd just disembarked the plane.

Are you from San Francisco?

Berkeley. I'm a retired psychologist. I'm waiting for my husband. He went off to find a cart.

Psychologist! I thought. Maybe this is why I came. I was supposed to meet her. Maybe she can help me...

What about you? she asked.

Yeah I live in San Francisco.

What are you doing here? Are you by yourself?

Yeah, I'm by myself. And I don't know what I'm doing here. My girlfriend and I broke up, and I hit kind of an end with my job, so I decided to come to Paris. But I already feel like it was a mistake.

Oh, I should've sat next to *you* on the plane. We'd've had lots to talk about.

Yes! She got it!

How long are you here? she asked.

Three weeks. But I don't know, I said. We'll see how long I last.

I was already thinking of cutting it short.

How 'bout you?

We're here three weeks too. One in Paris and two in Provence. What happened with your job?

I gave her a brief rundown on the museum and what had happened, and while I was explaining baggage finally began tumbling from the gaping mouth of the conveyer belt and making its way around the carousel.

Oh my *husband* used to work there! Years ago. Oh you'll have *lots* to talk about.

59

Good news, thank God, there's vital sign renewal from the feared dead!

The Jardin des Plantes is very close to where I'm staying. Today I thought I'd go have a look.

It got hot early this morning and by the time I reached the gardens the sun was high and bearing straight down on the city. Upon entering the gardens I took refuge immediately in the shaded narrow paths winding through the trees, and began slowly walking. I saw nothing of real interest at first as I went along, but it was nice to be among nature, out of the sun in the cool of that shade. After walking for some time I paused at a meeting of paths, deciding which way I wanted to go, and as I stood there a young woman and her boyfriend crossed before me. I went totally still as they passed, but as soon as they did my chin dropped straight into my chest and my head just hung there swinging like a loose hinge. Back and forth it swung in disbelief at the unearthly beauty I just saw. My decision was made.

I allowed the couple to stroll ahead a bit, then followed. He was tall and walked to her right. She was petite beside him and held his hand. She wore a thin skirt so short it only covered the very tops of her thighs. Sunlight where it broke through between treetops and fell dappling the path flashed once or twice through the thin, loose material, and I could see the lovely joining of those thighs. Burnt-orange leather boots with three inch wooden heels rode high and snug up her shapely calves, and the skin of her legs sparkled creamy white in the sun's flashes. She walked, and my eyes clung to her body's every movement. Not a twitch of hip or bouncing shift beneath that skirt escaped me, and I wanted so badly to touch what I saw, to squeeze the springy firmness in that skirt between my palms. Why didn't *he* touch it, I wondered, hold her there?

Then he did.

He slipped his hand from hers and placed it where I longed for mine to be, caressing as he walked beside her as I would have done, and the small pink purple and white flowers patterned into that thin skirt lifted a bit, just a touch higher up the back of her thighs, but that was enough. Her bottom was barely covered now and his fingers dipped rubbing between the crevice, lightly pressing there.

As I moved behind them watching her, and that hand, and the way her long lightbrown ponytail batted about her back swaying and swinging with each of her steps, smooth and shiny it swung, teasing me to take hold of it like a silky handle, teasing me to take hold and tug it, watching her I became suddenly aware of my own body now, my own balled-up flesh rubbing confined inside my jeans, and slowly, little by little I could feel it. They walked and I walked and I could feel it happening, inching along my inner left thigh. I slipped my hand into my pocket to encourage it along. It was working. She moved and I moved, watching her, and it was working, gaining strength with every step. Then finally it felt so strong, so ready, ready like it finally remembered what it meant to be that ready, and blood pumped hard through me. I was alive. *It* was alive not dead after all. She moved, and that hand patted now, patted and bounced on and off that gorgeous cushion with the rhythm of her stride and I could almost feel it myself, feel the solid spring in that flesh as if it were my own hand doing the patting, and I watched it, watched that hand now like a tail-twitching cat eyeing a sparrow through a window pane. And then, slowly, gently, the patting subsided into a cupping, pampering rub, as it began, and the hand finally sought hers again, and hers his, and they resumed walking in that way. But it wasn't over.

The material of her skirt remained locked in the channel

where his fingers had playfully lodged, defining those luscious globes, and I could see their round shape so clearly now as they shifted in their soft undulations, and I was bamboo. I was steel. For the first time in weeks...*Yes*. Oh yes...

A kiosk, a little green shed-like structure stood blocking the pathway ahead. They came to it and stopped. There was a window, and with arms around one another now the couple joined a short line before it as I continued my pace, slowly drawing near. Closer, I had to get closer to her, see her closer.

Approaching now, coming as near as I stealthily dare, my senses drinking deeply of her, deep as they were able barring the ache of touch, I crossed closely behind them to the other side of the kiosk, to another window over there on the left, swinging my face in toward her, toward her hair pinched and falling in the glossy luster of that ponytail, doing my best to breathe her into me as I passed. The sign on the glass said there was a menagerie past this point. I saw there was an admission fee I didn't want to pay. But no attendant was behind this window so I stood feigning interest, as if debating, while surreptitiously absorbing the presence of the woman beside me wrapped in the arm of the man beside her, until at last I watched them pass through the turnstile and enter the grounds of the zoo. I watched until I could no longer see them, see her, and then when she was finally out of sight I turned. Alive, I was alive again, and I turned from that kiosk to hurry home not to waste it, that new life, where I could be alone with her, the memory of her on that shaded path, just her and me now on my thin mattress in the heat up here filling the rafters.

Oh here he is. *Ted!* Ted over here!

The woman extended her arm and flapped her hand downward, and then I saw him. He smiled as he made his way toward us through the crowd gathered around the carousel. He had snow white hair to match his snow white beard, but I was surprised at how young-looking he was compared to his wife. She seemed his elder by 15, 20 years. We all introduced ourselves when he reached us. She was Eileen and he was Ted, and at first Ted didn't seem pleased at the sight of a stranger talking with his wife. I got the sense this happened a lot—Eileen engaging strangers in conversation Ted was then forced to interact with as well. I thought I caught a twinge of this in him just before we were introduced, a here-we-go-again look in his eyes. I knew that feeling well. So often after returning to her seated at a bar or restaurant table somewhere, returning from a trip to the restroom, she'd be engaged by another man and then similar introductions would be made, or in most cases were not made, and in me always was that oh-here-we-go-again feeling. I'm sure it showed on my face at times, too. The difference, though, was that the men I encountered plainly hit on her, taking the opportunity of my absence to ask her out, and she'd make a point of telling me so later. The exasperation of this was overwhelming. The disrespect of those cunts...But she played into it too, that's what got under my skin at times. Her energy was so open that understandable misinterpretations would occur, portraying her as ripe pickings for one deft enough to pluck her, and so many it seemed felt tailored to that task. If a woman really wants to deflect unwanted attention she knows how to do that, and that's all I asked of her. There will always be the occasional obnoxious idiot to break through the shield out of sheer imperviousness, but for the most part women are very skilled at deflection when they want to be. Somewhere inside her I believed she craved this attention, for whatever reason, and unconsciously encouraged it.

Roman works at the museum where you used to work, Eileen said.

Worked, I said.

Oh, is that right? Yeah about thirty years ago I worked there, Ted said.

I thought I'd recognize him, from the photos I'd seen in the office maybe. There were old black and white photos of crew members who worked at the museum in the 70s taped up in there. I used to study them a lot, wondering about the faces in those photos, what became of those people. I looked at Ted closely as we chatted but nothing struck me.

We were still waiting to spot our bags on the carousel. Our eyes kept a darting watch as we talked, mostly about the museum, Ted mentally dredging to exhume names from the long-forgotten graveyard of his memory. He mentioned them one by one as they surfaced in his mind. Some I recognized, most I didn't.

It was one thing and another on this topic, which was the last thing I wanted to talk about actually, but he kept going on with those names, and about what he used to do there and how he eventually left. It was a touchy subject for me because it was all so fresh to my life. But then, after listening to his story, I began to feel like I was supposed to meet him too, the same way I felt about Eileen, that our mutual work history and his eventual fate could somehow help straighten my current fork in the road situation.

Ted described his depression after leaving the museum, how he didn't know what to do. He curled up on his couch for months collecting unemployment checks. Until one day he finally got himself together, took a class in real estate appraisal, got a job, then eventually opened his own appraisal business, which changed his life, and that's when he met Eileen.

That's what I was looking for, I explained, a new direction. I felt like it was over for me, that kind of employment, that that chapter was closed, but I didn't know what I'd do next.

The conversation was given over to this now, how Ted had made his transition, and it was clear this topic was going to remain dominant. And as grateful as I was for this interaction (the coincidence, the affinity and empathy, the feeling that this was somehow supposed to happen, all that stuff was good and I took comfort in it), what I desperately wanted, however, was to talk more with Eileen. I felt the real boon of this meeting was to have met a psychologist, and I was silently crying out to her. But whereas before she was garrulous, with Ted's presence she was deferentially quiet.

They were taking the RER, the train that takes you into Paris, and so was I, and after our bags were collected we set off in search of it.

Having just been to Paris six months earlier and taken the RER then as well I felt I could lead the way. My memory of the ticket terminal and entrance to the train platform was still pretty strong, and where on that trip I found the train quite easily, we had arrived to a different part of the airport this time and were much further away. Ted briefly consulted his paper fold-out map and then we began following overhead signs, but Eileen insisted on asking for information along the way. There was a man in an airport uniform. She broke from us and walked up to him.

Which way to the RER? she asked. Do you know?

She was unabashed in posing the question, with no concern or inhibition toward the fact that she was in a different country now, where people spoke with a different tongue.

Do you speak English? she asked with that same demanding tone.

Yes, the man replied.

Which way to the RER then?

He pointed to the signs overhead we'd been following and with a thick accent said, Thaire, *that* way.

How far? she wanted to know.

Long way still, madam.

Thank you.

We continued winding our way through the airport, following the encircled RER signs that had an arrow next to them pointing up. We passed an information booth. Eileen went to the window. Better ask, she said, and delivered her question with the same brusque approach.

It just wasn't my style. You at least make the acknowledgement first that you're speaking to someone of another language, on their turf. A *bonjour*, a *pardon*, a *s'il vous plait*, merci, *something*. But there was none of that. She was American and she didn't speak French and she was playing no bones about it.

Same response, follow the signs.

Finally we reached what was recognizable to me. There were the ticket machines, which I avoided because I found them confusing in past experience. There was the ticket counter behind a wall of glass, and I directed us over. A huge line was snaking out through the door. We joined it. While we waited Eileen got a whiff of cigarette smoke. Probably came up the train platform escalator, which wasn't too far from us.

Smoking! Eileen said with alarm, striking a finger up into the air and stretching herself at least two rigid inches taller. *Hello!* she called, still standing that way but looking around now with those jerky, birdlike head moves. Bad for my *LUNGS!* she shouted out finally into the vast space about us, swinging and tilting her eyes like a falcon on a downtown ledge looking for the culprit.

They do that a lot here, I said in a lowered voice, huddling down close to her.

I know, she said, nearly whimpering now, dropping her finger and easing the starch out of her spine. But I'm a housewife from PC Berkeley, she whined, and I'm not gonna be too *good* with that.

Soon she began talking with the young man who'd joined the

line behind her. He was lanky and had a baby face with a gap-toothed smile. Once I overheard he was from Poland I disengaged.

She was first generation Polish. Her parents had arrived to Chicago poor but with a large community of well-established fellow countrymen all around them, and with their help her folks eventually prospered. She was the middle girl of five daughters, and there was one son. Her family strongly retained the pride of their roots (she could even speak Polish), and she was very close to them, especially her sisters of course. Not a day passed, if she was not with them in Chicago, that she did not speak to one or more of her sisters several times throughout the day on the phone. I couldn't look at this guy now without my stomach churning, so I did my best to keep my attention averted as he and Eileen continued to talk.

Did you hear that Ted? Roman? Eileen said. He's Polish and has been traveling all over Europe. He just came from Germany.

I turned my back to them all.

Finally we had inched inside the ticket room, and mostly as distraction for myself I began instructing Ted on the procedure as Eileen continued chatting with the Polish kid. I pointed out that, although there were a lot of ticket windows, only a few of them sold the tickets we wanted. The rest were for the outlying provinces or suburbs. To the left were three attendants seated in booths. To the right of the booths was a long counter of partitioned open windows, and all these, except the very first one nearest us, were for tickets to other places. We wanted the glass-fronted booths, or the first window at the counter.

And here's what you say, Ted, I said, showing off a little now. Un billet pour Paris, s'il vous plait.

Wouldn't that be deux? he asked. I'm buying Eileen's too.

Oh, yes, right...I said, sinking like a tire pissing air.

Space at a booth opened and Ted walked up to the window. From my place at the head of the line I faintly heard him ask for his tickets.

Two to Paris, please.

I couldn't understand it, but it was their business. I felt better to at least make the attempt. And so I made my purchase en français, then met Ted and Eileen outside the ticket room and led them over to the escalator and on down to the train platform.

A train on the right was just pulling out and one was waiting with doors open to the left. As usual to past experience guys stood in the doorways of the train and waved, signaling to come in. But one guy stood in the doorway of his car and was waving so emphatically I became suspicious, so I chose the door to the car ahead of his. When he saw I was leading Ted and Eileen away from his door he began shaking his head signaling *no* while still waving us toward him, which seemed a little ominous. I didn't fully understand this until we were settled on our car. The man in the doorway of this one had been more relaxed, and helped Ted and Eileen lift their bags onto the train. After we were seated he passed them a piece of blue paper the size of an index card. I remembered now.

What's this? Eileen asked.

I watched her face as she read what was printed on the paper, and smiled as she slowly absorbed it.

Oh...she laughed. He wants money. I thought he worked here on the train, as a porter or something...Oh well, he's smart.

She and Ted both laughed.

He helped us, Eileen said. Ted, give'im something.

Ted reached into his pocket and handed the man some coins. The man bowed his head and moved off.

We were seated at the rear of the car. Ted and Eileen sat together facing forward and I sat facing them. The train pulled out of the station, and as it rolled and rocked over the rails through the countryside, late morning sunlight streaming in through the windows, I couldn't believe I was here again, taking this train ride again, my third time now, into Paris. It felt so familiar, except this time the scenery was greener. The trees along the train tracks were full with their shaggy dressings of late spring, as opposed to the dark skeletal figures I saw standing a naked vigil along the tracks my first two trips—the first, years ago in early March, and the second so recently but at the end of October. Both beautiful and exciting in their separate ways, but this time it was altogether a different ride into the city, despite its familiarity. There was life outside those train windows as we rolled through the suburban countryside, there was life and love and excitement in the eyes of the older couple seated before me, but there was nothing but unhappy dread in my deadened heart. This time, I had exchanged roles with the trees.

I did my best to conceal my emotions from Eileen and Ted. They beamed with happy foresight as they sat together holding hands, discussing their travel plans. Eileen's cousin Micah was going to meet them at the train station in Provence during the second week of their stay and drive them to the hotel he'd picked out for them.

I was very specific, Eileen said. I told Micah I wanted a clean, quiet place with a balcony and view. Very important I told him. I definitely wanted a place with a balcony that opened onto some kind of beauty. Trees, a garden, *some*thing. I wanted to be able to open the balcony doors and let the spring country air in. I hope it's not like that place in Italy. Remember Ted? There weren't even any *windows* in that room in Italy. Oh how we fought about that. You said they'd told you they had no other rooms. I said I didn't *care!* I'm not staying *here!* It's not *romantic!* I didn't travel all the way to Italy to stay in some place that wasn't beautiful and *romantic!* We stayed in that room one night and I said let *me* talk to them. And I did. I speak a little Italian, and I could tell they had other rooms, they were just saving them. Remember the room I finally got us Ted?

Ted nodded turning away from his wife with a slight smile parting his lips, his teeth showing a bit, and it was then it hit me. Looking at Ted in that instant, at his smile and the angle of his head, I knew I *had* seen him before in one of those office photographs. He was standing in a group of four or five people holding his head in exactly the same way he was holding it now—slightly turned and looking vacantly off to the left. His hair was dark then of course and a little longer, but had the same wiry fuzz quality it still seemed to have. And he wore a beard at that time too as he did now. It was him, and it was amazing how it came in a flash like that, like being sucked through a window of time. But I chose to keep a lid on the excitement of this revelation. I didn't want to reopen and be restrained by that conversation again now we'd finally shed it. Plus, I kind of enjoyed the secrecy of the moment. I'm like that I guess. I like to hold little secret thoughts sometimes like that, for the richness it infuses a moment with in me.

Micah said he found us the perfect place, Eileen concluded. We'll see. I hope so.

They mentioned that at the end of their last week in Paris, before they left for Provence, they were planning a day trip to Monet's Garden in Giverny. That's when I saw my chance and pounced.

Monet's Garden? I said. That sounds wonderful. Would you two mind if I join you for that? I mean, I don't want to intrude, but—

No no we'd love to have you come, Eileen said. Wouldn't we Ted?

Sure.

Ted, make sure to get Roman's information before we get off the train.

It was agreed then, I was going to tag along to see Monet's Garden.

Monet was not among my favorite artists, but I wanted to take a day trip out of Paris myself as well, and here was a chance to do that and not be alone. But even more than this, I asked to join them because I saw it, I had *hoped* anyway, as an opportunity to talk to Eileen again, *professionally* as it were. I needed help. I was unraveling, and the mounting desperation within me could not let the serendipity of this moment pass without at least making an attempt. It was over a week away, but it gave me something to hold on to through the frightening isolation I anticipated for myself in between.

I hated feeling so desperate, There was a growing sense of fear invading me inside like strange warfare. This was something new and alien, this was not me. I was not a fearful person. Previously I spent my life in contempt of fearfulness in others. I reacted fiercely against it. Now I was eating so many words hurled so arrogantly in the past.

No, I needed help and I knew it, though I wasn't sure if Eileen could do anything for me. She seemed pretty wacky herself, the epitome of the psychologist spawned by the need for her own therapy. But if chance brought me all the way to Europe to encounter help I was going to open myself to it.

This was the main reason I'd asked to go along, the darker one, but there was a lighter one as well—one I thought held a glimmer of hope. The writer in me was kicking in, and he knew a potential source of material when he stumbled upon one, and if these characters were going to a place so enchantingly, so perfectly literarily named *Monet's Garden*—what a great title that is for something, I thought—then he wanted to go along too to see what might happen.

There's something about 20 past the hour that's been following me around for years now. Not quite sure when it arrived. Sometime during the wasteland period though, I'm sure of that. But the majority of the time when I get to wondering what time it is, and then check to see, it's usually 20 past the hour exactly. And if not exactly, then only a minute or two within range. I mention this because when I sat down to begin writing this morning I checked my cell phone for the time, which is on the table next to me, and it was 9:20.

There was a photo I took on my second trip here to Paris. It was taken within the first few days of my arrival when I was wandering around alone. Walking along the Seine one day toward the 13th (for some reason, for something new to do that day I chose to explore that district) I was taken with the composition of the view of one of the bridges to my left. There were modern, overhanging streetlights in a close successive row across the bridge that formed a nice curving perspective line leading, at the end of the street, on the other side of the river, to a clock tower. I took the shot and it came out quite nice, like an image you'd see in a travel book. But later, weeks after we'd gotten back home and I was showing Lain, one of my coworkers, pictures from the trip on the office computer, I noticed something I didn't see when I took the shot.

Oh my God, I said, and leaned in closer to the computer screen. I turned around to look at Lain. Lain looked closer too, then locked eyes with me. We smiled at each other and shook our heads, and Lain got up and left the room.

The hands of the clock on the tower in the photo were frozen precisely at 12:20.

Lain knew about this thing, this specter following me. We often worked closely together on projects, and when I'd pull my cell phone out of my jeans to check the time it would most likely be twenty past. We laughed about it often, but this photo was spooky, a frozen visual document of the specter. It was as if we could now see it as an entity manifest. That's why Lain left the room like that.

We were at Palace Hotel, her third stay now in the city since we'd known each other. We had just made love and were lying in each other's arms, drifting away lightly, blissfully to sleep. But I couldn't stay, wasn't properly prepared for work the next day, no fresh clothing, and I didn't have my ID badge. I needed to go back to my apartment and knew it was getting late. I started wondering about the time.

Lying there beside her in the dark I said, I wonder what time it is?

Then, remembering, *it*: Oh yeah, I said, it's probably eleven-twenty.

She rolled over to look at the time on her cell phone charging on the table beside her, then turned back to me with wide eyes. A huge smile stretched her face. She looked frightened.

What's wrong?

In a very slow, precise manner she said: It's exactly eleven, twenty.

Of course it is, I sighed, and rolled over to drift a little more.

How'd you *do* that? she asked.

I explained then, and from that moment on the specter invaded our relationship. She became infected with it too. We'd be driving along, for instance, when suddenly she'd call 3:20, or 5:20, or whatever 20, after having looked at the car clock on the dash. She'd smile then, and I'd shake my head.

Oooh Romannn, she'd singsong. What have you *done* to me?

The specter is obviously still with me, can't seem to shake it whatever it is, but I wonder—has it abandoned her now that she's cast me from her? Does she miss it, remember it even, that it was ever there, squatting over us?

That night at Palace Hotel will never be forgotten in me.

Can I give you a bath? she asked. Let me give you a bath, she said.

My knee was hurting, my right knee, one of those pains picked up on the job that came and went. After lying in bed for a certain length of time, as my leg lay bent in the sheets it would start burning. And when I'd slowly straighten it out it burned even more. Hurt like hell. We'd been lying in bed long enough now for this to start happening. I guess I'd said something about it.

Let me give you a bath, baby. Come on.

No lover had ever said these words to me before. I didn't know how to respond. It sounded wonderful, glorious, but it also made me uncomfortable, as if I were her child. I lay there and didn't speak, didn't move.

Come on, she said again, and got up from the bed and went into the bathroom. I heard the water in the tub start running. She came back, moved through the room, her naked form backlit by the light pouring out from the bathroom. She sat down next to me on the edge of the bed.

Come on, baby. The water's nice and warm. It'll help your knee.

You don't have to give me a bath, honey. I'll just get in and soak a while myself.

No, I want to give you a bath. Please. Come on. And she put her arms around me and led me out of bed into the bathroom.

For such a grand hotel the rooms at the Palace are strangely bland. Or the one we were in was anyway. Downstairs on the first floor it looked like Versailles. Tall mirror-glassed French doors, sumptuous banquet halls, ornate gilded moldings, polished marble floors, low hanging crystal chandeliers. Upstairs in this room we might as well have been at Best Western. No matter. Just an observation as I climbed into the tan-colored bathtub and stretched out in the hot water rising around me. She unfolded a white towel onto the floor and knelt down beside the tub. From a little plastic bottle she dropped liquid into the roiling faucet stream and white foam sprang up consuming my toes. The water kept pouring in rising higher and higher and soon the foam was a blanket of froth covering me. She rolled up a small towel and placed it like a pillow under my head where it rested on the edge of the tub, then turned off the faucet.

Wait a minute, she said, and got up.

She walked out of the bathroom, then came right back, shutting off the glaring overhead light as she reentered. Now a soft glow came to us from behind her through the bathroom doorway, from the other room where she'd switched on a bedside lamp. She knelt beside the tub again.

Better, she said.

I smiled up at her beautiful face.

She soaped a washcloth and began gliding it over my body. I let her go anywhere she wanted, wash anything she liked. Then she told me to sit up.

From another small plastic bottle she poured more liquid out, into her palm this time, and rubbed it over my head. Her fingers worked the lather into my scalp and it felt so good my eyes closed to the silky massaging and I was floating away on that feeling when suddenly it stopped and I felt water fall over me. I lay back down then and slipped all the way under to remove the rest of the shampoo. When I emerged I wiped the soapy water out of my eyes with my fingers and looked up at her smiling down at me. I reached for her and she leaned over into the tub into my arms and we held each other tenderly that way, until finally she rolled in altogether and lay entwined with me. For a long time we did not speak. I couldn't. I could only hold her there against my body in the warm suds and feel the joy it brought me.

Then, finding words finally, I said, or think I did anyway, maybe I only dreamed it, dreamed any of this ever happened: I'm afraid of this. It doesn't seem real. I'm afraid *you're* not real, and I'm gonna wake up one of these days and you'll have changed your mind and be gone.

What, she said, do you think I'm just gonna disappear?

The train entered the Paris subway now and the stations began reeling off. Ted took out his old fold-out map to find the stop he and Eileen needed. He'd been referring to that map since our meeting at the airport, when we began looking for the RER together, said he'd had it with him the first time he came to Paris over 20 years ago. He and Eileen were staying in the Marais, the 4th arrondissement, and according to Ted's map the nearest Metro station to their hotel was Châtelet, which was coming up in a few stops. I took my notebook from my shoulder bag and wrote down the phone number and address to the apartment, along with my email. I gave them the apartment address because it seemed likely they'd be coming to the Mouffetard at some point, being a popular tourist spot with all the restaurants and everything. Having my address they could stop by if they wished should they find themselves in that part of the city. I was sure I'd appreciate the company.

I tore this piece of paper from my notebook and handed it to Ted. He then pulled out a yellow legal pad from his black nap sack along with a folded white sheet of paper and copied something from it onto the pad. Then he tore this bit of information from the full sheet, handing me a very small fragment of yellow paper containing his email address and hotel phone number.

I won't give you the hotel address, he said, because I don't think it's necessary.

Oh...That's, that's fine.

For a second I considered explaining why I'd included my address but decided to let it go, along with the embarrassment I felt for having perhaps appeared to Ted as overeager—for having just exposed the desperation gurgling in me like a black spring.

A moment later Châtelet came and the train doors opened. Ted and I hurriedly shook hands and Eileen and I waved warm smiles at each other as they quickly made their exit. I watched through the open train doors as they stood on the platform gathering their bearings amidst the rushing crowd. The doors slid closed, and through the glass I saw Ted finally make a move to the left, Eileen lurching after him. But then abruptly Ted changed course and went right, bumping softly into Eileen as he reversed himself, and then the train moved on and they left my sight, and I was alone. Alone in Paris.

It was about 1:00 on a Tuesday afternoon. Two stops more and I got out at Luxembourg, at the entrance to the Gardens. It was the Metro station I exited my very first time here seven years earlier with the one who started all this, gave birth to this brokenhearted monster.

We had reservations at Hotel Gay-Lussac around the corner, a couple blocks down from the station. My God, the moment I ascended those steps that day and emerged for the very first time onto the streets of Paris, the *sensation* of that moment, will live with me forever. As I wound my way through the jaundice, labyrinthine halls of the Metro, making my way toward the exit now, the strap of my heavy leather bag digging into my shoulder, my right hand cupped beneath it for support, to ease a bit of the weight, trailing the bloated carry-on on wheels behind me newly purchased for this trip, my first ever piece of luggage on wheels, trailing it behind with my left hand, my black leather jacket tucked under my right arm wedged against hip and shoulder bag, walking laden like this through the station halls the memories started fucking with me. I saw that day seven years ago very clearly in my mind. We rode the escalator with our bags up to the street. Slowly the world above became visible. We'd already had our first difficulty at the airport trying to get tickets for the train. Ticket machines were only in French and we had trouble navigating the system. Frustration mounted and we snapped at each other as each of us tried and failed again and again to purchase tickets. Couldn't seem to make it work. Reluctantly we finally asked a man in a blue uniform. His English was good enough so that he understood and walked us through the process, the infantile monolingual Americans. Once we were on the train there was an accordion player who helped set the proper mood and we relaxed, watching the French suburban landscape roll along our windows as the train chugged from Roissy toward Paris. As we rose out of the Metro sunlight bounced toward us, reflecting off the buildings and washing down to greet us. Then we were on the street itself standing in that flooding light, and I was reminded immediately of San Francisco. Similar quality of light, I thought. That was the first impression of Paris upon me— the light. Next were the buildings, of course, bleached yellowish gray limestone that threw the light blindingly and stood angled and disjointed and stunted, happily disorienting at first encounter. Over them the sky lay blue and clear. The sun was warm but the air still sharp. It was early March. There weren't many people about, mid Thursday morning. We walked a few steps with our bags. I was carrying mine, hers was on wheels. We saw that we were on the right street, Gay-Lussac, and walked straight ahead in the direction we thought our hotel should be. About a block up there was a building at the triangular tip intersection of three streets, its window opened onto the sidewalk. In the window was a big tray of cellophane-wrapped baguette sandwiches. I stopped at the window and put down my bag. Looking over the selection I uttered my first words ever to a Parisian, reading the card next to the sandwich I wanted.

Rose bef, s'il vous plait.

I was handed the baguette and I gave some money and we moved on to find our hotel, pleased with the success of my first

Paris transaction.

The hotel was only another block; we could see its sign now running vertical to the building. We went in and registered. The woman behind the counter was a bit hulking in a Julia Child way and was pleasant enough, though she never smiled. She had dry gray hair cropped flaring at her shoulders and black eyebrows and spoke to us in lightly accented English. We were given our key and went to the elevator to the right of the desk. It was small and resembled a cage. I pulled the bars of the accordion-styled doors closed and we ascended to the third floor. The hallway outside the elevator was paneled with rich dark glossy wood. Once inside our room we moved through it, checking it out. There was a balcony and I opened the doors and stepped out into the sunlight and lit a cigarette. I turned around smiling with the pale yellow Paris sun shining on my face, the black slant-roofed buildings standing behind me, cigarette burning between the fingers of my right hand poised on top of the black balcony railing, left sunk deep into my pants pocket, and she snapped my picture. In my ratty gray scarf and beat-up black leather jacket and black Ben Davis pants and sunglasses I looked like a bohemian but I felt like a fucking king. My secret ego was out of control. I felt like an errant son finally come home, like I could do anything, that my life was finally on track. I was an artist. I had a band. My words had just been released to the world on our first cd and there was more to come as far as I was concerned, much more. I was sure of it. Someone would hear our music and we'd get picked up by a record label or producer, how could we not? And now I was in Europe, in Paris, with my girl, my love, we were together in Paris. It felt so incredible I could hardly stand it.

I ate my baguette. I wasn't tired in the least, quite the opposite. I paced the room, busting. I suggested we go out right away and take a walk. Adrenaline raged through me. She freshened up a little and we set out. Not far at first, just within a few block radius of the hotel. We stopped at a café on a narrow street and sat outside at a little round table on the sidewalk and had a glass of red wine in the sun. There were more people now. We watched them, tourists and natives alike. We got a bit turned around on our way back to the hotel but we made it, got into bed and made love with the warm noon cusp of spring sun streaming softly in through the thin white curtains of the balcony doors, muffled beeps and rumblings of light traffic moving sleepily below, then settled in for a long delicious nap. By mid afternoon we were back on the streets.

Notre Dame was first. It wasn't far, ten blocks or so up rue St. Jacques. Our hotel was just off the intersection of Gay-Lussac and St. Jacques, and we found ourselves on that street a lot during our short stay. There were shops there where we bought food and wine to bring back to our room. There was a little butcher shop, and from our travel book I learned to say un demi poulet, s'il vous plait, and I'd say this to the little old man in the white apron behind the glass case housing bright red slices of meat and he'd take a chicken from the rotisserie behind him and cut it in half, wrap it in brown butcher's paper, and pass it to me over the top of the case. Merci monsieur, I'd say, and he'd nod twitching his gray mustache. As ignorant as I was I was adapting relatively well to the culture, I thought. The simplicity of this life suited me very well.

It was my first experience with Europe. I was exploding. It was as if a curtain had been thrown back on paradise. I wanted to do as much as possible in the ten days allotted us. I was constantly on the go. Up early and ready to hit the streets to absorb as much as I could—as *we* could. We were there to do that together after all, I thought, weren't we? I pushed and dragged her along as much as I could before realizing this was not why she was there. She'd been to Europe before, traveled solo through the continent at the age of 19, some 15 years earlier. She'd shown me a photo of herself taken during that adventure when she had looked like a young punk chick. Asymmetrical short haircut, red bangs long and sweeping across her broad face, muted green bomber jacket and purple tights. I'd heard stories from that trip: drinking wine in Tuscan villages with a group of German boys, wine dipped up from wooden casks and ported back to the villa in the jug brought for that purpose, skinny dipping, her eventual seduction of one of those boys, and once, on a train, an old man masturbating in the seat beside her beneath the newspaper on his lap, the rustling finally getting her attention and when she understood quickly found another seat. That must have been a very intense time for her I could imagine, that trip. But this time, I learned, this time she was there to relax, which meant sleeping in, moving at a leisurely pace, taking it easy. But like so many other things I didn't know, I did not know this was her agenda before we arrived in Paris. And then, oddly, there was her fear.

Even after having traveled abroad before, and now arriving with more maturity, more financial stability, and with a partner at her side, she was uncharacteristically frightened.

While walking hand in hand near Notre Dame that first day a woman suddenly emerged from the crowd and began speaking earnestly to us in French. The spindly fingers wrapped in mine instantly clutched, digging their nails into my flesh. Unable to recall how to say je ne parle pas français in that instant like I'd practiced, it all happened so fast, I merely shrugged and we walked on, simple as that. But her grip was a lingering sting. She didn't relax until we were well away. That was the first time I really felt the depth of her fear. I didn't understand what was going on with her and it frustrated me. Communication, as always, could've saved this love.

There was a lot I didn't understand. She chose everything, planned the entire trip, which for me was part of the frustration. When I had asked to be more involved in the planning stages I was rebuffed. No, I got it babe. I got it all worked out, she'd said.

She wasn't being mean she just liked doing that sort of thing, planning, arranging, organizing. She probably thought she was doing me a favor.

Alright, fine. So I let her take it all on, and we never spoke in depth of the specifics of the trip. All I got was a loose itinerary. Arrive Paris at Roissy-Charles de Gaulle. Three and a half nights Paris, then catch an overnight train from Gare d'Austerlitz to Barcelona, sleeping compartment. Three nights Barcelona, then on to Madrid. Two, three nights Madrid, then back to Paris. One more night in Paris, fly home in the morning.

Who knew within that simple map of activity we'd find the death of our love?

I was hungry. I was always hungry during that trip. This was a major problem. I like to eat, and had a ferocious appetite while in Paris particularly because we were expending so much energy walking the city, eating lightly as we went, baguettes mostly, because they were cheap and readily accessible and reasonably easy to order. I say that because she was thoroughly intimidated by the language barrier. She said she'd rather starve than go into a place and try to order food. Food for her was considered a nuisance, an inconvenience. She did not share my enthusiasm for it. I was intimidated too but I'd make whatever effort I could to communicate. I was not going to starve. And she was already too thin, I was not going to let her starve either. Not in Paris. Not with such great food surrounding us. But whatever nourishment we consumed quickly burned off and I needed more. And then of course there were the restaurant menus. This I admit was one of my greatest mistakes.

I was interested in the Paris cuisine. During our walks through the city I would stop and look at the menu of nearly every restaurant that caught my eye, to see what was offered out of curiosity. And if my interest was piqued and if it wasn't too expensive I'd mentally file it away for later as a possible dinner choice.

This didn't go over well at all, and I know I over did it. There are a lot of restaurants in Paris and they all looked good. I was stopping every few feet.

But I was *excited!* Surely she could forgive me that. If not at the time, then at least when we got back home to our little apartment in San Francisco. Couldn't we laugh about it, at how ridiculous I was? I can understand being annoyed, but couldn't it just be chalked up to a quirk in my personality?

Apparently not.

I rose hungry one morning, the day before we were to leave for Spain, and I was careful not to wake her. I did not want to mention food again. She lay on her stomach, her thin bare freckled arms and back exposed, elbows extended angular and sharp from either side of her head, her long red hair stretching across the white of the pillows like an aged violent stain. I dressed and quietly slipped away in search of breakfast.

In the early Sunday morning cold I wandered up and down rue Gay-Lussac. It was quiet. I was out way too early and could find nothing open. My breath blew lonesome fog, wasn't a soul to be seen. The streets of Paris were mine alone. I was freezing but my God I was thrilled. Yet at the same time I felt foolish, out on the street freezing all by myself looking for something yet again, always looking for something and never able to find it. A roaming restless searching heart unfulfilled, that's me, constantly afraid I'm missing something, out there, always somewhere other than where I am while what I already have escapes from all around me, her lying there in our room warm and content, and now gone forever too.

While walking I remember seeing a billboard for the band Linkin Park and shuddered at the sight of it. I didn't want to be reminded of anything American, especially rock music. My band had just released a self-produced cd, and two weeks prior to the trip delivered our debut performance. It was also my debut per-formance singing in public, and I was still riding high on that experience. I had arrived in Europe with a handful of cds, hoping to selectively distribute them throughout our stay, to clubs, bars, really to anyone who I felt might be interested, trying to establish contacts for possible future gigs. Big thoughts, big ambitions, but I had to take advantage of my presence in Europe. Our music was not such that would be readily embraced by an American audience. To our minds our potential market was Europe. A band like Linkin Park was our nemesis, feeding the formula back to the already formula saturated culture, and now here was a big billboard pushing them. Ruined my whole Paris-streets-are-mine fantasy and brought me back to cold reality: I was wandering freezing alone for nothing.

I huddled in my black leather jacket and scarf. I wasn't imitating a Parisian that's how I dressed. Leather jacket, scarf. In San Francisco at the time that was usual daily dress for me. The weather there welcomes it. In Paris I blended right in. To my delight I was mistaken for a Parisian or at least a Frenchman more than twice in our short stay. I was proud of that, that I didn't stick out as an American.

It was just days before the US invasion of Iraq. We were wary of the timing, aware that it was just as an unpopular move with the majority of the rest of the world as it was with us, and we thought we might receive some grief from the European community simply for being Americans. Of course this was a large part of her fear, but I wasn't aware how deep it actually ran until that woman came out of the crowd at us by Notre Dame. She thought it was a preamble to an assault.

I really wasn't that concerned about the whole thing myself, and in fact we never received any problem of any kind from anyone except each other while in Europe. That's the sad truth. We saw a couple protests, in Paris as well as Barcelona, but no one in Europe was rude to us as individuals. We reserved that honor for ourselves.

In the end I gave up and went back to the hotel and ate in the café downstairs, which I had somehow missed on my way out. The windows were steamy and it was warm and cozy inside. When I finished eating and tried to pay I was asked if I was a guest at the hotel. I said I was, and then there seemed to be no charge.

How great, I thought. What a wonderful city. How gracious and accommodating.

I went upstairs to our room. She was just waking. I told her about my free breakfast.

When we checked out the next day on our way to Barcelona the price of my breakfast had been tacked onto the price of the room, which went on her credit card. She gave me a hard-mouthed smile.

Yes, of course. How savvy. How civilized. How naive of me.

Everything in Europe to me was better than in America. Everything, that is, except us.

When we returned home I accepted her time away without much complaint at first.

She just needs some space, I thought. We'd spent so much time together on the trip.

I understood that. It was an awful trip; we were awful with each other. One night she got crazy angry because I was drinking wine on the street from the bottle we'd purchased earlier, out of a little plastic cup, and I bellowed up into the quiet night sky: *Where on earth can I drink wine on the street if not in PARIS!*

By the time we got to Spain there wasn't much left. I wandered Barcelona and Madrid alone while she mainly stayed in. I felt sick about it, but she would rarely join me. When we got back home I thought we'd eventually talk, figure out what went wrong and make amends. Never happened. And for an entire year, the last year of our relationship, I miserably endured life living apart from my lover while residing with her. She just hardly ever came home.

The cat and the vacant pillow became proxies. In the gray

light one morning not long after dawn I heard the apartment door. The lock turned softly, there was the click of a boot heel stepping onto the hardwood floor from the carpeted silence of the hall, then the door gently latched closed again. I lay in bed on my side, eyes open facing the tall rectangles of the windows watching the birth of light strain through the mini blinds, a pillow lodged between my legs. This was a recently acquired habit that somehow eased her absence. When I went to sleep the pillow began cradled in my arms parallel to my body at the side of my head, to my right where ordinarily she would be, then during the night made its way slowly down to rest against my chest, between my knees and up against my groin. I lay there staring blankly, numb. I'd been lying awake that way for some time watching the light slowly creep into the room, feeling my life bleeding away into the emptiness of the bed. There were more muffled boot steps; she was trying to be quiet. Then they stopped.

The apartment was small. You could hear things pretty well. There was the sound of a long zipper, followed by another, and a clunk, then of clothes rustling. Was she going to curl up on the couch or come to bed? She'd chosen the couch before in these instances. She was actually home earlier than usual. It was ordinarily sometime in the afternoon on the weekends, after I'd already been out for the day, when I'd come home and discover her asleep in bed—if she came home at all. I was glad at least this time it was only barely dawn.

Soft padding of bare feet now came toward the bed. The cat was stretched out next to me, along my back. Since there was so much room the cat had taken to sprawling out on the bed next to me at night. I'd cuddle her a while, then like lovers we'd separate and settle into our own sleeping space beside one another. I felt the warm fur lift now and a dangling paw brush my shoulder. There was a sleepy mew in protest, a weight suddenly deposited at the foot of the bed. I felt the comforter lift behind me then and her body slip in. She quickly settled and molded herself to my shape. Her skin was cool against my back and I reflexively winced. We lay still a moment, silent. Slowly then I felt her hand round my hip, hold there, then slowly dive. I moved the pillow aside. She began to caress and stroke me. When I got hard she gently rolled me onto my back and shifted herself between my legs. Crouching, she bent over me. I heard a soft thud hit the floor and knew the cat was taking its leave, displaced by the activity.

This I knew was not her thing. She was not one who naturally enjoyed performing this way, unlike myself. I love it, love doing it, and she knew that but rarely afforded me the pleasure. Ironic, considering. And likewise she rarely afforded the pleasure of performing on me. It was viewed as a chore, it seemed, something obligatorily done to appease or apologize, depending upon the situation. Regardless, I never sensed joy in the act.

Instinctively I knew which one this was.

I let her do it. I loved her. I hated her.

After a while she tried to stop but I held her head and forced it back down.

More, I said. And she continued.

I needed more of an apology than that.

Really what I wanted though was for her to say something, to hear the words, but she was not going to say them. In the five years we'd been together I'd learned this about her. She did not apologize with words. She apologized with blowjobs, with money. That's what was underlying this whole crumbling.

Maybe I should have said something, told her to fuck off or somehow force her to acknowledge her behavior verbally, but some deficiency in me wouldn't allow it. I craved her, longed for her to come to me this way, into my arms and love me, love me again and stop this pain. So I took this one, what felt like a supposed gift. But was she coming to me with love or a mixture of guilt and easy lust? She knew she could get off with me, knowing how I wanted it. That was my weakness. She knew what she was doing, how she was killing me. Pride would not let me address it more than I already had. It'd been going on for months by now. When it first started I asked her to at least call if she knew she wasn't coming home. I had questioned her, let her know how upset I was, and then I waited. Waited for a change that refused to come. Once or twice she did call, with a gloating tone, but no longer deigned the courtesy. She was staying out on purpose, doing things with other friends instead of with me, deliberately cutting me out of her life, willfully committing emotional murder.

The next time she released me I let her and she climbed up in an eager straddle.

It was getting harder now to tell if this was purely an apology or if she had actually come home turned on by something or someone she'd encountered earlier in the night. Where had she been, what had she been doing?

I wanted to make love with her, fuck her, whatever this was now we were up to, it'd been a long while since we had, but I was so conflicted I didn't want to give her any pleasure. I wanted to hurt her, let her feel my hurt. I grabbed her round full ass with both hands and pulled her down upon me, sinking deep inside her, and began to thrust hard.

I looked at her smiling face. No, she likes this too much.

As we moved I pulled her ass cheeks apart and inched the middle finger of my left hand over, worked it inside the tight twisted flesh. She liked this too though she pretended she didn't, as if she shouldn't. But I liked it myself.

She pushed my hand away at first, but I put the finger in again and this time it stayed, in recompense.

I didn't really want to hurt her and knew I wasn't, not really, but I wanted to make her feel something other than just pure pleasure. With this she felt just enough for her to feel the difference.

I slapped her ass with my free hand once quick and sharp, then rapidly again and again. The impact crackled through the room like rogue electricity. She smiled broader with the sting of it.

It was no good, all these things she liked.

I smacked her again, this time with added frustration.

UH! OK, she said. And I thought she finally felt it then, my pathetic wrath.

Paris, I was eventually told, Paris, city of lovers, was where she'd said she'd fallen out of love with me.

I've slept with all my guy friends, she said, and looked at me with fierce defiance, flicking a quick smile from the corner of her mouth.

It wasn't going as easily as she thought or hoped it might. I wasn't going to give it to her like that. I was fighting, and she was going to have to work harder.

She did. She was relentless.

We've been together five years, she said. That's long enough.

And on another occasion, a few days later, she spun at me with eyes narrowed like a reptile's and hissed a whisper as if oozing battery acid. The words came in one devastating rush, running together in a quick fizzing corrosive sizzle. *Idon'twanta-boyfriend.*

After five years she decided she didn't want a boyfriend? And she could just say that, after five years?

She followed this up with: I want to be with a *girl*.

And then: I'm leaving, what are *you* gonna do?

I looked at her. Her grayblue eyes looked the same but they were hollow. They belonged to a cold stranger. And I heard the words this familiar stranger said but didn't know what they meant. It was too simple for me, confused me. I didn't know how to respond to any of it. The wintry clarity with which these words were spoken, each time they came, like buckets of ice water tossed on me, threw me into a shock. How do you respond to your lover, the one you've considered to be the love of your life, the other part of you, your life's mate, how do you respond to her saying these things?

Out of all the ugly verbal blows she served that one about being together five years and that that was enough, that one struck deepest.

Time limit? There was a time limit to this she was secretly holding that I wasn't aware of, and now she's imposing it? Was she embodying some arcane philosophy in emulation of David Bowie, her musical idol—*Fiiive yeears...that's all we got...*—and nothing lasted beyond those five years for her, could exist with any life beyond those five years? Is that what she meant? Or was it simply that she'd been dealing with my ass for five years now, the struggling embittered artist, and she was through dealing finally, tired of me at last. Was that it? She could just shut it off and walk away like that, after so much time, without ever trying to address the heart of the issue? I mean, wouldn't she even want to try, after such an intensely connected relationship, to work out the things that had gone wrong? She could really just say those words without any regard toward the damage they caused and walk out of my life? She could. She did.

I'm leaving Roman, what are *you* gonna do?

She had begun the packing process. Boxes accumulated about the apartment. She was sorting through her things and making piles. I'd come in one evening and found her at work in the living room. She was alluding to the fact that she paid two thirds the rent, and what was I going to do to secure my life without her? I was working at the museum on-call part-time and getting by on that, but I couldn't do it alone and she knew it. It was an obvious dig and I resented it. And then there was another one.

Why do you choose to live in the most expensive city in the country, she asked, if you can't afford it?

Before we moved in together I had asked if she was sure she wanted this, because my income was low and housing being what it is in San Francisco, expensive and competitive, I didn't want to get screwed if it didn't work out. I didn't know what I'd do if it didn't work out. She said yes, that she was sure, and I would only have to pay what I was paying at my garage space, which was about a third. For four years prior to our moving in together I had been living in a garage in the Parkside, near San Francisco Zoo and Ocean Beach. It was Spartan existence. No heat no kitchen. The carport was my living room. But there was a separate room off the carport that became my bedroom, and I had a hotplate and microwave and mini fridge and a bathroom and I only paid $300. It got old to be sure, but it served its purpose. I got a lot of work done there, a lot of writing. She raised my portion of rent a bit from the original agreement about six months in, but I was still getting a deal. She began resenting that. And now look what was happening.

Why did you say you were sure about this if you really weren't? I asked. Why did we move in together?

I did it to save your *life!* You were *dying* out there in that garage.

Oh…I thought you wanted to move in together because you loved me.

It was true. The garage had become uninhabitable. Black mold had begun to consume it and I was getting sick frequently and repetitively. My immune system was breaking down. I had to get out, but couldn't quite afford another place. When she suggested we get a place together I thought the time had finally come for us to make the next step, because we loved each other and it only made sense, now that I absolutely had to find a new home, that we take it. I was wary though. Certainly I loved her, but there were issues. It was the first time I'd heard that she thought she was saving my life, however, and my heart sank at her words.

I don't want you to go, I said. I love you. Please stop this.

You don't love me. You're just scared to be alone.

I thought a minute. Sure I was afraid to be alone again—it'd been about eight and a half years since I had been single, when you added my previous relationship to ours. There was only a two week span between the two. First time in my life that happened, when one relationship ended and a new one began so quickly. Usually it took years for me to enter something new. I don't fall in love very easily. Up until then I never respected that in others, that quick jump from one person to another without a proper grieving or transitional period, but here I found myself in that exact situation. It was an accident. I'd stumbled upon her through an acquaintance days after my break-up and something got my attention. Maybe it was after I'd learned that she was a Scorpio too, and that our birthdays were only two days apart— maybe that's what first piqued my curiosity. I'd never been with another Scorpio, but I thought if her sexuality was anything like mine, *look out.* I kept an eye on her that first evening we met at the Crow Bar, in North Beach. I wasn't even sure I was so physically attracted to her. She was very thin and kind of flat-chested, slightly boyish in dress with her hooded sweatshirt and suede Vans, long lank red hair. Not really my taste. The more I learned about her though the more there was a psychic-knocking at the back of my brain telling me to pay attention, that there was something going on in her direction I needed to be aware of. There was a kind of spiritual tugging toward her. I never felt that before. Turned out we worked near each other in the financial district—she at the Bar Association, me as an office services clerk at the Law Offices of Undercutt & Hang. I'd run into her once during lunch break shortly after we met at a little Japanese place down the street from my building on Kearny. There was a long line inside waiting to order at the counter. I'd gotten something for to go and was squeezing through the crowd toward the door when I passed her standing in the doorway. Her rust-colored hair shone in the sun. She was wearing more femi-nine office clothes. I didn't recognize her at first and did a double take as I slid by.

Oh, hi, I said.

She smiled.

The next time I ran into her I asked if she wanted to have lunch sometime, and she gave me her work number. I called and we had lunch. During lunch I asked if she'd like to have a drink after work, and so we did. North Beach again. Romolo first, a dark place in the Basque Hotel. Too early. No one in there but us and the bartender, who was beginning to flirt with her. I had to do something. I suggested we go down the street to Crow Bar instead, the place of our first meeting. That's where things took off. We were sitting with our drinks at a low table talking. She was about to stand up to go to the restroom and I stopped her. Wait, I said, and she settled back down. As she did I reached and touched her face with the fingertips of my right hand and leaned over and kissed her. She later said it was the best first kiss she'd ever had.

We held hands as we walked together down Kearny toward the train. As we talked the similarities kept ticking off, and I'd look at her with more unsure intensity with each new discovery. Her father had a '57 Chevy when she was young too. She had a chicken pox scar beneath the corner of her right eye too. She had a slight case of scoliosis too. I even learned later there was a sunken indenture in her chest like mine, though mine is more severe. I learned this on our second date, when I saw it for the first time. Our demeanors were similar as well, quietly intense and intuitive, and I recognized early the otherness in her in a way that never existed with any previous lover.

Shortly after we moved into the apartment we hosted a house-warming party. The afternoon before the party I took a long solitary walk, wound up in the Upper Haight. There was a shop that sold wares from India and I stepped in, suddenly feeling like I wanted to get her a present. There was a skirt, purple and like a veil, silk with gold trim. I bought it, guessing at the size, brought it home to her. She was happily surprised and wore it that evening at the party. At some point that night I overheard her talking with a girl friend.

It was exactly what I had in *mind!* she said.

Huh…the friend replied, seemingly baffled as to what to say.

How did he know? she asked. How did he know this was the kind of skirt I had in mind? I told him I'd been looking for something new to wear for tonight, during the week, but couldn't find anything. Then in he walks with *this!*

No, she was wrong. I didn't know how to be single anymore and I didn't want to be, but no, it wasn't out of fear of this that I didn't want her to go. All I wanted in that moment I remember was for time to stop, for everyone and everything to just stop, so that we may be plucked from the flow of the world's motion, so that I may somehow make her believe me and want to change things, believe that there was something more profound at stake here to protect and maintain and we shouldn't let it go, because to let it go meant it did not exist, didn't happen—yet how could it have not existed? But the deposit had already been placed on a studio apartment and there was no reversing the march toward the inevitable. Helpless, I said nothing and left the room, leaving her to her packing. Two days later I came home and the apartment was empty except for the few things that were mine. The kitchen table, a dresser, some books.

I reached the stairs leading to the street now, folded down the handle of the carry-on and turned it on its side. I could see the soft blue sky at the top of the steps and felt the warmth of the day up there radiating downward. I picked up the bag by its handle and began climbing. With each step I became very conscious of trying to decide how I felt.

How does it feel to be climbing these steps again, I asked myself, up to Paris, to the place you've loved so? How does it feel now, this time?

I couldn't deny there was a flutter, a faint pulse of something stirring within me, kind of like a toad waking.

At the top I set the bag down and righted it, extended the handle once again, then stood there a moment catching my breath, looking around.

Here it is again, I said.

Then I repeated myself.

Here it is again...

The station is at the intersection of rue Gay-Lussac and Boulevard St. Michel. I saw the goldtipped spikes of the gates surrounding Luxembourg Gardens across St. Michel behind me. I saw the squat rounded limestone buildings with their black wrought-iron balconies midway up. To my right was Gay-Lussac. I could just make out the yellow-lettered sign to the hotel down the street from here. There was the red-awninged McDonald's across the street ahead of me and to the left. Crowds of people moved about, mostly young people. The Sorbonne is nearby so there are a lot of students in this area. It was lunchtime. There were people everywhere. The sun was warmer than I'd hoped it would be.

Here it is...I said a third time, and taking a breath I crossed the street finally joining the flow of traffic, and rounded the corner to Soufflot. There was the dome of the Pantheon ahead. Immediately it all started attacking. I had to get to the apartment.

I knew the general direction toward the Mouffetard, had a vague route in mind, but first I needed to get to St. Jacques, which was a couple blocks up. It was so familiar. It was all so fucking familiar.

Then I found the street I wanted off St. Jacques and took that to the left, and it became less familiar. I knew the apartment was only about five blocks from the Luxembourg Metro, I was very close, but I stopped now to consult my *Plan de Paris* for the rest of the way. She'd purchased this for us, ordered it online for our trip last time, saying that it was the best map of the city there is, that even the Parisians carry it. Red vinyl-covered book that fits comfortably and inconspicuously in the palm of your hand. She'd kept it, but when I told her I was coming back here to Paris I asked to borrow it. She gave it to me the day she'd met me in Oakland to go to the museum, at the top of the stairs in the train station. Holding it now was like holding her face in my hands. Sweat soaked through my tshirt where the bag's strap pressed tightly into my body. I could feel rivulets rolling down my back. There was no shade. I stood cooking on the street in the hot spring sun as I looked at the map. Then I put the book away, back into my shoulder bag overflowing, and walked on— sweating, exhausted, tears rolling now behind my sunglasses like the crooked streams trickling along my spine.

W e're gonna get you over her, she said.
We had just seen a movie at the Castro Theater, our second date, if you could *call* them dates. *I* did, but maybe she'd say different. Anyway, we were walking up Market Street after the movie to have a drink at Lucky 13.

Yeah...I said, not quite convinced.

We are. We're gonna get you over her.

She smiled wide at me. Light bounced and shined off her in the night, off her teeth and full glossy lips and brown eyes. She was wearing a short dress under her winter jacket with tall brown leather boots with a high flat heel. She'd met me right from work and was still dressed from her day. Got out of the cab at Market and Castro and came walking down the street. I stood under the theater marquee and watched her move toward me, swinging her hips with each purposeful, booted stride. The movie was about to start, but she needed a slice of pizza first. Said she hadn't eaten all day. We went across the street to the pizza place there, got a slice to go for her, and came back to the theater, slipping into our seats just as the trailers began to roll.

I'd told her the story the night before over dinner at the German restaurant, told her everything: how after our trip to Europe she didn't come home for a year, how I started dying inside then, and how she ultimately left to be with women, and that the pain was horribly still with me going on five years. The movie we'd seen was *Milk* with Sean Penn. It premiered at the Castro Theater, and although I wound up living in the Castro after the split (that was another residual irony), truth be told, against my better nature all things gay still rubbed me wrong. Every day, just due to my neighborhood environment, our acrimonious end was a constant sock in the nuts.

At first I'd resigned myself to the fact that she left to be with women with the small consoling thought that I simply could not compete with the absurd strength of feminine beauty. As a heterosexual male who loves women as much as I do I could understand that. But she wound up with someone who looked like an unattractive *man* and was still with that person, and to me Sean Penn in the movie resembled the woman she was with and I could hardly watch because of it, and I'd just told her this while walking to the bar.

Yeah...I said again. Maybe I can be your San Francisco lover. Maybe that'd help.

I was joking, but I was also testing the water.

She didn't say anything, appeared to be thinking though.

She'd told me her story at dinner too. She and her husband basically had no relationship. In the months she'd been traveling, while in Chicago during the brief stints between trips they'd slept together maybe twice, she'd said. And the thing was, according to her, he wasn't even aware that there was a problem— seemingly oblivious to her physical and emotional absence. Why didn't she leave the marriage then? I'd asked. He was such a deep part of her family, she said, like another son to her mother and father and a brother to her siblings, that if she did, if she got a divorce, her family would essentially disown her. No, really? Yes, she said. That's how close he was to her family.

It was hard for me to grasp, but that's what I was made to understand. Her family was so tight, so traditional and so catholic, that they'd actually excommunicate her if she sought divorce. So she chose to simply live her life unfettered while remaining married in name alone. Had the situation been otherwise, if she was married in the usual full sense of the word, I might have still slept with her let's face it, but I never would've gotten involved the way I did. Little by little, though, I was being captured by her.

After our drink I escorted her back to the St. Francis, as I'd done the night before after dinner. That night when she invited me back to her room I was under a certain impression. At one point, as we sat there talking and listening to music on her laptop, she in the swivel chair at the desk and me in a chair across the small room, I got up and walked over to her, put my hands on either arm of her chair, and bent down to kiss her. Why else was I there? Her eyes widened at my approaching face and she turned away. I went back to my chair chuckling through my embarrassment. I'd only encountered that once before early on in the wasteland, and there's no worse feeling than going to kiss a girl, thinking she wants you to, waiting for you to, only to see what feels like revulsion in her eyes as she turns her face from you. I laughed then as well, a hardy laugh, to cover the humiliation. Now here it was again.

This night after the movie I was a little surprised she'd asked me back up, but I went of course. As we rode in the glass elevator that traveled up the building from the outside and looked out onto the sparkling lights of the city, ascending high up to her floor, we stood untouching next to one another. The elevator lifted and I could feel gravity pulling in my stomach and legs. I turned to her and she turned to me, then we both looked away, but we both could feel it I think—the pulling toward one another. My body drifted slowly sideways over to her, closer and closer my shoulder came to hers, almost unconsciously, then I straightened again. The elevator doors opened and we went to her room. She changed into jeans and a sweater. We watched another movie that she'd downloaded from the TV menu. This time we sat next to each other on the bed, propped up on pillows against the head board. I did not make another attempt.

After the movie I left, but before I did I made a comment at the door. Her jeans fit tight and straight on her legs, and she was barefoot. As she held the door open for me, I said: I see your toes.

She was self-conscious because the polish on her toenails was chipped and nearly grown off; she'd kept her flats on while we watched the movie and explained this was why. When I got up to leave, though, she had slipped her flats off and went to the door barefoot. She squealed softly with a big smile when I said it, curling her red-flecked toes under into the carpet and quickly closing the door, our first intimacy broached with that sighting of her rather thick toes in need of a pedicure.

That was Thursday night. The next night I met her in the hotel lobby and she came down with that copy of *The Little Prince*. We had sushi at a restaurant near the hotel that served floating-boat style, then again went back up to the room. That same pulling feeling in the elevator, the same silent resistance. Again we watched a movie on the bed, but this time I did kiss her as she lay curled on her side facing me, a light kiss on her unsure lips. And then once more at the door when I left.

Saturday was her last night in town. This time we met in the upper Haight at a brew pub. She said she used to know the owners but hadn't been for a while and wanted to see if she could reconnect with her old friends, and did I want to go? Yes, of course I did.

The pub had changed apparently from the time she'd known it. Her friends were no longer affiliated. We stayed for a beer, then left for dinner.

What do you feel like? I asked.

Mmmm...I feel like avgolemono.

That's very specific. I don't even know what that is.

I know...Suddenly I have this craving though. It's this Mediterranean soup you squeeze all this lemon juice into. I love lemons. And I love that soup. I really want it right now.

Hmm...

I thought a minute.

OK I have a place. I can't promise they'll have your soup, but it's a pretty good Mediterranean restaurant.

We got in a cab, rode down to my neighborhood again to the restaurant at Noe and Market.

They did have her soup. I tried it, and I like lemons, but it was way too tart for me.

We sat across from each other at a table against the wall. Another couple was seated at a table next to us to my right.

How do you like the soup? the man asked her. He was right beside me.

It's great. Love it. But it could be a little more lemony.

I looked at her.

Oh my wife and I love that soup, he said. We come here a lot. I always get that soup. Where you two from?

It was obvious to me then. My left hand was hidden against the wall, but her ring flashed plain as day from where the man and I sat. He thought we were married, to each other.

Chicago, she said.

Oh. Visiting?

No, I work here.

Oh...he said.

I kept quiet and he didn't follow up, but now I was very aware of that sparkle on her hand and tried very hard not to look at it.

After dinner I walked her down Market to a European flavored wine bar I knew, brown brick walls and dim inside, hidden on a little street called Rose.

She ordered a bottle of champagne and we sat drinking it on a black leather couch in the backroom secluded from the rest of the bar. When we first sat down we were alone back there. She looked very sexy this night, wearing a low cut dress and those brown leather boots again. I got to touch them now, soft soft leather thin and tight on her calf. I ran my hand up and down that leather, and grabbed the heel in my fist. I'd kissed her, and she turned to lie facing me across my lap. I cradled her there. We kissed and kissed. Then I let my finger slip under the inner lip of her dress open in a wide V on her breasts, stretching tightly across them. I ran my finger all the way down to the crotch of that V deep in her cleavage, then pulled the cloth to one side to let her nipple out. I flicked it with my tongue and circled it with the tip of my thumb and, slickened now, it swelled easily under my touch. But as it did, over her shoulder I saw a few people enter the room and sit in the leather chairs along the wall per-pendicular to our couch. I covered her with her dress again, but she did not move. She stayed right there draped across my lap like some inverse, hedonistic pieta as we kissed and drank our champagne.

Let's go back to your hotel, I said.

No. Not tonight.

What? Are you crazy? *Especially* tonight.

No. We're not going tonight, she said.

We kissed some more and finished the bottle and I said it's crazy we don't go back to your room. It's just *crazy*.

No, she repeated. I'm gonna take a cab back alone. But call me when you get home, K? Call me.

I put her in a cab and went home. It was about midnight. I took off all my clothes and shut off the lights and got into bed with my cell phone and did as she asked.

She was naked in bed too, on her knees, she said. Her ass was in the air and she was playing with herself. She was spreading her pussy wide between two fingers. Oh it was so *wet* she said, I'd made it so *wet* she told me. Now she was putting the middle finger of her left hand into her pussy, putting it deep in there, and now another finger too *uhhh*…they were both in there, and she was fucking herself. Oh my God oh my God she said, she was fucking herself, could I hear it? Yes I could, I could hear it. Now…now…now she was slipping a finger into her asshole and, and…

My God where did she learn this, how did she get so good at this, so uninhibited? Was it all that time away from her husband while she was traveling? Was this what they did to cope with the distance? I'd never experienced anything like it. I'd had plenty of phone sex in the wasteland, but not like this. This…this was…*skilled!* It drove me wild…

When we were done she told me to meet her at the hotel the next morning. She was leaving for Chicago, and she asked me to have breakfast with her before she left.

I was there by 8:30. We ate in the hotel restaurant. Over breakfast she lowered her eyes and said: You make me feel lonely.

What do you mean?

I didn't know I was lonely until you met me, she said, and looked at me with a sad smile. I cupped her cheek in my hand.

After breakfast we went upstairs and dry humped like teenagers till we came together in our jeans. Then I left, to allow her to finish packing. She returned to Chicago to celebrate Christmas with her family, but on New Year's Eve she was back and staying at the W.

E verything was as described. There was the large arched barn-like, sky blue door at number 7 on the narrow rue du Pot de Fer. I entered the code into the electronic system on the right, and the smaller entrance door, cut into the larger one, unlocked. I stepped through over the threshold, *over* because the bottom of the door does not reach the street itself but is six inches above. Just inside to the right was the stairway. The apartment is on the fourth floor, the very top of the building, but there are five twisting flights up to it. Off the top of the stairs to the left down a short hallway there was the door to the apartment on the right, the same blue color as the outside door downstairs. And there was that little gold knob in the middle of it. All as described. I inserted the key that Richard had sent me in the mail and opened the door.

I knew it was small, I was under no illusions otherwise, I just wasn't prepared for how small it actually *was* at first sight. The floor is octagon-shaped terracotta tile, painted chimney red on top of it and fading in scraped-off areas. Three or four steps in and you are standing in the middle of it, in the middle of the floor, in the middle of the entire apartment. There's the wooden ladder to the left leading straight up to the loft, directly vertical. Just ahead of that is the white futon couch, with the ceiling angling drastically above it. And just off that to the right is the red table in front of the window, and the kitchen sink a step to the right of that, under the ceiling drastically slanting above *it* on that side, so that you cannot stand erect before it. Those slants give the room a feeling of being folded over at the sides, like pastry.

The bathroom is immediately to the right as you enter. Everything but the toilet is in miniature, and your knees rub against the white cabinet of the sink when you sit on it. The tub is even smaller than the one at the apartment on rue St. Julien. This one is maybe half the size of an American tub, and narrow, but still very deep. The sink is the size of an airplane sink, and all around the upper halves of the close walls are covered by mirrors.

Basically there is just enough room in the apartment for a body to turn itself in a tight circle, and that is it. It is a cell, a penitent's cell, and in that way it is suitable to me. But at first sight I couldn't help but be horrified. I walked in and immediately felt suffocated. I left the door open on the hall to relieve the welling sensation of claustrophobia.

There were very specific instructions that came with the apartment. When I arrived I was to find the laundry ticket that was supposedly left by the previous tenant on the red table, retrieve the laundry from whichever neighboring Laundromat the ticket said it was from, and when I left this was to be done in reverse—bring whatever laundry for the apartment I had to the cleaners, pay for it, and leave the ticket behind. I walked over to the red table and opened the window. There was the ticket with the address of the Laundromat printed at the top, just like Richard said. I looked at it. It was like a grocery receipt. I set it back down on the table, then climbed the ladder to look at the loft. There was a bare single mattress resting on a sheet of plywood nailed to the beams protruding from the wall that faced the outside hallway. A white comforter was folded up and sitting on top of the mattress. I climbed back down the ladder.

A tall white cabinet stands against the wall behind the ladder, directly to the left of the door as you walk in, and I looked through it. There were stacks of unopened packages of laundry in clear plastic bags on the shelves. I tore one open and dug out a faded lavender sheet. I climbed with it back up the ladder, grabbed the comforter and threw it down to the futon, and crawled onto the platform. On my knees and ducking beneath the slanted ceiling up there, I spread the sheet out on the mattress and tucked the ends underneath, and then crawled backwards back to the ladder and on down. Again I looked in the cabinet and found two small pillows and two pillow cases. One case matched the sheet and one was white. I put these together, shut the door to the hall, grabbed the comforter from the couch, and went back up with all this to finish the bed. When the comforter and pillows were in place I stretched out on my back on top of it all and pulled off my boots. The ceiling hung low over me like a tomb lid and I looked at the raw beams angling sharply down to my right. It's a tree house, I thought. I've rented a $900 tree house in Paris.

I looked at the round window in the wall to my left and tipped it open. Warm air came in. I let my eyes close on it all and fell asleep.

After a few hours rest I felt better, woke refreshed and hungry. I climbed down from the rafters, sitting at the edge of the platform with legs dangling a moment till I got a sense how to navigate the transition to the ladder. It's perpendicular to the platform, which requires a reach and twist of the body as you swing onto the rungs. I managed the first attempt but worried about climbing down in the dark of night to use the bathroom, probably still drunk, I predicted, and mixed with the blur of sleep...I was gonna break my leg, I was sure of it, and then what? Who will be there to help me then but no one?

I took my clothes off and got into the shower. It was like standing in a washtub, deep and small. And I had to duck a little to get under the stream of water, which was cold. I'd forgotten to check to see if the hot water switch had been turned on. Richard had mentioned that, that there was a switch for the water in the white closet. Later, after I'd adjusted the water temperature, I realized the faucet was a handholdable faucet and I'd take it from its cradle on the wall and place it anywhere I liked. Feels particularly good to shoot it upward between my legs, I found.

After my shower I pulled some fresh clothes out of the carry-on, dressed, grabbed the ticket from the table, and set out.

The Laundromat was a couple blocks down rue Mouffetard. As I wandered down the street, I noticed a man in a seafood shop on the left wearing a white double-breasted chef's smock. I recognized him. On our trip six months earlier, while we meandered down the same street one Sunday morning, I took a photo of this man as he leaned out his window, elbows resting on the railing just beyond the pane, overlooking the street with a pursed face and a contemplative countenance. The picture was taken just as he swung his eyes directly down into my lens, and was one that'd made it into the book. I'd looked at it many times, wondering what thoughts were behind that face, remembering how I'd captured it. A face I thought I'd never in the world see again but here it was. His hair was slightly longer now, I noticed. Further down the street I found the Laundromat but it was closed until the next day. I turned around and went back up rue Mouffetard and stopped at a charcuterie I'd passed with roasting chickens outside on the street. I asked the man at the counter for a half and he took one from the rotisserie and cut it on the counter before me and wrapped it up. I took the receipt he handed me with the chicken and went inside to pay. Then I kept walking back toward the apartment. There was a grocery store. I went inside and bought a bottle of red wine and broccoli. Now I was set.

Back at the apartment I cooked some broccoli in a pot on the hot plate (there is no stove here only a single electric burner and a small microwave—microwaves I loathe and do not use) and cut the chicken in quarters and ate the large leg and thigh with the broccoli along with half the bottle of red wine. While seated at the red table I sat chewing, looking out the open window before me at the trees and courtyard out there. It was quiet, with a steady hum of machinery working somewhere. It was a very peaceful feeling but I felt so very alone. It was so solitary, sitting by myself in this tiny room freshly arrived, looking out this window on a strange new place, like I'd just been transferred to a stay in a new facility of habitation, an institution of some kind. Fitting, I thought. My own little cuckoo's nest.

*

I put the remaining food into the white mini fridge that stood beside the sink. Wasn't much room in there, remnants from previous tenants were taking up most the small space. There were two cereal boxes (who kept cereal in the fridge?) that I immediately tossed out. Now the chicken and broccoli fit. I left the rest alone.

It was around 6:00 now and the sun was still high but would be coming down soon. It was time for a real walk. I put on my black Dickies jacket, slung my brown shoulder bag around me (I jettisoned most of the stuff in there earlier—the books except *Plan de Paris* and my notebook, the laptop, *hers* I reluctantly brought but had no choice mine would not fit in this bag, and whatever else was in there I did not need on my daily walks) and back down the winding stairs I went, back to rue Mouffetard, which was half a block up from the apartment, but I went left this time, toward the Seine.

There was the circle plaza surrounded by cafés and bars, Place de la Contrescarpe it's called, just up the street. I remembered that. Up ahead was beautiful St. Etienne church to the left. At rue Descartes and rue Clovis I saw the church's bell-shaped tower jut up into the sky behind the buildings facing the street. And then there was the other, smaller circle a block further, where rue Descartes forks into rue de la Montagne, where that restaurant sits that we drank beer in on our last night. We stood at the small, dark wood bar having demi pints of Stella, and were amazed at one point to see the bartender, an average-sized male, step down with ease through a tiny door behind the bar among the cooler doors that you would have thought only a very small child could fit through, and descend disappearing into the cellar as if by secret escape hatch. And across the way from this place was the restaurant where we had our late last night steak dinner; there was the window we sat in by candlelight. Soon then I was at St. Germain, and there was the charcuterie and other shops we loved, and the Metro Café across the street where we ate breakfast the morning she arrived, and it was like I'd never left. And I was becoming a bit excited now, seeing these things, but I could not help but see her as well. I walked on, to rue Lagrange, and here I had to be careful because this was very near to rue St. Julien—this was our neighborhood on our stay—but it was unavoidable. I maneuvered away from Lagrange, however, down a very narrow side street that emptied onto the quai running along the river, on the back side of Notre Dame, which I was in no hurry to see. In fact, I forced my attention away and did not look in its direction when I reached the quai. Then I walked, away from the church, along the river. The city glowed golden as the setting sun buttered the trees and buildings, and I was growing more excited as I walked. I even found myself smiling now. I was really here again…

I remembered a café we discovered on the last morning of our trip that I liked very much, and headed for it. The café was on Ile St. Louis, on Quai D'Orleans. I crossed the river at Pont de l'Archeveche, which is at the back of Notre Dame, and as I strode across the bridge I saw it, *us*, standing there in that spot posing for that picture together. It was the morning of our last day. We were going to the Marais, taking a route neither of us had strolled before. The air was crisp beneath a sapphire sky. An Italian couple asked us to take their picture as we passed on the bridge. She took their camera and they stood against the railing and she snapped their smiling faces. Then they insisted they take our picture with our camera. We traded spots, and I stood there with my arm around her waist on the side of the bridge with regal Notre Dame behind us. I saw it, saw *her*, her *face*, that *smile!* I clamped my eyes tight and grit my teeth and turned my head and kept walking, averting my eyes from the church altogether as I passed.

Then I was crossing Pont St. Louis to the island. This is the only place you cross the Seine in three spots to get to the Right Bank. At Pont de l'Archeveche. At Pont Louis. And, on the back side of the island, at Pont Louis Philippe. It's a beautiful walk. And as you cross the second bridge, Pont Louis, the café is there to greet you. It's on a corner, and the door sits at an angle to the street facing the foot of the bridge. I walked in and up to the small zinc bar and stood there. I felt better already. I ordered a Kronenbourg and the man behind the bar poured it from the tap. The waiters wore white short-sleeved shirts and black vests with black ties and black pants, and here was the second man this day, my first day of arrival, who I recognized now—the waiter. He was working the day she and I stopped in and he looked exactly the same—short salt and pepper hair not unlike François on the plane, long nose, mischievous twinkling eyes. He did not serve me my beer but ran in and out from behind the bar serving the tables in the back, and I wanted to squeeze him, plant a big kiss on his cheek and say *I'm back!* I did not forget you! And now here you are again. And never in your life would you ever recognize *me*, monsieur, but I know *you!* You lived with me in a very tiny attic room inside my head in America and now I live in a very tiny attic room in Paris!

I stood there ordering beer after beer, watching through the big open windows night fall over the river and the people sitting out front at a train of round tables. A guy had an acoustic guitar and was singing French songs, and sometimes the others would join in. I liked they were there. It felt so casual and warm, just folks gathered in the springtime on a Tuesday night at a café singing for the joy of singing. There was a core group of friends, a few couples primarily, but strangers were welcomed too. Passersby stopped, contributed their voices to a chorus or two, sat and listened and talked here and there, then went on their way. People rotated in and out. Made me feel good to see that, to watch them. The fun they were having seemed to pet back the ears of my sadness.

Finally the singing came to an end, and slowly two by two the couples trickled off into the quiet night. I decided to do the same before I got too drunk. Crossing Pont St. Louis again, in the darkness, this time I decided to walk the street that ran along Notre Dame. For the third time tonight I did not look at the church, though now I walked directly beside it.

I crossed in front of its magnificent face, and could certainly feel its mighty presence snorting down my neck, but would not look. I needed a new book, and Shakespeare and Co. was right across the river. I went over Pont au Double, the bridge that leads directly to and from the entrance to Notre Dame, crossing Quai Montebello toward the bookstore, and as I did I started to shake. There was rue St. Julien straight ahead; there was our street. The store is directly around the corner from it, on the quai. Fixing my eyes hard to the right, I went inside.

I'd been in before but never fully browsed extensively. Tonight I did, discovered a second level and went up the steps. There was a little room up there toward the front of the building where some kind of lecture or salon had just ended. There were pretty young women standing around chatting in English and people gathering their things and leaving, passing me in the hallway as I approached. I was sorry I'd missed it. I went back downstairs and continued browsing.

I chose a novel by Leonard Cohen called *Beautiful Losers*. I'd always wanted to read one of his books but never came across any. It was a stupid choice of course because, although I was excited at first to read it, I found later I just couldn't.

A year before she and I went to see Leonard Cohen perform in Oakland at the gorgeous Paramount Theater. He played two back to back nights there. She bought tickets for the first night and we sat in the third row to the right of the stage. Fantastic. An absolutely fantastic concert. I happened to have had my new digital recorder with me in my bag. I carried it always in order to capture ideas for songs as they came to me as I walked the city, singing vocal rhythms or lyrics into it so I wouldn't forget. It was a gift from her. Suddenly remembering I had it two songs into the show, I took it out. The device is small, the size of a candy bar maybe, so I was able to discreetly record that entire concert. She downloaded it on her computer as did I and we listened to it often, together or separately. Three hours of beautiful music I'll never play again.

That show was a very pricy ticket, especially to sit where we sat, but she loved it so much and was so excited that when it ended and we were on our feet applauding with everybody else she said with a big enraptured smile *I'm coming again tomorrow night!*

She looked at me while still applauding, almost as an afterthought. You wanna come?

I thought she was joking. I said of course, sure.

The following night we sat front row center, the *very* front row, five feet from the stage.

Before the show we had dinner at a restaurant in the old part of Oakland. Beautiful redbrick Victorian buildings there. While at dinner, she had taken out the tickets at some point and set them on the table. She wasn't aware of this, but when she left to use the restroom I looked at the price of the ticket listed at the top corner: $251—a piece. She'd said she'd gotten them at face value from someone selling his seats online, and this on top of the tickets from the night before, which had to be a similar price...I was floored.

I brought the Cohen book to the counter and while I stood there I thought I'd attempt a little networking. I told the British girl ringing me up that I was from San Francisco, and at first she received this information rather coolly. Oh yeah? she said.

Yeah, I said. And I know this store and City Lights are sister stores, and City Lights is great, but I much prefer *this* sister.

Oh. Well...*Wow*, she said, warming up a smidge with that one. Thank you very much.

You know, I just got here today. I'm gonna be here three weeks. Can you tell me where some English-speaking folks hangout?

Oh, I dunno, she said, furrowing her brow. I don't actually do a lot of hanging *out*, really. You could just come by the store, though. There's always loads of people who speak English here.

Right. Sure, I said.

I wasn't completely satisfied with that response, felt like she was holding back, protecting the secret spots I was sure she must know, but I guess I couldn't really blame her. She didn't know me. I might've done the same thing. I took my book and put it in my bag and left in a good mood anyway. Maybe this was going to work out after all.

I started heading down the quai past Notre Dame again. Now it was around 11 and though my energy was high with excitement, underneath I was exhausted. I decided to just head back to the Mouffetard. As I walked along the quai on the river's side, just past Notre Dame, my eyes still avoiding it directly, I recognized someone else. A young blonde man with a ponytail glided by and I knew him. I stopped and turned, watching as he walked down the street away from me, then ran to catch up.

Christophe! Hey, *Christophe!*

He stopped, turned around.

Hey Christophe, do you remember me? I'm Roman.

Romon. Yes. I just *e*mailed *you*.

You just emailed me?

Yes, about the apart*ment*. I was out of town when you wrote. I just sent it a few minutes a*go*.

I couldn't believe it.

Is it available? I asked. The apartment?

Don't know why I asked that, didn't matter now anyway.

It was, yes, he said. But not now.

I told Christophe where I was staying, and asked if he'd like to get together for a drink one night. He said he would, and I gave him the apartment phone number. My cell phone was not yet operational in Paris.

112

We shook hands and parted ways and I turned toward the Mouffetard again, smiling.

I showed up at her door at W Hotel with two bottles of sparkling Spanish wine. She was dressed sexier than I'd ever seen her. Low cut dress again and boots, different kind this time, black with high pointy heels, and she wore a smoky, gunpowder shade of eye shadow over her soft brown eyes. I was glad she liked boots; I've always loved women in boots.

The room was quite homey, more like a little apartment in the sky than a hotel room. We sat at a low round table that was set in a kind of nook. It gave the illusion of a living room. There were green wooden shutters on the windows and she had them folded back to allow view of the city lights' jewel-like shine in the black of the window glass. The W was a much hipper hotel than the Weston St. Francis, catered to a younger clientele. There was even a glowing velveteen plastic Buddha in the hall on a shelf near the door that changed color from a rich royal blue to deep lush purple, and back again.

She ordered a pizza from room service. I'd never had room service. We drank our cava while the other bottle went on ice. It was like a white cyclone twirling in our flutes and for a $10 bottle it was delicious, even she thought so, and I had the feeling she had drunk a lot more fine wine than I had.

The pizza came and we shared it. That was very good too. All this was great and all I needed. I couldn't believe I even had *this*. There were vague plans to go out, nothing special, just go out for drinks somewhere, but my evening would've been complete staying right there in that hotel room. When we finished the pizza and the wine we left, ended up at Lucky 13.

It was kind of quiet in there for the night it was, but we were together and there was something happening between us. I felt so special to be with her. We laughed we kissed we held hands, got drunk and rang in the New Year, and then we went back to her hotel.

In the room's softened light our clothes came off easily and we climbed onto the large bed. Her body was firm and smooth, everywhere, and was built like a plastic doll. That's what it reminded me of it was so close to perfect, even her skin.

I was not prepared for what I was about to encounter. She was a dynamo. What had I found? She employed fascinating combinations of technique and could do things with her tongue I'd never before experienced.

My God, she's a porn star…

After languishing in her adept hands for a good long while I relieved her, turned her on her back and returned the favor, savoring her salty-sweetness. It was the smoothest thing I'd ever touched, as if naturally no hair ever grew there. What came next, though, was very troubling.

Attempting to enter for the first time I worked and worked, pushed and rocked and pushed and swirled and pushed and pushed again. Oh no…Please no…I want this so…

I kept at it, doing everything I could think to do to and trying my best, but only managed to get partway. I just didn't seem to fit.

After a while we did it a second time and it went a little further, not much though. I felt myself losing confidence and becoming sad. Shit this isn't gonna work out, I thought, disappointment washing over me as we fell asleep finally in each other's arms.

In the morning we tried once more, different position, and *yes!* Took some effort like before, but made it all the way this time. Our mutual tacit worry of physical incompatibility vanished. We stood a chance after all. It was still incredibly snug and my skin was raw from all the previous exertion to enter, but what a difference...I was in, I'd made it in...

She ordered room service—scrambled eggs and sausage. We ate it wearing smiles and the hotel's white terrycloth robes, sitting on the side of the bed. It was delicious. *This* was delicious, to be with her in these twisted white sheets up here in the sky with the green wooden shutters and a fat blue Buddha smiling and glowing on his shelf, as if blessing our new year to come.

No matter how good I went to bed feeling that first night, when my eyes opened on the beams above the first thought was of her and my eyes flooded again. I lay there sobbing with hot tears charging down my neck into the pillow. I had no idea what time it was because I didn't bring my alarm clock with me from my suitcase when I climbed up to bed, but I knew it was early, just passed dawn maybe. My body clock unadjusted to the time change I was wide awake, but all I could do is lie there and cry.

I went drinking Thursday night after work. It was just four days after she ended it. The second shot and beer had arrived and I was a couple sips in, beginning to feel her slip ever so slightly now from my thoughts, when I got a call.

Hey I want to drop off your stuff tonight. Is ten alright?

You want to drop off my *stuff*? What are you talking about?

Yeah I have it all loaded up and I'm heading out. Thought I'd come by later and drop it off. Will you be home at ten?

You mean, you're driving around with my stuff in your car right now?

Yeah.

You gotta be kidding me.

Whatever.

You're seriously driving around with my stuff, and you want to just come drop it off? How about *asking* me instead of *telling* me you're gonna do that? I thought I'd come get my things myself.

Whatever. Will you be there at ten?

Where are you going that you want to come by at ten o'clock?

Cal Academy. You know, *night life?*

The California Academy of Sciences had recently reopened in their brand new beautiful building in Golden Gate Park. As an attendance booster they started doing this thing on Thursday nights where the museum stayed open late and there was music and interactive exhibitions and cocktails. It's the latest thing in the museum world. It's meant to be a hip alternative evening to the usual scene, something educational and interesting. She'd gone once before during our time together, by herself, when she was upset with me for some reason. She didn't call to ask me along, wanted to make a point of going alone. Made sure to show me the pictures in her camera from that evening afterwards, though. Among them were shots of a huge centipede must've been a foot long crawling up her arm. And there she was dancing with a freak in funky costume and white-faced makeup, on stilts. Two or three shots of that—her dancing.

And who had taken those pictures?

I never asked.

This thing was called Night Life at the Museum, but I wasn't aware of this at the time. I thought she was saying, you know, *night life?* like that, to be smart, to rub it in, that she was having fun, a night out, a date maybe. Her tone of voice sounded like this was what she meant. Her tone of voice with me was altogether different now. Cold. Removed. And it hurt so much.

I should be done by ten, she said.

I can't believe you're telling me you're gonna come by and drop my stuff off.

Whatever. I'll see you at ten, and she hung up.

The last two nights I had long conversations with her on the phone. Hours of pouring my heart out to her, begging her to change her mind. She would not soften or budge, and her voice remained ice.

You don't know how it's been for me, I said, how hard it is for me when you're away. All the stuff in the back of my mind rolls forward and really starts fucking with me. The fact that you're not technically mine. I mean, here's the woman I love and who I think of as mine and who I want a life with, but when it comes down to it you're *not*. You're *not* mine. You technically still belong to someone else. And your family, your family will never accept me even if you *do* become mine. These are the thoughts that attack me every time you leave and I'm alone. And I just miss you so much when you're gone I can't stand it. I get so *lonely…*

Well you don't have to worry about that anymore, was all she said to that.

You don't have to worry about that anymore…It was a blade that sliced right through me. Now this…I continued to drink. From that bar to a Mexican restaurant for a couple of tacos with my margaritas. Then to another place. Another shot and a beer. And then there was a shot on the house. By this time I felt on my way, but I didn't realize how far I'd actually gotten.

By the time I got home it was around 10. I had just arrived and was getting settled when she called. I had almost forgotten she was supposed to come over. Maybe I wanted to.

Hi, I'm on my way, she said.

Oh *yeah?* Really? I said, and launched into telling her just how I felt about that, about how much I didn't appreciate our previous conversation, how offended I was, how I thought I'd be able to at least come over to collect my things myself, peacefully and amicably with her, etc. Somewhere during this I began to notice that she wasn't saying much, and there were sounds, a car door beeping, raspy scraping on pavement, sounds like that. I thought maybe she'd stopped to get gas or something, when suddenly she said: Your things are on your steps.

Slamming shut my cell phone I bolted from my room down the hallway to the front door, swung it open and flew down the long cement stoop 2, 3 steps at a time out of the 22 that exist, dodging the big plastic tubs left there in the way as I came down. Somewhere mid stoop I felt my knee snap but kept flying down those steps afraid she'd drive off any second and I could not allow that to happen. *And this is how it ends...*I remember these words flashing through me...*And this is how it ends...*Like a roadside warning too late it flashed through my mind as I came running down those steps till I reached her car parked in front of my house. She must have come from the right because she was parked driver side to the curb. My body hit her car with a thump, snapping back her side view mirror but thankfully not breaking it. I remember being glad for that, not breaking it. Almost upon impact I flung the car door wide and reached in...Oh God, I reached in...

The light in the car went on and I saw her flinch surprised by it and I reached in and grabbed her by her jacket collar, her new bright red rain jacket she'd worn on Valentine's day a month and a half earlier, I recognized it, I grabbed its collar in my fist and shook it, oh God, shook her, screaming *What the fuck are you doing you fucking lunatic!*

Dropping her collar then as if that red held forgotten heat and burned, I stood up in the swung-open doorway, stood there looking down at her behind the wheel, looked at her who would not look at me.

What the fuck are you *doing?* You dump my shit on my steps and you were gonna just drive *off?*

You knew I was out here.

No I *didn't!*

Yes you did. You could hear me.

I heard *something*, but I didn't know you were out her unloading my shit on my *steps!* What the fuck are you *doing?* Why are you *doing* this?

I'm done. I'm done…

I couldn't believe this, this was not happening. This was something that'd slimed its way out of a nightmare.

I was about to call nine one one, she said. Don't ever touch me again.

I wouldn't have hurt you, you know that. I'm sorry I grabbed you. You know I'd never hurt you.

Now I see the real you, she said.

No you don't. You see the *pissed off* me. What *was* I to you? Tell me. What was I to you?

My voice was low and husky as I spoke, coarse.

What's that voice? she asked.

I didn't know. I didn't recognize it myself.

It's the same voice you've been giving me, I said. It matches yours.

No it didn't and I knew it. Mine was meaner than hers now, full of more pain, and thick with angry offense. It was like a beast speaking through me.

What was I to you? I asked again. Tell me. What was I?

I needed to know, needed to hear her say it.

I feel like I've been fucked with for a year, I said.

Believe what you want.

That's just it. I don't *know* what to believe. Tell me, what was I?

Someone great, she said softly, almost like a whisper, and inside I shattered. You were someone great. But you could never get over her.

You're wrong, I said. You're wrong. I *am* over her. *You* got me over her. You were far superior…Far superior…And you've just destroyed me. I'll never get over this.

Whatever.

You've just destroyed me, I repeated.

Don't call me again. Don't email. Don't bother, she said, and closed the car door and drove off. And never, not once through all of it, all of that ugly and painful exchange, never once did she look at me.

I turned around to the steps and stumbled. My knee, it had no strength left to it. I could walk, barely, but in a pathetic hobble. I'm limping still, roaming Paris in a slight gimp. As I slowly climbed the steps I picked up two tubs and carried them stacked one on the other, as they were, up the stairs. I knew these tubs, was with her when they were purchased. Now I'd inherited them. The front door was still wide open as I'd left it. My roommate had walked up out of the night during the heat of it all and went inside, but left the door as it was. I carried the tubs down the hall and into my room, then went back and got the other four, one by one.

Later, upon waking in morning's sober light, I realized what I had done. I'd turned into her worst fear right before her eyes.

She had a secret phobia that at first might seem silly, but when you think about it makes perfect sense. She was afraid of The Incredible Hulk—that enraged green mountainous mutant. It wasn't so much the Hulk himself, but what he represents, the unbridled rage he erupts into, and that's what she saw in me when I reached into that car and laid hands on her. That's what scared her so.

I did it without thinking, without even knowing I was going to. It was crazy what she did, so brash and undeserved, so unfair and hurtful to me as she must've known it would be, my instinct was to just get her attention, to shake some sense into her to get her to look at what she was doing. And it was just one shake, a grip at the collar and a shake that was all, but that was more than enough. And the next day I couldn't get it out of my mind. I sent an email from work, snuck extra time on my morning break and wrote an apology to her. There was no response. I wrote another one, Sunday night two days later, from my room. *On My Knees* was the subject title, because I literally wrote it while down on my knees at my computer. I explained and begged and pleaded her forgiveness, poured all my shamed and remorseful guts into it. The next day, again during morning break, I checked my email. There was her name. I took a breath and clicked it open. Just three words greeted me: I forgive you.

That's when they began, when I read those three simple words. The tears that streamed down my face when I read them have not stopped falling since.

Eventually sitting up in the gray light of the loft, ceiling inches above my head, I tried to make some sense of my surroundings. Through the crescent hole where the ceiling and floor of the loft meet I looked down into the apartment at the window above the table to get some indication of time by the light. Early, that's all I could tell. No matter. My face still wet I crawled to the edge of the platform and let my legs dangle, then swung onto the ladder and climbed down. I was naked and it was chilly, the tile floor cold on my feet. I sat on the futon with my head in my hands and it started again.

The next morning this repeated, waking at dawn, crying, climbing down and crying again, but this time from the futon I took my notebook from my shoulder bag and brought it to the table and sat down and began writing. Writing to save my life.

I t was the Palace after the W, and then she stayed one more time at the St. Francis. When it was time for her to leave again from there it was very early on Sunday morning. She dressed in the dark, then came to me to say goodbye. She sat on the edge of the bed in a hooded sweatshirt that had ILLINOIS printed in orange across the front. I lay half asleep. We kissed, and I pulled her down to me. She told me to sleep as long as I wanted, and to order room service if I liked. Then she was gone, back to the ungodly winter of Chicago.

When I woke, I did order breakfast from room service. But when it arrived I had to sign for it, and I'd forgotten about having to do that. The server called me Mr. _____, giving me her last name, and that felt very creepy. Now I worried about signing. It would be evidence that could be used against her in some way—if only by her employer. Yet I had to sign.

In a sloppy but still legible hand I wrote: *Jack Kerouac*.

Later I told her about it, how I had to sign the room service check and hoped there wouldn't be any repercussions because of it, and she said not to worry. People had signed for her before.

Oh…

The next time she came to town she rented the first apartment.

That place on Telegraph Hill was thrilling, but it was this very first place she rented that was the best, in Cole Valley, on Shrader and Carmel.

She moved into it in February, a cozy yet spacious place; a *home* actually, someone's home. I don't know where these people went and why they abandoned their house but it was still full of their things, decorated with their furnishings, with tasteful artwork on the walls. It was a split level blue house. Downstairs was the garage, full of every thinkable garage item. There were laundry machines in there. And down a short hall from the garage was a studio apartment in back, which was vacant when she first moved in.

Upstairs was the main house. Living room in front off the left of the stairs which connected to a large sitting room, converted I guess from what was once the dining room. There was a zebra-striped kidney-shaped divan in one corner overhung by a tall drooping palm plant. This room then connected to the large kitchen toward the rear.

Down the hall to the right from the landing was a split bathroom. The first door was the toilet and sink, and the next was the shower room with dual sinks sunk into a long single counter. The shower was custom built. Round stones had been imbedded into the tile floor and sloped downward to the drain in the far right corner where you stood under the spray, partitioned from the rest of the room only by a swinging piece of glass. Very unique and we loved it.

The bedroom was at the end of the hall. To the left of the bedroom was the kitchen again.

This kitchen was something special. It had an expensive professional gas stove, all the appliances, utensils, and dishware needed and then some, and all of high quality. A large rectangular country-style table was at the far end of the room where the back wall was glass, and just outside was a deck overlooking a nice sitting garden with a hot tub surrounded by small cypress trees and ferns. Off the side of the deck was a metal corkscrew staircase that either led down to the patio/garden area and the hot tub, or up to a rooftop deck with an expansive view of the surrounding area. The hills that loomed up off to the left looked like a lush jungle, and way off to the right you could see the towers of the Golden Gate Bridge. We didn't spend a lot of time up there, but it was nice to go to on occasion while sipping a glass of wine.

She rented this place on Shrader for three months and we fell in love with it. It felt like it was ours. It was where we fell in love with each other.

Our sex life was on fire ever since the first time at the W and the flame only turned up now.

One night while lying in bed together, this was when she was still staying at the Palace Hotel, she said with a big smile: We've had so much sex that I'm beginning to *hurt*. When I'm at work I cross my legs and feel it, then I think of you and just smile.

She looked at me then, beaming.

I'd never had such incredible sex with anyone as I had with her, and definitely not with such frequency. The only thing that came close to it was when I was 19, with my first real lover, who'd taught me and explored with me so much I become enflamed still to this day when I let myself fully remember her. But this…This was all together something else. I'd finally met my sexual match.

Where you planning on coming? she asked.

She lay on her back, knees drawn up cradled wide over my arms, toes tight and pointing to the bedroom wall behind me. I looked down at her, elevated above her on my knees looking into her rich brown eyes. We seemed so serious and intense in our gaze, and we were.

I *wasn't* planning, I said.

Oh…How unlike you…

She'd gotten it into her head that I was some kind of planner, that I planned nearly every move I made, which was absurd, but there was no changing her mind about it. Just because I'd often wake up thinking how we could spend the day together and toss off suggestions as they came to me, because I wanted to make full use of the time I had with her, knowing she'd be leaving again soon for wherever—somehow this implied to her I was a planner. Somehow in this way my spontaneity eluded her and there was no shaking her conviction.

I suddenly pulled from her and rolled her on her side and slid down behind her, keeping her left leg high in the air. I put it back inside and fucked hard now, harder, lying that way. She began to slip from the bed with the force of it and fell halfway off. I held onto her by her hips and she supported herself with one hand on the floor as I kept at it. I showed her then where I wanted to come.

And that...is why...I can never be...a lesbian, she said, huffing out the words between breaths as we both lay panting afterwards. The allusion was obvious.

On another occasion as we lay in bed talking one morning, having just finished, I asked her about toys, if she had any, was she even interested in them? It seemed that with a sexual appetite like hers, and her travel life, she'd need something to get her through.

Unyielding plastic holds no interest for me, she said. There's no emotion, no...

No personality, I proffered.

No soul, she continued.

You on the other hand, she added, have more soul than I know what to do with.

Yet you're doing pretty well with it, I said.

I'm glad you think so.

That's always stuck with me, her saying that. *You have more soul than I know what to do with*...and I wonder about it now. One more thing to wonder about.

But what she said about having no interest in unyielding plastic made me uneasy. What did she do to feed her appetite then while she was away and only the real thing would suffice? With the comfort of secrecy distance allows, and sexy new locations and hotels, and businessmen more her economic equals also cloaked in the comfort of travelers' secrecy, and with her beauty and openness and charm and desirability and *talent* my imagination ran wild and I prepared myself for the worst. From the very beginning I was holding onto my walls and was determined not to let them come down—I could not, *would* not survive another crumbling I was sure of it—because I sensed it, sensed the danger of what lay ahead and must steel myself against it. I knew what was going to happen eventually, and I was protecting myself. Or so I thought. Slowly though those walls dissolved in the heat of our passion and the beauty I saw in her heart.

I'm glad I met you, she said.

I told her I didn't know how I got so lucky meeting *her*, and she said: You feel lucky? I smiled and nodded. *I* do, she said.

She did? *She* felt lucky to be with *me?* All this was too good to be true, and a part of me distrusted it as an anomaly, a dream that would soon go poof and I'd wake up and resume my rightful fate. But she made me so thoroughly believe it, believe her love for me, that I let myself go over to her too, as love demands. But not yet. As much as I felt myself going to her, for the time being I was still holding my walls in place.

When she first moved into Shrader the apartment downstairs was empty, as I said. The first night when she brought me with her to the place (it was the first time she saw it too) we moved all through the house exploring, including the downstairs apartment. The door was unlocked and we entered. It was very nice as well, but very different from upstairs.

It was all one big room. There was a sunken, hardwood floor living room space, a desk and office area, a double bed across the room from this, and then the small, humble kitchen in back. There was a backdoor in the kitchen that opened onto the patio and the hot tub, which was right outside the kitchen window. It was furnished and decorated with a simpler, more bohemian taste, and there were shelves of good books lining the walls, fine literature. I would have been ecstatic if this place was mine. It seemed perfect for me.

Shortly after she moved in a woman moved in downstairs. I never saw her but she was described to me as average and frumpy, a school teacher from the Midwest who was in San Francisco doing research of some kind and took the apartment for a couple weeks—through the end of the month. They met one day at the washing machines in the garage. The woman was

126

collecting wash, and she came down to start hers. Something got mixed up in the woman's clothes that didn't belong to her.

This must be yours, the woman said, dangling black thong panties from her finger. I could never get into that skimpy thing.

Yes, she said, it is, taking the panties from the woman's finger with a smile. Thanks.

And that was it. The woman went down the hall and into the apartment.

That poor woman…She was subjected to the sound of sexual gymnastics tumbling regularly over her head, especially on the night of Valentine's Day.

We had spent the afternoon drinking champagne downtown. Then I took her to Bistro Clovis for dinner, a French restaurant which was a block down Market Street from that wine bar we went to the week we first met. More wine. When we got back to Shrader we tore into each other, first in the living room on the couch and the floor, then on down in the bedroom. It was endless. We thumped for hours above the head of that woman downstairs, and then in the morning too. She heard it all no doubt and it must have driven her crazy.

The next weekend we woke to moaning beneath us. Moaning and squeaking and squealing. The woman's boyfriend was visiting (they had met again at the washing machines a couple days before, and the woman had mentioned he'd be coming to stay the weekend) and this was her attempt at revenge. We lay quiet a moment in the morning light listening, then turned to each other and laughed. We couldn't help it. We could tell the woman was being extra loud on purpose, and we felt a little sorry for her then, realizing what she'd endured.

Soon the apartment was vacant again though and we carried on, growing deeper and deeper into one another.

We had wonderful dinners at home together. She was a terrific cook. Pork loin was a delicious specialty of hers, with a sour cream mushroom dill sauce, and she prepared it often. At my request she once made fried chicken. She'd never made it before, had to research a recipe. Hot oil splashed from the pan and striped an indelible scar across the top of her left wrist, a permanent brown slash marking her forever, for me; she'd wanted to roast but changed it at my suggestion to please my mercurial tastes. I felt terrible but she did not complain, and the chicken of course was excellent. She began making lunches for me in the morning with leftovers from dinner, pork loin sandwiches for example, with raspberries. Or she'd boil eggs while I was in the shower to bring with me for breakfast, timed just right so that the yolk was bright yellow and flaky. Tucked away along with the eggs in the paper bag she put them in would always be a special spice mixture she'd prepared—salt garlic powder black pepper paprika. There's never been a faster way to melt me than to do things like these. I was melting.

One morning I joined her in the kitchen with a sigh. She was squeezing oranges for fresh juice to go with breakfast that we were about to cook together. It was Sunday. I was feeling a little down, thinking about how far removed I felt from my writing, how I was once so dedicated to it, really worked hard at it, either writing songs or other things, I was constantly at work on something, but now it felt so far away…

She looked at me. What baby? What's that sigh?

Oh…I don't know where my words went, I said, looking out the window.

When did you lose them?

Long time ago now, I said. Five years…When I lost faith in them.

Five years earlier after she'd left I shut down, began consciously pushing my creativity away. It was the cause of what happened, I felt, of her leaving. I was too strongly focused on trying to succeed as an artist. And the more elusive success proved to be the more frustrated and single-minded I became, and that overflowed onto the relationship. After she left, and then a year later after the band stopped and I no longer had a creative platform, I decided to take a step back from it all and do some work on myself. I needed to learn to be less intense, more open, more giving. And learn to laugh more. So I poured my creative energy into myself, in developing more as a person and focus less on being an artist. My art now was creating myself, I thought, and that's what I tried to do. Learning new social skills became part of that.

They'll come back, she said. When you're over her your words will come back.

She often made references like this, to my former girlfriend. I tried to ignore them.

I'm afraid they're too far gone to come back, I said. *That's* what I'm afraid of.

As I stared out the window I had an image in my mind then of birds, and I was the sky. A few birds still flew erratically through me but the rest had migrated far away. I thought of sharing this with her, but I didn't.

I saw that she looked downcast now and tried to kiss her, but she would not offer her lips.

Hey, what's the matter? Why won't you let me kiss you?

I'm afraid you're saying we have no future.

I took her face in my hand and looked into her eyes.

There you go again, I said. I wasn't saying that at all.

She had begun saying things like this now too, misreading me at times and the things I'd say.

I know you didn't in words, she said, but I feel like that's what was behind them.

If my words come back, you would be the one to help them come back.

You're the only one that can bring your words back, she said.

I know. I said you'd be the one to *help* them come back.

M y second night here in Paris I reached the apartment door just in time to catch the phone ringing. It was little more than a faint chirp and at first didn't register in me, but then I ran inside to the far end of the futon and snatched the receiver from its cradle.

Hello?

Roman?

Yes…

Roman it's Richard.

Yes Richard, hi. How are you?

Oh I'm fine. I was just calling to check in. You made it alright, then.

I've never met Richard in person. All our communications and transactions have been conducted via email, post, and telephone. His voice is very soft and he sounds very kind. Before I left we'd had a long phone conversation in which I'd told him my situation. He knows how depressed I am. I was telling him I didn't think I could go through with it, the trip. I just didn't see how I could do it. This was only three days before I was scheduled to leave. He said he understood, that I'd gotten hit pretty hard, but he said he thought it would be good for me, and I should go. Everyone said that. Everyone I talked to about it said I should go. I was the only one, it seemed, who knew just how bad an idea it really was.

So, how's it going? Richard asked. His voice was cottony, his words padded from any sharp edges to soothe and protect, as if I were some brittle thing.

Well, it's really *small* Richard. I mean, I knew it was, but I didn't realize…

I stopped myself. My voice still sounded dead to me and I'm sure it did to Richard too, but it managed to let disappointment seep out, and I did not want Richard to think I was complaining or dissatisfied. He'd been too nice to me, making all kinds of recommendations for things to do while in Paris, even writing an email of introduction to an American expatriate friend of his who puts on weekly soirees in her home so I could make some English-speaking connections. He'd gone out of his way to help me, and I appreciated him and his friendly efforts. Still though, I couldn't help it. I *was* disappointed. I'd been spoiled from my last trip and I knew it. No matter how I had tried to prevent it I'd been spoiled by her in many ways, and what I found when I arrived in Paris this time just couldn't begin to compare to my experience last time. Plus, the toilet was leak-ing. It was a new thing that started that morning after I'd flushed. A little stream springing from the base of the commode rolled across the floor through the bathroom threshold into the main room.

But it's fine Richard, I said. Really.

Yes...Yes it is small...Richard said.

And the toilet's leaking, I said.

Oh no, Roman. I'm so sorry. Is it bad? I didn't know there was a problem. The tenants who just left didn't mention anything, only that you need to hold the handle in a certain way when you flush. They said they left a note about that.

They had. I found the note on the table next to the laundry ticket when I arrived, and was following the instructions that were written there. That wasn't the problem. This was different. This was a leak.

Yeah, I know about that, I said. But this morning water seeped out on the floor when I flushed. Way out near the futon.

Oh no, Roman, Richard said again, and still his words were cushioned and placating, as if wary that any tinge of alarm in his voice might trigger greater trauma in me. I'll call Patrick and see if he can look at it, he said.

Patrick was the handyman. Richard had mentioned him before I left San Francisco and gave me his number in case of any problems. Did he speak English? I'd asked. No, no not much, Richard said. I didn't see how that was going to help me then if something did come up.

Thanks Richard. That might be good.

How's everything else? Did you find the laundry ticket?

I did, yes, I said.

Good. That's good, Roman.

I felt coddled and I hated it, hated that I provoked this tone of voice in him.

Did you find the hot water switch in the closet? he asked.

Yeah. I forgot at first, and when I took a shower the water was cold. But then I remembered you told me about the switch, and changed it.

Good. Yeah, it's green for hot and red for cold. Kind of counter intuitive, I know...

Yeah. Yeah I got it, I said.

OK Roman, good. Well, I guess I'll let you go then. I'll try to call you again in a few days. You take care.

OK Richard, thanks for calling, I said and hung up.

And since I was home now and it was around 10 o'clock I thought I'd just settle in on the couch for the night and read. I picked up *Beautiful Losers*, got half into the first chapter, and it was good, but I realized it was impossible. I put it down and have never opened it again since.

Even before we entered the Paramount Theater that night for the second Leonard Cohen show I knew I was going to see her. We had that. We could sense each other. Maybe it was because we were Scorpios, and that our birthdays were two days apart. Or maybe it was what I'd always suspected and what made our relationship so intense, that we were soul mates and connected somehow psychically. I don't know, but we had it, whatever it was. There are numerous incidences that illustrate, but one night four years ago, nearly three years after she'd left, I ran into her. I was in a funk this particular night. Something, a bad date the night before I think, set it off, and I started really missing her. I was out wandering the streets, found myself on Divisadero walking with tears in my eyes thinking thinking of her. I stopped for a drink at a place, then kept walking. I reached Page and Divis and decided to stop again at the bar there, but they were very busy. I ordered and waited, and when it became clear they'd forgotten about me I left. Down Page I went and then over to Haight Street. I tried another bar and got a drink easily. Then had another, all the while with her on my mind and feeling incredibly sad. Then I left and walked down Haight, heading toward Church and Market and the train there, and as I was reaching the corner of Duboce and Church I saw a group of four people round the corner toward me. Though we were 30 yards or so apart, and it was dark, the streetlight above threw enough light for me to see and I quickly recognized her among them. Although I looked at no one but her, I could see she was with a male and another female, and her person. She was bringing up the rear of the group, to the right. I cocked my head when I saw her, looking at her, not knowing how to behave or what to do. First instinct was to turn around or somehow alter course, but it was too late for that now. That would have been embarrassingly obvious. Should I just keep walking right past her, like I'd told myself I'd do if this situation ever occurred? The thought flashed through me just as the realization began to really sink in, that it was HER, the person I most wanted in the world at that moment, there she was walking toward me in the night, and if I had altered a single thing I'd done earlier this would not be happening right now, and I could still hardly believe it actually was. I decided to stay my path, and they stayed theirs. I could see now that she saw me too. I both looked at her and averted my eyes downward as we approached each other. I took the sidewalk wide to the left as I passed the group, only using my vision peripherally. I saw her fade back slightly and cross toward me, a bit hesitant at first, as was I (I still wasn't sure what I was going to do) but when she got close to me I automatically scooped her up in my arms and hugged her tight. In my arms, she was in my arms…How familiar her thin body felt. My arms wrapped completely around her like a coil and as I squeezed her to me I heard her ask softly: How are you?

Before I even knew what I was saying I murmured, I miss you.

I know, she said. I've sensed it.

We loosened our embrace, aware we were being observed by the others who stood waiting for her just up the street. Our hands fumbled together as we chatted, our fingers interlocking, dancing playfully, carefully. Those thin fingers…so delicate. My fingertips recognized their touch instantly. We looked into each other's faces. She released her gaze now and then, but mine was riveted. She glanced up the street. They were waiting. I could tell she'd been drinking.

I gotta go, she said. We're going to a party.

I nodded, then pulled her to me and held her in my arms again, held her tightly. When we disengaged we still locked fingertips at arm's length and looked into each other's eyes.

I sensed I would see you tonight, she said. I knew I would.

And with these words she turned, as did I.

Without looking back I walked on. I didn't want to see her with them, with *her*, her person, but I was glad they saw her with me. Glad they saw our embrace and our hands touching and me sweep her up in my arms and hold her tight. I imagined them saying to themselves as they watched us: Wow, that guy really *loves* her, whoever he is…

We entered the Paramount and she needed to use the restroom. The theater lobby was humming with people clustered and hustling about. Having just been to the theater we knew that the bathrooms downstairs would be packed, as we discovered they were last time, so we walked up the flight of stairs ahead of us toward the mezzanine restrooms, where we felt they'd be less crowded. She joined the long line waiting for the ladies room and I lingered in the mezzanine lobby. There was a bar at one corner there and standing at the far end was Sean Penn. Though he wore a baseball cap with the bill pulled low over his eyes, I recognized him right off. I'd seen him a couple times during the filming of *Milk* in the Castro. The most interesting time was when I passed the window of the old shop where the real Harvey Milk worked and where some of the film was shot. Security held foot traffic at first as I approached, but when I was released I glanced inside the window in passing and there was Penn staring intently through the glass, taking a breath between takes I assumed, and for an instant we locked eyes. I felt that was significant, the meeting of two intense artists' eyes—those of one famous and recognized, and those of the obscurely anonymous though no less recognized in the eyes of heaven.

Anyway, there he was standing at the bar trying to be incognito wearing a baseball cap too small for his big head, he has a really big head, and I turned from that moment and wandered over near the stairs to look out at the beautiful, resplendent art deco lobby, all emerald green and gold. Suddenly I remembered my camera (last time I recorded the show in audio, this time I was taking advantage of our front row center seats to record it visually) and took it out of my jacket for a shot of the colorful lobby.

After I snapped my picture I happened to glance across to the railing on the right side of the stairs, and there she was, taking her own photo of the lobby, her person standing right behind her.

My heart skipped and I became almost embarrassed for some reason; again I didn't know what to do. Immediately I turned away, not wanting them to see me looking at them, but then I turned back and looked again. Now she had spun her back to the lobby and turned the camera on her person. I say it that way, her person, because it's hard to think of her partner as a woman when she so closely resembles a man. She appears to be a synthesis of both sexes, each canceling the other out to near sexlessness.

I turned away again, and seeing a fixture on the wall of a golden Capricorn (my present love was a Capricorn) I distracted myself by taking a couple photos of this image. A moment later she passed before me in the crowd, alone. I took a look around and didn't see her person anywhere, so breathed deep and quickly caught up. When I tapped her shoulder she turned and gave a surprised little laugh, and we embraced.

She felt terribly thin in my arms, even thinner than before, unhealthy, like I could easily snap her into pieces. I could feel her bones. She wore an odd outfit—some kind of 40s style hat that clung contoured to her head like some fat exotic laying hen, a tapering bluegreen feather curled from it curving down along her long red hair. She had on false eyelashes, thick and black and batlike, which I'd never seen her wear before, and black fishnet fingerless gloves à la Madonna circa 1983.

I knew I was gonna see you, I said.

Yeah? That seems to keep happening, doesn't it?

Yeah...

We chatted awkwardly a moment. Then, in the middle of telling her how she was in for a treat, how I'd seen the show before and how great I thought it was, suddenly, looking over my shoulder as I spoke, she goes: Here comes my girlfriend. Are you going to be nice?

Oh no, I didn't mean for this to happen. I never wanted to meet this person, and now here it was finally coming.

And then there she (she?) was, standing at her side. Much shorter than her, with short black hair pressed curling out around the brim of a black bowler, wearing an oversized man's black blazer. There surely must be more than meets the eye, but what she saw in this person I'd never know.

We both said hi, uncomfortably, and that was it. I looked away.

She laughed then, at my obvious uneasiness no doubt, and to break the awkward silence she explained to her girlfriend that I was just saying this was my second time to the show.

Well, he must've really liked it if he's seeing it again, her person said.

I did, I said. It was amazing. And I'm fortunate enough to be able to see it again.

For a second I thought of mentioning my front row seat, but that would've been unnecessarily rude, so with that I wished them good night, saying that I had someone waiting for me. I was proud of myself for keeping my mouth shut about the seat.

Flash forward to intermission now an hour later.

We went to the lobby for a drink. She disappeared briefly while I stood ordering at the bar. I had just placed my order when I heard *Roman!* Get me one too!

It was her calling from the corner of the bar.

I asked what she'd like, then added a white wine to my champagne/red wine order.

Now it's her turn, I thought, gathering the three drinks in a triangle shape and stepping away from the bar toward the center of the lobby. They both joined me at about the same time, and I made the introductions. My former girlfriend did not hear me properly when I gave her name, so she addressed her directly.

And you are? she asked.

His girlfriend, was the response.

Again she didn't hear properly and asked for the answer to be repeated.

His *girlfriend?* she said, a little louder this time, her voice lilting into a giggling question as a flush colored her cheeks and her eyes darted at me.

My girlfriend? I'd never heard her refer to herself this way before, and I liked it. Especially in this instance. I smiled too.

I was looking for a *name*, my dear.

Oh this is getting good, I thought.

Her name was given again and this time it stuck.

I couldn't believe it, this moment I was in, one on my right and the other on my left. I watched them talk. One looked beautiful, young and feminine. And the other looked, well, odd in her strange outfit. I hated to think it, but she looked a little aged, too, and I wondered why.

Then the question came.

Where you two sitting?

I'd managed to avoid mentioning it before—now there was no getting around it.

Wow! she said, astonished.

I showed her some of the pictures in my camera I'd taken during the first half of the show.

Those are great. Who took those, you? she asked her.

I did, I said.

Again she was surprised. I didn't take too many pictures when we were together. She asked where we sat at the other show.

Uh, close to the front, I said. But on the side.

Another wow, more subdued though this time, and a strange, almost hostile suspicion crept out from behind her smile with that word. She asked how we'd gotten the tickets, and I explained that my girl was really good at getting things...that she wants, I added, and then worried how that might've sounded, but not too much, because a moment later the lobby lights flashed and it was time to get back to our seats. I did my best not to rub anything in, and I didn't, but right then I felt *great!*

Before she parted from us we clasped hands lightly. No, more accurately, she dipped her fingers into my hand genteelly, like a debutant at a cotillion or something, she all but curtsied. Then she looked me in the eye and said: Ro*monn.*

Ro*monn?* She never called me *that* before. Ever. I was left with the same unanswerable question swimming inside me that I had been unable to get a handle on for five years: Who was she? Who was this woman who had consumed my life for so long?

Before she let go of my hand she looked over at my girl pleasantly, offering a farewell glance to her with the thin smile stretching across her pale face, and then she turned toward the stairs. As I watched her ascend to the mezzanine toward her upper balcony seats, there seemed to be a faint glower clouding her face, and it felt like this time I had won, that fortune had finally smiled on me for a change and I won before her this time. For the very first time since she left me, this time *I* won, and I thought my life was finally changing. And just like that the spell was broken. The noxious, all-consuming haunting spell of her was shattered, and I felt free for the first time finally in five long years. Five. Long. Years. Turns out though one haunting had just been exchanged for another.

That was such a special evening, unforgettable in so many ways, and as we were leaving the theater after the concert one more special thing happened.

We were filing out of the theater's side exit, right of the stage, and as we neared the door a woman was standing there holding a white sheet of paper. Drawing closer we heard this woman say: Now let's see, who can I give this set list to?

The woman's eyes roved the flowing line of passing faces, and then settled.

Would *you* like it?

Yes! she said. I would! Thank you very much!

It was a printed list of the songs Leonard Cohen performed

that night, which were exactly the same as the night before; the whole concert was, right down to the stage patter. We smiled about that during the show but it didn't matter, it was still glorious, a magnificent show, just like the one before. She handed me the paper and I carried it in my hands for her to the car like it was a fine and precious piece of art.

A couple nights later the phone rang again. It was Christophe suggesting we get together.

Great, I said. Sure. When?

Mmtomar*row* night? I'll come to the Mouffetard and peek you up. What street ahr you on?

I told him, asked if he knew it. Oh oui oui oui, yes he knew it of course. He'd call me when he reached the neighborhood, round 9.

The next night at 9:30 the phone rang. He was on rue Mouffetard and du Pot de Fer. I went down and walked up the street to meet him. He was with his friend Julien.

Julien. How the names in this tale keep overlapping, I thought.

It was a warm night, warmer than I thought it was going to be. The weather has fluctuated from pleasantly sunny to cool and overcast to scorching afternoons followed now by muggy nights. Each morning I've woken to a different climate. I was wearing my leather jacket with a brown tshirt, and Christophe a tight-fitting white tshirt with his jacket draped over one shoulder like a cape. Julien had on a thick tan shawl-collared sweater, made me itch and sweat just to look at him but he seemed comfortable enough. He was tall, about Christophe's height, and thin, with pale skin and fluffy brown hair. I got the feeling he came along to check out the American. People in Paris are curious about Americans I've learned. Nearly everywhere we went Christophe and Julien introduced me as an American. They said French girls love American men. Well, that didn't seem to be the case with me. I couldn't get any French girls in Paris to even look at me so far. Oh they're like that, they said, French girls. They ahr like rabbeet, Christophe said. Easily scaired and 'ard to catch. He liked American girls, Christophe. Blondes. That's nearly all he talked about. Blonde American girls. Next best was Canadian for him. Everything was about girls for these guys.

We set off wandering down rue Mouffetard, stopping at a bar before we left the neighborhood for a quick shot Christophe ordered, some sweet French concoction. I don't like sweet drinks but I drank it. We walked on, turned onto rue Lanneau de Polytechnique and into a bar on that street. It was an American-style bar, they said.

Well, they had photos of American rock stars on the walls and played American music on the juke box, so I guess it was, but it just seemed like a dull low-ceilinged average bar to me, with not much going on. I had asked that they show me around a little, take me to some cool Paris places that they surely must know, being both born and bred Parisians. Maybe it was coming, but they seemed a bit at odds as to where to go. Christophe bought a round of beers here and we talked. Julien asked why I was in Paris. I did my sheepish best to explain, and he said *What?* You come to Parees to get ovair a broken *'art?* You don't come to Parees for *zat.*

I know I know…I said, keeping my head low. I didn't mention the writing part.

Parees ees too roman*teek* for zat.

Yeah, I know…

I mean, go to Thailand if you want to get ovair a garl. Zat's whaire to go.

Alright, yeah, I know…

I mean, zair you can walk up to any garl al*most* and…you know…'Ere…'Ere zee garls are all scaired. You don't come 'ere for zat.

Al*right!* I *know!* Don't rub it in. It was a dumb move I know that already. Let's move on…

They laughed. We laughed. We finished our pints and left.

As we continued walking down Polytechnique Julien pointed out the building ahead. Zat's whaire Christophe and I went to school, Romon. Zat's whaire we met.

Ah, I see…I never would have guessed that was a school, I said. And though I was glad he shared this (I was enjoying myself with these guys, beginning to forget myself a bit) those were the last words I said for quite a long while, because seconds later on the same street we passed a restaurant named *Le Petit Prince*.

Suddenly I dropped out of conversation and they talked to each other in French. I felt myself sinking away again. She even had him tattooed on her lower back, the Prince, an image from the book—that's how much she'd loved it. In a long coat fanning at his heels he stood at the base of her spine holding a thin sword pointing downward, as if in proclamation, of her, his terra firma. I saw it the first time we were together of course, but I really got to examine it at Shrader. It was so old, done so long ago and was so badly faded it now resembled little more than a large squashed turquoise and yellow bug. When I first saw it I wouldn't have known what it was if she hadn't already told me about it. At one point she decided to have it removed and began treatment in Chicago during her frequent returns—treatment with Dr. Brian. Or rather, *hot* Dr. Brian as she referred to him. She described her first session, it would require a series of them over time, which was not finished by the time we were. While lying naked face down on the table Dr. Brian examined the area, pulling her skin taut and pressing down over the tailbone, and she said she almost came right there. Apparently the good doctor had unwittingly hit the spot, *my* spot, the one I discovered all on my own. Perhaps it's already known to man and antiquity but I and the women who've come into awareness of this spot had neither heard of nor experienced it prior to experiencing it first hand, through *my* hand, and so it has been dubbed (not by me) the R Spot. I'd found it years ago, with *her*, the other one, and over the years my discovery remained a greedily guarded secret, though I demonstrated freely with opportunity. I see the time has come now to document my find.

If you apply pressure at the tip of a woman's coccyx, I'd say 8 out of 10 times it unleashes a small fury in her, and I'd proved it yet again with this lover. Once I'd applied my technique and the sensation had been released it was easily triggered, so Dr. Brian's fingers had little trouble arousing the spot when they stumbled upon it beneath her worn-out tattoo, the skin of which had been turned crinkly with laser treatment. The Little Prince was being erased, and is he gone yet? He is not gone from me…

After passing that restaurant I didn't say a word the whole time we meandered down the turning streets, silently shutup and lost in the ghost-swollen world of my memories. Like a balloon on a string I simply trailed along through the night in the hands of Christophe and Julien, silent and unseeing, oblivious to every-thing around me. But when we reached Place St. Michel, and then hung a left down St. Andre des Arts, recognition somehow seeped in and I suddenly snapped to. Wait a minute, I said to myself, not this street again. I knew this street all too well, one of the many I've wandered over and over and now try very hard to avoid. I wanted so desperately to go somewhere new and unfa-miliar I wanted to scream it. Holding to my patience though I walked on with them, thinking perhaps it was yet to come, we were just walking this street to get there—but I was wrong.

I followed them into a place I'd been before, *we'd* been before, last time. Tonight there was live music, a guy with his guitar singing American pop songs. It was busy, a lot of young girls standing in small groups at the bar and dancing on the low coffee table in front of the window.

We bought beers and listened to the guy sing. He wasn't bad I just wished he was playing something else. Christophe and Julien eyed the girls. I did too, but with the knowledge that they were all too young for me and that I couldn't speak to them. Christophe swore this was not a problem, seeing how French girls love Americans and all, but it was a problem for me. If I can't speak to a girl I feel like an idiot and it doesn't work.

Julien went to make his move. He joined a circle of three girls and started chatting with them. Then Christophe began talking to the one next to him at the bar. I stood and drank my beer. It was loud in there and they were all speaking French. The only thing I understood was the pop songs the guy was singing, and I didn't like the words. Julien seemed like he was doing alright. I even thought he knew them the way they all talked, so easy and friendly. Then he was back standing with me at the bar.

Do you know them?

No. Zey ahr *stu*dents. *Too* young.

I could've told him that. He went out for a cigarette.

Christophe came over, tried to encourage me to approach a girl. Come on Romon, you got to at least try...He shoved me over at one, said I was American, but that's as far as it went. I shook my head and drank my beer. I had no heart no stomach no balls no *any*thing for *any* of it. I just didn't care.

We left there after a while and walked over to St. Germain to get something to eat. The guys were hungry. I wasn't. We walked into a place with a long glass case full of sandwiches and pizza. They ordered a couple slices. A few black guys came in, Americans, dressed like jazz musicians with brimmed hats and goatees. They ordered in typical American fashion—loud, de-manding, and in English. They got served promptly and swiftly. That's when I learned it didn't matter if you tried to speak French or not while in Paris. In fact the real lesson I took from it was that it was better if you just spoke English. Seemed to command more respect for some reason. Alright then, fuck it. I decided to switch my attitude right then and there and from now on was going to follow that example. No more trying to blend in, making the attempt. I'm American and there's no getting around that in the end.

Christophe and Julien were still hungry. They went next door to another shop and got falafels. We walked Boulevard St. Germain slowly back toward Place St. Michel while they ate their wraps. They'd talk to me in English a bit, then to one another in French. I didn't mind. I thought they were really nice to hang out with me at all, this drag of an American. At one point Christophe asked if I understood them when they spoke to each other and I said un petit peu, which was true I thought—thought I got the general gist anyway. But he smiled at me when I said that, and I wondered then what they'd actually been saying.

Near Place St. Michel we wandered through the narrow tourist-choked streets again and ended up at the corner of St. Julien and rue Galande, around the corner to the apartment. Christophe still lives there, of course. In fact I've learned that the apartment we stayed in was actually *his* apartment, used to belong to his father, but he rents it out so often to supplement his income he rarely gets to stay in it himself. He keeps the small apartment across the way and stays there most the time. I didn't like hanging out there at that corner, it was too close. There are two bars there in that spot on Galande straddling St. Julien. One I really liked—Le Caveau des Oubliettes. Discovered it on my very first trip to Paris; the first place I left my band's cd in the hope of securing a future gig.

Off the street as you walk in from Galande it appears to be just a simple drinking establishment, but there's a whole other level and aspect to it. Down the winding stone stairs through the doorway to the right of the restroom is a cavern where live music is played—mostly blues and jazz and classic rock. They love blues and classic American rock in Paris. Story is this cavern used to be a dungeon where prisoners were left to perish in iron shackles chained to the walls (iron rings are still visible in places anchored into the stone). Now they play music down there to their ghosts. I loved it immediately the time she and I went there on my first brief visit to Paris. I gave the bartender upstairs a cd on the way out, fully expecting to come back and play that cavern someday. Who knew I'd wind up six years later staying in a beautiful apartment around the corner from it, for two weeks? Or that I'd see it yet again six months after that? I wanted to go in now, but Julien was talking to a blonde outside the other bar across St. Julien, on the left corner. This was a piano bar. I'd never set foot in the place and we didn't now either, it was just the tall blonde Julien was talking to that kept us standing there. Again I was introduced as the American, as some kind of impressive tactic on the girl I thought. She looked at me clearly without interest and said nothing, and I said nothing back.

I was sorry to disappoint them, that I couldn't be the kind of charm for them I think they hoped I'd be, but my shriveled spirit just wouldn't allow it. And so I bid goodnight to Julien and Christophe here and shuffled across the street into Le Caveau for one last one on my own.

Down in the cavern the space was tight and as usual stuffed with many young faces. The stone was cool where I stood leaning against it, but the air was stifling, dank. I liked being in there all the same though, better than where we were earlier anyway for sure. Carved like a grave marker into the wall beside me was the image of a saxophone with the date 1920 chiseled next to it, and I smiled as if at an old friend. This was one of my favorite places to drink last time, particularly the first week when I was alone, and I'd sit with my beer and stare often at that carving and think about the lively era it evoked and the swirling jazz and shadow lives that once swelled this underground hall. It kept me company in my thoughts to look at it then. I smiled at my old catalytic companion and drank from my chalice of Stella while listening to the music now. A little guy in a black beret was leading a band through blues tunes, singing in English, and I let myself drift with the languid rhythm. After a song or two they took a break. The little bandleader came over and stood near me by the bar, having a beer and chatting with patrons. Though he slipped in and out of French I could tell he was American, had an East Coast accent. Something came over me, a sudden urge to sing. I saw myself standing up in front of this blues band in this dungeon singing before these young strangers and these silent polite spirits, like I did the very first time I laid eyes on the place, saw myself singing up there within this belly of rock then with *my* band; my band was gone now, dead and gone like everything and everyone else I've loved, but I could still sing, I still had that, that was mine, and I'd had enough to drink by now to feel like I wanted to. So I watched and listened to this bandleader as he talked to those around him. He seemed friendly enough the way he interacted, and I understood now that he played here regularly, a house band, and he was inviting a girl to come up and sing with them after the break, a young pretty brunette with bright red wide lips. They were talking about standards, which song she'd sing. Deciding upon one, she walked off, but he was still standing there by the bar chatting and enjoying his beer. I went over and asked him then. He looked up from under his floppy cocked beret.

Uh sure, you sing?

Yeah.

Whahtaya wahnna sing? Know any standuds?

Not enough to get through a whole song, I said. I wanna sing one of my songs.

Can't do that man.

Yeah, one of my songs. I'll show you, pretty simple...

The band can't play a song they don't know, man.

No they're pretty easy. I'll hum out the beat and melody. They'll get it. We'll wing it.

Can't do it, he said.

How 'bout Moonlight Drive then? You do that one?

But by this time the little bandleader with the beret was edging through the crowd back to his musicians and then he introduced the brunette and she sprung up from her seat and got behind the mic and she could sing, but I didn't care. I finished my beer and set the glass down and wandered up the curving stone steps away from the dense sweaty air of the cave, and the music and the voice got smaller. When I reached the threshold to the bar upstairs and walked through the air floating free and light up there the sounds melted away behind me altogether, and out into the dark I went, back onto the cobblestoned street and up the hill, back to the rafters in the empty night.

She stopped wearing her wedding ring while at Shrader and every day it felt like she was becoming more and more mine, that we were becoming each other's. My wardrobe began to expand here. She was continually picking new articles of clothing up for me, and soon I'd owned a whole new separate batch that grew ever larger over the months. The six plastic tubs deposited on my stoop that night contained these things, as well as others. Here is where she also gave me my brown suede shoulder bag, and my little digital recorder I'd carry with me in my bag. And here is where so many beautiful memories were born.

Many times coming home at night from being out on the town we'd stand in the kitchen having a last drink together, talking, listening to music. Sometimes I'd sing to her, songs from my band that I'd written, or sometimes it was one of my favorite songs by The Doors, *Moonlight Drive*. I loved singing that one.

These were some of the most special moments with her there—standing and singing to her in the kitchen with a glass of wine in my hand. Sometimes we'd get in the hot tub with champagne and that was nice too, to be naked in that hot jetting water with her under the ferns while cool fog rolled over us. But standing and singing to her in the kitchen felt most special. She seemed to love to listen to me sing.

Our drive to work from Shrader in the mornings was less exciting scenically than what we'd later encounter driving from North Beach, but it was very pleasant just the same. We took 17th Street, which cuts dipping up from Cole Valley and dumps you all the way over the hill onto Market Street in the Castro, and at one point coming down the hill just over the hump at Clayton the dustwhite and tan fossil-like cubes and planes of the city's corpus lay in a jumbled spread before you, rimmed by the waters of the bay and Oakland's mammoth hills ranging in the distance beyond that, and your breath catches a little with the beauty as fleeting contentment washes up and trickles over you, which for me was augmented and prolonged by her presence at my side. It was brief, and the view and the color of the bay changed frequently with the weather and the light, some days were prettier than others, but it was the high point of the drive. One morning as we descended 17th, sunk below this vista, swinging onto Market, she told me something that momentarily jostled this feeling of contentment. She'd had one other extramarital relationship prior to ours she said, with a friend of hers named Todd, and he was in town. He wanted to see her. Oh…I said, not knowing how to immediately receive this information, preparing myself for more.

Yeah, she continued, he lives in Honduras. On an island *off* of Honduras actually. But he's in town this week and he wants to get together.

Oh…I said again, my mind shuffling to accommodate this

new input. O, K…So…What do you want to do?

I haven't responded. He left a message, but I haven't gotten back to him yet.

And?

I'm really happy in the place I am with you, she said. And I think it's better to leave the past in the past.

Yeah?

Yeah. I just wanted to be honest and tell you what was happening. I don't plan on calling him. I want you to know that.

I kissed her on the cheek as she drove, breathing a little easier. I'm happy in the place we're in too, I said to her, obviously glad she'd made that decision. But to tell the truth, glad as I was, still I couldn't help feeling a little bad for Todd as well. And if that was the case, if she didn't intend to call him, why'd she feel the need to mention it at all? To gauge my response?

I don't know their story, what happened between her and Todd, but I know our story, and how it ended, and I never thought in that moment I'd turn out to be someone in her past. Someone she may never speak to or even *think* of again. I never thought *I'd* be Todd.

Again the next night as I reached the apartment door there was the chirping. Hurrying inside I picked up. Hey *hey! Con*tact!

Hi Ted! I'm glad I caught the phone in time, I just walked in.

Well I've been calling but it just rings and rings.

Sorry, there's no answering machine. And I'm out a lot, of course.

I write regularly in the mornings at the red table, but I'm also writing all over the city during the day on my walks—cafes, bars, parks. Presently I'm sitting in the shade on a bench in the Luxembourg Gardens. A teenage couple sits across the fine, gray gravel path from me on another bench, furtively making out. I caught his hand in her shirt twice now.

No sweat, Ted said. So listen, Eileen and I are still thinkin' of going to Monet's Garden tomorrow. You still thinkin' you wanna come along?

Sure. Yes, I do.

OK. We're thinkin' we could meet up at Metro Sully-Morland, that's about halfway between you and us. You know where that is?

No, but I'll find it. What time?

Thinkin' nine. We leave out of Gare St. Lazare, I think it's called. Catch a train to a town called Vernon. We need to leave a little cushion of time because we transfer trains in the Metro to St. Lazare, so try to get there as close to nine as you can, awright?

OK. Yeah. Sounds good. See you tomorrow morning at nine then.

Great. See ya.

I took out the *Plan de Paris* and found Metro stop Sully-Morland. I decided it was close enough that I'd just walk it instead of taking the train.

It was a beautiful morning, sunny and clear and still. I walked down rue Monge, the broad street two blocks over from rue Mouffetard. There's a Metro stop right at rue Monge and rue Ortolan, which is the street du Pot de Fer becomes once past rue Mouffetard. I could have taken the train easily, would have taken me directly to Sully-Morland, but I preferred to walk. This station at rue Monge was the one Richard suggested I use when I arrived to Paris from the airport, but I would've had to transfer from the RER and I didn't trust my transferring abilities then. I opted to play it safe and chose what I knew, the Luxembourg stop.

Many restaurants and cafés and shops line rue Monge. My second day here I walked this street at lunch hour and felt myself overwhelmed with the realization that I was indeed in Paris. I'd never been on this street before and there was scant tourist traffic. These were real French people moving on the sidewalks around me living their everyday lives in Paris, and I was suddenly terrified at my complete foreign aloneness among them, at my complete aloneness in general. Felt as though I was being devoured, from without and from within, as if the city itself would gulp me into its dark viscid bowels as I felt gobbled up and interred within my own. I had to quickly flee to recognizable ground. Heart pounding, I'd cut back over to rue Mouffetard where I eventually calmed down and continued on to territory less threatening. This uncharacteristic move was symptomatic of my new self, I recognized, and was sickened to see it. Walking rue Monge now at this hour, though, Monday morning, was quiet; too early for most the shops to be open and hardly anyone else out there. Plus, it was a holiday. I don't know what it was but all of Europe celebrated it, and all of Europe came to do this in Paris, it seemed. The streets had swarmed that weekend with masses of people. They must've all been sleeping it off.

I thought I'd pick up a baguette to have as a snack later on the trip, if I could find a place open. Luckily as I neared rue Cardinal Lemoine a boulangerie had its door pinned back. I went inside and bought a ham and cheese baguette, stuck it in my bag, and went on my way. I crossed the Seine at Pont Sully. The river appeared to still be asleep as well. I'd never seen it so still and smooth. The water mirrored the sky and the trees and structures of the bank. I paused on the bridge a short while to take it in. I was taking my time enjoying my walk, though I knew I was running a few minutes late. There was still plenty of time though, I didn't feel like rushing. I was only going to see the beauty of this moment once.

Finally I approached the Metro and from a block away I saw them standing on the sidewalk. They seemed anxious; maybe I was later than I thought. I took my phone out to check. It was 9:19.

I waved as I approached. They saw me then and smiled, squinting in the sun.

Sorry I'm a little late, I said, shaking hands with Ted.

Yeah, we were just beginning to wonder. It's OK though, we got time.

Hi Eileen.

I bent over to give her a little hug and when I did she kissed me on one cheek and then the other, greeting me à la française, and I followed suit. She smiled maternally up into my face. It was comforting to see her, see them both, but especially Eileen.

Hi Roman. It's nice to see you.

Likewise, I said, and we went down into the Metro station to catch our train.

As we sat together on the Metro out of Sully-Morland, catching up on our trips so far, that feeling of comfort was transforming into the feeling of having made a mistake. It was like being embarrassed to be seen with your parents in public, which was what they kind of represented to me I must admit—surrogate parents. God how pathetic is that. No way in hell I'd've been caught dead with my own real family here if my state of mind was at all healthy, and here I was clinging to two stranger substitutes. But archetypal rivers of consolation and safety run forever deep, do not dry up in us with time's advance as we believe, for I'd tapped again these ancient and embracing yet bygone waters and saw the difference in me, this weird adolescent if not infantile shift, and slouched down even lower inside myself with the sight of it.

I don't know how I might've thought it'd be otherwise, guess I didn't think about it, but here seated with me were two very obvious, typical American tourists. Ted had on shorts and white tennis shoes and a black baseball cap, and he was brandishing his well-worn folded paper map, slapping it against his palm and bare hairy knees. All that was missing was the Hawaiian shirt. Eileen wore a plain, peach-colored long sleeve pull over top, light blue loose slacks, and a large white visor. Surely the visor could've been saved for later, I thought, when we were actually outside in the sun and it was needed. But no, she wore it ready and down tight over her eyes. And, they were loud—both of them.

The train was sparsely populated and the few people who were seated among us were tucked silently into their own thoughts or conversed quietly. Ted's and Eileen's voices, however, boomed, particularly Ted's, and again I couldn't understand it. They seemed like intelligent, sensitive people, how could these things elude them? Or was it just me and my hypersensitivity that made them seem so loud? I looked around at the other passengers. Some were looking at us. There was something in their eyes, a twist on some of their mouths. There were some who were turned away altogether, forcing their attention elsewhere, perhaps not noticing or caring anything about us, or perhaps they did. Perhaps they were doing their best to ignore us. Either way, our fellow passengers were all quiet and two voices filled the train car. No, I didn't think it was just me.

We made the transfer and arrived at Gare St. Lazare, where we waited in line at the ticket desk. It was long. Eileen began talking with a girl ahead of us in line. She was American studying in Paris. She and her friend were going to Monet's Garden too. Both girls were plump and about 22. The girl Eileen was talking with mentioned a park that she said was her favorite in Paris—Buttes Chaumont, she said. None of us had heard of it. I filed it away in the back of my mind as a new place to explore.

After we bought our tickets and were waiting to board, Ted went off to use the restroom and Eileen and I bought coffee at a little snack counter. I remembered why I was actually there, but I didn't know how to broach the topic. Fortunately as we sipped from our paper cups Eileen did it for me.

So what happened with your girlfriend?

Well, it's kind of a long story, I said.

Good, we have forty-five minutes to Vernon. It'll pass the time.

So I began, and slowly the story unfurled in pieces.

Finally time came to board our train. I was expecting to continue our talk en route to Vernon but Eileen chose to sit with two college students instead—different ones than before. These were two young guys who had just returned from Amsterdam and told Eileen all about it. She later told me and Ted all about it too, whether we wanted to hear it or not.

I sat opposite Ted. He wanted to talk more about the museum. I didn't, but I obliged.

The train pulled into Vernon, where we were to board a tour bus that would shuttle us to Giverny and Monet's Garden, another 15 minutes outside of Vernon.

By now the sun was high and hot, hotter than it's been in Paris even. We stood along the road in a long single file line with all the others. There were a lot of people waiting to board those buses, three large white monsters parked waiting along the curb. It was the second line of the day. I hate waiting in line. Particularly long lines composed of tourists. I never wanted to be perceived as a tourist. Traveler, yes. Tourist, no. We stood there, us tourists, baking in the sun. I'd brought my hat, the one she'd bought for me as a parting gift from Paris. I'd given her the sommelier and she got me this nice Stetson cap I'd found in a chapeau shop on rue Dauphine and had had my eye on all through the trip. I brought it back with me on this one. I knew there'd be sun and I was going to need some head protection at some point, and my hat helped, but not fully. The sun was so penetrating that day it found its way around my hat and my ears and neck were beginning to burn.

While waiting for the bus I continued with my story. They both heard it now, now that Ted was with us. He'd come into it a little late at Gare St. Lazare, but I was already feeling he was in too deep for his taste, and I couldn't blame him. Then after a long while the line started moving and we got on our bus, which caused a natural pause in the tale, and because I was becoming self-conscious of Ted's feelings I was resolved to end it there. Once seated, though, Eileen asked me to resume, so I did.

It's a good story, right?

It is, Eileen said. I wish I could meet this woman, she sounds like she's something.

You don't even know the half of it, I muttered to myself.

When I told her about the night she dumped my stuff on my stoop Eileen's face puckered with pain and her eyes clamped tight and her head wagged in empathy before me, as if what I was telling her filled her with pain too and shook her head to ward away or cast off the memory of it, to make impotent its power, sensing the hold it had on me. My eyes welled a little then, but I caught them thankfully.

Now I was very conscious of Ted and was determined to cap this thing here.

Awright, I'm gonna shut up now. We're supposed to be enjoying ourselves. I don't want to spoil our trip with all this.

Right, Ted said. Fuck her. She's fucked up, you're not. So let's just forget it.

I knew that wasn't a completely accurate assessment, but I let it be and tried to leave it at that. Eileen had more to say, though, and I guessed this was what I'd been waiting for, why I was there in the first place.

Well, Eileen began…the question is why do you keep sabotaging your life?

That went right through me, right through my gut.

You have to look at that. The first thing I'd tell you to do is to get into a twelve step program for your drinking. Sounds like it played a part here.

I had to agree with that, that alcohol was an issue at play in my relationships, but not entirely, not enough to seriously consider the program stuff.

I'd even look into some kind of co-dependency group, Eileen added. That seems to be an issue here too.

And again I guessed I had to agree, but there's still more, much more that went into all this than these tossed off prescriptions—which I wasn't going to do anyway—could aid. But there was no addressing it here in this moment with Eileen. No, she couldn't help me, nor can anyone else. I alone am the one to look to. Somehow I have to find a way out of this pain myself, find something to help that doesn't involve methods matriculated into mainstream solutions, but what I don't know other than this that I'm doing. I have to get this worm out of my chest that's consuming me, remove it slowly with my words so that it comes out whole. If it breaks as I pull on it and a part remains inside it could regenerate and begin again. I have to tear it out of me whole and bring it into this world to prove its existence if I am to heal, but it is a very tricky process. How does a heart heal when it's been so thoroughly mutilated, and a fragile and uncommon mind step back from the wavering edge? How am I ever to be the same again? Could I, *should* I be the same, should I even try?

The bus finally reached its destination and parked in a large lot. We tourists filed out of the buses and across the lot and through an underground walkway that took us beneath the road where we then emerged onto the sidewalk on the other side. We walked for a short ways along the highway toward a narrow entrance road to the left. The air was thick with white puffs like feather down. They floated all about, coming from the surrounding trees. Dreamy little tufts snowing gently down upon us as we walked, nesting in hair and eyelashes and clothing.

The narrow road came to a T and we rounded the right corner and joined a long unmoving line along a stone wall. We stood and stood there, in direct sunlight, not moving for probably a half hour. The white tufts still floated about but greatly thinned now we were further away from the highway and the trees. We stood and waited. After a while a man walked along the line saying something in French to us tourists. Some people left the line then and turned around to walk in the other direction. The line tightened up a little and we moved six feet forward, then stopped and stood. Twenty minutes more and the same man passed again. We still had not moved since the first time we saw him and people walked off. He seemed to be saying the same thing to the line he said before. This time Eileen stopped him.

Look here, she said, what are you saying? Do you speak English?

Yes.

Then what are you saying? Tell me. In English.

I am sayinguh zat zair ees anozair entronce around zee cornair, and you should go zair.

Thank you. Why didn't you say that in the first place?

I deed, Madam. You deed not undairstand *me*.

But you said it in French.

Oui. Zat ees correct Madam, he said with a smile, and kept walking.

So we and many others turned around and went in the direction the first wave of people went after the first time the man came by. We joined another line along a different side of the stone wall, but closer to the entrance to the garden. This made the fourth time today I'd lined up like this among people I never wished to be identified with but here I was one of them. I wanted to shoot myself and get it all over with.

This line moved, but was painfully slow.

Eileen did a little reconnaissance and discovered that our line had a double, and its brother seemed to be shorter and more active. She wanted to move over there. We left our line and added to this new one.

The gate had two entrances. The line we abandoned filtered through the left entrance and the one we just joined filtered into the right, but they both met at the same box office. This was the part that Eileen missed in her excitement to switch lines. She could not see over the wall (none of us could) and she did not peek inside the entrance past the line to see where the line led. All she could tell was that it seemed to be shorter. When we got in our new line, in a moment our old forsaken line started moving, and the people who stood behind us had now moved ahead of us inside the entrance. Ted and I looked at Eileen.

Well it *seemed* to be moving faster over *here*, she said.

We waited.

Finally we were at the box office, a little green wooden closet that stood just behind the stone wall we'd waited before and was at the center of the two converging paths of entrance. A man sat in there at a window behind thin bars taking money. We paid and followed those ahead of us on the path to the right. It was a little dirt trail leading through trees and shrubs and flowers, very pretty, very green, but not terribly exciting, particularly because we were on the heels of other people, as others were on ours. This is why I typically avoid tourist activities exactly like this one.

We started down the trail together, but slowly I let Ted and Eileen drift ahead. I wanted them to have their own experience, and I wanted a little space. I started to get hungry and remembered my baguette. There was a bench ahead and when I reached it I sat down. People filed steadily by. I took the baguette out of my bag and watched the people as I ate my sandwich. The bench was positioned across the trail from a little bridge, and there was a tall woman in an orange dress posing for a photo at the foot of it before a backdrop of dark purple flowers. Eileen, passing this woman, was struck by her dress and stopped to admire it. She began talking.

That is a *beautiful* dress, she said to the woman. Really a *lovely* color on you. Really.

The woman was a statue but flicked an eye down at Eileen and offered her the smile she was holding for the camera, then trained her gaze back on her photographer. Eileen stood there looking up, smiling admiringly at the woman, looking her dress up and down.

I saw a dress like that the other day, Eileen continued as the woman stood motionlessly ignoring her, and I *llloved* it, she said. Just adored it. I went to try it on and wouldn't you know I...I...oh...oh I, I see, oh you're, you're having your pic...oh...oh, well...Eileen sputtered, and hurried on across the bridge to catch up with Ted.

I couldn't help laughing at that.

Finishing my baguette, I got up and rejoined the herd and crossed the bridge myself. We circled the famous pond now.

So this was where Monet painted his water lilies, huh? Smaller than I imagined but very pretty of course, no wonder Claude found solace here—a peaceful oasis for an artist. If all these people weren't choking the place I imagine it a very serene spot.

I felt as though I was part of a mob trampling over holy bones.

The pond was hooded in refreshing shade. Sunlight danced in checkered sparkles on the water through the scrim of leaves. The coolness of the spot was a greatly welcomed relief and pleasure, but I had to keep moving. There were others right behind me who wanted a look too.

Back in the hot sun, next we were walking through a large flower garden. Rows and rows of beautiful flowers neatly staked out like vegetable plants. There was row after beautiful colorful row, and I walked among them along with the others, up and down every path, and pretty, yes it was, but by now I was ready to leave. I swung my eyes across the grounds scanning for Eileen and Ted. I didn't see them.

The flower garden was outside the brown brick house where

Monet lived, a portion of which was now a gift shop. I wandered in there to get out of the sun, thinking maybe Ted and Eileen had done the same. There were two large panels of water lily paintings hung high up on the walls. I looked at these a while, browsed a little, but no Ted and Eileen. I went back outside to look for them, hoping they were ready to leave now too—couldn't see them anywhere. I wandered the rows of flowers again. Still couldn't find them. I went back into the gift shop, maybe they were in there now. No sign of them. Again I walked back outside into the sun, and on the path leading to the gift shop there they stood with quizzical expressions.

You done looking in there Roman? Ted asked. You keep going back in there. You walked right by us twice.

I *did*? I'm sorry.

Am I that far gone that their recognition didn't even register?

You ready to get going? Ted asked.

Yeah. You?

Yeah, he said, we were waiting for *you*.

We exited through the other portion of the house and headed back down the narrow entrance road to the sidewalk along the highway. The tufts again, still waltzing like a carnival of fairies in the breeze as we walked to the corral of buses. We had to wait a little while before there were enough people to fill the bus where it made sense to the driver to make the trip back to Vernon, but soon there were and we were on our way to the train station. Once there, there was another wait. The train to Paris wasn't due to arrive for 30 minutes. I figured I had time for a beer so I went across the street to a brasserie and had two demi Stellas, enjoying a few minutes to myself; I'd needed it after that long day of lines and crowds.

Finally we were on our way. On the train I sat alone a few seats up and across the aisle from Eileen and Ted, who were sitting together. I turned to look back at them. Eileen was in the aisle seat, resting with her eyes closed and holding Ted's hand,

and it hit me. Mr. Magoo. That's who she reminded me of. Mr. Magoo the cartoon character. That's what it was that'd been bugging me. She'd reminded me of something, *someone* else other than that old girlfriend's mother from the moment I met her but hadn't been able to put my finger on it, now I had it. It was the shape of her nose and eyes, the brows like inverted reversed checkmarks, her whole physiognomy in fact made me think of the character, and now I had it I couldn't help but laugh again remembering that incident with the woman by the bridge. It just seemed too perfect now I'd made the association. Then another association formed.

Riding the train back into Paris now suddenly I was returning from our trip to Chartres. What a beautiful day that was. Must've taken close to a hundred photos that day alone of the cathedral's architecture and the transfixing stained glass windows inside. At one point while within the darkened interior we'd witnessed the sun move across the southwest façade, watched the windows above the main entrance slowly ignite panel by panel in the sun's path and glow brilliantly rich with cobalt blue and wine red light. It was—and I never use this tired, purloined word but it seems the most powerfully succinct choice, so I will reclaim it here and restore its weighty origin—it was *awesome* in the truest sense, as if a deeper radiance lit-up inside me right along with that colored glass. We climbed the winding stone Rapunzel staircase up the cathedral's left tower. There was access to the exterior of the church through open doorways throughout the climb that led to parapets, and we foraged out onto them. It was like wandering the turrets of a castle. From these lookout points we took shots of the village below quaint and colorful and small way down there nestled in the colors of autumn, and the fields beyond with a bruised rolling sky stretching out above. We took photos of the exterior of the church itself, of gargoyles and stone bishops presiding off the sides and corners of the building. We took pictures of each other standing on the parapets. I snapped one of her smiling down at me over the edge of a short wall, long brown hair blowing, and there was my darkhaired Rapunzel.

We probably spent two hours exploring that church inside and out, and then we wandered the town itself. There was a square with many shops in a row. We passed a woman's clothing store, and prominently displayed, clearly visible through the doorway, was a navy blue nightie on a headless mannequin. We stopped and went in to have a closer look. It was roughly in the style of an antique bathing suit, with fluttery short sleeves and a scooped neck. I thought it very sexy. She bought it. Later we went into a little restaurant across the street from the cathedral and had dinner. Naively we ordered côte de boeuf, which we thought would be a large steak the two of us could share, and it was, but it was so large that the carnage brought to our table and carved bloody before us lasted three days. We took the leftovers back to Paris and with them made baguette sandwiches to bring along on our daily walks through the city.

On the train home it was dark now, the windows were black mirrors studded and wormed with droplets of rain that'd begun falling as we left Chartres. We took a whole portrait series of ourselves sitting together in our seats reflected in the glass. Such wonderful, romantic photos. How in love they seemed, that couple, together in the glass. How from another time they appeared. She in her olive flapper-style hat, and he in worn black leather and black scarf lost deep in thought or as if in supplication, head bowed toward fingerlaced hands. What phantoms they are now to each other.

Back at the apartment she bathed and afterwards joined me in the living room for a glass of wine. Her thick long hair was wet, and she sat across the room in a chair facing me in the dim light as we talked. She was wearing the nightie she just bought in Chartres, and she looked so beautiful sitting there in it, with her wet hair. I remember distinctly saying to myself I should take her picture, but I didn't. I never got up from the couch. I looked and looked at her as she sat there, knowing I should take that picture, but somehow I just didn't—the one I regret most out of the entire trip having not taken. In my mind though, the image remains just as vividly as if I had.

Ted and Eileen were off for Provence the next day, and on the Metro we made vague plans to meet once more when they return to Paris, for dinner or a glass of wine perhaps, before our return to California.

I have the strong suspicion that's not going to happen.

I feel like taking it easy tonight, she said. I'm gonna stay in. We were just pulling away from Shrader on our drive across town to work. Friday morning, cool and sunny. It was going to be a beautiful day.

Oh, OK. That sounds great to me.

You wanna come over?

Of course.

That was the extent of it. Nothing more on the subject was said.

It did sound great. By the end of the workweek I was beat, and Friday nights my energy left quickly. I was more inclined these days to take it easy those nights anyway. I was happy to hear she wanted to stay in. I envisioned making dinner, wrapping round one another on the couch to watch a movie.

Later that evening I arrived at her door. I rang the bell to let her know I was there, then let myself in with the spare key she'd given me. As I mounted the first step to the stairs she called down *Wait!* Hold on! Don't come up yet.

Puzzled, I stepped back down and waited by the door. Min-

164

utes went by, then I called up the stairs.

Hey, whataya doin' baby?

Just a minute, I'm getting ready.

More minutes passed. I stood there.

Hey c'*mon!* What's going on?

Just a minute!

I waited some more, growing impatient, then called up again.

Babyyy? What's happ'nin?

OK. You can come up.

When I reached the top of the stairs I found her in the living room. It was darkened, flickering with candlelight. She was standing there dressed as I'd never seen her, in a black pleather bra and panties with silver studs, black thigh-high stockings held by a garter belt, black stilettos. She had that gunmetal eye shadow on again, and her hair was crimped in ridges. She stood there in the middle of the room looking at me with a kind of defiant, steely eye.

Baby? I said. What's goin' on?

What's it look like?

Slowly I entered the room. She seemed to be someone else. A porn was running on the TV, candles were everywhere. There was an open bottle of champagne on the coffee table and two flutes filled and bubbling. Furniture had been removed; there was more space in there. She'd turned this rather bourgeois French-provincial living room into a sex den.

She picked up the glasses and handed me one.

Sit down, she said.

I took the glass and slid into the big chair in front of the window. She got on my lap and we drank some of the champagne, then she took my glass and set it back down along with hers on the table. She climbed back onto my lap. I took it from there, but I was not wholly turned on or at ease. This was interesting, but it felt so forced, like she was trying too hard. It wasn't even my taste, that studded underwear she was wearing. I like natural simplicity; I'm very easy that way. I like what is real and genuine and tasteful. I thought she knew that. She could have just been sitting there naked when I came in, or naked in heels, or in a teddy even, and that would've done the trick way better than this. Way better. This only confused me. Was she trying to tell me something? Was another side of her surfacing? Was she trying to show me she had other unfulfilled desires and tastes I wasn't aware of? Was our sex life in need of such a drastic boost already only four months in? That was hard for me to believe, but did she think so? She sensed something of all this in me when we finished, but she misinterpreted and slipped into a simmering withdrawal.

I guess you don't like surprises, she said finally. Now I know.

Wait, that's not true. I just…I just wasn't prepared for all this. I thought we were gonna have a quiet night. You said you wanted to take it easy, so I came over thinking that. Thinking something else.

I'm sorry I caught you unprepared, she said, then got up and shut the TV off and left the room. I followed her into the bedroom where she was removing the rest of her clothes and putting on jeans and a tshirt in the dark. Then she went into the bathroom and closed the door. I heard water hit the sink. I walked in worried circles in the kitchen waiting for her. She came out and went into the living room. Through the kitchen doorway I watched her blow out the candles. I walked in there. She'd washed her face.

Listen, I'm sorry. I know you went to a lot of trouble tonight. I mean, preparing and everything. But it…it was too much. You didn't have to do all that. I mean, I love you, I love having sex with you. I don't need a whole lot of—

You just don't like surprises, I got it.

That's not true, that's not what I'm saying.

But just like I couldn't convince her that I was not the planner she believed me to be, now I couldn't convince her that I did not

not like surprises.

She remained upset into the next day, and the following Sunday morning she returned to Chicago. She'd left the flat ahead of me, and when I was gathering my things to leave, to go home, I found a postcard by my bag on the divan in the sitting room. The illustration on the card was of a girl, old pin-up style, sitting astride a green toy horse wearing sheer thigh-high stockings, an orange fringe mini skirt to match the orange kerchief tied around the back of her neck and dangling loose over her breasts like a big bib, and white cowgirl boots offsetting a black cowgirl hat. She was slinging a lariat behind her, and beside her was a very tall thin D with these words printed beneath it: is for dress-up. On the back of the card she'd written: *Let's try it again one day—more notice to you next time…I promise.*

I was still confused and she was still operating under a misinterpretation. I didn't realize it then, but that was among the first of the misinterpretations she was to hold regarding me that would plague us, and they only multiplied from there.

I enjoyed the route I'd taken to meet Eileen and Ted so much I decided to walk it again the next day, going further into the Marais this time. Past Sully-Morland I walked rue du Petit-Musc, which I'd never been on before, and which I'd discovered led to rue St. Antoine, a street I'd walked many times. Rue du Petit-Musc wasn't remarkable in any way, and St. Antoine is a large bustling street that held no interest for me at the moment, so I kept walking, down rue Birague. I knew it must be near here but I certainly wasn't looking for it, and had I known rue Birague was going to take me there I would not have chosen it, but as I reached the end of the short street I began to recognize what lay ahead.

Suddenly I found myself wandering into Place des Vosges, and I began to shake again. It was one place I planned not to seek out this trip because it was the last great scene of the previous one. Now she was all around me, and though I knew I should spin round and get out of there as quickly as I could, now that I saw it again I could not turn away. I was drawn further into the square, memory pulling and repulsing me simultaneously as I went.

Slowly I moved forward, past the row of shops on my right to the end of the square and the café on the corner, where we had lunch that day. There was the table outside along the sidewalk against the gray stone pillar. She was sitting there holding her wine glass with both hands and looking back at me over her shoulder, smiling. Oh…My hand went up to cover my mouth and behind my sunglasses my face was wet. I stepped away off the curb to cross the street, to the park side on my left, and as I did I looked to my right and there was the cutlery store over there where I bought her sommelier. I shut my eyes and turned my head fast and made it across the street and walked along the black wrought-iron fence caging the park. There were the trees I photographed, now bushy and full instead of half nude as I captured them, branches like that of a water fountain flowing downward. I caught the sunlight that day coming through the few remaining yellow and green leaves stubbornly clinging at the ends of the bottom branches, while in the background the park's actual water fountain spouted thin streams falling in the shape of the trees. Knowing I shouldn't, I entered cautiously through the turnstile and into the park onto the tan dirt path inside the fence. *Oh…*My hand covered my mouth again. There she was standing in her cream wool coat, double-breasted and belted tightly at the waist, short skirt peeking out just below, a white paper shopping bag from the lingerie shop we had just left around the corner dangling delicately from her right fingertips, dangling along her legs clad in black tights and tall black leather boots, feet together as she stood there in the sunlight letting the sun drench her, absorbing it into her face thrust unsmiling upward to the warmth, her big black mask-like sunglasses covering half her face but behind them you knew her eyes were closed in the pleasure of receiving that kiss from the sun, as they were as she stood at the balcony door of the Telegraph apartment, her dark hair a kinky tangle now, wild with lack of attention the way I loved it, it fell all about her shoulders, framing her face, and there she was my favorite image of her from our trip, the photo I loved the most, there she was standing there before me again...

And now I knew I must hurry, had to get out of there. It was a haunted hall of mirrors. She was all around me and nowhere to be seen. I turned and walked back through the fence and up the street, quickly now, as quick as this bum leg allowed. I passed a young couple. The woman wore a bright red jacket, like the one I clenched in my fist. *Oh*...I walked away from the square and turned left down rue des Francs Bourgeois. *Red jacket! Another one! Oh*...And I stumbled now in near blindness, eyes blurred with underwater vision, but still managed to navigate through the crowded streets. It was a cool and overcast day, and it must be a very popular color this spring for women's jackets, that red, because there was another one coming toward me as I zigzagged along in my fight to escape out of the Marais. I had to get out of the Marais. But there were people everywhere and everywhere I looked now I saw a bright red jacket. Jesusmotherfuckme*christ!* They kept coming, flaring up out of nowhere at me like battle fire, as if under attack, as that horrific memory twirled in a loop in my head. Breaking away from the crowd finally I ducked into a very small street, somewhere, I no longer knew where I was, but I was alone and that's all that mattered. I rounded a corner and leaned palms trembling against the stone of the building and let it go completely now out of my shaking and convulsing body, let the gush of tears spout and flow onto the ground, flow out of me like the fountain flowed in the park.

In May she had to move. Shrader had been rented for the next two months and wouldn't be available again until July, when she planned to move back in. What I mainly see in my mind when I think about this next place is brown and white. It was one large living room, a bedroom, and a bath, very modern in décor. Dark brown laminate floor, brown kitchen cabinets and appliances in the same room unobstructed, brown entertainment unit, brown leather couch and coffee table. White were the walls, the large shag rug in front of the couch, the hanging paper orb lamp that drooped in an arc into the room from the floor beside the couch on a long metal rod, like the palm plant at Shrader arced hanging over into the sitting room. And white was the bedroom, walls and bed, and the bathroom, which glared with light. The bathroom was so bright I called it the alien autopsy room. You'd hit the light switch and *POW* you were on the spaceship.

This apartment was in Ashbury Heights, just up the hill from Cole Valley. The place on Shrader and this one were only about seven blocks apart, and it was nice enough, but I remember it most for the new discovery that occurred here.

We were at it on the couch one night after dinner (she'd made king crab legs). All our clothes were on except her panties, which I'd removed from beneath her dress, and my shirt. My pants were around my knees, and my feet were on the floor. She rode astride me as I lay back on the couch, and she was getting there, I could feel it, and when she did suddenly a gushing force of warm liquid splattered against my abdomen.

Oh my God. You can *squirt?*

Yeah, sometimes, she said, panting.

Why didn't you mention that before?

It hasn't happened for a really long time. It must be your position. You're hitting the spot.

We kept going, and spurt after spurt soaked me, coming in thinner sprays than the initial blast but they were many and it pooled on my belly and chest. I'd experienced this only once before in the wasteland, beneath a fog-shrouded oyster moon at the Marina beach one night with a girl I had a spontaneous date with. Or at least I've gone on the assumption since then it was this. When I went down on her in the sand some trickle of something came in a mist at me anyway. Wasn't anything remotely like what I had here, however.

The next day at work the excitement of this discovery may have been detectable only in the far-away grins that kept breaking out across my face, but inside I was shouting *My girl can SQUIRT! It just keeps getting better and better!*

That was the only time it happened though, at Ashbury, until we got back to Shrader in July. We had one more night of it then, different position this time on her back. Over and over a silvery arc shot at me in the dark, in the moonlight coming through the window, but never again after that night. A temperamental geyser it seemed.

It's just over a week now that I've been in Paris. At the moment it is raining, and I am again sitting at my little red table watching the rain through the window. I realize the luxury of this moment, waking leisurely in an apartment in Paris, eventually boiling eggs and water for tea after you've taken your time to shower and dress, and the rain that fell gently at first begins falling steadily with more force, which allows you secure excuse to stay in and write, and after a night of making love on top of it…Well, I guess it doesn't get much better than this in the romantic notion of it all, which brought me here in the first place. I realize the beauty of this moment as I listen to the rain pick up and dance harder on the roof above my head and on the slategray tin slanted rooftops outside my window, I realize the beauty I'm experiencing, but the sadness relentlessly keeps gnawing away at me.

I still wake each morning up in the rafters of this room, staring at the brown beams like ancient ribs of a long ago fallen beast protruding from the vanilla skin of plaster slanting over me, enclosing my chamber up there, as my ribs are beginning to protrude through my own skin—each morning I still wake with the immediate thought of her, the memory of her loss, that she is now with someone else, and I crumple in pain all over again. This morning was no different. Rain fell and I woke to its pinging on the tin roof above me, and there it was.

The rain reminded me of not so long ago, in the fall when the rainy season begins in San Francisco, when we'd wake together to that sound and she'd say, if it were a weekday morning, I can't wait to sleep in with *yooouuu*, drawing that word out in a way I loved, and she'd curl up in my arms for a couple more precious moments before having to rise and ready for work. And when the weekends finally came we'd lie in bed in the leaden morning light making love beneath that sound patting on the roof and ticking against the window. I saw and heard it all so clearly with the sound of that rain, felt it all so deeply within me, the wailing began instantly.

That's how I spent the first hour upon waking, crumpled in pain, as I did yesterday and every day before. Had to force myself to leave the apartment yesterday, eventually made it to the Pompidou like I promised myself I would. There's been too much aimlessness, too much wandering the same routes seeing the same things, so I made a plan to give my time a little more structure, and the Pompidou was a place I'd not yet gone. But it was the same. I wandered the exhibits in a daze, untouched or unmoved by what I saw. Not even the views of the city outside the gallery windows touched me. I leaned a shoulder to the glass as I stood numb looking through the window at Paris, at the beauty stretching before my eyes, pressed my face very close so no one could see, and let my vision swim again in the waters that ceaselessly flood it.

When I left Pompidou Center the rain came and I walked unshielded in its fall, though I've begun carrying my umbrella with me now in my shoulder bag. It was a welcome thing to me, the rain, and I was thankful for it.

Since my arrival the heat had steadily increased. The first few days a spring coolness still lingered and you needed a jacket in the evenings. I like to wear jackets. The night I went out with Christophe and Julien the weather had begun to shift. By the end of the week things really heated up. The sun burned down from clear blue skies and made things miserable. I don't like hot weather. The searing sun, the sweaty heat, that's for other people. I like cool temperate climates, like San Francisco. So I was thankful for the rain coming to cool things down.

It began the night before, the night after I came back from Vernon. It came in a sudden cloud burst. There was thunder. Flashes of meek lightning. I had just left an English-styled pub around the corner from Place St. Michel, along the Seine, where I'd whiled away a couple hours drinking beer and chatting with the cute bartender there named Lesley. She's a student studying French, been here two years, from Missouri originally, brown hair brown eyes my favorite combination. It was nice talking with her. She gave me her email address, but I think she only did it to be nice when I asked if she'd like to show me around a little. I don't intend to write her. Anyway, I had a few petit Stellas at Happy Hour price, €2 a pop that's not bad, though that's still almost 4 bucks for a small beer. Had a cheeseburger, my first in

Paris ever and it hit the spot, and although it was prepared by a Frenchman it tasted very British to me. He'd added quite a bit of Worcestershire sauce to the meat I think, that's what it was. Not really my taste but I enjoyed it. I think I was feeling a little homesick and the burger helped, along with the conversation with Lesley. She had a down to earth quality to her that you often find in Midwestern girls. I like that. And even though she's living in Paris she seemed to retain this. The moment I walked out of the pub and approached St. Michel the rain started and fell hard fast. I crossed the boulevard as fat raindrops bombed the street.

Since there'd been no prior indication of impending rain earlier that evening when I left the apartment, my umbrella was still back there in my suitcase. I crossed St. Michel, shoulders hunched and head bowed against the downpour. When I reached the other side by the Metro, there was a broad, inviting café awning and I ducked under it, right at the corner end, and stood there a moment. The rain pounded down. I watched it and wondered how long I'd be allowed to stand there before the waiter asked me to leave. There were three people seated at two small round tables right next to me. They were all talking with one another so I assumed they were together. They were young. Two girls sat next to each other at one table, and a guy sat beside them at the other. There was only one empty chair that I saw, and it was next to him. I saw no glass or setting there, so I quickly plopped down. I didn't know if a fourth friend was going to return any second from the toilet and I'd have to surrender my seat, or if the group was going to somehow object to my joining them so opportunistically, but I took a chance. They were speaking English. Sounded American.

I hope you don't mind, I said to the back of the guy's head. An empty chair, the rain…

He turned from his conversation.

Oh no, go for it dude, he said.

We started talking. His name was Steven. He was a flight attendant. They all were, on a layover from New York. Arrived that day and returned the next. He asked about me. What did I do, why was I here in Paris?

Struggling writer, I said.

Oh…Anything I may uh…?

Unpublished, of course, I quickly added.

Oh. And you're here just on holiday, or what?

Sort of, I said, and I told him my story.

Wow, that's tough man. I'm sorry.

Yeah…

No, really. That sucks.

Yeah…I'm trying to write about it. It's perfect, isn't it? Man comes to Paris heartbroken and alone, trying to write. Oooh the ro*mantic* irony…I laughed. And if it weren't true I would've really laughed, instead of what I was actually doing.

No, that's pretty good, he said. You could do something with that. Depending upon how you write it, of course.

The waiter came and I ordered a pint of Stella. The rain was still coming down hard. We watched it while dry under the awning, watched it flood the streets and pour down into the Seine across Quai Augustins. It was wonderful sitting there, watching the rain. There was another café to our right, with another awning, which kept filling with rainwater and sagging. The waiters had to dump it now and then, pushing the sagging bulge with their hands to spill the water off onto the sidewalk. It fell in big sheets over the awning's side.

Steven told me he's been trying to get over a girl too, in New York. His story was very different from mine of course, and he was much younger, and his scars didn't reach anywhere near as deep as the canyon carved through me, but I could see he carried a little pain over it, the usual kind. The normal kind when some-one breaks up with you. But he was going to be fine, of that I was certain. He was young and attractive and had a sexy job. I thought of that French flight attendant on the plane here. I'm sure they both did just fine for themselves. Look at the girls he was sitting with now, both young and pretty. They didn't want to look at or know anything about me, but he was their type, that was obvious. No, he'd be fine. But I'm not so sure I can say the same for myself.

I just don't know with any certainty what can be said in this regard, and what the future may hold for me. I see it as one big open leading question, open on Eternity...And I feel it waiting with wide and embracing arms, Eternity, waving me onward...

The beer the waiter brought was in a tall glass and cost €9. I nursed it while Steven and I talked, watching the rain. It was still coming down, but eventually it slowed, and by the time I finished my beer it had stopped altogether. Through the sky's thick gray sea of clouds I noticed sunrays breaking and shining goldenred on a singular spot along the buildings of the Right Bank, across the river. It was close to sunset, and this was the last light the sun was going to emanate today, creating the only place of color to be seen in the dreariness surrounding us in that moment. It was beautiful to see, a kind of last gasp of hope breaking through. I pointed it out to Steven, who then pointed it out to the girls. Steven seemed to get it, but the girls couldn't care less.

My cell phone vibrated in my pants pocket. I finally, earlier that day, took care of setting it up with the Orange network, the mobile phone service in Paris. A very nice man at a shop very close to the English Pub where I was before the storm hit helped me set it up. He was Israeli and spoke English. I went to two Orange stores before I found this man's electronic shop, but the young French people working behind the counters shook their heads and pretended not to speak English when I asked parlez-vous anglais? One store was on Soufflot by the Pantheon and the other on St. Michel, both near the university so I was pretty sure they could speak English, they just chose not to for some reason.

After that I wasn't sure what to do. Then I thought of Christophe.

I stopped by and rang his buzzer on rue St. Julien. The second time I'd returned to that spot. I remembered the code to enter the street door, which got me into the anteroom. You need a key to go further from there, but the mailboxes and apartment buzzers are right inside that door. I rang a few times, waited, but there was no response. I took the notebook out of my bag and tore a sheet from it to write a note explaining to Christophe why I'd stopped by, asked him to call me. I folded it and stuck it part way into the mailbox that had Christophe's last name handwritten on a label below. Christophe's last name is the same as the street that's around the corner, I remembered that from last time—another strange coincidence. Then I got out of there.

Part of me was thrilled to enter that door again, but physically I felt nauseous. As I turned to leave I saw her outside through the window of the door, in the photo I took of her from there, standing outside, hair windswept, shapely eyebrows arched looking at herself in the glass, unaware I was taking her picture. I got out of there fast.

Shortly after that, as I was walking the quai past St. Michel, I found the Israeli man's shop and took care of the cell phone business myself with him.

I took my phone out and looked at it. There was a text message.

Hey where are you? Would you like to meet?

I had done one smart thing before I left San Francisco. I'd placed a posting on Craigslist Paris with my photo announcing that I was going to be visiting, and would any English-speaking women be interested in meeting up during my trip? When I checked my email after the first couple days of arrival there were two responses, one from an American girl living in London visiting Paris and one from a Turkish girl who was a recent transplant from Istanbul. Though they were both interested in getting together, the Turkish girl was the only one who came

through. I had emailed her my new cell phone number that afternoon.

Yes I would, I typed. I'm at Place St. Michel.

Where would you like to meet?

How about Place St. Michel, by the fountain?

OK. 10 min?

Sure.

A few minutes later I said goodbye to Steven, shaking hands
with him and waving at the uncaring girls as I got up to leave. I
walked across the boulevard and down to the fountain. Night had
fallen completely now. People once again filled the wet streets
after the rain, and the pavement shimmied with shiny reflected
light. A crowd surrounded the fountain listening to the musicians
that had gathered there to play. I approached looking at the faces,
trying to recognize her from the photo she'd included in one of
her emails. Suddenly I saw a girl with long black wavy hair
wheel out from the crowd, coming at me. It was as if she was
coming to assassinate me, stick a knife in my throat, the way she
was bent so resolutely forward as she moved, arms outspread
behind her as if restraining companions who wished to get at me
first, all the while holding me with such fixed, intense eyes. Then
just like that they were jumping up out of the crowd before me,
those eyes, dark and penetrating and glinting like razors in the
night.

Roman! she said.

Yes. Hi...

I refrained from using her name because I wasn't quite sure
how to pronounce it. We kissed each other on either cheek. I was
following her lead.

Well where would you like to go? she asked. For drink?

Sure, I said, and she instantly whisked me off.

To the right of the fountain we went, down rue St. Andre des
Arts, that street again. She was all energy and walked quickly
ahead speaking rapidly all the while and I hurried to keep up,

dodging the tourists and threading along as I struggled to hear what she was saying. Her words were delivered as if to someone in front of her and only occasionally spoken directly back to me, so I missed most of them. She was fresh from the last day of her French class, out drinking with classmates afterwards. That much I caught. Then she stopped for coffee before meeting me, and the caffeine on top of the alcohol had her a little amped. So that explains the chase, I thought, but as I trailed after this crazy fireball down this clogged, tired street I also thought *not this again*, and began fading, lagging back a few steps. But then abruptly she took a left and I was following her down a different route, a route new to me suddenly and I didn't know where I was, and I was so grateful for this I perked up and followed now happily.

We wound up at a place in the Odeon, tucked away off of Boulevard St. Germain. I bought a couple beers and we sat at a table near the bar and talked.

She said she'd been in Paris six months. Had dated a couple French men, but found them too feminine for her taste.

They are like woman, she said. Too soft. Too...she made a droopy face here and mouthed mmlaa mmlaa, then righted here expression again. No, I don't like, she said.

She said people in Paris don't use Craigslist, but she thought she would try. When she saw my picture she said she thought I looked nice, so she would try. So now here we were.

She asked about me. I gave her a very abbreviated version of my story.

Oh you broke up. And now you are sad. Yes I think. I see. And what for you come back here?

Again, short version.

I see. And what are you lookink for?

A friend, I said. To just have companionship, see the city with someone.

I see. I think you want sex.

179

Well if that happens great, I said, but it's not a necessity. I'm looking for a friend to hang out with. And you? What are you looking for?

I don't know. We will see. Maybe sex.

We had another beer, then left. We walked St. Germain this time. She lived near Luxembourg Gardens so we had a nice long walk together in the same direction. It was kind of late now and the streets were quiet. I was keeping a respectful distance as we walked on St. Germain, then abruptly she stopped. I stopped too. We looked at each other.

I think you are gentleman, she said, and I knew what that meant.

I took her face in my hands and kissed her, long and sweet.

And here I am kissing a strange girl on the streets of Paris. The thought sailed through me while she was in my arms. *Look at me, kissing a girl I just met, in the night, on the streets of Paris.*

We continued walking, holding hands now. At St. Michel we turned right, toward the Gardens. We reached Soufflot and stopped. Again we kissed.

Goodnight, Roman, she said.

Goodnight...and here is where I ventured her name for the first time, and mispronounced it.

Ma-tee-*chay*, she corrected. Not Matisse. That is the American pronunciation. It's Matee*chay*, Matice said.

Mateechay, I repeated. I got it.

Good. Goodnight, Matice said, and we kissed again, a quick little one, and then parted with plans to see each other the following night.

At nightfall I met her in the same spot, St. Michel and Soufflot, but diagonal from where I'd left her, across the street in front of the red-awninged McDonald's I so loathe the sight of. We walked toward the river. I thought I'd take her to my café on

Ile St. Louis.

We sat on stools facing each other at the bar and drank beer, our knees interlacing and hands fumbling as we talked. She was wearing white jeans and a light blue button-down Polo shirt, long-sleeves rolled. It was a warm, pleasant evening. With waist-length, shiny black hair falling in tendril waves down along her breast she looked very sexy in a natural way, and I was much more attracted to her now than the night before. I looked down into her lap, and her eyes followed mine.

What are you lookink?

Nothing, I told her. I was just getting turned on.

She smiled.

We left the café and strolled along the quai. The river sparkled in the night. We stopped at a shadowy spot and stood at the low stone wall looking out over the river and began kissing. She spun her back to the wall and leaned against it. I pressed my body into hers and we kissed some more. She began loosening my belt and unfastening my jeans. Then they were all the way open and she dipped her fingers into my underwear and extracted my hardon, stroking it lightly in her soft hands.

It was *back* thank God, ever since that girl and her boyfriend at the Jardin des Plantes, and this was the first time I was going to get to use it in two months. I was very excited.

I felt my pants beginning to slide down off my hips and I reached back to hitch them up as I spread my legs wider, making it harder for them to fall again. I had the sense that what Matice was doing was less about pleasure and more about investigation. She wanted to see how big my dick was before we went any further. Sure, why not. I understood that I guess. Satisfied, I felt—and I felt this because she gave a soft little *hmmm* with a pleased smile on her lips and a twinkling in her eyes—satisfied she tucked it back inside my pants. I fastened them again and we hurried back across the river, back here to the rafters.

Afterwards, after the first time, before we actually made it up the ladder to the loft, she was coiled up naked on the couch, seemingly lost in thought. I asked what she was thinking.

I'm thinkink how many times I can fuck you before you go.

Oh? You like? I asked.

She smiled.

I like, she said.

We woke in the white of the bedroom at Ashbury. A diffused pale light coming through the window covered by a thin white drape engulfed the room. The light seemed to expand the already existing paleness surrounding us into an ethereal haze. The sheets and thick comforter covering us also white. We were floating in a cloud, it seemed.

Lying beside me she asked: Are you happy?

I smiled.

Yes, I said.

A little bit? she asked, as if not hearing my reply.

I nodded and smiled wider. Yes, I said again.

She kissed me on the cheek. Good, she said. Now tell me something nice.

There was a long pause before I spoke. I wanted to say the right thing.

How about...How about I love you, I said. Will that work? That's what I was thinking when you kissed me.

That'll work, she said smiling, and lightly pinched my chin between thumb and forefinger. Then she rolled out of bed and went into the bathroom.

And it was true. I'd never known what it was to feel that kind of happiness before.

*

Later that month I'd read in the newspaper about an exhibit happening in New York I told her I'd love to see, and wished I could. It was a Picasso exhibit, a show of his later work.

She had an idea. She was going to be in New York on business the following weekend anyway, she said, why didn't I meet her there?

She flew me out on a redeye, on her surplus of mileage points. I left Thursday night after work and arrived at Kennedy Airport around 7 the next morning. I don't know what happened, maybe the pilot took the plane too quickly into descent, or maybe I had an infection of some kind I wasn't aware of, but when the plane began to lose altitude my ears plugged and would not release no matter what I tried. Then my left ear was stabbed with excruciating pain and I jammed my finger into it, sealing the flap tight while violently shaking my head. In absolute agony I turned to my fellow passengers, was anyone else experiencing this torture? Everyone in my line of vision sat relaxed and easy in their seats, I alone was writhing and squirming and shaking my head, popping my jaw like a gasping carp. I wanted to tear my face off, rip the ears right from my head.

As the plane slowly lowered from the sky the pain steadily built like an air raid siren in my skull, like the most masterful Hitchcockian suspense transposed into sheer breathless physical torment, until I was about to crawl out of my skin. Clawing into the armrests I tried to brace myself for the horrific climax. I was sure my eardrum would explode any second.

Finally, it seemed to take forever, but the wheels touched down and there was relief. Slowly the pain subsided as we bumped down the runway and rolled toward our gate, though the pressure was still there and I couldn't do anything about it. I could hardly hear and I left the plane that way, and then the airport, thinking it would correct itself any minute, but the release stubbornly refused to come. Then I was standing outside on the island waiting half deaf for the town car she hired for me.

It rolled up long and gray. The driver got out and opened the back door. I got in and told him the Parker Meridien Hotel, did he know it? It felt as if my words were coming from the bottom of the Hudson. Yes, he said, of course he knew it. I told him about my ears, that they were stopped up from the plane and I could hardly hear. He said something I didn't catch, but I sensed his sympathy as he drove. It smelled funny in there, like stale cologne and Parmesan. I called her at the hotel to let her know I'd landed. I told her about my ears, and the smell.

First she laughed about the smell, then we talked about my ears. I was serious, and she caught the tone of my voice.

Oh that happened to me once, she said. Plug your nose and blow, she told me.

She was very faint in my ear—my right ear. I was afraid to use my left, afraid to have sound get that close to it, as if close range sound would injure it further. I was sure it was irreparably damaged. I did as she instructed, held my nose and blew. Nothing happened except a squeal that came out of my left ear mixed with another sharp stab of pain.

There was a squeal that came out of my ear, *I heard it*. Ears should not *make* sound!

I was frightened, kept popping and popping my jaw. I was afraid to, but I tried plugging and blowing once more. This time there was a slight release, but it quickly filled again with pressure.

I hung up with her. The driver drove. We tried talking a little but we both lost steam there, and I was preoccupied with my ears anyway. Would I ever hear properly again?

We were snarled in morning rush hour traffic. The driver decided to detour through Queens. I'd never been to Queens so I didn't mind. This happened to be the driver's neighborhood and he talked about it. I could hardly hear him, but I appreciated his guided tour and listened. He pointed things out as we drove, this and that, and after a while I noticed I could hear him a little better now—just a little—or so it seemed anyway. My ears were still plugged, but a little less so now I thought. An hour and half later we were in Manhattan, on the Upper West side, pulling up in front of the Parker Meridian. She'd gotten a suite.

From San Francisco I'd called her while on the plane just before takeoff. It was about 2 AM New York time. She said she was walking, that she had just left a porn shop. What? Why? I asked. Why not? she countered. Well, I don't like the thought of you going to those places alone. Who said I was alone? she said. She was joking. That was her sense of humor. It took me a while to get used to it, and looking back maybe I never fully did. A lot of times, although I knew she was supposedly joking, I couldn't tell if she actually was or not. This was one of those times. She thought the remark very funny, though. I didn't. I couldn't tell if she was joking about having gone to the porn shop, and if she *had* gone if she'd gone alone or not. Which part was the joke and which wasn't? Or was it all a joke? If she had gone, why had she? I became annoyed. I was tired from working all day and it was late and I wasn't in the mood to hear such things, joking or not—things that only made me wonder. We'd hung up with tension between us.

From the car parked outside the hotel I phoned her. She came down.

There she was with that smile, looking beautiful as usual. There was my girl.

She came to the driver's door and he got out. She counted a stack of bills in her hands and passed the lump over to him. I climbed out of the back with my bag and hugged her on the sidewalk, then we went inside the hotel and up to the room.

For a suite, I wasn't that impressed. It was certainly nice, and very modern, but it was quite small. She said that's what you get in Manhattan, that the suites there were like that. I figured she was the world traveler and took her word for it. It was my first time in a Manhattan suite. I'd pictured it larger, that's all. The only other hotel in New York I'd ever stayed in was seven or so years earlier, with her. It was an old school place in the East Village, and had that kind of charm to it. Black and white marble walls in the lobby yellowed with age and history. It was a little shabby, but it seemed nice enough during the day when we checked-in. Later when we returned to the room at 3:30 in the morning and flipped on the light switch the walls and furniture were rife and crawling with dark brown cockroaches, large and small.

In this elegant modern suite now we went at each other like monkeys. I stood in the middle of the room in front of the couch and had hold of her by the hips as her legs winged around me. I held her like that and let her head and shoulders and arms dangle on the floor as I fucked her with all my life. It had been a few days since I'd seen her. Then we went into the next room and drew the blinds and crawled into bed together. It was 9 AM, but with the blinds closed it became terrifically dark. I was exhausted, and my head still felt like it was in a bucket because of my ears. I was ready for sleep and knocked out right away. By 1:00 we were up again though, and ready to hit the exhibit.

She'd decided to wear her new boots over jeans. They were high, vinyl, and ruby red, sort of equestrian style. She said she always got comments on those boots whenever she wore them, and sure enough a minute later as we rode down to the lobby in the elevator a man riding with us felt compelled to speak.

What great boots, he said.

He was staring down at them, couldn't take his eyes off them. He seemed smitten, transfixed. These boots did hold strange magic. Or more correctly, enhanced the magic of the one who wore them.

Fantastic. Really fabulous, he went on, bent over and staring as if he were speaking to the boots themselves. We looked at each other as he kept looking down at her feet. She smiled. I grimaced.

Men were always making comments to her, talking to her, touching her. She told me this repeatedly. Repugnant as it was, that guy in the elevator was nothing in comparison to some. One time, she told me, she woke in her seat on an overnight flight as a man was rubbing her bare feet. She had stretched out on the two empty seats beside her, feet toward the aisle, and when she woke up he was standing there in the darkened plane rubbing her toes.

I had witnessed the phenomenon first hand many times myself of course, guys trying to hold her hand, caress her arm and other places in my presence. She said it happened so frequently she'd begun to desensitize to it, barely entered her mind that it was even happening. I on the other hand *was* sensitive to it. When she'd go with me to Caffé Greco in North Beach, for instance, at a certain time of day, one particular Guatemalan barista there, a very nice and charming man, he'd been serving me for years, but when I'd go in with her and he was working the counter he had to come out around to hug her. He did not know her prior to her coming in with me, and they had not established any kind of special rapport that I was aware of, but upon just seeing her he was compelled to hug her, to touch her. After the first hug was established he took it for granted that it was allowed each time he saw her, and so it continued every time we came in and he was working. We started avoiding his shift times, when it would be safe to go sans hug, because it just got to be too much—even for her. And then there were those who'd blatantly hit on her or ask her out when I left the room— that shit bugged me the most, and that was what I most wanted her to control and squelch. It was a constant irritation to me, and it seemed like something that shouldn't be too hard to address. Just remove any possibility in the question and for the most part it would disappear. It seemed an easy solution to me. But rather than somehow trying to dissuade this stuff she laughed about it instead, treated it as an uneasy joke, and reacted disdainfully toward me as if to someone who fastidiously refused to play along, as I suppose I was.

It left me spinning at times though. Why would she not try to discourage these things, I wondered, if just for my sake? Alright, in the least case of it, it was just a hug from a café barista. But that hug's a breach of protocol. In all the years I'd been going to that café I'd never seen him do that to another female customer. Man to man we know what that stuff means, and I didn't like it. But what could I do? My only recourse as I saw it was to let her know how I felt, and leave it up to her to somehow alter things. With the barista it was a simple fix, but with the others it was harder to contain and it put me in an awkward spot. If I became aggressive or defensive I'd be viewed as possessive and rude. If I said or did nothing I'd appear docilely passive, which would send the wrong signal in both directions—that she was free for the taking, and that I didn't care. A no win situation for me. So it was her place, I felt, to do something about it when she could. Other women did, I saw it all the time. But I could tell she both liked it, this male attention, thrived upon it I came to see, and was uneasy with it, because it seemed to wield so much power and chaos.

While in Paris with her one evening, as we were headed back to the apartment after a long walk on the Right Bank we were winding our way through rue de Buci, which leads into rue St. André des Arts, and because that's such a narrow bustling street, crowded with restaurant tables as well as pedestrians, I was walking ahead of her. After we passed a long row of outside tables and those dining at them, she caught up with me and blithely said: A guy just grabbed my ass. God *damn* it! I said. Did you say something? *React* in any way? Give him a piece of your *mind?* No, I didn't, she said, and looked at me as if I was crazy to even suggest such a thing. To her, a man was sitting there and saw a piece of ass pass in a dress he wanted to touch, so he did. Simple as that. That's the way things worked. I believe she took it as a compliment.

By addressing the issue with her, over time, only made her feel like I was insecure and controlling, like I wanted to change her, and a secret brew began boiling within her.

I felt like it wasn't that much to ask. While she was away I had all but stopped going out to my favorite spots at night. I had no interest in the women I'd see around me because I knew I had someone very special beyond them, that was obvious to me and I wasn't looking for anything else. But as I said before, in recent past sometimes women just appeared, and I was afraid that my loneliness for her just might make me slip into something that I'd regret happening, and I didn't want to chance destroying what I had. I stopped hanging out with friends like Jari and a couple others too, because they were single, and what do single men do but look for women. I knew that more than anyone. I didn't want to be even that close to it.

Looking back it was an overreaction, I know that now, but I did it for her. I was trying to change my life. I no longer wanted to continue living the way I'd been living in San Francisco; I didn't want to be a barfly. Drinking culture in San Francisco is so strong, like a dark magnetic current pulsing through the streets of the city, I'd gotten snagged in it over the years and recently awakened to the cold realization that I'd become a barfly, but I didn't want to be anymore. I never wanted to be. Sometimes life takes over, though, and your dreams die, and all you want to do is live, live the way you're dying inside to live but you no longer know how. She made me want to try to live again.

There was something inside me, I knew it, I've always known it, and she was drawing it to the surface once more. At least the *desire* for it to surface was surfacing, and I liked this feeling. I needed it. And now that I had found her I wanted to be *better*, to feel worthy of her, and I wanted nothing more than to shed all that wasteful apathy. I'd had years of it, and I was sick to death of that scene. So toward the end of our relationship I had fairly isolated myself from everyone and everything that was a part of my ordinary social activity before she entered my life, which fed into my loneliness while she was gone. As it turned out this added one more ingredient to the secretly generating poison in her—my isolation. It said to her that I was antisocial and boring, and if I was that lonely while she was away I needed to get some new friends, get a life beyond her.

This was never overtly said while we could've done something about it, but it came out in the end when she was running down her list, which came like a litany, and featured among the many things hurled at me, each taking me by surprise—I didn't tell her I loved her enough, or compliment her enough, and I never took her dancing or to baseball games or to other places she never expressed interest in going while we were together—featured among these things, and many more as well, was that I had tried to change her, and she felt she was losing her identity to me. My grimace in the elevator that day met by her smile was a harbinger of all this.

The exhibit was at a gallery in Chelsea. It was a ways from the hotel, but the weather was beautiful and it was New York, so we walked.

It was an exciting show—rarely seen paintings and prints done toward the end of Picasso's life, when his powers had all but been written off by the critics as long past. But this work proved he was still vital and relevant to the end. And the old goat still retained his lascivious spirit, too. It was a very sexy show, full of nudes and voyeuristic dreams of copulation. He still had it alright, if only in desire and will alone, and that sexual energy came through. We both left the gallery very turned on.

But as we were leaving, she had me step outside and wait for her. I didn't know what she was up to and it took a long time, whatever she was doing. She did this kind of thing sometimes and I never knew what she might be about in these instances, and my mind would race. Finally she joined me outside, but she wouldn't tell me what she had been doing and why I had to wait for her like that. Again I became a little annoyed with her then.

A week later a package arrived at my door. I opened it and found a thick hardcover book with a big black and white picture of Picasso staring almost accusatorily at me from the dust jacket. It was from the exhibit, and included all the paintings and prints we'd seen in the show, and now I understood. She had seen it at the desk as we were leaving the gallery and decided to surprise me with it as a present. She had gotten me again, and I felt bad for getting upset with her that day. After the exhibit, after having lunch and hanging out on the town a bit, we'd made it an early night and went back to the hotel. When I took her clothes off, again in front of the couch, I discovered the first surprise she had for me.

She was wearing new pink and black sheer crotchless underwear. This was why she had gone to that porn shop, she'd said, to buy something new and sexy for me. She lay on the floor as her fingers twinkled through the open slit in the panties, staring up into my eyes as I watched her from the couch. Her eyes were molten glass as she watched me.

Look at her, my baby, my girl, down there…There's my girl… My God…

I stood up and hot snakes of mercury rained upon her.

My ears were still blocked and bothering me the next morning, although less than the day before. Still though, they bothered me enough to pose a concern. She suggested I see a doctor, and called the concierge desk. A few minutes later the room phone rang and she answered. It was the house physician. She described the situation, and because he was unavailable, it being Saturday and all, the doctor referred her to a medical office in the vicinity of the hotel he said would be open. We went.

The woman behind the desk looked up from her magazine with some surprise when we opened the door to the small office. It was very quiet in there and no one else was in sight. The woman stood up right away and welcomed us in. She was black and thin and wore her hair in a nest of spaghetti braids. Long, curving colorful nails tipped her fingers. Sickle-like, each was about two inches or so and painted a different color. As she handed me the standard forms to fill out she held her hands fingertips upward and never let them drop, as though all the color would drain from them like freshly dipped paint brushes if she did. I finished the forms and after sitting in the lobby a minute I was called into the back.

The doctor was tall and around my age. A light German accent dragged in his voice. I told him what'd happened, about the stabbing torture I experienced during my flight's descent. He looked in my ears with a metal instrument. When he looked into my left one he said he saw a little irritation, a slight discoloring of red around the drum, but no damage. I'd be fine, he said.

That was a relief. Hard to believe, but a relief to hear. The trouble was, I explained, I had to get on another plane tomorrow, and I was afraid the same thing was going to happen again during descent into San Francisco, and did he have any suggestions to prevent this feared hell?

Try popping your ears, he said.

Brilliant. Thank you doctor. Keen insight and advice.

After wasting a portion of the morning on that nonsense we got in a cab from there and headed to the Upper West Village. She was excited to show me the famous Zabar's deli.

She knew it well, and escorted me through the entire store. She brought me to the fish counter and showed me how the man hand-sliced the lox. So thin, so rare to see, she said. She showed me the amazing cheese section and we tasted samples. It was an impressive place to those culinarily inclined, like us. She bought lox and fresh baked bagels and cream cheese for us to make breakfast with, and a baguette and salami and cheese and olives for a snack on our walk later.

From the West Village we walked toward the Metropolitan Museum via Central Park. As we neared the museum she led me in a detour to something I never knew existed, an obelisk of stone called Cleopatra's Needle.

Gazing up at the stone, she asked: How old do you think that is?

I don't know...I said. Three, four hundred years?

Nope. Try about four *thousand.*

We read about it together then, on the plaque at the base.

I loved that she showed me this. I'd been to New York a few times before, enough to become familiar with the city generally speaking, but I'd never had the experience she was creating for me.

We ate the food we brought with us from Zabar's after that, sitting on a short wall at the edge of the park, then went into the Met.

I'd been here before too, on my first trip to New York, just a month before the twin towers were annihilated. In fact, I'd come specifically to go to the Metropolitan Museum.

Very similar to the inspiration for this visit to see Picasso's work, the first time I went to New York was to see a William Blake exhibit.

Again I'd read about it in the paper, recognized it as a rare opportunity. I'd mentioned it to my girlfriend, the other one, and she very graciously bought me a plane ticket so I could go. I loved her for that. She was not rich by any means, but she had a decent job that paid well, and splurged so that I could have that experience. She knew what Blake meant to me.

I combined the trip with a visit with my older brother, Sam, who had recently moved from Miami to Manhattan to pursue his fashion photography dreams, but more recently, somewhat deflated, had relocated to Jersey City. I stayed with him over there across the river during that trip. He and I went to the Metropolitan together. He was showing me New York City, and I was showing him art. We walked the museum and I explained what I could about the works we saw. And where he was confused about the significance of certain pieces or artists I tried to help him have a better appreciation. I remember explaining Jackson Pollock to him, for instance, and the drips and splatters he was seeing seemed to open up before him and take life. I could see it in his face.

I wandered many of the same galleries in the museum with her now, and many others I didn't get a chance to see before with my brother, and I had to explain nothing. She didn't have an art background like I did, but being from a metropolitan city like Chicago she was well versed in perusing museums—the Art Institute being one of the greatest in the world. Outwardly she had the kitten sensuality of an up-scale stripper, an image made even more savory by the fact that she wasn't, but armed along with this arsenal of a trait, worldliness aside she was whipsmart, and she held me captured now. My walls had become rubble, and I was hers.

When we were done touring the exhibits we had a glass of wine on the museum rooftop terrace overlooking the trees of Central Park. From there we went back into the park and had a glass of champagne at the Boathouse Restaurant—another place of which I was unaware. We sat under lowhanging trees beside the small lake and with her BlackBerry she took a photo of our flutes glittering in the sun, resting like lovers' heads next to each other on our table. The image seemed to say something to her, and she looked at it on the screen of her phone with a lovely, serene smile.

After that though, after that beautiful day together, the night began to fall apart.

By the time we reached the Parker Meridien I was starving. We were going out to eat from here, at her favorite Italian place in Greenwich Village, but she needed to shower and get ready, and I needed food—now. The hotel had a burger joint in the lobby that was very popular citywide, she suggested I try it. But—although I knew my body in situations like this, could feel I was going down and needed to eat—I thought I should try to tough it out.

No, I said. If I eat a burger now I'll spoil dinner.

It's gonna take me a while to get ready, she said. And those burgers are great. You need to have one. Don't get any fries though, K? Just get a burger. They're kinda small. You'll still be able to eat dinner.

OK baby, if you say so.

She headed upstairs in the elevator and I went over to the burger place. It was in the left corner of the lobby behind a thick burgundy velvet curtain. That seemed too swanky to me, and at first I didn't want to go in, but behind the curtain was a dive diner with graffiti and street signs and stickers on the walls. It was hopping, and I had to wait in line a while to place my order. As I stood there, I watched people eating at their tables. Now I felt famished, and the food looked great—especially the fries. I couldn't help myself, I had to have some. I ordered a cheeseburger and small fries. I didn't eat them all, but I ate too many, because when I was with her now at the restaurant I had zero appetite. I tried to hide it, but eventually I had to confess. She was livid.

My plate came, sole in white wine sauce with vegetables— the lightest thing I could find on the menu. I choked down half of it but that was all I could take, had to leave the rest. We left the restaurant and she was quiet. She wanted to go to Rocco's across Bleeker Street and have cannoli. She'd raved about this cannoli, it was her favorite anywhere. We went but it was packed, a line through the entire café and no place to sit. I couldn't do it. I said lets come back later, and I meant it and thought we would, but we didn't. We walked a while. I suggested the White Horse

Tavern. I'd been before but I wanted to see it again—the place where Dylan Thomas got drunk for the last time before nodding into a coma back at the Chelsea Hotel and dying. We headed over there; we were very close to it. Again this place was packed. The door guy wouldn't even let us step inside. It started lightly raining. There was a little bar down the street from the White Horse. We went in there and somehow got to talking about the night we'd met, at Jari's party, and how we had *actually* met, I told her, the night before at the 500 Club, but she didn't remember.

I had just walked in the 500 and ran into Jari on his way out with a beautiful girl at his side who had a big dazzling smile, and another guy who was a regular at the bar trailing along with them. I was briefly introduced, and then they were all off to another bar in the Mission. From the moment I saw her I was set aflame. I guess that's how most men reacted to her. But when I sat down next to her at the party she did not recognize having met me the night before, and didn't know she had until I told her so then in that bar in New York.

And then she asked what I had been doing at the 500 Club that night, and I told her I'd gone there to meet someone, and as soon as I said it I knew I'd put my foot in it. When she asked who, I refused to say.

It was something I wasn't very proud of, I told her, I wasn't very proud of myself to be in the situation, and I didn't want to tell her the person's name. I didn't say this to her then, but it was possible we could run into this someone sometime in San Francisco, and I didn't want her to know the person's name because of it. I didn't want anyone to be uncomfortable if that should happen. I didn't feel like it was that big of deal, not to tell her. It was over. That was the last night of it, that night at the 500 Club, and it did not involve us, didn't touch us in any way. The next night we'd met at the party, and from there it was us.

But she wouldn't let it go, demanded the woman's name. I refused and kept refusing. To tell her meant telling her the situation, and I was ashamed of that. It was a byproduct of the wasteland, when I cared for or believed in very little and few boundaries were sacred. But I did not want her to hear this from me, so I refused to give the name and because of this she felt like it must surely still be going on and I was nothing but a shit and wouldn't believe otherwise.

We left, went back into the night in the rain silent with one another. Back at the hotel we simply went to sleep.

In the morning I found the pink and black underwear she had bought especially for me in the bathroom trash can.

By now my ears were better, but here I was on the plane again, together now with her seated side by side, not talking much, and about to descend into San Francisco. I could feel the pressure building and I was getting nervous. She had told me that when a friend of hers had this problem he drank a bottle of water during descent. I had a big bottle with me, and I sucked at it like a newly dropped calf at its mother, but it didn't help. I shook my head and twisted in pain from the same stabbing in my left ear, the only difference now was that she was there beside me to witness it, and I was embarrassed for her to see me that way.

Although she did me the honor of keeping her attention buried In her magazine, somehow I couldn't help feeling that a part of her was enjoying knowing that I was in pain.

I've lost more weight. Even with my belt fastened at the last hole pants still slink down my hips. Matice doesn't know the difference, though. My build is naturally slender but contrary to her perception I'm not normally this thin. She hasn't mentioned my physique and I haven't said anything of course, but I know the difference in my appearance from how I looked with *her* to how I now appear. I see my body as I step into the shower each morning, the walls lined with mirrors, and I see the internal devour happening, see myself growing more and more gaunt in the glass. Last night I went to have dinner, thought I'd try one of the places on rue du Pot de Fer. There's restaurant after restaurant right outside my door. I walked out onto the warm street and perused the menus posted along the windows but couldn't decide. Many had the same things, plates that sounded good, but the similarities made it harder to choose. Which one would be better? The prices varied only slightly, all relatively high for me. If I were to pay those prices, though, I wanted to make the better choice. But how could you tell which was the better choice? And what did I want? I didn't know what I even wanted…I was afraid of wasting my money on the wrong thing. I watched the people eating at their tables on the street, walked back and forth looking at the food on their plates, hoping what I saw would tell me what I wanted and help me decide. Up and down the street I went, then narrowed it down to two places right in front of my big blue door, and stood there leaning off to the side against my building feeling hunger's chasm, its quaking open pit, but still I couldn't decide. Just like at the airport when I stood looking at the young man and woman inside the money booth, I stood paralyzed, planted in inertia jumbled thought screwed me into, rooting me, unable to make a move. I must've stood there staring at food going into the flexing mouths of diners for twenty minutes or so before realizing how long I'd been there, and how I must look just standing staring in the street. So I went back upstairs and forgot about eating altogether, just swallowed the hunger deep into myself. Is this how I wish the vanishing to come?

Matice and I walked the Right Bank today for something to do together, in the rain, and I couldn't help remembering when I'd roamed over there six months before, with her. It'd rained that day too. Though I tried to squeeze the memories out of my mind, Matice still felt something. The distance in me already showing now the first lust has been satisfied.

We didn't do much, Matice and I, got as far as the Opera House when it started coming down so hard we stopped at a café for a beer to wait it out. The downpour passed relatively quickly and we continued walking, not much further though, and then circled back around near the Louvre. We came back on rue de Rivoli, the broad street that runs along the Louvre, walking through the long congested row of tourist shops. Matice thought I wanted to see that for some reason, not realizing that it's the thing I detest the most.

I learned more about Matice as we walked. She lives with her brother, who's a lawyer; they share an apartment on rue Gay-Lussac. The place is too small though, and they'll be moving soon. Matice has been looking at apartments. She's found one she likes, only just down the street from where they live now, but the landlord is giving her trouble. He wants proof of income, and Matice is unemployed. Her brother works, but she does not, and it's been difficult to get across to the landlord that in Turkey it is different.

When daughter is unmarried, Matice said, her father helps her with money. It's nothink there. It's *nor*mal. Here is different. Landlord doesn't understand. So I have to have my father call heem. It's fine. But what for my father has to call? He should *trust* me. But no. So my father will call, and we will get the apartment.

What about your brother? I asked. Has he seen the place? Does he like it?

My brother? *Pah*...He doesn't care. He's leaving to me.

But what about his income? Isn't that enough for the landlord to see?

My brother is lawyer, but he doesn't earn that much money yet. Soon, but not yet. We just moved here six month ago. My father helps heem too.

I see, I said.

What you see? You see nothink…You think you are clever. I am more clever than you.

We came back here to the apartment and fucked on the futon and then standing up over the red table. I looked out the window over Matice's head at the yellow lights of the apartment across the courtyard as I worked from behind, wondering about the couple I've seen over there. There was a shiny black guitar leaning on the floor against the bookcase in the living room and brown beer bottles scattered around it on the stone tiles. They had a party there the other night. I watched it from here in the dark for a while before I went out. Matice has a nice smooth pussy too and I thank God for it but it only reminds me of hers. And as far as the sex goes, which I also thank God for, I've had the absolute best I've ever had and every woman from now on has a lot impossibly to live up to, and I am fucked now because of it. Afterwards Matice and I sat together naked on the futon and talked some more, drinking wine.

You should meet people here in Paris, she said. You didn't come here just to fuck me.

I explained I knew Christophe, and now I knew her, and although I'd love to meet more people it's very difficult, unable to speak French.

Is not so difficult, she said. You are shy, that's all. You should try. Maybe you meet more people, you like, you stay… Why don't you write your story here in Paris?

She knew I was trying to write, but not to what extent I've already been writing.

I'd love to stay, I said. There's nothing for me in San Francisco anymore. I just don't know how I'd make that happen. But I promise, I'll try to meet more people.

You should. But don't do for me. Do for you.

I poured another glass of wine for each of us, then we got

dressed and I walked her home.

We took the route by the Pantheon. It's lit-up at night with a strong bluish-white beam that makes the dome and the pillars supporting it look as if they were a giant model of a building and not an actual one at all, almost as if it were made of clay. It's very beautiful that way. There are some really great photographs in that book she'd taken of me during our trip last fall, standing on rue Soufflot with the Pantheon lit-up in the background like a set-builder's construct. Grainy in the night I stood there in those photos in my black leather jacket, slouched and leaning my right shoulder into a wall like some anachronistic street punk poet, my back to her, looking uncaringly in profile to the left while the Pantheon loomed beyond glowing blue and gray and ceramic. They're all I see when I see the Pantheon now, and I pass it every day and night on my walks—those photos, that book, that night with her…I passed it again on my way home after I separated from Matice on the corner, but by then the beam was no longer illuminating the building. And when it is not lit, when it's squatting there huge and majestic and sprawling in the dark you can actually better sense the lofty dead it houses lying silently asleep inside behind its gates. You can almost hear their dreams and opinions as you pass small and mortal, a mouse in the night.

I actually did meet someone else, prior to Matice, the Sunday before I went to Monet's Garden.

In the hour just before sunset I went to sit by the Seine. The light slanted a golden patina over the cobbled walkway and upon the stone walls and buildings of the Right Bank across the river. Walking along I saw a girl sitting alone on the edge of the bank reading a book. She reminded me of a young, swarthy Elizabeth Taylor. She had short black curly hair and skin the color of tarnished brass enriched by the declining sun and a little up-turned pointy nose. She even had a black mole on her left cheek, the side of her painted by the sun, like Liz, near the corner of her mouth. I noticed this when I sat upriver from her, about 10 feet away. I wasn't being obvious about it but I was looking at her of course. She was aware of me, or rather, aware that someone had sat down near her, but she didn't notice me yet. I took out my notebook and started writing. After a few minutes she closed her book and lit a cigarette. I seized that moment.

What are you reading?

She said something but I didn't understand. Couldn't tell what language she said it in either. I made an indication that I didn't catch what she'd said. She repeated it. I made a face and cocked my head, though now I could tell she spoke English. I got up and moved a little closer. Then once again she said it.

Soci*ology*, ah…Got it, I said. Sorry, I couldn't hear you over there. Are you in school?

She said she was, an internship, moved back to Paris from Marseille to complete her studies. What about me?

I told her my story, partially, and much condensed.

Oh…she said. I'm sorry.

Yeah. What's your name?

Sarah.

Sarah…I have a sister named Sarah.

She smiled.

What was she doing sitting here by herself?

Sometimes she just liked to be alone she said.

What was she doing from here? Would she like to get a drink or something?

She said she would, but she's about to go meet some friends in St. Germain. And she was really busy this next week, she'd said, but offered her phone number. I had her write it down in my notebook.

Then her phone chimed and she answered. She spoke in French. It was her friends asking where she was she told me after she'd hung up. We slowly rose and walked up to the quai together, then parted there on the street. And it felt so easy, and she was so beautiful, the kind of girl I'd hoped to meet—dark and petit, smart, and seemingly soulful. I floated from there back toward the Mouffetard. I felt so good I stopped for steak frites at a place on St. Germain, across from the charcuterie by rue Monge.

Sarah was the real impetus to get my cell phone working in Paris. The phone in the apartment only receives calls. Whenever I've tried to dial out an automated voice comes on informing me of something I do not comprehend and then the line goes dead. So the day after returning from Monet's Garden my first action was to take care of my cell phone. When I got it working I sent a text to Sarah right away, asked if she was free that night, or some night soon.

She wrote back that it turned out she was actually much busier that week than she originally thought, but when things quieted down she'd call. I'm still waiting for that call but I'm not holding my breath. If she's anything like the girls I remember encountering in San Francisco my rational mind tells me I can pretty much write it off.

Another little part of me, though, can't help lifting its tender glistening eyes out of the shadows, and with a rippled, beggarly brow offers this humble but infectious susurration: Ah, but you're not *in* San Francisco. Maybe girls here will turn out to be otherwise?

Yeah, maybe. And that tiny, hopeful part of me is holding on to this guarded whisper, but ever, ever so loosely…

Matice knows nothing about this meeting and I'm not going to tell her.

After New York something happened to us. On the surface we were very much still the same, same passion, same love as far as I could tell, but a ghost-tap of some undercurrent had been turned on now, and bickering and arguments began spouting between us. They were rare and sporadic at first, but as time went on misunderstandings escalated, and fighting came with more frequency.

She moved into the Telegraph Hill apartment. One morning I was awakened by her coming at me through the hall into the bedroom.

From some far-off, vague place I heard: Oh, Roman…You have *condoms* in your *bag?* Then, closer, a little clearer: Why do you carry condoms?

I shook off sleep and tried to focus on what I was hearing. By this time she was in the room repeating the question, seated at the edge of the bed next to me looking directly into my face.

Why do you have condoms in your bag?

I don't know. When you gave me that bag at Shrader I just shuffled everything out of my old one into my new one. I had almost forgotten they were in there. I had condoms in my other bag from before I met you.

When she and I first started, aside from the first night at the W, we used condoms until she went on the pill. I remember the night we went into Walgreens together on 18th and Castro to buy them. We got a big box of 40. After we paid and were walking out she said to the clerk with a big smile see you *tomorrow* night! We went out laughing. Those condoms in my bag were leftover from that batch I carried with me then, as well as a few from before her. To this day the majority of them are still in a drawer in their box in my room in San Francisco.

She was angry and took it as a sign of infidelity. I asked what she was doing going through my bag anyway. This to her was inconsequential. I removed the condoms from my bag.

Another time while at the same place the same scenario; I

woke to her coming at me upset through the hall with my phone in her hand. This time she asked why I had called her, my ex-girlfriend.

She had gone through my cell phone, she said, because she needed to call Jari to let him know she was going to be working from home that day, and wasn't able to drive him down to the office. Her phone was dead and she couldn't find her charger. Realizing I had Jari's number in my phone she thought of using mine to call. In doing this she found I had made a call myself. What this had to do with finding Jari's number and calling him I wasn't sure, since that process was a different application than going into calls received and dialed in my phone, but this was irrelevant to her when I asked.

I had made the call, undeniably true, but it was not like she was making it out to be.

The week prior, while she was out of town, I got to thinking about the recording of that Leonard Cohen concert I'd made, and what a treasure trove I felt it was, and what a shame I couldn't share it with more people. Then I thought of her. Knowing the music aficionada she was, and actually having been at one of those concerts, I thought she might like to have it as a memento. That's how profoundly those shows touched me. I thought the experience that special.

As a gesture of friendliness and goodwill, I thought I'd offer to share the recording with her. That was the true and magnanimous answer to the question why I had made that call. The more selfish one was that I was curious about her response to meeting my new girl, and I deviously, secretly wanted to gloat a little. I didn't get a chance to get this part out, though. She didn't want to hear any of it. To her, I'd made a great transgression and offense to our relationship. She said she'd told me she'd chosen not to see her friend Todd because she wanted to leave the past the past, and that she'd done that for me. She took it for granted I'd do the same. She said she'd told me how she felt about *her*, and never wanted me to speak to her again.

This I had no memory of. I couldn't recall her ever saying anything like this to me, but I got it now loud and clear. I didn't think it was right or fair, but I'd heard her, and I never made another attempt at contact after that. The meeting I had with her, though, was significant.

We met at a tea parlor near where I live. I was just from work. She, I believe, was between jobs at this time and was in the process of sending out resumes. I knew next to nothing about her life now. What she did, where she lived, how she occupied herself and interacted with life—all that was a mystery to me. *She* more than ever now was a mystery to me. She seemed just as thin as when I saw her at the concert two months earlier. *Thinner* actually, because she wore a tight teal cotton turtleneck and I could really see her form now. I was worried about what I saw.

Aside from the ecstasy we'd done a handful of times together she'd never been into drugs while I knew her, but maybe the change of lifestyle had changed her decision on that. I didn't know, and I didn't say anything about her weight, afraid she'd take it as another one of my famous criticisms. So I swallowed it. But again she looked odd to me. She'd cut her long red hair once again (the first time she did this was shortly after she left me, and when I saw that she had I knew how permanent her decision of leaving was), and underneath her black wool sailor's cap it fell just above her shoulders at the base of her neck. The oddest thing about her that day, though, was that she was wearing earrings made from the clipped ends of peacock feathers. More feathers…I thought, the teal color of which matched the color of her turtleneck, she was very well coordinated, but I'd never seen her wear anything remotely like that, and those earrings distracted me the entire time I was with her.

I was dying to hear what she had to say about her, and I just knew she was dying to talk about it, but I also knew her pride and reticence. So I took my time. We talked about what I'd been up to workwise, the museum and the renovation, how I'd been working full-time for basically the last four years, the last two with benefits finally. None of this she was used to hearing about me. I hadn't worked full-time since we met, when I was at that law firm. I'd quit not long after when I received $9,000 out of the blue from my father, from some insurance money he was owed. He split it all among his children. We each had received $9,000, and with mine I felt I could exist six months in my low-rent garage and stay home to write, so I did. After that it had been a struggle for me and my employment life, as it had been before the law firm. But I did not regret the decision. Then eventually the museum work came around, but it was part-time and I eked by at best, until now.

I asked what she'd been up to, but typical evasiveness prevailed here and I learned next to nothing except that she was making books. Photo books. She'd learned a computer program that allowed her to assemble and manipulate images, and print and bind them in hard cover. She made them for friends and they sold for $200 each. I was impressed, and couldn't at the time visualize what her books may look like, until I was given mine made by someone else containing photos of a trip to Paris. I thought of her instantly when I was handed my gift on my birthday, remembering the books she said she'd learned to make. It was the same program used to make mine.

Then I gave her the recording. It took up three cds and I set the stack on the table. Wow, look at that, she said. We talked about the show we'd seen, from different perspectives. I did not mention this.

Circling…Circling…

Finally then we zeroed in on it.

We met at a party, through a mutual friend, I answered.

Well, she makes a lot of money, I said. That's how we got those seats.

No I am *not* being spoiled rotten, because I've told her. I've told her how susceptible to that I am and I'm doing my best never to be accused of that again. She's just really generous. But I've impressed upon her how important it is to me to contribute, and I make it a point to. Plus, I said, I deserve it.

She cocked an eyebrow.

That's right, I said. After five years of being alone, and working on myself to make changes, I deserve this.

And I truly believed it, that Providence or whatever had finally smiled on me, that all my hard work and the pain I'd endured over the last few years had not all been in vain because it blossomed now—blossomed into my beautiful, amazing new lover.

After we parted and I'd turned to walk home, it dawned on me what I'd really been up to with her. When I thought about it, I realized I'd been testing to see if I was really over her, if her power over me had really lifted—that's what I'd been doing. And I'd gotten my answer. I felt so good walking away from her that evening, so free, knowing her spell had been broken. I felt entirely at ease and happy and turned fully forward without doubt toward the prospect of my new life. And that was the *whole* truth.

But she did not want to hear it, and so she never did.

T he phone rang. I was staying in with my notebook, and when the phone started chirping I turned toward it. The red, digital numbers of the electric alarm clock beside the phone read 11:33. I walked over from the table and picked up the receiver. Slow and soft the voice.

Hi Roman. Howya doin'?

Hi Richard. Fine. How are you?

I'm good. I wanted to see how things were, and let you know

that I spoke to Patrick. He's gonna come by to look at the toilet.

Oh...OK. But it's stopped leaking, thankfully. It stopped the day after we talked last.

Oh, that's good Roman. Glad to hear that. Well, he'll probably come by anyway. Sometime in the next few days, I guess. How's it going otherwise?

Oh, fine. I'm getting out, met a couple people. Things are fine.

Good. Glad to hear that. Have you called Leticia yet?

No. Not yet.

Leticia was his expatriate friend he'd emailed regarding me. I've meant to contact her, out of politeness anyway, but I haven't gotten around to it.

Well, you really should give her a call, or send an email. She's a good contact to have over there. And her parties are really pretty fun.

I'd gone to her website where information is posted about her salons with photos taken from past parties. I wasn't sure about it. None of the people I saw in those photos seemed unemployed and in questionable mental state. Quite the opposite actually. Most of the faces I saw were smiling cheerfully and seemed somewhat affluent. Maybe I was misreading them and letting my hypersensitivity get the better of me again, but I didn't feel so sure I'd make the best impression at her party, particularly under the circumstances. I'd read that new guests are asked to introduce themselves before the group. I could see it...Hi everyone. Heartshattered, starving mental case writer here, from San Francisco. Newly unimpotent, thank Jesus. I'm thinking of trying to make a go of it here in Paris. No, I cannot speak French and I have no real marketable skills to speak of beyond my uncommercial artistic talents, and I shake and cry a lot, but if any of you have a lead on something I might be a fit for, please let me know. I'll be over there in the corner again, watching you all. Any ideas, come *chat*.

Yeah, I will, I said. I'll make a point of doing that Richard.

Good. Well, alright, I should get going Roman.

OK Richard. Thanks for calling. I appreciate it.

Sure. No problem. And like I said, Patrick should be around in a day or two.

I put the receiver back in its cradle. A few minutes later it chirped again. It happened like that. The thing could be silent for days, and then when it started ringing it didn't seem to quit.

Hello?

'Ello, Romon? Ees Christophe.

Yeah, hi Christophe.

I got your note. I'm sor*ree*, I wazuh out of town.

That's OK.

You need 'elp wizz yoair cell *phone*?

I *did*, yes, but I've taken care of it. Sorry, I should have called you about that. I took care of it myself.

Oh, OK. What ahr you do*ing*?

Oh, I'm…I'm just reading.

I didn't want to say I was writing for some reason. I've neared the end of my third notebook, and each time I go to the stationary store at Place St. Michel and buy a new one I think it'll be the last, I can't possibly fill another after this one, but it keeps coming, this worm, slowly. I didn't want to jinx it.

Do you want to get togezair mmmay*be*, for a drink or some-*sing*?

Oh that sounds good. We definitely need to do that, I said, but maybe another night would be better.

I've run into Christophe three times on the street since being in Paris. By Notre Dame my first night. The day after he and Julien and I went out, near St. Michel and rue de la Harpe, when I'd just left an internet café there. And once on Quai Montabello by Shakespeare and Co. This type of thing means a lot to me. It's the kind of thing that used to happen between me and my close friends in San Francisco. I'd run into them all over town at random times, because we were that unconsciously connected I thought. When this started happening with Christophe it signified to me that he and I were becoming friends. But tonight I just couldn't face walking those streets all over again, forcing a public guise. Earlier, before picking up my notebook, I'd been crying. More crying...Working this way is the only thing that helps beats that back, and now that I was into it I was dug in. I couldn't deal with any more pretending. It took too much effort. I put Matice off earlier too when she'd called, especially Matice. It's hardest to keep pretending with her. We'd gone out last night to a couple places on rue Dauphine, to a club, I forget what it was called, and then just to a quiet brasserie for a couple beers. When we met that night she said to me: Don't you miss me? I don't think, she said, looking into my eyes. No, you don't.

I made a fainthearted protest.

Then why don't you *tell* me? she said.

 It struck such a deep chord. Of course I didn't miss her, I see her too often for someone I don't love to miss, but I tried to be nice and lie, and choked on it. But it resonated within me because of what I was told by *her*—that I didn't tell her I loved her often enough, or how beautiful I thought she looked. I did tell her those things, but not enough for her taste as it turned out. It was so obvious though, I thought, in the way I touched her, looked at her, held her close to me when we walked down the street in San Francisco. I thought I showed her these things, how I felt about her in these ways, in the flowers I bought for her each time she came back into town the last five months or so we were together. I preferred to try to show it than say it, but I thought I did both.

 It was not a new criticism. I'd heard it many times from other women. Something in me just prevents me from dishing out the sweet stuff, the little things they love, the compliments and sugar-topped words. I don't know why, other than when I've heard men use those words so liberally with women it's just rung so falsely in my ears it's made me sick. So somewhere in my psyche, somehow unconsciously, I'd decided to really mean them when they are said, and their infrequency would carry a great deal of weight when they are heard because to hear them meant their sincerity rang true. To say I love you to someone really meant that I loved her, and for me to say it meant there couldn't be anything truer. I took it for granted in the other person that this was understood, if we were close enough to exchange those words. Once I've said them there's no turning back for me. But to keep saying it as frequently as it seemed she needed to hear it, on top of my trying to show it, ran counter to my understanding of the concept of love. Why did she need to hear it so often if she knew that I loved her, and how could she not have known that? Isn't there a point when two people can relax within the knowledge of their love for each other without the words, or less of the words I mean, and just accept and embrace that quiet knowledge as it exists? Isn't that what love is, not having always to say I love you?

As I say, this was all an unconscious process. I've never put it together in my mind quite like I've just expressed it, but now that I have I know it to be true this way in me. Can there really be conflicting styles of love, enough to tear love in two? Both welling ostensibly from the same emotional reservoir, but different approaches in drawing it forth can taint the drink?

To hear Matice ask last night if I missed her told me we are already getting too close. Tomorrow we are going to explore Buttes Chaumont, the park that American girl mentioned in the ticket line at Gare St. Lazare. It's in the 19th arrondissement, and neither one of us has been to the 19th. It's one Matice's been warned away from, which attracts me even more.

Before our time at Telegraph Hill was up, the last weekend of June we got out of town. That's when Gay Pride hits San Francisco. I'd begun preferring to leave town for the event.

It started the year before, when I was still alone but making regular money now. I knew that Pride weekend was coming and began scheming as if a tsunami was on its way. This year I had the means to escape, and decided I wanted to rent a cabin somewhere in the woods. I wanted nature, peace and quiet—the opposite of what was going to be happening in the city. I was going to try to do some writing, I told myself.

I went online and found a couple prospects in my price range, then I found the one.

It was in Big Sur, and surprisingly affordable, and luck was with me because it was free that weekend. I booked it.

Since she'd made the shift in lifestyles I'd begun hearing reports of her from friends surrounding this weekend.

Guess who I saw riding on the back of the Dyke March float? I was asked.

Hey, I saw your ex on the back of a motorcycle riding with the Dykes on Bikes in the Pride parade, I was told.

She was only two years into this change, two years after us, when I'd started hearing these things, and it really tore into me to hear them. And the harsh stupid twist of my living in the Mecca neighborhood of the whole thing, that topped it all. I had to get away from it this year.

The cabin was a real find, a little jewel of discovery that I held in secret after my first visit. It was going to be my special get away place of retreat forever, I hoped.

Well, that time of year approached again and I told her about my cabin and idea of getting away for the weekend, and she loved it. I made the initial contact, reminding the couple who owned and rented the cabins (there were actually two) of my rental the year before, and was there availability for the same time this year? I asked. Lucked out again. The same cabin was open and I snatched it up. From here I handed things over to her. She took over the business arrangements and transactions directly then.

Both cabins were charmers, different in layout but essentially the same. The first one, that is, the one you come to first as you drive down the very narrow gravel path behind the owners' home, was A frame. The second a little further down the path was more secluded, nestled among young redwoods, and was the epitome of the image I hold in mind when I think of a cabin—roughhewn and square, a little raw shell of shelter. This was the one I'd rented and this was the one we had together now.

It had everything you needed, from a fully stocked, very basic kitchen (you'd have to bring your own food of course, but all the pots and pans and utensil etc. were there, right down to spices and wine glasses) to robes, soap, and a fire place. Rustic comfort they called it.

The cabin was perched at the edge of a deep ravine. Cutting through the ravine, barely visible through the overgrowth, was a gurgling stream. A wide deck ran around the cabin that overlooked the ravine, and there were lounging chairs and a round, pebbled-glass-topped table out there. On the far right of the deck, behind the cabin out of sight, were the bathroom facilities. There was simply a toilet and an open showerhead attached to a thin pipe jutting up from over the back of the deck's railing, that was it. You were completely exposed to the elements. But it was fun to use these things before a strange audience of redwoods, silent in their front row watch among the clouds and the stars in their upper tier seats. But best of all, independent from the shower and anything else back there, stretching out like a throne unto itself was a white, cast iron, clawfoot bathtub. This was the real star of the place. I'd described it all to her, and at first I was worried the outside open bathroom might put her off, but she thought the whole thing sounded wonderful.

We got into the Prius Saturday morning and headed south. Somewhere just past San Jose, in a quiet moment between us, I was looking out my passenger side window letting my mind roll along with the freeway scenery and began thinking about the fact that she always drove when we went anywhere. I'd asked to drive a couple times, but because the cars were rented in her name and I wasn't insured on them as a driver, she'd never let me. I said what did that matter? But she was a stickler for rules and safety in a way I was not and refused to let me get behind the wheel.

She suffered from debilitating migraines. The first signs of them coming on were loss of vision, literal blindness, followed by vomiting, and the first time I became aware of this condition in her was while we were driving. It was in the early days of the Shrader place, and we were cruising along the Embarcadero one night. As I sat beside her in the passenger seat she suddenly said I think I'm losing my vision. I thought she was joking, but that's when she told me about the migraines, and the symptoms. I told her to pull over. If she thought her sight was going she needed to pull over and let me drive. She refused. Even then she would not release control, preferring to race across town in the hope of making it home in time before she either crashed us or puked all over the dash.

I'd been in relationships before where the woman always drove, and after a while it starts to feel a little emasculating. I wasn't making a big deal out of it, but as we drove along toward Big Sur I turned suddenly from the window and said to her: You know, one of these days *I'm* gonna drive *you* somewhere.

She smiled her big smile and gave her head a slow shake.

What? What are you smiling at?

I was just going to ask you to do that, she said.

I smiled then too and watched the road ahead again scrolling up the windshield.

We'd begun having this over the past few months. Though ar-

guing was unfortunately a part of us now, that indefinable psy-
chic communication, like that which existed between me and the
other *other*, the other one, was also becoming part of us. So often
now I did this to her, answer her before she spoke, and it
frightened her a little each time, but it only reinforced my belief
in our connection. These things only happened between deeply
connected minds and souls, I believed, and are taken seriously in
me. It might've surprised and frightened her, but I was used to
this occurring between myself and the one I loved.

We'd been following directions from a printed email the
owners sent upon receipt of deposit. I vaguely remembered the
route from the year before, but I told her how to go from the
email as we went. Now at the end of Carmel we stopped at the
Safeway to the left of the highway. I did this last time too. This
was the last place to get supplies before reaching the cabin,
which was just up the road about another mile and a half. From
there you make a turn and drive a twisting road through huge
redwood trees to the couples' home.

After our pit stop we were back on our way. There was the
turn, I remembered it, and we climbed the narrow route through
the cool shade of the big, primeval trees. Another fifteen minutes
of this maybe and there was the house. The couple's name was
on the mail box.

We rolled into the gravel driveway and parked. A shaggy
gray and black dog wandering loose on the drive in front of the
open garage stopped in its tracks to bark, pointing its snout up at
the sky. They were slow, sleepy barks, the kind to let someone
know there were strangers about. We got out of the car and stepped into the hot sun. Walking up to the door of the house I rang
the bell. We stood there together, and the door opened. There
was the woman. She looked exactly the same as she did before—
short gray hair in a kind of grown-out spiky butch cut, pleasant
smile to match her pleasant eyes squeezed into smiling slits.
There was a slight southern drawl to her speech. The woman's

name happened to be the same as hers, and she faintly remembered me. I introduced them and they shook hands. She said her husband was out just then, but she welcomed us. We paid the remainder of the amount for the weekend and were told to pull our car down around to the cabin.

We got back into the car and I showed her where to go. The gravel path was just to the right of the driveway. She turned onto it and drove us down to the cabin.

There was the first one, and a little silver car parked just ahead of it at the end of the path pulled tight along the banking hillside to the right. The path widens out at the end to allow turnaround, and beyond the turnaround was our cabin. We parked behind the silver car, which we figured must belong to the renters of the other cabin, and began to unload.

I stepped onto the deck and opened the cabin's screen door, and then the green wooden door behind it, and entered. It was just as I remembered, and it felt great to be back. It felt particularly wonderful to be sharing this special place now with her. The last time I was here Big Sur was being consumed by fire. It raged nearby, but out of range from immediate danger as of my arrival. Ash fell like fat dirty snowflakes and heavy smoke filled the sky. The sun strained to punch through it, turning the light an eerie amber color. I'd never seen that kind of light in nature before. It felt very apocalyptic, with the strange orange light and the ash coming down like fallout. Firemen in firefighting gear constantly roamed the quiet, main road. Late into the next day, although enjoying myself despite it all, under threat of evacuation I decided to leave, worried I'd never see my newfound little retreat again. But it survived, and here it was. Here *we* were.

We got situated, put the groceries away, opened a bottle of wine. Soon evening came and we made dinner. There was a small grill outside on the deck beside the screen door. The woman said we could use it, but if we did to be sure to slide the square piece of tin they had leaning against the cabin underneath to protect against fire. I found a bag of charcoal in the kitchen closet and brought it out. I put some in and laid the tin down and set the grill on top of it and lit the coals. When the fire burned off and the coals were hot I put the two filet mignon steaks we bought on to cook. She also wanted crab legs (she cooked those often) so she prepared those in the kitchen along with a salad. We ignited the fire in the gas fireplace and lit the candles about the cabin and ate at the table beneath the window to the right of the door in that warm glow. Outside the windows it was pure black. We had music from her laptop (the cabin was equipped with wifi) and it played softly. After dinner we took a candle and our wine outside and climbed into the clawfoot tub and lay together in the sudsy bubbles beneath a smear of diamond dust stars. Wrapped in each other in the warm water, we stared up at the glitter twinkling through the dark redwood canopy above in the black velvet sky, relaxing now after our long day—but not for long. Ferociously, as if starved for one another, we made love out there in that tub under those stars. The water churned in a marine life feeding frenzy and sloshed over the tub's edge. And then, because it was too cramped in the tub, we stepped out and continued standing up on the deck at the railing, looking out into the darkness of the ravine as the stream sang its rippling chant up to us, cheering us on from its blind roll.

The bed was thick and high off the ground. There was a wooden stool of two steps at its side to help climb up to it. We came back inside the cabin through the sliding glass doors that opened onto the backside of the deck, climbed up into bed under the heavy pink and white patchwork quilt, and slept sweetly together in utter black silence.

The next morning we woke leisurely. There was a scratchy, shuffling sound above us, and I could see, blurred through the opaque plastic of the skylight, the forked images of a bird's black feet prancing around up there. Probably a blue jay, I thought. I kissed her as she lay beside me and she smiled tenderly just before opening her eyes and stretched her bare arms out from under the quilt and over her head.

After making breakfast and cleaning up, we simply relaxed the day away under the redwoods on the deck, reading, chatting, and saying nothing. It was Sunday now, and we had to leave in order to get back to the city for work the next day, but we were enjoying our little haven in the trees for as long as we could.

Shortly before we left I was lounging on a deckchair looking out into the ravine, listening to the birds twertling and the stream down there, when she came out and handed me something, then went back inside. It was a journal bound in the softest cocoa-brown leather, clasped with a leather thong knotted into a loop, which was attached through the leather at the spine and cinched tight with a wooden bead. Slid under the thong was a large white envelope with my name handwritten in large letters on it. I slipped it out and read the card inside.

Something to help find your words while in Paris.

I was stunned. We had already hatched the vague plan to go to Paris in the fall, and this was an offering from her to help encourage my writing. I opened the beautiful notebook and looked at the empty ruled manila pages inside. What was I going to do with this? How could I ever fill these wonderful pages? It was too beautiful. I couldn't imagine sullying its paper with my pen, my words. I loved it, loved her for giving it to me, loved her without it, but this book was an art piece itself, handmade in Italy, and I had no words then good or true enough that could do it justice. I held it in my hands, rubbing the softness with my thumbtips, and felt emotion rise all through me.

I got up and went inside and held her close.

On the wooden bar that separated the cabin's kitchen from the rest of the small, one-room space, laid a guest book. People wrote messages in there thanking the proprietors for the pleasure and privilege of their stays. I wrote one on my first visit before I left, and she wrote one for us now, but would not let me read it.

No, read it next time, she said. When we come back.

This didn't make any sense to me, so I kept at her. Finally she allowed me to look.

> *Thank you so much for this wonderful experience.*
> *I am leaving here even more in love with the man*
> *who brought me.*

Because it was easiest to reach the 19th taking the train from Place Monge, Matice came to meet me this time. She called from the street at my door and I came down the long, turning stairs.

From the Pink 7 line we caught at Place Monge, we transferred at Châtelet to the Brown 11. The 11 stops a few blocks from Buttes Chaumont, but it seemed less complicated and faster to take that line than connecting to the one that would have let us off right at the park. We got off at Pyrenees and walked the rest of the way.

It was cool and the sky was a white sheet, giving the light a finish so soft and pure it seemed to create no shadows, as if emanating from all around you. The sadness I woke with attached to me like an infected second skin and I couldn't salve it, but did my best to hide it. I did OK at first, but as the day wore on Matice began to sense something.

From Metro Pyrenees we walked rue Simon Bolivar into the

park. It was very green, and with the light the way it was the grass and the trees looked very lush. Slowly we walked the empty road leading us into the park, and wound our way up onto a little hill where there were benches. We sat for a while and looked out over the greenery before us. There was another couple up there sitting on another bench. The girl sat across the guy's lap with her feet dangling above the ground and had her arm draped around his neck. They just sat that way, talking and smoking cigarettes.

There wasn't much to see up there beyond the trees, and we weren't talking much, I had the feeling Matice was getting a little bored, so we got up and walked back down the hill. We picked up the same road as before and walked further through the park. It was nice, but I didn't see what that American girl was talking about. There was nothing I saw that made this place special among any other. We must've been missing something. But I guess Matice and I weren't particularly in the mood to explore in depth, so we just followed the road till it led us out of the park.

There was a café across the street from where we exited Buttes Chaumont, and we sat with coffees at a table outside. A heavy mist began falling but we were safe under a long orange and yellow striped awning. I watched the light-gray pavement beyond our chairs gradually darken with the thick spray.

You're not happy, Matice said. Why? It hurts me *here* to see.

Matice placed a hand beneath her throat, on her chest.

I gave a sick smile.

Oh…That's in the *past*…She's in the *past* now, Matice said. You have to let go.

But that was just it—I *know* she's in the past now, and it hurts so to think of her this way. The period of transition when someone you love slips from present to past is a purgatorial torment. There's neither life nor death, all is merely detached floating mechanical misery as you watch helplessly the recession occur…

What happened with your girlfriend? Matice asked, then answered her own question. I think you are selfish, she said. I can see. Yes. That's your problem.

That ripped a chunk clear out of me. Another principal item on her secret long list was that she felt she could not ask me to do anything for her, that to ask me to do her a favor was to put me out in some way. She did not use the word Matice just used, but that was the implication. How she came to this judgment is still a mindtwist of a mystery to me. I would have done almost anything for her, nearly anything she asked, but she felt otherwise for some reason and it was not the first time I'd heard it. Another lover had recently told me the same thing. I felt wronged and perplexed then, but to hear it again from *her* was crushing. Why am I perceived this way? What is it in me that breeds such insecurity, that translates into this signal I seem to send out and that Matice is already receiving? I looked at Matice and said nothing as she squinted a hard, measuring look back at me.

There's somethink wronk with you, Matice said, her words slow and speculative. A man more than forty who never marry… No! she concluded abruptly, definitively. There's somethink wronk…

I couldn't argue with that. There is something wrong with me. Not because I've never been married but because I keep losing the people I love. What is it in me that produces this loss over and over? How did I lose her? How *could* I have when I loved her so much? Is it me, or some bad sign, a malign star I was born under that prevents love from staying in my life? And why am I the only one demolished when it leaves? I cannot fathom, if the sentiment is really true, that real love simply vanishes, and I will never accept how a person can so easily shift from one to whom such grand professions were made to another and leave the last as if never there. How is that possible in a human heart?

Everything Matice was saying touched on something, nailed

down what I've been told by others but have not been able to see as true within myself. She's known me for such a short time, days, yet she's already seeing into my soul. What makes me like this? What makes me such an unacceptable reject in the eyes of love?

In this case the answer is easy. I do not, cannot, will *never* love Matice, as much as I appreciate her, and so therefore my energy with her is detectable and her response to it understandable. Yet much of what she says to me has come also from those I *have* loved, and that is where I am caught. That's where I know she's right. There is something terribly, sadly wrong with me, and whatever it is I don't know how, or even if it's possible, to correct it.

You should meet more people here in Paris, Matice told me again. You need to know more people than me.

I said that I agreed, and again promised I'd try, not knowing how I'd actually go about doing that.

The waiter came out then with our check on a little round black tray the size of a drink coaster. We paid and then moved on. The drizzle had stopped now.

We roamed the streets of the neighborhood near the park. Matice began noticing Turkish shops and restaurants, and was excited to discover a place in Paris that reminded her of home. Now she knew where to go, she'd said, when she wanted Turkish food.

But at the moment she wanted frites, so we stopped at a place and sat at another outside table under another awning, although this was more of a patio space in front of a restaurant. The restaurant sat at a very busy corner where many streets converged. We ordered a plate of fries and two beers. I watched the street beyond the railing of our patio as we ate and drank. It seemed to be a neighborhood where many people from other countries lived, many from the African continent. There were thin black men walking around swathed head to ankle in blue cloth and white cloth, for instance, and clumps of dark women enveloped in black flowing robes covering their bodies from the top of their foreheads over their hair and around under their chins, leaving the oval of their faces exposed, all the way down to their shoes. Many passed dressed that way with small children in tow. And then there were some where, frighteningly, the only freedom from the cloth concealing them was a slit to peer out through at the world.

The foot traffic at this corner was equally as heavy as the traffic in the streets, and exhaust fumes were thick. The air was chewy with it. I was looking forward to getting out of there.

From that restaurant we slowly walked south, meandering down through arrondissement 11 on Boulevard Richard Lenoir, which took us all the way to the Bastille. This was all new to me, and though the streets were nearly empty now as we moved through the 11th, particularly Boulevard Lenoir, which was a wide street with a thin median separating two lanes of traffic on either side, and though Matice and I didn't speak much, still it was a welcome change to the streets I've grown so weary of walking.

Lenoir led us right to the gold statue-topped column at Place de la Bastille. I'd never gone beyond this point so suggested continuing left in that direction, past the column. Narrow streets, restaurants, cafés, bars—more of the same like everywhere else. After a rest over a short beer, we turned back. There was Place Bastille again and we crossed into the 4th now, the Marais, on St. Antoine. It was Happy Hour, which called for a more substantial break from all that walking.

Because Paris is so expensive, Happy Hour is when most people here do most their drinking. Drinks are usually half price, and Matice and I stopped in a place now on St. Antoine.

It was a large bar, really a late night club not a place for Happy Hour, though they had it, and there it was as we passed feeling like a beer so we went in. There were two sides, two large rooms, and an upstairs. We were on the left side from where we entered off the street, sitting at the bar—the only one in service presently. It was very quiet in there, only a few other people besides us and the bartender. He slid us a little dish of peanuts when we sat down. I ordered two large Heinekens and paid for them. Matice was a little surly now. She looked at me over the tall beer glass and said, I feel sorry for you, and took a long drink of her Heineken.

Oh yeah?

Yes. I feel sorry for you. You're so sad. You come here with your broken heart. Other people have broken hearts, too. It's not just you. Why are you here? This is not a movie.

She drank again looking at me. She was faintly smiling, but there was maliciousness in that smile, and I could tell looking at her that I was failing in my role as temporary lover, because I am in love with someone else, who no longer loves me, and for whom the scattered shards of my heart quiver and pulse like small dying animals. Matice was realizing now just how short-lived this is. She was holding it up in the light before us and peering into it, as if she were holding up her beer glass and peering through the color inside. She was seeing it fully now for what it is, the distraction it is for both of us, and was both embracing it and snarling sadly at it. I will return to San Francisco in a matter of days to my empty, directionless life, and she will continue here in Paris, for perhaps another two years she has told me, she's going to give it that long of a chance she said, trying in her own way to find happiness here. She was looking into our separate futures, and for me at least she was sympathizing in advance for what she saw there.

Her movie reference made yet another cut into me. I do tend to observe life as I live it, in order to write about it. Maybe that's what others have sensed in me as well, this interactive distance I hold with life. Maybe that's why these misinterpretations happen, even with the ones I love. I am there with them, but a large part of me, even if my heart is truly engaged and present, is still elsewhere. And what I felt Matice was saying to me was that this was real, this was happening right now, that she, *Matice*, was here and real, and I was once again missing it. I didn't think there was anything left inside me to break, but I felt another little bit of myself drop off inside when she said it.

This is not a movie.

She said it again, staring and smiling at me behind her big beer glass, for emphasis I guess. She is both flirting with me and lamenting me at the same time.

I feel sorry for you.

Over the next round of beers Matice suddenly said: Maybe I visit you in San Francisco. Why not? You are hawt. You will probably have girlfriend, but so…

I said she was welcome to come to San Francisco of course, but when I protested that I most probably will *not* have a girl-friend, she said yes, why not? You are hawt, she said again. You will see. Maybe I come September.

OK, sure, I said. And we left it at that.

We finished our big pints and continued walking. After sharing a nicoise salad and another plate of frites at a restaurant that was very much like an American diner, near Pont Marie, we crossed the river again and came back to the rafters. We'd stopped for a bottle of Bordeaux at a little grocery when we reached the Mouffetard, and I poured it for us. Matice had soft-ened again by now and her clothes came off eagerly. We by-passed the futon this time and climbed straight up the ladder to the loft. Through the open window the sky was darkening. The light was becoming anemic blue and I liked it, so I lit no lamp or candle. When we finished Matice curled up beside me and quickly fell asleep. In the murky, bluish light filling the apart-ment and rising up to us like smoke, I lay listening to her breathe. It came in a raspy, heavy sound, as if she was breathing through her mouth, but because she was curled facing away from me I couldn't tell.

This was the first time Matice ever slept beside me. She doesn't sleep with people, she'd told me that. But here she was, though I knew this was only a nap. I knew soon enough she'd wake and walk home for the rest of the night. But at the moment I listened to her heavy breathing while staring up at the beams slanting over us. I'd opened the porthole and a nice cross breeze pulled through the room, up from the window below. I stretched my leg up out of the comforter and touched my toes to one of the beams. That's how much space there was over me—a leg's worth. Over Matice, lying to my right, there was maybe a foot.

The hallway light suddenly came on and shined yellow through the porthole. I heard a door squeak open then close again somewhere in the hall. A lock turned, the click of heels re-sounded on the hardwood floor, then on the stairs. I listened as the reverberating clicks grew fainter in their descent. Sounded like a woman to me—like high heels. I listened until I heard the street door latch closed and it was quiet again.

The hallway light is on a timer, and after a minute the light returned to the blue hue I liked, though it seemed darker now. I thought about what Matice said earlier as I lay there. This is not a movie, she'd said. I feel sorry for you…The words ran like hamsters around the sphere of my skull. This is not a movie… This is not a movie…This is not a movie…

Somewhere in the beginning of July, after the Telegraph apartment, she returned from Chicago and landed once again at Shrader. We were ecstatic to be back. This was our place, and we didn't want to be anywhere else. But it must've been rented to some pretty rowdy people while we were away. The big palm plant hung broken. She eventually cut it, and threw the long, dead fan of the branch out. And the thermostat in the hot tub no longer worked. The water refused to heat above lukewarm. There was a feeling of violation, marauders had come and desecrated sacred land and we swayed in their dark wake. Things were just a little different here now. Still, we were glad to be back.

She spent a lot of time out of town that month, and our time at Shrader went pretty quickly. It was unavailable for August, but the studio downstairs was free, so she planned to switch to that space at the end of the month.

On our last night upstairs, it was Friday night, we'd been out and returned home a little drunk and high-spirited. I started singing to her in the kitchen again, over wine.

Let's swim to the moon, uh huh
Let's climb through the tide
Penetrate the evening that the city sleeps to hide
Let's swim out tonight love it's our turn to try
Park beside the ocean on our moonliiiiight drive

While I was singing she had switched off the overhead light and switched on the red warming lights on the hood of the stove. That's how high-quality that stove was—it came with warming lights, like you'd see in a restaurant. The kitchen glowed ruby red now and she was feeling sexy. Her laptop was on the counter beside the stove and she pulled up a supplemental site we'd used before. While she was turned around working the computer and making her selection, I had already gotten started. I'd slipped her panties down from under her dress and was at work kneeling behind her. Then I stood up and gently nudged it in as the video flashed naked bodies on the computer screen. After a minute I backed out to remove my clothes and she pulled her dress up over herself. I helped her with her bra, unsnapping and tossing it aside with one hand in one flourish of a motion almost and was back searching for the spot again when, suddenly, she ran over and hopped up on the big kitchen table and lay back across it. I found the spot again over there instead.

It was a warm night, and when we came home we had opened the back door to the deck to let in some air. The door was still that way now as we went to the table. A couple weeks earlier new neighbors had moved in next door—a woman and a man and a large dog. We'd seen them, waved at each other, but had not been introduced. It was only around midnight, and except for the new neighbors' dog that was barking in gappy, broken-paced *row row row* triplets, it was quiet outside. Sound easily carried through the neighborhood at this hour, and if we had our door open chances were the neighbors had at least windows open too. But no thought of neighbors' ears prevented her from loudly moaning my name over and over and over into the night while stretched across the table in the red glow. The table moved under us, shimmied and jumped across the floor and up against the wall like a burdened, cornered creature, jogging something loose from above that slid crashing down at the far end, and a chair fell over behind me with a loud thwack, but there was no better way to say goodbye to our favorite home together than like this. It was only afterwards that it crossed her mind.

Well, she said, I guess the neighbors know your *name* now.

In the morning we moved our things to the apartment down-stairs. Although it was the same house, with the same backyard and same now nonfunctional hot tub, this apartment had a com-pletely different feel than upstairs. It was like the funky graduate student's room in the basement of his parents' house. It was cozy and interesting, and like I said it would have been a perfect liv-ing space for *me* if I were alone without her, but together *with* her, as *her* space, the low ceiling became a little claustrophobic, and the funkiness a little too much in comparison to what we were used to upstairs, and it was a little too dark. And then, somewhere mid August, we started hearing a scratchy, digging sound inside the wall beside the bed. Eventually one night we came home and discovered chewed-open food packages on the refrigerator and countertop, with big black turds mixed in among the debris. This place had rats.

Luckily the discovery came near the end of the month and she'd already found a new apartment in the Castro to move into, near me on Noe and Market. But the last few nights here were spent with the unnerving knowledge that rats lived in the wall beside our heads as we slept, and their scratching shredded any chance for rest or comfort.

I fully expected to help move her things into the new place on Noe Street, but she said Jari helped her after they came back into the city from their office in San Jose. I thought that odd, but I didn't dwell on it.

After work on the first day she moved in I walked down from my place, only four and a half blocks, and saw it for the first time. I rang the bell at the black metal gate caging the building's entranceway from the street. Beyond the gate there was a short stoop with two doors at the top. Both doors were white, and each had windows that were like half a pizza—four triangle pieces fanned into a semi circle. She came out of the one on the right. Her landlords—a gay couple—lived upstairs through the left one. This apartment did not come from the service she'd been using up till this point. After the rats in the studio at Shrader, and the slow repair of the hot tub, she decided to take a break from that property company.

The couple upstairs at Noe owned the building and rented out the bottom space as a short-term rental—maximum four months per renter. She took all four months, and it was here our lives dramatically changed.

Haven't heard from Matice in a few days. She'd told me that she and her brother got the apartment they wanted and she was going to be busy moving. It's the beginning of the month, June, and the landlord said they could move in right away. Her mother and sister are also due to arrive this week from Istanbul, and so she's preparing for their visit as well. She's very busy.

Meanwhile, as I dubiously promised Matice, I did meet someone new, though it had less to do with trying and everything to do with arbitrary chance.

One place I had not yet revisited here in Paris was Montmartre, and like a lot of places this trip I wasn't sure I wanted to. Yesterday though, I felt like it might be nice to see Sacre-Coeur again.

Since it was a sunny day I thought I'd sit on the long steps of the church and watch the sun go down over the city. The weather the way it was it promised to be a spectacular sunset. From the high hill where Sacre-Coeur sits in Montmartre you get one of the best views of Paris.

I'd spent the morning writing. At one point I looked up and saw a plane cutting across my open window, leaving a long chalky white trail in the square of blue before me. I was seated at the red table, and in exactly a week I was going to be sitting on a plane just like the one I saw now flying over Paris back to the nothingness of my real life waiting for me in San Francisco. Ten and a half hours on my ass again in a cramped seat. I could see it already as I sat there looking at that plane from my chair at the table. I could see myself jetting through the morning sky looking down on Paris, and I knew I'd be sitting there wondering what I just did with three weeks of my life in one of the most beautiful cities on the planet, which I've now killed in my errant return.

Christophe phoned while I was watching that plane. I'd called him the night before to see if he'd like to get a drink. He didn't answer, so I'd left a message. He called back now suggesting we get together later. I said I'd call him around 9.

I headed out mid afternoon. From Place Monge I took the train to the 9th and got off at the Cadet Metro stop. Sacre-Coeur is in the 18th, the district just north of the 9th. That was part of the plan. Walking and exploring is always part of my plan here. I don't know how else to enjoy Paris than like this.

I'd walked through the 9th arrondissement before, last time, with her, but not this part of it and not in the daylight. Cadet seemed near enough to my destination to be a logical starting point, yet unfamiliar and far enough away to allow for something new. From Cadet Metro I slowly wandered up rue de Rochechouart, which was pretty much a straight shot into the 18th and Montmartre.

By the time I hit Boulevard Rochechouart, which bordered the two arrondissements and intersected with the street I was walking that confusingly shared the same name, I was feeling hungry. There was a restaurant there on the corner and I sat down at an outside table against the big front windows to the left of the open doorway. The waiter came and without looking at the menu I ordered in French a glass of red wine and a nicoise salad. I couldn't really buy not making the attempt, couldn't just speak English like the others. It felt wrong.

The wine came right away, and then the salad a few minutes later. I took a bite. The girl sitting at the table to my left, on the other side of the doorway, who I had certainly noticed, and who was actually a deciding factor in my choosing this restaurant (I had seen her sitting there as I came walking by with my appetite, she was very pretty, but at the moment I had not been paying any attention to her)—this girl suddenly said something to me now in

French.

Je ne parle pas français, I said back. Parlez-vouz anglais?

I do, yes, she said without a trace of accent.

Oh...Hi. You're American.

Canadian, she corrected. I asked how your salad was.

Oh, fine. It's good.

Are you American?

I am.

Where you from?

We proceeded to get acquainted, and when the inevitable question of why I was in Paris came I told her briefly my story. But this time this girl had a story too, and the first part of it at least closely resembled mine. Recent bad break-up, nothing left for her in Toronto, tired of her job and what she was doing there, so she picked up and came to Paris. Very much like my story in some ways. But here is where her story veered from mine.

Being from Canada, where of course French is the prevalent second language, she could speak French pretty well, though with a Canadian patois. Some French words in Paris, she found, just didn't translate into her French-Canadian understanding of them. And likewise the Parisians often didn't understand her version of French. But for the most part, especially in comparison to me, she was greatly ahead of the language game. She had never been to Paris before, and her presence here was not just a visit. She came to Paris with the intent to stay.

Her name was Chantal. She had walnut brown hair and wore it wrapped up in itself at the back of her head in a tight round roll. She said she'd arrived in Paris three weeks ago with next to nothing, only a few clothes other than the ones on her back. In fact that's why she was in this neighborhood. She had just been shopping at a bargain store nearby that someone had tipped her off to. They sold clothes dirt cheap, she said, and showed me the skirt she'd just bought there. She carried it in a blue plastic bag. There's a restaurant hostess job someone told her about that she was going to apply for, but she needed new clothes. She was staying across town in the 14th, Montparnasse, with a famous American expatriate. She gave me his name but I'd never heard of him.

In Toronto, when the inspiration for Paris came to her, she did some online research before deciding to make her move. She came across this man in her searches, this famous expatriate, and what she read about him excited her. He's apparently quite renowned in Paris, in fact all across Europe. He opens his home every Sunday to guests from around the world. He owns a villa of sorts in Montparnasse that can accommodate several people at a time. Large dinners are cooked at these events and shared in communal fashion. People hangout and party and talk and play music and dance, or give readings, stagings even, of their work. Many often stay the night or for days at a time, depending on their circumstances—if they're traveling and in need of a place to crash. According to Chantal he's famous for this, this American expatriate, for his embracing accommodations of not only people but of life itself in the grand salon tradition.

Chantal had contacted him from Toronto, notifying him of her plans, and he invited her to come to his villa if she came to Paris. The night she arrived she showed up at his door. They talked, and he allowed her to stay the night. The next morning they continued to get acquainted and, apparently taken with her, he said she could stay indefinitely—rent free. The only condition was that she cook an occasional meal for the house.

There was someone else who also lived in the expatriate's villa, another woman. Her name was Gabriella, and she was as brilliant as she was hot, Chantal said. Long black hair, dark eyes, and a body to kill for, according to Chantal. Gabriella was a doctorate student in political science from Portugal. She also held master degrees in art history and psychology. You'd love her, Chantal told me. Even *I'm* in love with her, she said.

I was certainly intrigued, but thoroughly intimidated already.

Hey, Chantal said, what are you doing next Sunday?

I said I didn't know. That was almost a week away, and it was my next to last scheduled day in Paris.

There's a dinner every Sunday, Chantal said. Unfortunately I won't be at this next one, Gabriella and I are going to a show this Sunday, but you could still go. You should, Chantal said. You're the kind of person that should be there, I can tell.

It no doubt sounded interesting, just what I was hoping to stumble onto while here in Paris. It sounded way better than what I'd read of Leticia's salons. But to show up to an event like that a complete stranger without Chantal there to at least introduce me, to provide some small social crutch...out of the question. If I were someone else, as I often wish I was, there'd be no problem. But me being me, and particularly the way I am now, the thought of it was impossible. I absorbed the information, though, and feigned to entertain the notion.

Chantal was having a glass of chardonnay without food, and ordered another glass while we talked and I finished my salad. I told her what I had in mind, that I was walking up to Sacre-Coeur for the sunset, and asked if she'd like to join me.

Well, she said, I'm supposed to cook dinner for Jim tonight (that was the expatriate) but...Oh, I don't think he'll mind. In fact, if I told him I met a cool guy he'd probably want me to go. He's all about letting life lead you, being open to possibilities and seizing chances when they come along. He's always talking about that. So...Yeah! Let's go.

We paid our bills and set off walking the boulevard.

I was a full head plus taller than Chantal when we stood up to leave. She was tiny, maybe 5 feet, if that. I didn't realize she was so small as we sat talking, and finding that out actually kind of turned me off at first. But she was well built and very pretty, and as we walked I kept a step or two behind her pace and could see her nice round bottom in her snug jeans sway before me. I knew then I wanted her. Thing was though, I couldn't tell if she was interested in me the same way or if I just afforded her the chance to roam spontaneously in the company of a stranger, for the fun of it. She kind of seemed that way to me, the type to do this just to do it without further agenda, but I just couldn't tell. My instincts have been woefully dulled, and she was not coming across with any overt signals. We walked, and I stayed on the lookout for any sign where this may be going.

We headed down the boulevard toward Clichy. There's a wide tree-lined median in the center of the boulevard and we walked that in the shade. Soon we were passing strip clubs and sex shops. This is the red light district, but it was late afternoon and the sun was still high and hot, so not much was happening. It created an undertone though, for me at least, seeing neon signs advertising pussy everywhere.

Since it was Happy Hour I suggested we stop for a drink. There was a place sandwiched between strip clubs and we went in. We sat at a table in the front where the windows had been retracted to the street. The open air and sun poured onto us. I ordered two Affligems. Chantal'd never heard of it, but the Belgian beer is one of my favorites. We sat talking and I looked at her face slathered with sunshine. Her hazel eyes turned the color of honey in it, and they looked very beautiful. I decided to tell her this, to perhaps help get a sense where she was coming from, but all Chantal gave in response to my compliment was a tepid thank you. I thought about trying to kiss her there, in the warm sun shining on us, but that flat thank you was not very encouraging, and I did not want to embarrass myself so soon. With Matice it was easy. When she accused me of being a gentleman that first night I knew that that was a challenge, and I picked it up gallantly. But now, with Chantal, I was stuck in an aimless drift. Either she was being too subtle and I too meek, or she was playing it cool and I no longer remembered how to seduce to warm her up. Or—and this was the one that messed with me the most and I was afraid may be the real truth—or, I thought, she was just plainly not into it the way I was trying to make it.

But it's Paris, and we were a man and woman who just met, sharing a drink while waiting for the sunset to come so that we may bathe in its glory—how else was I expected to try to make it?

She talked more about Jim, the expatriate, and where previously I couldn't tell if they were lovers by the information I was given now I knew they weren't. Jim was in his seventies and theirs was a patriarchal friendship, but she obviously liked and respected him a great deal. By the end of our beers I was still no closer to warming her up. We left together and continued walking.

Along the way, not far from the bar, Chantal began regretting having not eaten at the restaurant where we met. She said it was too expensive there and had opted to save her money at the time, but now she had an appetite. The idea of a picnic began to form. We passed a supermarket and went in. Now we were shopping together. I was grocery shopping with a strange girl from Canada in Paris who I just met and we were going on a picnic, I recapped to myself while tailing Chantal through the aisles. How wonderful!

We bought a baguette and brie and sliced packaged salami and she absolutely had to have rillettes. I had no idea what that was, but we scoured the store until she found it. We also got two bottles of red wine, and plastic cups to drink it from. Oddly though, the store did not carry wine openers, and we needed to buy one if we were to drink our wine. We walked on down the boulevard in the shade of the median, but now began shifting gears.

How would you feel if we went to the river instead of the church? Chantal asked.

Fine, sure, let's go to the river, I said.

But we still needed a wine opener.

Ah! There was a store, along the boulevard to the right of the median. It was a cheap gadgetry store, with electronic devices and pocket knives and souvenirs. We went in and they had them, cheap and flimsy, but it'd do. I bought the wine opener and gave it to Chantal to keep. Now we were set and headed for the train at Place Pigalle.

The closest stop this train went to the river was the Tuileries Gardens, so we got out there and walked through the gardens to the Seine. The sun was still bright and hot in the sky but ever so slowly now had begun its descent. There was a bridge straight ahead and we went toward it. It was a thin bridge, for foot traffic only, and had benches in the middle of the span. One was empty and we sat there with our backs to the sun. I opened a bottle immediately and poured wine out into our plastic cups red and rich in the sunlight as Chantal took the food from the paper bags we'd carried from Montmartre. She tore a piece of the baguette and I watched her plunge it into the container of rillettes, which looked like a Haagen-Dazs container—same shape as that but much smaller. She took a bite of bread now and went mmmmm, told me to try it. I tore my own piece of baguette and dug in. At the top was a pure layer of white fat, but when you plowed through that there was the pink minced pork underneath. It was good, but very rich, and I could feel my arteries clogging with each bite. Between the two of us we ate it all, but she had most of it. We sat eating and drinking the wine and talking, looking at the river. The sides of the bridge were caged with metal grating. We started talking about the padlocks hanging from them. This was something I'd noticed while walking across Pont de l'Archeveche as well. There were padlocks clipped onto the metal grating of that bridge too, and I didn't remember them being there when I walked that spot with her six months ago. They were new and mystifying to me. To Chantal, too. We sat speculating on what the locks could mean.

Maybe they're some kind of memorial, Chantal thought, to someone who jumped off the bridge.

Or maybe, I offered, maybe they were put there by lovers, and the lock represents their love.

(I'd noticed there were names written on some of them when I'd gotten up at one point to look closer, names with hearts drawn between them.)

Yeah...Chantal said, not sounding too convinced.

Just then though a teenage couple came walking up and stopped at one of the locks. We watched them. The girl bent over and fiddled with the lock till it sprang open in her hands, and when it did she stood up without hesitation and tossed it over the side of the bridge into the river. Before the lock even hit the water she'd turned and was looking up smiling into her companion's face, slipping her arm around his waist as his slipped around hers, and off they went together like that smiling in the sunshine. There was a sense of both cruel finality and new beginning about them, as if that lock were a body they'd just dumped into the river.

Uhhh...Chantal drew in her breath. You were right! They *are* for lovers!

It was as though that couple stopped by just to deliver a French dramatized version of my life, and I didn't want to talk about it anymore. I poured more wine and tried to redirect our conversation back to what we were talking about earlier.

Chantal had been explaining that once she'd made the decision to come to Paris, to stay, and committed to that decision, things have been opening up for her here. Taking the chance and arriving at Jim's door the way she did, and his opening it to her so welcomingly, giving her a free place to stay, has opened all kinds of other doors since. Through him she was meeting contacts all around the city. That's how the news of that hostess job came to her, someone he knew who worked in the restaurant told her about it. And because she wants to sing, through Jim's

Sunday dinners she's been meeting musicians who've offered to include her in gigs and sessions. And she's made friends already, Gabriella and some of Gabriella's friends have embraced her. They go out and do things. She feels so happy and alive. And all she did was make the decision to do it. And she said I could too, encouraging me to take the leap of faith.

I'd told her how I felt, how life in San Francisco seemed over for me now, that there wasn't anything left for me there anymore, the same way she felt about Toronto, and I was toying with the idea of trying to live in Paris.

Chantal said all I had to do was to make the decision and commit. Everything I needed I already had, she said, and promised that the business of tidying up my life back in San Francisco could all be accomplished from right here in Paris, online. I'd never even have to go back. I could hire movers to clear out my room and put my stuff in storage and find someone to move in and take it over, all from here online, she said.

And I listened to Chantal and I knew she was right. I *could* do that. And for a moment I became excited by the possibility of what Chantal was saying and began to seriously think about staying in Paris. That is something I *could* do, that *could* happen, I thought, and for a moment I believed it really could. Then I came to my senses. If I were someone else...

I was realistic enough to believe that I was not going to have doors magically open for me like they were opening for Chantal. No one was going to give me a free place to live. No one was going to hook me up with a job. These were things that happened to a pretty young woman not to a sad middle-aged man of limited skills and means and fading charm, who did not speak French. And yes, in theory I could learn. But would I really? And how long would it actually take? How many months? And how would I get by in the mean time? And again, in *theory* I could orchestrate a move from here, but in reality that would be a disaster. My things were not in order in my apartment, not nearly in any state where I could rely on strangers to come in and collect them properly and successfully. I had manuscripts and notebooks and loose papers of work and other things scattered about in my room. I had artwork in boxes in closets, as well as other boxes buried in there, containing so much I hadn't seen in so long but still had significance to me, and I would not want to lose it, and I was sure it would be lost. And then there was the ethical question. I would not feel comfortable leaving my room-mates in the lurch by suddenly splitting. That wouldn't be right or fair to them. And then there'd be the expense of maintaining a storage space indefinitely in San Francisco while struggling to stay afloat in Paris. Who had the funds for that?

No. Like I said if I were someone else I believed it was pos-sible, but I am unfortunately only me, and I could see for me it was not. Not that way. However, the idea of making a go of it here became sufficiently lodged in my brain, and I did begin thinking how that could be a realistic possibility. I tried to get the conversation back here on this track, and we were starting again when we were again distracted by the locks.

There was a man with two little girls on the bridge. Chantal and I watched all three of them now playing with the locks, many of which hung like grapes in clusters while others were more solitarily attached, hanging on their own apart from the bunches. Some of the locks were combination style and some took a key. The man and the girls, together and separately, went from lock to lock as if hunting for one in particular, pulling at them and turning the combination dials and then tugging again. Chantal and I watched them as we talked, wondering what on earth they could be doing.

Finally, when the man seemed to tire of whatever game he and his girls seemed to be playing he gathered them around him, they were only about 5 and 7 I guessed, just little things, and they all started walking away. As they passed us, Chantal spoke to the man in French. He had dark skin and a short wispy black beard and wore a red velvet fez-like hat.

Monsieur? Parlez-vous anglais?

The man shook his head so Chantal continued in French.

Sir, what were you doing there? With the locks?

Trying to break them, the man said.

But why? Why do you want to break the locks?

To show them that love doesn't last. Things happen in life that makes the love change and break. It's not all happiness, he said. You can't lockup love. They need to learn this too.

It wasn't clear who the man was talking about. Was it his children he was trying to teach this lesson to, who were equally involved in the game of trying to break the locks, or was he referring to the young lovers themselves who placed them there? I would have liked to have known, but Chantal didn't ask.

Then the man asked about us. Were we lovers?

We were not, Chantal explained. We had just met, and were watching the sunset together.

Ah, he said. Then you're not lovers *yet*.

Chantal translated all this for me after the man and his little girls walked off. She blushed and laughed telling the last part of what he said. I didn't know how to take that. I simply could not read her.

I started wondering about the mother of the two little girls. Where was she? Was this man still married to her, or were they perhaps divorced? Had she died, or worse walked out and left them all alone? Was he trying to break those locks because he himself had been broken, like me, his illusions squashed with the pain, or was he some kind of severe saint trying to teach the world a harsh lesson? I opened the second bottle of wine and thought about it but didn't mention any of this to Chantal, and a stretch of fat silence snuggled its way in here and sat wide between us. Whatever romantic energy that may have existed initially, if any, if only in my mind, had been dissipating ever since we reached the bridge and was quickly leaving now. As our time together wore on I could feel Chantal slipping through my fingers like sand. I just didn't know how to get to her, how to break through the invisible wall between us.

The sun was much lower now and golden but still a ways from setting. We finished the food and kept drinking. Chantal began talking about having recently gone with a friend to a club, some meat market place in the Marais that I didn't know, and about all the cute French boys there. She was telling me about it and suddenly said you know, sometimes you just wanna *fuck*. And when I heard her say that word, and the way that she said it, hope flinted off a spark in me. I listened to her closely.

She was talking about this one French boy who came on to her that night, and how they started making out. After a while he wanted to take her home but she didn't go, and now she regretted that. It's been a while without having any she said, and she was getting horny, and she regretted not going home with that French boy. Because sometimes you just need to fuck she said, using the word again, and because she used the word again I felt like she was using it deliberately, as some kind of sign. Then she said she felt like it was time to take a lover in Paris, and that was my cue I thought. So I swallowed the bait.

And does this lover have to be French? I asked

Yeah…He kinda does, Chantal said, sensing I think where I was going.

Oh…

That did it for me. I wasn't getting anywhere with Chantal and was beginning to feel stupid for even thinking I had a chance at all. My ego receded like a beaten old mongrel looking for a dirty ally to circle up in and die. I drank the wine.

Although the sun hadn't completely set, we both felt we'd had enough. It was time to move.

Chantal and I walked together along the Right Bank of the Seine. Golden light threw long stretching shadows ahead of us and we pursued them toward St. Michel, and it was beautiful,

Chantal was beautiful in the golden light, but there couldn't be less sexual energy between us now than if I were her brother. Less maybe even. And I couldn't believe I'd let her get away like this, that we were walking together now like this with so much deep, dull, unbridgeable distance between us.

While walking beside Chantal along this path by the river I remembered the day I walked it six months earlier in the opposite direction, on our way to explore the Right Bank. It was a chilly gray day. Light rain fell intermittently. But as we walked along the river in this same spot then it was not raining and I was taking pictures of her, a short video even, of just her in close profile strolling in her olive green flapper's hat along the Seine. She looked into the camera with a sassy air, defiant and sexy, then looked casually away again as I hurried dancing the camera around her easy stride. You can't lockup love, the man on the bridge had said. She'd accused me of just that, resting comfortably on my laurels as if I'd felt I had it all sewn-up—her, our love, our future—had it all conquered as mine when all it seemed I was doing was constantly waiting, worrying for her to be, dancing along her stride until ultimately she strode easily on over my tripped, tangled heap. She bloomed in my mind now, her face, that look she fed me through the camera, it opened and grew and kept growing, ate up all space in me, the cavity maw I now carry within, as I walked defeated beside Chantal in the warm, sinking sun.

It was a long walk to St. Michel and Chantal and I moved passing very few words between us. It seemed she couldn't wait to be rid of me, and I couldn't wait to get rid of this feeling of failure choking me while walking beside her.

Finally we reached the Metro at Place St. Michel, where Chantal was catching the train back to Montparnasse. Before she went down into the station we exchanged email addresses and embraced, but we both knew we were never going to see each other again. I felt like I'd turned out to be such a disappointment, to Chantal, to myself. I didn't have it anymore. Seduction requires a nimble freedom of heart that I no longer possess. I'd given it away. I'd given it all away in the belief of one last chance. I'm just a fool—a tamed abandoned fool.

I called Christophe.

L ittle by little her things had accumulated. Now, along with her clothes (and my clothes too, the tshirts and long-sleeve pullovers and underwear and socks, the things she was always picking up for me to save me from having to constantly carry clothes when she was in town and I'd stay with her—they were mostly work clothes, but there were some nicer things mixed in) along with these bags of clothes that would move with her from place to place there were also her kitchen supplies—spices and oils and cans and containers, the odd accoutrement—that stuff kept getting added to and expanding as well. And there were books too, boxes of them she'd had shipped from Chicago. She was slowly making the transition to San Francisco, and there was quite a pile now. That's why I had expected to help her with it, help move it from Shrader to the new place on Noe Street, and that's why I was surprised to hear that she'd already had Jari do it. I knew they were friends, but that seemed like my job. Why would she ask him to help instead of me?

Her employment now was also changing. The interview process had begun for the position in San Leandro. She basically already had the job, but formalities had to be met. It went on for weeks. It was her ex-CEO asking her aboard, who was the CEO at this place, so that made it pretty much a done deal. But there were of course others in the company she needed to meet. She needed their approval as well. So one meeting after another on up the chain to get to where they already knew they were going. In the end it mostly came down to negotiation, which was apparently her forte. She was actually being hired because of her negotiation prowess. The company had to now negotiate with a master negotiator, and it had to be hardball or the company may begin to second guess their choice in hiring her. In the end she was confident she'd get everything she wanted—from an even higher salary than she was already pulling down, to moving and relocation costs and the first six months rent of her first permanent apartment. She left me out of all details, of course, but I knew whatever the San Leandro company was going to give her was going to be a very sweet deal indeed. Toward the end of the month the deal was closed and transition complete. Now, instead of dropping me off at the train on her way to San Jose, like she'd done on and off for the last seven months, we were taking the train to work together. San Leandro was on the same BART route as mine, three stops past Lake Merritt. We'd catch the MUNI (the train system that runs within San Francisco) a block away at Castro and Market, then transfer three stops down the line at Civic Center to BART (the interbay rail system) which took us to the East Bay. For the last six years that was my daily morning routine, now she was a part of it. It felt odd. It felt absolutely wonderful.

She didn't ride with me every morning by any means. Her schedule was more flexible than mine. I had to be at the museum every morning at the same time. She could go in later or earlier, depending upon the structure of that particular day and her workload. But I loved it on those days she did ride the train with me—standing with my arm around her waist on the crowded MUNI, sitting silently together on BART reading the paper beside one another, chatting now and then, kissing her goodbye at my stop—all a pleasure to me. If I had to go to work, I couldn't think of a better way to start my day to do it. She, on the other hand, was still trying to make the adjustment to having to be in an office practically every day instead of jetting around the country. She said her friends back in Chicago were taking bets on how long it'd last, how long she'd hold-out before going nuts and need the travel again. She said they were wrong, that she was looking forward to the change, but in retrospect that comment seemed to say a lot about her—that her friends were betting how long she'd last.

I was made to believe I was a factor in her taking this new position. Would it have happened anyway if I weren't in the picture? Quite possibly. She was fed-up with that job in San Jose. She said she was tired of traveling so much and wanted to change that, for her own sake, but it was also hoped that traveling less would alleviate the stress it created in our relationship as well. But, although there was much less involved in this job, travel was still a part of it. There was another branch of the office in Florida she was required to work with too, which meant going there often, every other month maybe, sometimes even more frequently, depending. Overall though, her work travel schedule was greatly reduced. However, there were still her frequent trips to her family in Chicago. Every couple of weeks she went back there. Combined she was still gone quite often, much more than the average person in any relationship experiences. Even so, this change of employment and this new place on Noe Street brought some stability to us now, and we were getting closer to a life together.

I was there almost every night, even when she was not. I couldn't stand being at my own place now. Being in the space we shared together, even while she was gone, made me feel closer to her. And even though I was alone in it I preferred that to my own cold empty room. It was my new alternate residence. We were unofficially cohabitating, although I was very careful to respect it as her space. I never assumed she wanted me there every night, and often asked if she wanted me to come over, or deferred mentioning it altogether until she'd ask me herself.

Are you going to stay with me tonight?

The words came in that by now familiar lilting cadence unique to her Polish-Chicago accent. She almost skipped along the words in syllables of two—areyou going tostay withme tonight?—and enunciated each one of the words fully. It always struck my heart with a kiss and a smile to hear it, to hear her say those words. If I made no reference to going over, always the same lovely question would come in the same lovely way— areyou going tostay withme tonight? I hear it just as clearly now as I did then. It just rings so clearly in my mind...

Areyou going tostay withme tonight?

Yes, I am, I'd say. If you want me to.

I want you to, she would say.

She wanted me there every night, as I wanted to be there with her every night.

In comparison to most of the other places we'd stayed to- gether, this one struck me as rather vapid. When I walked in and saw it for the first time I was a little disappointed. No character to the place at all, I thought, and it was poorly deco-rated, in a bad hotel kind of way. That's how it felt at first, a little like a hotel instead of a home. But I got over this quickly and never let her hear these impressions. Main thing was it allowed her a place to be with some regularity, to break this nomadic cycle we'd been caught up in for months. She needed that. *We* needed that. And it was so close to my place, so easy to get to her, to be with her, what was I being critical of? Who cared what it looked or felt like? It became our place, and I was soon just as attached to it as any other we spent time in together.

The rooms were large, and maybe that was part of the prob- lem. There was a lot of space but it wasn't used well. The living room was immediately to your right when you walked in, a big room that faced Noe Street. A huge brown leather couch curved in the middle of it, a massive crescent that surrounded the big flat screen TV against the wall. Behind the couch though, the other half of the room was empty for a small wooden table in the window. This table was never used by us, except later when I sat alone typing at it in the evenings after work. Other than that the only traffic and flow that room got was to walk in to and out from the leather couch waiting for you like a big chocolate hug to watch TV on, which, regretfully now, I unfortunately did a lot.

The next room, again on the right sharing a wall with the living room, was the bedroom. Big again, and a big bed on a wooden frame sat in the middle of this one, headboard against the far wall as you entered. Long brown dresser to the right low against that wall, and a small closet to either side of this. She used the one on the right, I used the one on the left. Hanging above the dresser were two framed Disney drawings—one of Pinocchio and the other of Snow White. They were pencil sketch drawings of these characters and were hung oddly on the wall, low and in staircase fashion above the dresser. They confused me. I didn't understand them at all. Why were they there and why were they hung like that?

To the left as you entered was another dresser sitting tall along that wall, and on the last wall, to the left of the bed and about 4 feet from it, was the window with mini blinds. Above the bed was the ceiling light with a big fan attached. That fan came in handy the first month or so as the hot weather hung on. We'd lie under it and let it cool the sweat on our skins after feverishly making love. Our sex life took off again here, particularly in September and October.

Across the hall from the bedroom was one bathroom, just toilet and sink, then a niche space and large closet where she kept her books in loose order on the floor, then the other bathroom—toilet, sink and tub. This opened onto the kitchen and the dining area. An excessive round table sat here. It seated about eight and took up most the room, but there was still a lot of unused space surrounding it. To the left of it was a brown and black granite-topped bar, which wrapped around the kitchen walls as its counter. It was a nice, spacious kitchen, very modern. That was a selling point for her of course, lots of counter and dark wood cabinet space.

And that was it. At the back wall of the dining area was a glass sliding door that opened onto a small deck and a stairway leading to the backyard and the garage below us. There was a hot tub here too, in a little gazebo, but we only used it once. And in the garage were the laundry machines, like at Shrader. It was a very convenient and functional place, but like I said, at first the flow of the space threw me. We quickly settled in though and I no longer cared.

Most of our time in the beginning was spent in the bedroom and kitchen. Something came over us. Maybe it was the lingering heat, maybe it was the fresh start at a brand new place that gave us resurgence and even more vitality, maybe we were just simply in love and hot for each other, but on the weekends we'd lie in bed and make love for hours.

She straddled me on the bed in late afternoon light. It was a gray day, so it was dim, heavy light. She slipped me inside of her, and softly in a near whisper said: Tell me something you've never told me…

The breath of her words in my ear made me shudder.

I held her ass in both palms, pumping, while my mind searched.

I don't know what to say, I said.

You've told me that before, she said.

Rocking pumping thrusting, my mind sifting through memories as we moved, seizing upon one, then another, weighing and then rejecting each as they came to me, realizing how tricky this kind of thing was. I didn't want to give myself away completely or serve-up fodder for a grudge or later attack. It couldn't involve another lover or a fleeting encounter or risk jealousy, or worse, revulsion, yet it had to be titillating. That's what she was after. She wanted spice.

Moments went by as we wordlessly moved and moaned together, then finally I had it, or thought I did. Again I weighed the memory, considered its possible reaction. It involved no one but myself, and I was much younger so there was the distance and cushion of time to soften from any present context, and it had that naughty appeal I felt she wanted. Another moment passed as I decided. Her silence told me she was waiting. Slowly the words were released.

I…once…masturbated…on the steps…of a church.

The words came and flowed with the rhythm of our bodies.

No response, so I continued.

It was a long time ago, when I was still living in Illinois.

The words were more even now. The water had been tested and the initial plunge past. Now I was in, I let the current take me.

How old were you? she asked.

Young. Twenty-four…Twenty-three maybe. I'd been drinking, walking around one night. It was summer. I just laid down on these church steps and jerked off.

How did you feel when you came?

Like I was breaking a taboo, or at least I had the illusion of breaking a taboo. And slightly perverted. At that time I was still looking for experience, hungry for it, trying to break down barriers of consciousness and limits. I felt like Rimbaud.

What were you thinking about while you did it?

I don't remember that, of course, it was a long time ago. But it wasn't like I was really turned on and needed to get off. I did it on purpose. I was drunk and just lying there and there wasn't anybody around and it was dark so…

So you just took it out…

Yeah, I just wanted to do it there, on the steps of a church, for the experience of it. I later used the image and put it my book.

Do you remember it?

Yes, she said. I think I do...

This happened around the anniversary of having completed that book. It'd been written many years earlier, and I'd brought it over to read to her from, at her request. Though she had read it herself months before, she wanted to hear the author read from it on the anniversary of its completion. She even gave my book a birthday card. On the cover of the card, befitting the nature of the book, was a satyr being led into a stream by four naked nymphs. I recognized it. I was given the exact card by my former girl-friend on the first birthday I shared with her many years before. Inside this card now her inscription addressed the book by title, preceded by *Happy Birthday!*

> *I wish I had met you*
> *closer to your birth.*
> *Perhaps I could have*
> *nurtured you in some*
> *small way. Perhaps I*
> *still can. I'm glad that*
> *you are in existence.*

How could you not love a woman who'd do something like that? For one reason or another we never had that reading, but I did recite to her the opening lines in bed one morning when we woke. She said it was mesmerizing to hear the words come out of me. I of course was hoping to impress her, but she said it was *mesmerizing*...

As I spoke to her now, describing the scene on the church steps, I did my best to mentally relive the experience that took place 20 years before. I could see myself lying on those short steps leading to the side door of that red-bricked church, lying there in the darkness of the warm soft summer night and con-sciously deciding to bring myself off. The steps were covered in green Astroturf, and they were narrow, rough and scratchy on my skin. My body was slightly wedged between the railing as I lay parallel along the doorway on the stoop. These things I remembered. Beyond this though, the interior details that led me to make that decision, and what coursed through me while I went about it, remained faded in my mind—all but one that is. I remember I had a vague feeling that what I was doing was sacred rather than profane. Profane would have been to piss on those steps. What I was doing was a consecration. As I wrote in my book regarding this image, it was like *chalking God Lives! with semen on the doorstep.*

I masturbated in the choir loft of a church, she said, breaking the silence we'd sunk into and temporarily, separately lost ourselves in as our bodies moved.

You did? I asked, suddenly opening my eyes, instantly retrieved from that summer night. How'd you do that? Were you in a choir?

Yes.

And what did you do? Sneak your hand under your robe and play with yourself?

I was envisioning her now sitting among the other members of the choir, her hand somehow secretly under her robe, which I saw as gold for some reason, in my mind her robe had been gold and there she was fingering her clit beneath it as the choir rested and the service went on below.

Yeah, she said. I was early, and so I was sitting up there alone. And it was so quiet, and light was streaming in through the stained glass windows. I suddenly felt this really strong urge to come.

Why didn't you take care of that at home in your bed before you left, or didn't you have time?

Probably not. Or maybe I had done it then too, but I wanted to do it again. I don't remember.

So what happened?

We were both breathing heavily now, our lovemaking invigorated by the imagery forming in both our minds.

I was sitting there alone, and slid down in my chair, and opened my legs, and stretched my feet out. I lifted back my robe, and raised my skirt, and slid my panties aside, and started rubbing my pussy.

I thrust deeper as she spoke and she moaned between words. We both did. The image she was creating of herself in my mind enflamed me. I shut my eyes and let it unfold in my brain like a film as I gripped her ass tight and fucked, fucked.

How old were you? I asked, looking to flesh out further the scene playing in my head.

I was a freshman in high school, so fourteen, I think. No, fifteen.

And weren't you afraid someone would come in?

The steps to the loft were really old and creaky. I knew I'd hear if someone was coming. I wasn't worried about that.

What color was your robe?

Blue. Dark blue, she said.

Blue…And you sat there with your legs spread beneath it, rubbing your pussy?

Yes *uh*…Yes baby yes…

Yes…Yes…

The rain started early that season. By the end of September, and all through the fall, it was often coming down in the morning when we'd have to get up for work, which would make us curl up deeper into each other and wish we could stay there that way. The rain ticked at the window in the wind, and somehow she'd muster up the will to leave the covers, she always got up first, but before she did, through the sound of the rain on the window she'd often say, while still lying warm in my arms: I wish it was Saturday. I can't wait to sleep in with yoouuu…

She'd get up then and take her shower, then come back and

sit on the edge of the bed next to me and gently rouse me from the sleep I'd inevitably fall back into while waiting my turn. Time to make the doughnuts, she'd say. Nearly every morning that's how I'd wake, with her coming to me damp and wrapped in her towel to lift me out of sleep. Her hair was dark now. She'd changed it while living at the studio on Shrader. It hung wet in limp black tentacles around her smiling face as I opened my eyes.

Often she'd still pack a lunch for me. She'd be at it when I came out of the bathroom. As much as I loved her for doing that it was so maternal it made me a little uneasy, like when she wanted to give me a bath at the Palace, and it worked on me in a way that I wasn't aware of till later. Things can come out of you in the strangest ways sometimes. Could I really allow myself to be taken care of this way? Was it all being reversed in me? I felt something happening inside, but couldn't quite recognize it. Or I was unwilling to allow myself to.

Fighting began to escalate, slowly at first, but steadily. There was something about the way she'd interact with Jari that would set me off. The three of us would get together at times, for dinner, for drinks. Things became different between us when we were together with him. The chemistry changed. I felt I was the same, but she was not. The two of them together became a different, separate entity that fed off one another. Not much of substance could be said. Jokes. It was all jokes and laughter, usually of some suggestive variety, and I never found them that funny. Not that they were flirting with each other. They weren't. It wasn't like that. But there was obvious connection there, and obvious love I felt that came from her toward Jari. She thoroughly enjoyed being in his presence—precisely because it was all fun and games, I think. The way some straight women love to be around stereotypically gay men for their outrageous frivolity and sniping humor, Jari generated similar attention without being gay. His shtick was less frivolity though and more the outrageous mock angry curmudgeon, sniping with a sardonic gripe about this or that. And now because they no longer worked together, it was even more special and fun for her to see him. She was deprived now of those 45 minutes in the morning alone with him in the car, and then on the drive back too. She'd picked him up almost every morning to ride with her down to San Jose. They had a rapport that she missed and needed. But when we were all together I'd begin feeling excluded from their energy, their intimacy, and often I felt ganged up on. Things I would say they would disagree with, and the things they seemed to jointly think or believe I disagreed with. It was like she was his girl-friend now, and I hardly knew her.

They wouldn't do this on purpose, they weren't even aware they were doing it for the most part, but I felt like a tag along when they were together. I found myself skulking behind, watch-ing and listening to them laugh and carry on as we walked down the street. She and I often laughed our heads off together, she was very funny, and I thought we both enjoyed each other's company, it seemed so to me anyway, but Jari appeared to sat-isfy a part of her that was hidden to me when we were alone.

When we got home later after these nights, or sometimes during them when we had a moment to ourselves, I couldn't help but say something. I would just feel so shitty. She wouldn't react well, though.

I don't think I can date someone who's so *sensitive*, she'd say.

But she knew I was sensitive, knew that from the beginning. Was she already looking for a way out?

People don't come to bars to have a *conversation*, she'd say, they come to have *fun*, to joke *around*.

Like our apparent disparate expressions of love, we had different styles when it came to this too that slowly wedged the tear wider. In all my years of bar life, conversation *was* a part of it. Real, intelligent discourse or exchange was fun to me, and

I've known plenty of other people who have felt the same. Of course there were jokes amidst it, but the other was just as present and fun too. Or there'd be times I'd simply sit quietly alone, saying nothing to no one as I drank, depending upon my mood. Sometimes I just wanted to sit there and think, or brood, and be bothered with no one. Sometimes I wanted to just be left alone and sink away anonymously into the social energy swirling around me, to feel it but not be a part of it. These were my varying styles. And we were OK alone together when we did this, went to a bar for a drink together, but with the addition of Jari we often fell apart.

Then there was the issue of my trying to recede from that life, from the scene at the 500 Club, because it had just been going on too long, and now she was with me I didn't want to be a part of it any longer, or certainly a part of it less anyway. I wanted to move into something new and better with her. But Jari was deeply steeped in that scene, and would always want to go to the 500 Club and rarely anywhere else. It was where his friends and acquaintances were, where he felt at home and most comfortable. It was where he and I first met too, and I understood that feeling. It was that way for me years and years ago, and still was to a lesser degree. But that was just it. That bar had been a part of my life in San Francisco from the very beginning. I'd been going there for so long that I just couldn't stomach it anymore. I'd like going in for a drink once in a while, and I did still, alone after work on my walk home, or when I was on my own when she was out of town, and *with* her too now and then, but always with Jari we'd end up there and it would become something else. She was aware of this, how I felt about not going there as much, and would support me when I tried to sway Jari to other places. But he'd feel uncomfortable because these places were unfamiliar to him and we'd wind up back at the 500.

Jari was relatively new to San Francisco. He'd moved there maybe four years ago, from London. That's where she knew him first, actually. They worked briefly together in some capacity that I don't remember. Maybe Jari worked for another company then that her company was trying to do business with, and they got acquainted that way. I'm not quite sure, but that sounds about right. Jari was living there in London with his wife at the time, but after they divorced he needed a change and somehow wound up working for her company in San Jose. That's how he came to San Francisco. Besides, Jari hated London and wanted to leave there anyway. And the English, Jari said to me once, well you know how I feel about them. No Jari, I don't, I said. How do you feel about the English? I don't *cah* for'um, Jari said.

Jari's Australian, not that that had anything to do with his impressions of the English, that's just how he came to feel about them while living in London. He didn't care for them, and that was that. Part of Jari's appeal, apart from being a very sweet guy at heart, was the admixture of Australian colloquialisms he'd salt his conversation with, things no one in San Francisco had ever heard before. Phrases like *get a dog up ya!* and *fat salty cunt!* for instance, and words like *snappah* and *growlah* flowed along with his regular discourse

As it turns out, *snapper* is Australian for a girl's cooch, and so is *growler*. But where one may apparently be addressed or referred to by *snapper*, like—*how ya doin' theah snappah?*—the same does not apply to the word *growler*.

You can see how this stuff may get people's attention and brighten things up a bit. And along with the forced griping—*I'm gonna wrahte a lettah of complaint to the head office! You wait'n see, you fat salty cunt!*—and the handshakes and back-slaps he'd greet you with, he endeared himself to the hearts of many. And when he found the 500 Club he found a home.

I liked Jari too, and wanted us to be able to do things together with him as well—she and I came together *through* him after all—and we *had* been getting together with Jari now and then for months, but he never knew what a thorn he'd become in the side of this relationship. Or I should say in *my* side of the relationship. And I let it get away from me and hurt us.

In the end I decided I'd excuse myself from the equation and just let them hangout on their own. And for her part unbeknownst to me she started declining more and more of Jari's invitations, which were many I found out, much more even than I was aware of, and the unhappiness this caused found its place of prominence among her list when it came. And after she bestowed this precious tidbit of information that day, she added with a joyful smile of relief: I love that man. Now I can see him anytime I *want!*

Not only was the distance in our relationship an issue most people don't have to cope with, most people don't have to contend with someone outside the relationship continually crashing in and distracting it.

Why? Why couldn't I just have peace in my love with my lover like anyone else? She was gone so recurrently I wanted our time together when she was home to be our time; I wanted her to want to be with me as much as I wanted to be with her. But often it seemed she preferred Jari's company to mine.

And then there was that other little thing that never let up on me, the ever nagging knowledge that she was married—I found that extremely difficult to forget. She did tell me now that she had quietly begun divorce proceedings, but because there were a lot of shared assets the process was going to take a long time. How long I didn't know, I didn't ask, and that was my mistake. It was enough for me at the time though just to hear from her that measures were underway, and I did not want to push it. Through an email she'd sent, or perhaps it was a text, she said: Please hang in there with me. And I did. So I simply accepted what I was told and tried to be patient. Always though it worked ill in me, the thought that she was technically not free to fully be mine, and that illness became more dangerously terminal with time.

These things created a seeping that began to erode the ground beneath our feet.

One evening we met Jari for dinner. This was while she was still at the Shrader studio. We met in the Mission at a favorite Mexican restaurant on Valencia Street, a block over and around the corner from the 500 Club. He had a friend with him, an ex-comedian and a writer, published author of some variety, socio-political topics apparently. A friend with a common, three-lettered verb of a name. A friend who liked to hear himself talk, I remember. He talked and talked as we all ate dinner together. Finally he hit upon a topic that excited her. I forget now what it's called, but it has something to do with the third world, a system that helps the impoverished people of the third world. Something that works something like this: if you give a person living in one of these countries the gift of a small chunk of money, which allows them to purchase a cow, or seeds in which to plant crops, or some item they can use in some industrious way to improve their conditions and way of life, that small gift grows exponentially into the community and improves life for all there and thus ultimately the world. Now she took over the conversation with him. Jari and I listened to them talk. I remember he was staying with Jari for a few days, biding time before he went down to Mexico City, where he was going to be working on a new book, something to do with the political system there. After dinner we all went over to the 500 Club. There he and I chatted very briefly. He seemed harmless and nice enough, but that was my only experience with him.

A couple days later I'd stopped at this same Mexican restaurant after work for dinner on my walk home. While sitting at the bar I got a text from her asking if I'd like to go to dinner with her and Jari. They were on their way back into the city from San Jose. I told her I was already eating, but thanks. The next day she told me they, along with Jari's friend, had gone to dinner in North Beach at a place she liked on Kearny at Montgomery.

While they waited for their table she took them across the street to a peep show place called Lusty Lady.

You did what?

Yeah. They'd never been in there, so I took them.

The one time she and I went to this restaurant we did the same thing, at my suggestion. We went over there and fucked in a video booth, then came back and ate dinner. I remembered this, and I didn't like hearing that she took them in there too. I didn't think she did anything like that with them, but it was the idea of it. I know how most guys think, and to do something like that as a female with a male, *two* males, one or both of those males may then draw mental sexual associations with the woman who intro-duced him to that environment. And being a woman who already received way too much male attention, it stood to reason that one or both of those males would now have those sexual associations with *her*. And maybe this didn't enter Jari's male mind, but as a detached stranger I was afraid it most certainly entered his friend's.

She of course didn't see the problem. What was I making such a fuss about? It wasn't sexy at *all*, she claimed. How could anyone get exited in a place like that with those skanky women? she asked. It was absurd. A joke! It was all in fun! she said. We *laughed* about it. A *joke!* That's all it was!

She simply refused to acknowledge my perspective.

The next thing I heard about this friend of Jari's was that he had been calling and texting and emailing her. She told me this herself, with a voice full of bewilderment, maybe with even a dose of *uh-oh* in it. She would not tell me what he had been saying, but it was clear that whatever he said he was saying he wanted her, and was trying to court her right out from under my nose. And I knew it! *Knew* it would be so, that he would formu-late those ideas about her. How ridiculous was I *now?* I asked.

Somehow she made mention of it to Jari, who then conveyed my sentiments to his friend, and I was told the communication stopped. And we moved on. On to Noe Street.

Matice came over. It was a very warm day. I had both the porthole and the table window open, as well as the door to the hall for more ventilation. The heat concentrated up there on the top floor and made it uncomfortable. I had been out in the morning, but was back up in the rafters by mid afternoon. Matice called and said she was in the neighborhood, and would I like to see her? I said sure, come on up, and gave her the code for the door downstairs.

I was sitting at the red table when she walked in. I stood up and gave her a little kiss and a hug. Through her thin blouse her back was damp with sweat. She seemed a little irritable at first, probably the walk up the stairs in the heat did it, but she quickly brightened.

Ahchh...It's hhawwt. I no like hawt, she said. And then she asked: What have you been doink?

Writing, I answered.

I see. And who are your favorite writers?

I named a few, then I asked her the same thing.

I don't know, she said. Maybe you.

She smiled at me and I smiled back. That was very cute, I said.

I think, she said, still smiling and looking up at me with her dark eyes. She was seated on the futon now. She seemed to be in a good mood.

Just then a large man with gray hair and beard walked through the open door carrying a big box. Matice and I watched him. He glanced at us, but said nothing as he entered. He set the box on the floor and went right into the bathroom, leaving the door open.

Hello, I said.

Nothing came back.

I looked at Matice, then back toward this hulking man bent over the toilet. I shrugged and went on talking with Matice.

So what are you up to? I asked her.

Shopping. I need to go to de Ville. Want to come?

I didn't know where that was but said sure. It dawned on me later she meant Hotel de Ville. Her pronunciation threw me because she swallowed the Ls, *de Vee* she said, but I still didn't understand. I knew where Hotel de Ville was, just across the Seine on the edge of the Marais, a beautiful building, I've passed it many times in admiration, but the shopping part was confusing. I decided not to ask too many questions, though. I liked Matice's mood and didn't want to suddenly alter it somehow with questions. I'd find out soon enough. The man in my bathroom, however, had me very curious. Then that too dawned on me.

Are you Patrick? I asked.

Again no response, so I tried another tack.

Monsieur? Comment vous appelez-vous?

That did it. He stood up from handling the toilet and walked through the bathroom doorway.

Ah...Patrice, he said, lightly patting his chest with his big meaty paw. And to make sure I understood, he walked over to the closet and gestured toward a business card taped up in there that had his name and phone number on it. I'd seen it the first day I arrived when I switched on the hot water.

Patrice, he said again. Patrice.

Bonjour, Patrice. Je m'appelle Roman.

Bonjour, he said with a little smile and the faintest flutter of thick fingers. Then he shifted his blue eyes toward Matice and said the same to her with the same smile. Matice smiled back but said nothing, and I thought I'd quit while I was ahead so didn't attempt an introduction. I was quite proud of myself for pulling that one off. Then Patrice went back to work on the toilet, and Matice and I continued to chat.

The man I rented the apartment from, I said, told me someone would be by to fix the toilet. Guess we'll have to wait till he's done.

OKee, Matice said.

She told me her mother and sister had arrived from Turkey, and she needed to look for a bed for her sister. That's why she wanted to go shopping. She said it took her two days to move into her new apartment. It was just her, carrying her things by hand down the street to the new address. Ten trips, she said. Her brother didn't help at all.

I poured us a glass of wine while we talked and waited for Patrice to finish, but it didn't take much longer. He came out to the box and opened it. His big hands lifted something large and white out of there, a new toilet tank I could see. He set it down and walked back to the bathroom. Lifting the old tank and bringing it out he set it down beside the new one, then picked up the new one and went back to the bathroom. The connection only took a few minutes from there, and soon he was lumbering out with the box filled with the old tank just as silently as he came walking in. I stopped him.

Patrice!

Patrice stopped and slowly swung around.

Fini?

Oui.

Merci. Merci beaucoup.

Patrice gave a little nod then turned and slowly walked out. We watched him go through the open doorway and turn left in the hall, the only way he could go unless he was entering one of the other two neighboring apartments. There was another sky blue door directly across the way, and one to the right at the end of the hall, just a few steps down. I've never seen either of these two occupants, though I often hear them so I know they exist.

Matice and I finished our wine and walked through the doorway now too, and I locked it after us.

Matice didn't feel like walking, it was too hot for her, so we took the train from Place Monge to Pont Marie. It was just a short walk from there. Where she took me was actually across the street from Hotel de Ville, rue Rivoli at rue du Temple. Again I have passed this building many times without ever realizing it was a shopping mall. We went inside and rode the escalator up floor after floor. It was like any big shopping mall, but it was my first one in Paris, and I found it interesting. On the escalator we passed one whole huge floor devoted to art products. I couldn't think of one American mall I'd ever been in that even *had* any art products, and here was a whole floor of them. I found that wonderful, and to me it said a lot about the difference in cultures. The floor we were looking for was at the top—bedding and bath. As we left the escalator I saw a display of brown towels and I was back in San Francisco again, shopping with her for what we thought was going to be our new apartment. She had put a deposit down on a beautiful Victorian flat in the Mission, on 23rd between Valencia and Mission Streets. It was at the end of January, and we expected to move her in on the first of February, and I was soon to follow. Although it was furnished, we were going to make some changes. She began buying things, especially for the bedroom and bathroom. We spent a really long time deciding on the shower curtain. Finally we settled on one with the colors of white, brown and turquoise in staggered stripes. We moved on to towels then, and decided on brown. Do you like the light brown or the dark? she asked. I like the dark, I said. I do too, but I think we should have light too. Let's get both, she said. OK sure, whatever baby, I don't care, and we loaded up the cart. Oh, and what about this trash can? she asked, picking up a white tin one with a turquoise rim. That's cool, I said, but this one's better. It was turquoise with a brown rim. The walls were white, so I thought the colored one was a better accent piece. That's how into it I was, I was being aesthetic about a trash can. I was very excited to move into this apartment. Instantly when we walked in it felt like a home. How I wanted that, how ready I was for that. We'd looked at so many places together, weighing them in our minds and discussing how each might work for us or not, what we liked about them or didn't. This Victorian on 23rd was the first one to really feel right. OK, she said, and took the turquoise and brown can from me and into the cart it went. I was pushing the cart and we had quite a haul, sheets and pillowcases and pillows along with the bathroom stuff. A week later the man who was to rent this flat to her reneged on the deal and we lost it. She was in Chicago when she got the news. Right after the holidays her father was diagnosed with bladder cancer, so she was now going back there even more frequently. I received her call just after I had left a café in Cole Valley and was about to catch a train. I don't remember where I was going but remember wanting to just move from there. Her call came and I let the train pass to speak with her, that's when she told me. She was crying. She was very emotional over her father's illness because it sounded quite serious, and now she'd lost the apartment she was about to move into, and the only option was to ask her landlords at Noe Street if she could extend her lease another month. They had already extended it through January, but now she was going to have to ask for more time. Her things had already been moved down into the garage in storage, and she had scheduled the same mover to come back to move her into the place on 23rd Street. Now she was going to have to reschedule with him as well, and figure out something from there, where to go from there in the meantime while we continued to look for another permanent apartment. It was a sticky spot, and she was feeling overwhelmed. She wanted me to go to Noe Street and talk to the landlords, and I said I would. I tried to be comforting, I knew how upsetting the whole thing was, everything she was dealing with; I'm not the best at that, though. She was still sniffling, but everything she needed to say to me was said and I thought the conversation was over. Another train was coming. They came through there with large gaps of time in between. I wanted to catch this one. I said: OK baby, I love you. A train's coming so I'll talk to you later, in a little while (she was going to call back later to check on what she'd asked me to do) and I hung up. This later went on her list too, that I'd hung up on my crying girlfriend.

Matice found the beds. It turned out she wanted a temporary bed, the kind for guests, like an inflatable mattress, but what she was looking at were not inflatable mattresses. They were more like futon mattresses. But they weren't those either. It was for her sister to sleep on. She made a call on her cell phone and spoke in Turkish to her sister describing what she was looking at. Then she hung up and spoke in French with a salesman. They talked and talked, Matice asking questions. I saw and heard all that was going on but I was no longer there.

After the salesman left we did too. She was just looking today, not buying after all. We wondered what to do from there.

How about Eiffel? Matice suggested.

She pronounced it *A*ffel instead of *I*ffel. I'd never heard it said that way, and like her pronunciation of Hotel de Ville I pondered its correctness, but what did I know? She's been right about other things so why shouldn't she be right here too?

I wasn't excited about going to the Eiffel Tower but it gave us something to do, a direction, and the bus passing us on rue Rivoli was going right there so we jumped on. Traffic jammed the streets, it was a slow ride in the heat. Matice got impatient. She was changing her mind. When the bus turned onto Boulevard St. Germain after crossing the Seine at Pont de la Concorde she wanted to get off, so we did, at rue de Bellechasse. There was a café and we sat outside in the shade of big trees in front on the street and had coffee and smoked cigarettes. I'd quit smoking over a year ago, shortly before I met her, but began again a bit on this trip. I bum now and then from both Matice and Christophe when they light up. I don't feel like there's danger of relapse, it just feels good to join then in this sometimes. We were having coffee in the shade and smoking, watching the street, and that's when I told Matice that I had met someone as she'd advised.

Who? she asked. Who did you meet?

I told her about Chantal and how we'd had a picnic on the bridge over the river, how we'd met in Montmartre, and about the strip clubs and sex shops I'd seen but did not go in. She told me a story then.

Once in Istanbul she was taken to a strip club, a male strip club, by her friends. Her friends had bought a man for her, to have sex with, and Matice was led by him into a small room where he proceeded to grind in his g-string against her. She was mortified, started crying. To buy her this man, she felt, meant her friends thought she was too unattractive to get one herself. The man stopped grinding and sat with her and talked. He was nice, Matice said, but he was awful. He started crying then too, saying how he did not like doing what he was doing, working there. He explained how he wanted a nice girl, to get married, and Matice yelled at him. Told him to shut up! He'd been paid, so now he was going to listen to her! *She* was going to talk and *he* was going to listen. She sat in that little room and talked to this man in his g-string until it seemed long enough, then she went back out to her friends and made them think she'd actually gone through with it, that she had sex with the man. Later she went home and cried some more in secret into her pillow.

And you, she said to me, you're just for fun.

She became passionate. Her nostrils flared and her eyes focused hard on me, called me selfish again. I don't know why, she wouldn't explain, but I felt it go deep and I think she saw that because she followed up with another swing while I staggered.

I'm clever, she said. More clever than you.

And again I didn't know why she said this but tried a faint jab back this time.

I've never professed to be clever, I said, wondering how I suddenly entered this ring with her.

But Matice responded only with: Love...Love is like money.

She said that many times then over our coffee. She kept repeating it, interjecting it into our conversation like poetic punctuation, a refrain, peppering me into submission with it, that love was like money, and never explained why she was saying it. At first I found her association distasteful and tried to fend off the tireless onslaught of the phrase, but it was useless. Some of the blows must've obviously gotten through, because reflecting back upon Matice's words I think I understand now.

Like money, love is an abstract exchange, its value created by the choice of mutual agreement. Love comes and goes, can be spent freely or hoarded stingily, clung to or invested wisely. It can be given openly, or swindled and stolen. It's asked to be paid back, sometimes with interest, and sometimes it's written off and forgotten altogether. Sometimes love comes easy, and sometimes it is worked ridiculously hard for. Love can be withheld, or refused; it may come all at once or not at all. Love can be offered, returned, and taken back, or it can be a gift squandered. It can be seen as salvation, and freedom, but is always a necessity. Love strengthens and empowers, and its absence can rob the will to live. Sometimes love is found, and sometimes love is hopelessly, irretrievably lost.

Yeah, I had to think about it, but Matice was right this time too.

Matice took the bus home from there, wanted to take a nap, she was suddenly very tired. She'd see me later, maybe, she'd said. I slowly walked St. Germain thinking about things amidst the crawling rush hour sidewalks. The abrupt shift to being alone after that exchange left me woozy and wanting, I thought I'd just go home at first myself. But it was too beautiful to go back and be pent up in that little coop of mine. I think what finally did it was witnessing that young couple on their scooter.

I was walking along and happened to glance back over my shoulder into the boulevard. There was a couple perched on a scooter waiting on a car ahead of them so they could proceed with their turn onto a side street. While they waited, the young man driving the scooter, feet flopped and splayed like a fly's on the pavement at either side of the machine, steadying them as they sat idle in traffic, hands stretched apart and resting at the handlebar grips, this young man simply turned his head slowly round to the girl nestled up on the seat behind him, as if suddenly remembering she was there, and kissed her, slow and soft and luscious, and she, cradling his body with hers, answered with all herself, drawing him even further into her with that kiss, even when there was nowhere further to go she pulled him in deeper, gave herself back to him with all she could on that idling seat. They sat there on that scooter in the bright evening sunshine, white helmets strapped tightly to their heads, kissing. Kissing because there simply was nothing better in life to do in that moment with their time while they waited on that car to move than to kiss, and it was one of the sexiest things I have ever seen. So sexy I had to quickly turn away. But I was inspired now and determined to stay out, out and away from the rafters.

I bought a demi baguette at a boulangerie and some ham at a grocery store along with a tall can of Kronenbourg and went to catch the sunset at the river. I sit here now, writing this on my stone bench in the golden light. The cobbled bank is full of people drinking, picnicking, enjoying life. There are young bodies all about me. Everywhere I look bodies line both sides of the riverbank. San Francisco has Dolores Park for this, where the young have taken to carpeting every foot of that sloping hill in the sun, and Paris has the Seine. It's so beautiful, the light so golden as the sun sinks into the river behind Pont au Double and

Notre Dame. So beautiful...I almost forget I'm so alone.

I t's a sin, I mustn't tell it. But still I must. How could I not? How could I possibly not when it's so integral to this disin-tergration?

It was the middle of October, and we were leaving for Paris in a little over a week. Lain, my coworker, was also an artist and having a show. It was in a tiny backroom gallery in Oakland, on MacArthur. There was an opening reception on Thursday night. I had a couple hours to kill after work before it started so I stayed on the train past the stop and rode to Berkeley for a beer to wait it out. I was sitting at the bar with my pint when I got a call. It was her. She was in Chicago.

Hi baby.

Hi, she said.

How are you? How ya feelin'?

OK. I didn't have the surgery.

Oh, why not?

Well, I don't know how to tell you this, so I'm just going to say it.

Tell me what?

Roman I'm pregnant.

I almost dropped my phone, and for a moment my tongue wouldn't work.

Wha...wh *wha?*

Yeah. I'm pregnant.

She'd gone to Chicago to see her doctor. There was a minor procedure she needed to undergo, minor surgery, but in prepara-tion for this, through blood work, it was discovered that that procedure had to be postponed. Pregnancy was not a condition in which one may be operated upon. That's how she'd found out.

After a few minutes of speaking with her she said she'd be back in San Francisco the next day and we'd talk more then. I hung up and downed my beer and had another, trying to force the information into my brain. How could she be pregnant? She said she hadn't been skipping, never missed a day. Then how? We'd talk more when she got back...OK. But until then I went zombie.

I went to Lain's show, I mean my body did, and it stayed maybe ten minutes, then excused itself, said it had to go. It drifted out of that tiny gallery down dark MacArthur Street to the train station and somehow, through instinct, found its way home to its empty, alien room in the Castro. And when it woke the following morning it again drifted through its day's obligations until it got home, to her this time, and lay beside her in the darkness on the bed where it found her, where finally I slipped now back into the flesh shell.

What happened? I asked. How did it happen?

The doctor said you must have super sperm, she said. We're just that one percent this happens to.

I never wanted to have children. I mean, I never wanted to consciously try to have them. Just didn't think I'd make a good father. I felt ill at ease and awkward around kids; I never got on well with them. Then there was the painfully true fact that I was a lousy provider. I could barely take care of myself let alone a child. Trite as it may sound, my children were the products of my work, my art, that's what I'd always told myself and that's what I was dedicated to. And then this, which I held to be the truest of all and my most selfless reason to want to remain childless: if I felt life to be as painful as I did, how could...*why* would I purposely bring someone else here to crumple and blister in this fire? The best thing is never to have been born, Nietzsche wrote, and I believed it to be so. Now I was confronted with a burgeoning new life that had already begun its journey to this flame, and I was both scared to death and confused in my feelings. Someone, it seemed, was trying awfully hard to come here to us, through us.

We spoke quietly in the dark, with long pauses between words—questions, answers. We were both absorbed in our own heavy thoughts and took our time to speak. There seemed so many sides to any thought or decision, like the many facets of a finely cut gem. I'd turn each one in my mind and look at it, and a new reflection of a cut would glare up. I could tell it was the same for her as well. Finally, I asked it.

What do you wanna do?

She spoke slowly. Every word was so very heavy.

Well, I've done some research, and there are two procedures, she said. One is called medical, where you take a pill. I think that one's best.

So it was decided then, and I didn't know how I felt. It seemed the best thing to do, for everyone. She was still married. There was her family's reaction to also contend with. This wasn't said, but I'm sure it must have been a tremendous weight tugging upon her decision.

She found a place but delayed making the call. Every day that passed the life inside her grew and we both felt its measure increase, in our blood, in our hearts. Finally the appointment was made, three days before we were to leave for Paris. She asked me to go with her and I said I would, I wanted to. I had to clear it with work, but I said I would go.

They were being such sticklers at the museum regarding my vacation time, asking me to be positively sure I had enough hours available for the full two weeks I was planning to take off. They made such a stink out of it, being sure I had enough accrued hours to take off like I wanted. I did, with not many to spare—maybe three. Now I was going to have to use those to go with her to the clinic, and it was going to be close.

I told them I had a doctor's appointment and took the scheduled morning off. Said I'd be in by 1, after lunch. Lunch was always 12 to 1. Pressure was mounting over the progress of the reinstallation. My boss was becoming anxious; worried we were falling behind schedule. We had to be done in time for the museum's grand reopening on the first of May and he was afraid time was getting away from us. I felt obligated to do as I said, to be in when I said I'd be. I thought there'd be enough time.

She had told me once, near our beginning, about something she saw while in Thailand. She had been there during some festival and witnessed a ceremony taking place at night. She described paper lanterns that, illuminated inside with candlelight, were released from the hands of women and somehow floated skyward. It was so magical and beautiful, she'd said, watching those lanterns float away into the night sky. Her words conjured such a vivid image in my mind it stuck with me. I remembered it as we lay together in bed the night before, and reminded her of that ceremony. I want you to try to hold that image in mind tomorrow, I said. Try to think of those floating lanterns of light being released into heaven. OK? Can you do that, baby?

Through the darkness she whispered, I'll try. I held her in my arms, and we tried to sleep then.

The appointment was at 9 AM. We arrived at the clinic in a taxi. It was in the Fillmore district. She pressed the button at the door and we were buzzed in. There was a flight of stairs and we climbed them into the reception room. I took a seat and she walked up to the counter to check in. I could see the girl behind the counter glass and she was very pretty. I recognized her. Her hair was much longer and she'd dumped the cat eye glasses, but it was her. It was a face I remembered from the wasteland. We'd never dated or had any relations, but I had tried. She turned from the counter now and came over to sit down next to me. We held hands and I kissed her on the cheek. After a while she was called in and she walked through a door. I sat out there alone, flipping through a magazine. I glanced often at the girl behind the glass but she didn't glance back. It was typical of something that would happen to me, seeing someone I knew at a vulnerable and private moment like this. I slouched and shifted slightly away in my seat. I was in clear view of her and had nowhere else to go. Maybe she didn't recognize me, I thought. But then again I don't think she'd looked yet. She was busy and kept her head down when not addressing someone in the reception area. A young woman came in alone and walked up to the glass, then came and took a seat across from me. I forced my attention deep into the pages of the magazine.

Then she came out, it took some time, but she was back. That was just a preliminary stage of the process, she said. They just took her blood pressure and things like that, then told her to go back out and wait. We waited.

A couple more women came in, separately, and alone. They took seats. The first young woman who came in was asked back now, and was gone for a while. Eventually they came for her again, and I waited alone. I was the only male in sight and it felt strange, a bit like enemy infiltration. Slumped in my seat I glanced over at the receptionist and she was looking at me now. There was a little smile on her face, and she gave me the faintest twitch of her right eye. So she recognized me after all. That little wink was meant to both let me know that and, I felt, show approval for my presence. I gave a lame withered smile back. The other women who came in had been called behind the door while I waited and I was really alone out there now. I waited some more. I looked at the time and it was getting late. Finally she came back out and sat beside me again. The next time she went in, she said, was going to be it. I took both her hands in mine and we pressed our faces together. We waited.

But it was getting late. I began to worry about getting across the bay to work on time. It was almost noon. How could three hours have gone by already? I still had to pick something up to eat before starting work; I hadn't had a thing all morning and my stomach was beginning to ache. I couldn't work the rest of the day without eating. We waited some more, and then I told her I was going to have to leave. I didn't want to. I hated that I felt like I had to. I wanted to stay and be with her, to go in the room with her while she took that godawful pill, but they weren't going to let me do that, and I had to go to work now, to *work*. I kissed her hands her face her lips. I looked into her eyes. I told her I loved her. And then I dashed down the stairs.

When I got out onto the street and was walking toward the corner to hail a cab I suddenly stopped. My God, did I just leave her! I wanted to go back, but I couldn't. I had to go to *work*, to that *place*, and oh my God where I could tell no one where I'd just been and what was happening in my life and who and what I just left to come to do their work. *Their* work.

I had the cab take me downtown to a salad place I knew, to quickly get something for to go, and from there jumped on the train at Embarcadero station to Oakland.

When I ascended the stairs of the platform at Lake Merritt and was headed toward the exit I saw him. He was standing by the ticket gates, as if waiting for someone. Tall black man, young. He was just standing there looking spaced-out and dazed in front of the gates, inside. There was something wrong with him, I could feel it. He was trouble, detached evil waiting to happen. He looked at no one, standing there staring about unseeing. A yellowed plastic tip of a Swisher Sweet poked out of his mouth, the remaining cigar in it a mere burnt stub. With the salad carton in my left hand wrapped in white plastic and my brown leather shoulder bag draped against my right hip I passed him to exit through the gate, glancing at him peripherally and feeling his danger. His eyes were lidded and vacant. I saw them shift ever so slightly toward me as I passed. His skin was very dark— matte black in tone and texture. Light did not seem to shine or reflect upon it only absorb into it. I walked through the gate toward the escalator and before I stepped upon it glanced one last time back at him still standing numb inside the ticket gates, looking at no one, just as no one seemed to notice him.

Then I reached the top of the escalator, and as I took my first step from it onto solid pavement a great force suddenly shoved me from behind and I was thrown face first to the ground. My bag flung out around me though the strap was still looped across my torso and my lunch flew skidding out of my hand over the pavement but was still intact. Sprawled on my hands and knees, as fast as it happened and for the few seconds I was down there, all manner of thoughts tore through me in an instant. On this day of all days, the day my child was released and refused entry to this world, this day I left before that black job was done, out of obligation to the job of others, this day of my greatest sin, and now *this*, whatever this was, and whatever it was I deserved it, but I will destroy its insult and affront, on this today of all days. I collected my belongings, my lunch wrapped in white plastic and my spilled-open bag, and sprung to my feet, ready to drop them again and fight, fight who or whatever it was that attacked me. I sprung up and spun round. It was him.

Now what do YOU want? I screamed.

I looked straight into his dirtblack face. It was dead, expressionless. All I saw was a vacant stare, and that plastic ivory cigar tip hanging from the slackened mouth. I was expecting a second charge, but it did not come. We faced each other silently, squared off right in front of the entrance to the station. People passed, yet not one stopped or even seemed to notice what just happened. No one seemed to see him but me. And I looked into those deadened, half-shut eyes and knew who this was before me, I recognized him then. This was the Black Angel. He saw what I had just done and came to shove my face down into it, into the wretchedness of the earth, to show me that he had seen and that it would not be forgotten. This was Death himself come to face me, because I had called him upon myself. We looked at each other, and now he knew that I recognized him, now he saw

I understood, he just turned and walked away, as did I—to work. But I too had seen. I had looked into the eyes of Death and saw my sin reflected in the gaping cavern abyss of his face, and I too would never forget. I would never forget what had been done.

The day passed with quiet tears. I stayed apart from everyone and worked alone, or found an empty corner of the gallery where I could cry a little more as needed. When I got home to her, again we lay on the bed in the dark and I held her. We were quiet at first that way, and then she told me what had happened after I left. They had shown her a sonogram photo of the fetus, that's what happened when they called her in the second time, they took a sonogram. Then they gave her the pill to take. She was crying so much and for so long before taking it they almost wouldn't let her do it, she said. But then she did, and ran out of there. She said she took the sonogram picture with her, and did I want to look?

Yes. No. No not now, I said. I can't now. I would someday, I thought, because I believed there'd be a someday with us, but I couldn't look at it then.

Endless streams of soundless tears wriggled down my cheeks and neck and warm tiny pools collected in the cups of my ears. I couldn't help it, I told her then what I was thinking, that I never thought I wanted a kid but if it was going to happen I felt that was my chance, and it seemed like it wanted to come to us so bad…

In the darkness she suddenly reared up.

ROMAN I WANTED THAT BABY!

Out loud and mournful then the tears burst boldly into the room. She loved her nieces and nephews so, spoke of them constantly, I knew how she loved children, why had she not said she wanted our child that night when I came home to her and we had talked? Why hadn't she told me how she truly felt? Had she not known fully at the time, like me, did it only come to her too late? Had she been testing my reaction, and when it came, laconic and slow, acquiesced to the worst? Had she waited for me to speak first? Was that possible when it was her decision and hers alone ultimately? Silent questions and the impotence of regret crowded the room like thunderclouds settling in. What had we done...Oh God, oh Lord what had we done...

The people at the clinic said she wasn't allowed to travel for a week. I no longer wanted to go on our trip, but she would not let me back out. She said that everything had already been arranged, and she was not going to let me *not* go. She said she'd join me there in a week. I said my place was with her now, and that I wasn't going by myself. What the fuck would I do in Paris by myself? It was stupid; the whole idea was to go together. Besides, I should be there at home with her. We should be to-gether.

She would not hear it. She had bought a new carry-on, and packed it for me the night before I was supposed to leave. I kept telling her that I didn't want to go, that I wasn't going, but she kept packing. The bag had an expandable feature and it was extended to its maximum, and although it seemed quite large she was confident it would still fit in the overhead compartment. This bag was exactly the same model as the one she'd carried around the globe, which she still had and was planning to use when she followed, so by very good authority she should know. I'd told her my experience a few years earlier when I went to Buenos Aires and had to check my bag and how it had gotten lost. I'd spent the first two days there without my luggage and I didn't want to have to check my bag this time for fear of that happening again. She promised I wouldn't have to check it. We turned in early; it was a very early flight. I did not like any of this.

5:30 came and it was time to get up. I still felt this was wrong, it was wrong to leave her, but she ushered me through the morning. She'd called the cab. It was on its way. I was grumpy and still half asleep. I saw the leather-covered journal she'd given me on the dresser. She wanted me to bring it, but I looked at it and just couldn't. I loved it, but the thing frightened me. I felt I'd only ruin its beauty. I tricked my mind into thinking that there was no room for it in my bag, I was going to have to leave it.

The cab arrived and she jammed some folded bills into my hand and I walked through the black gate of the stoop. There was tension between us. I was unhappy she was forcing me to go and she was upset that I was going.

The cab drove down Market. The broad palm trees in the cobblestoned median fanned out over the street and seemed happy to stand in a new day. The sun had just come up and golden light flooded the city. The streetcar rails were solid gilt bars. My phone vibrated. A text.

I'm sorry that notebook intimidates you so.

She must've just discovered it still on the dresser. Then there was another message.

I wish you were here.

The driver asked where I was going and when I told him Paris he started speaking to me in French. He was an older man, said he'd lived in France once years ago, just outside of Paris. I told him I didn't speak French. My brain was still mush with lack of sleep. It was too early for me and my mental capacity was not yet there, and I was distracted with her. How could she be sending these things to me? I couldn't respond properly to even the simplest word or phrase the driver tossed at me. When he dropped me at the airport even his au revoir left me dumb.

As I was about to board, the woman taking boarding passes looked at my bag as I wheeled it by her. She stopped me.

You have to check that.

No, it'll fit, I said.

She acted like she didn't hear me and made out the claim receipt and handed it out to me. I wouldn't take it.

No, I said. I was told it would fit.

She ignored me, standing there with her hand out waiting for me to take the receipt. A man in a uniform was already grabbing the handle out of my hand.

It'll *fit!*

It's OK, bro, the man said. It'll be there. And as I watched him roll my bag away from the boarding gate I snatched the ticket from the woman's hand and walked through the passage toward the plane. I pulled my cell phone from my pocket and called her before I met up with the end of the line ahead.

They took it!

What?

My bag! They *took* it. Said it wouldn't *fit.*

I heard myself, sounded like a spoiled brat kid, but I couldn't stop. I wanted her to know she was wrong.

It's OK, she said. It'll be there. Don't worry about it.

You said it would *fit.*

I wasn't sure why I was making such a big deal out of it, other than she made me leave her when I didn't want to, *knew* I should not. I left her again, and this time it was her fault I'd left.

I'd been sitting quite a while on my bench along the Seine, and when I'd finished writing I needed to move, get the blood back in my legs. I got up to head home.

Walking along the cobblestones of the river, just as I started drifting toward the steps to the street, I crossed paths with Christophe. This made the fourth time he and I encountered each other this way. We walked toward one another with smiles.

What ahr you do*ing*?

Oh I was just about to walk home. I've been sitting here a

long time.

The sun had just sunk below the bridges of the Seine and was gone but the sky was powder blue, with some stars beginning to show. There was light still, but it was dimming fast.

You want to walk with *me*? Eet's a good time to look for garls.

This was Christophe's usual trolling spot, along the river at twilight, and there were certainly plenty of girls out there. Sure, it was worth a look at least, for the sake of a little companionship with Christophe.

We walked back in the direction I'd just come, our eyes skimming over the squirming river and the many people still lounging along its contained edge. We walked past the docked dinner boats, and further beneath the next bridge, which was under construction. Its underbelly was a wickerwork of wooden slats, draped and wrapped with big black plastic sheets. Beyond this point was a part of the river I'd never walked. Here there was grass and shrubbery on the grade beneath the quai instead of old stone walls and cobblestone. A lot of people were down here too, and I had the sense this was the real locals' spot. Locals were up river as well, but they seemed to be mostly students, mixed along with travelers and tourists. Up there was drunken revelry, partying, young people on the make. Down here was more of a blend of ages, families and couples as well as single friends, young and old. It was a little more sedate, yet still alive in a different way. There were circular platforms along the bank of the river made of gray stone. I counted three. They appeared to act as stages, and people danced on them.

On the first people danced apart from one another while doing the same movements, like line dancing. On the second there was tango, and Christophe and I watched this a while. Some very sexy women were out there on that floor, gliding and writhing and rolling in the arms of their partners, and the sensuality of the dance seduced us. We walked down river a little further. On the last platform people held hands in a circle and slowly rotated around the gray stone. It looked very strange and a little spooky, the way they moved so slowly in their linked chain of hands, like some coven. We turned and walked back from here, pausing a moment again at the tango stage as we passed.

Christophe was on his way to the Marais to see about a girl. She worked in a restaurant over there. He asked if I wanted to come.

Do you remembair what you asked me zee ozair night?

Yeah, about work?

The night I met up with Christophe after being with Chantal I told him what I was thinking. He was my only source of information in Paris so I thought I'd run it by him. I told him I was thinking of trying to stay in Paris to live, and did he have any idea about art handling, museum or gallery type work? He said he didn't, but he had a couple friends who did that. He'd talk to them. I asked him then what he did for a living. He was in property management—remodeling and construction, he said. He did very little of the actual remodeling himself, although he did say he had remodeled the apartment on rue St. Julien, what was his father's home. He said he'd done that himself, and I told him how impressed I was, that I really loved what he did with it. I remembered that sliding wall feature of the bathroom. But aside from that, he said he mainly assessed the jobs that came in and bid them. I told him I also could do that kind of work. I wasn't the best carpenter by any means but I could do small jobs, and I could paint. I'm a good painter I said. He said he didn't know, he'd think about it.

My friend say you must speak Fronch to work in museums, or work wizz ahrt. Zey will not 'ire you ozairwise. Sorree, but ziss ees what 'ee say.

OK. I figured as much, I said, and did not ask about possible work with him. I had no ideas other than these, and I knew they were long shots. I cannot do what Chantal has been able to do, and so I must go back to San Francisco and face the tatters waiting there.

We crossed the river at l'Archeveche. As we went, Christophe suddenly halted.

Deed you see *zat?*

What? I asked, looking around.

Zat *garl!* She was lookinguh at *you!*

Well don't sound so surprised, I said. It happens.

I didn't know what he was talking about. I've stopped trying to catch the eyes of women on the street here and wasn't paying attention. I was glad to hear it, I could use the uplift of morale, but the amount of surprise in Christophe's voice tempered the occasion. I suggested we stop for a beer at my café. I've come often during this trip. There's free wifi service so I could use the internet on the laptop, and they're accommodating to those lingering at tables. The waitresses are very pretty here too, that's helped as well. It's nice to be around them to look at. I've found it another nice place to work at times. I'd sit in back at one of the tables on a red cushioned Naugahyde seat. Christophe and I went in and stood at the zinc bar and ordered beers. He'd never been in before. He said he liked it. We had two and walked on.

We crossed from the island at Pont Louis Philippe into the Marais. We passed a church I remembered passing with her. Christophe and I were following the same path she and I took our last day when we went into the Marias. As we passed this church then the bells began ringing and nuns wove like scuttling seabirds across our path on the stone courtyard, flashing brightly in the sunshine in their white garb. I wanted to stop in now and Christophe followed me inside, but a service was in progress so we glanced around from the entranceway a moment and walked back out. I made a mental note to return for a closer look.

Deeper into the Marais we went. It was night now, and I just let myself coast along with Christophe without paying much attention to where we were or where we were headed. We wound up on a little street that was not a thoroughfare. At the end were apartment buildings. It was a street full of restaurants, and the girl Christophe came to see worked at one of these. It was very busy, and we milled around outside looking through the windows. Christophe wasn't positive she was working this night, so he was waiting to spot her before making a next move. The restaurant was rather large, and had two sides—two large rooms. We went from side to side looking through the big glass until he saw her, then he went in to say hello. A few minutes later he came back out and we sat at a table on the street at the far left side of the restaurant, away from the others in front.

The girl tended bar. Christophe met her recently at a party and wanted to follow up. She came out and asked if we'd like a drink. She was French. That kind of surprised me, and I thought it funny that I was surprised by that.

She brought us out a couple drinks, on the house. That was nice of her. Christophe and I finished those and she came back asking if we wanted another. I did, but before I said so Christophe spoke to the girl in French, then spoke to me.

Eef you want anozair you will *aff* to pay.

According to the drink menu drinks were €10. I decided to skip it, so did Christophe. The girl went back inside. Things didn't seem to be going so hot between them, she didn't seem too excited to see him, but maybe that was the French way.

She ees very bu*sy*. Eet's not zee best time to 'ave come. She ees 'aving a break *soon*. We 'ave a cigarette, and then *fffff*, he said, flicking his fingers. S'O*K*?

Sure man, it's cool. We'll have a cigarette with her.

A minute later the girl came out again. She had a long brown ponytail. We all stood together in the street away from the tables and smoked. Christophe introduced me. She smiled and said bonsoir and so did I but that was it. She didn't speak English. She and Christophe spoke to each other. They talked and talked and laughed and smoked, and I watched Christophe's eyes and they seemed to sparkle and flirt. I stood there walking in circles and toeing the street and looking up at the night sky while listening to a conversation in French, beginning to feel silly standing there, but not knowing what else to do I stood there, waiting. Finally the girl had to get back to work and went inside. As Christophe and I walked away I said: Well, that seemed to have gone well.

She ees not for *me*, Christophe said.

When I asked why he said: She ees scaired. Bor*ing*.

We kicked around the Marais. It was around midnight now. Had a drink here, drink there, nothing really going on. There were some girls Christophe started talking to sitting outside at the last place we stopped. He wasn't shy in the least. They were Dutch. They spoke English and French. The one Christophe was talking to was quite pretty, but distracted. Not too interested. They were young. They wanted to party. They were going to the Bastille. We didn't want to go there, and besides it wasn't going to go anywhere with these Dutch girls so we left them and walked back toward the river. We approached Notre Dame and walked along beside it. I allowed myself to look now. So beautiful. Stone demons protruded from its walls and leered ancient at us full of torture and evil and pain. We were not afraid. We embraced their glares and taunts safe from behind the black wrought iron gates and celebrated their fixed eternal and cherished existence. We crossed before the entrance to the church talking about it, its beauty, its mystery. Christophe has seen it all his life, even he still seemed in awe of it. The night before her arrival, when I was staying on rue St. Julien, I came out and crossed the river to sit in front of Notre Dame. It was 2 AM. I was all alone out there in the darkness, just me staring at that gorgeous structure. A rat scurried out from the planters near my bench and slithered by my feet. I looked at the church and thought of her. She was on her way here to me. I'd been alone in

Paris for five days, and now tomorrow she would arrive. I was so excited to see her, hold her. At first when I got to Paris I didn't know what to do, how to feel. I was empty and numb, and felt my existence unreal. There I was in Paris after six years, the city I'd been longing to see again for six years, and felt absolutely nothing for it. I remember that first night when I arrived sitting having coffee at a table on the quai just off St. Michel, looking at Notre Dame from there, trying to feel something, but couldn't. But the night when I sat alone before it I knew what a special moment that was. Who gets to sit all alone in the night staring up at Notre Dame? When I got up from there finally and was heading back across the river to the apartment a girl stopped me. She didn't speak English, but she was asking for directions to the Mouffetard. I knew where that was and through butchered French and hand signals I did my best to tell her. Now here I am living in the Mouffetard myself, temporarily. It's all so funny, my story with Paris, how my experiences have converged here. It's so funny it buoys my heart and sends a spike through at the same time.

Christophe was talking about the spire of the church, how he'd heard that the floor plan of Notre Dame is hidden in a compartment up there in that spire. That must've reminded him, because then he turned to me and asked: Deed you evair get your let*tair*?

I stopped in my tracks.

Letter?

Yes. Deed you evair get eet? I put eet in zee mail*box*. Deed you get eet?

Before we left Paris she had written me a letter. As we passed with our luggage on our way to the airport she placed a white envelope on the anteroom mailboxes, hoping the mailman or someone would mail it. It was addressed to my apartment. For weeks after our return she kept asking if I'd received it, but it never came. And she would not tell me what she had written.

Ever since we began, she wrote me cards and letters. Many were sent while she was away on her business trips, written from the plane. The return address on the envelopes read *10,000 FT*, or simply, *In The Sky*. Things like that. They were wonderful. She poured herself into her cards to me, it seemed, and there's a stack of them in San Francisco sitting on the mantel in my room. They're all I have now to prove that I had any impact whatsoever upon her life, and that she was ever a part of mine. Those, and that book of photos. Such marvelous things she would say to me in her cards. And when she was traveling less she still wrote them, with words or phrases written on the back like *Almost Heaven* with *Almost* crossed out, or *Bliss*, or *Wandering*. The night I came home to her after the clinic she had a card for me. She had a card for *me*. I did not readily think of those things, and if anyone should have gotten a card that night it was her, but I did not think of it. I was more concerned with simply getting home to be with her. In that card she said we were now spiritually linked for all of time, and she thanked me for being with her. It would have been much harder, she'd said, without me there. There was something else inside the envelope that made it bulky, an object. I pulled it out. A shiny metal thimble. That was an inside joke. I'd once teased her that the love she had for me was so big it could probably fit inside a thimble, and she'd put it in there to show me her love. In hindsight, that token was probably meant less ironically than I perceived.

No, Christophe. I didn't get it. *You* had mailed it?

Oui. Mmay*be* eet didn't 'ave enough post*age*? I don't know, he said, and shrugged.

No, I didn't get it, I said. And she never told me what was in it. Guess I'll never know now.

Oh…Christophe shrugged again.

We kept walking in the dark. As if by instinct I wandered in the direction of the Mouffetard. Christophe must have sensed it, how I was feeling, and walked with me. He stayed with me till just past rue des Ecoles, which is about halfway. We stopped there and talked a little more. I learned things about him I'd never known or realized before while we stood there talking in the quiet street. He is deaf in his left ear, he told me, but he didn't say why. I don't remember how that came up but he told me that as we stood there. And listening to him now, watching him as he spoke, I noticed that his face twitched and jerked when he talked, his eyes flinching in uncontrollable blinks. I knew a kid in high school who did that. And his words at times were either preceded with or followed by grunts, gentle monkey-like oo-ooo's just under his breath I'd never detected before, as if he had a mild case of Turret's. Why had I not noticed that before? I wondered.

I appreciated Christophe walking with me, but I wanted to be alone now. From where we stood we could see Boulevard St. Germain just over a block away down the gently sloping hill. Two blondes suddenly flashed by down there, in short white skirts, and Christophe went *aagh!* He couldn't stand it. He said: You want to go *catch* zem wizz *me?*

We couldn't even tell what they looked like only that they were blonde and female, but that was enough for Christophe. He was very excited.

Come on Romon, let's go *catch zem*, he said

Nah, go ahead, I told him. I couldn't give a shit, Christophe. I'm goin' home.

He took off in a trot down the hill, stubby blonde paddle wagging against the back of his stiff shoulders; he had a very erect running style. I watched after him until he quickly grew fainter in the night, his light hair turning darker with distance. And then I turned, and in the darkness slowly kept walking.

I'd forgotten my Sudafed. Since the New York flight I'd discovered Sudafed corrected whatever imbalance was happening in my ears and prevented the pain. The ear doctor I went to in San Francisco after that New York trip suggested it. I'd taken a flight back to Illinois to visit my family in September and it worked, but I'd forgotten it now, and as the plane descended on approach to de Gaulle I felt the pressure building and began to panic. I got up to use the restroom. On my way I asked a flight attendant standing back there if he had any suggestions.

Try popping your ears, he said.

Thanks.

I went through the restroom door and when I came out the same attendant was standing there holding two white Styrofoam cups.

Here, try these, he said, and handed me the cups. There were wet paper towels at the bottom of them, and I could feel their warmth through the Styrofoam.

Hold them over your ears, he said. The moisture from the hot water will help keep your canals open.

I returned to my seat and, after buckling up for the long descent, placed the cups over my ears. The warmth from the paper towels came into them. I felt stupid, but it was working. The pressure was decreasing. So in this way, Styrofoam pressed protuberantly to my head, I landed for my second time in Paris, without her by my side as planned.

I stood watching the baggage carousel intently until, with a great exhale of relief, I saw my muted green bag tumble onto the belt. I grabbed it up quickly and headed for the train, just down the stairs from the claim station. I got in line behind the two people ahead of me and walked up to the glass booth.

Un billet pour Paris, s'il vous plait.

Then down the escalator from the ticket counter I went and directly onto a train just departing. And here I was riding into Paris again, and I remembered this ride, and the leaveless trees and yellowbrick buildings along the tracks, and all I kept thinking was this was not how it was supposed to be. I was not supposed to be taking this ride alone. But alone or not here I was, and a sad excitement was building inside me.

And then my stop came, St. Michel/Notre Dame, and I ascended onto the street, on the Right Bank, and there was Notre Dame. I couldn't believe it. There was that spectacular church again. I stopped with my baggage and took out the camera she had bought for this trip and given to me to take. I brought it out from my leather jacket pocket and took a picture of the church, like any tourist, as the first thing I saw upon entry onto the Paris streets.

I wheeled my bag across the nearest bridge to the quai on the Left Bank and swung left and there was Shakespeare and Co. and rue St. Julien le Pauvre. *Here?* We were right *here?* This close to the river and the church? Unbelievable…

I wheeled my bag down the short street and found the number. It was Sunday morning, gray and chilly. There were people about but not many. I went to the door. I saw the box to punch in the code that would unlock the door and looked for a way to buzz this guy Christophe who was renting us the apartment. I didn't see one, so I took out my cell phone to call the number on the information sheet she'd printed from the confirmation email she'd been sent and from which I was following directions. I had set up my phone before leaving San Francisco so that it worked overseas, but the calls were expensive. I didn't know what else to do. No answer. I left a message. Now what? I rolled up the street and turned left, just to kill some time, to look around. Oh my God here's that bar! The one with the cavern downstairs where I left a cd! We're staying right around the *corner?* My phone vibrated. I answered. A voice with a heavy French accent. I told it I was at the door but didn't know how to buzz.

But you 'ave zee code, the voice said. I sent eet wizz my *email.*

I looked again. Yes there it was, I'd missed it somehow. I went back to the door and punched it in. But another door was inside that one. I waited there. In a moment a young man opened it saying he was Christophe. He looked like he could be a student in Berkeley, with his blonde ponytail and goatee and youth. He picked up my bag and nearly sprinted up the long winding wood and tile stairway. I had to walk fast to keep up, but I thought that a very courteous gesture. Around and around we went till finally there were no more steps, and two doors hung opposite each other. He set the bag down and opened the one on the left, leading me inside. Here? We were staying *here?* It was…*perfect!* I couldn't believe my eyes. Just as I'd seen on the computer, it was just as the photos showed, but to stand there was a different, more sensational reality.

This young man with the ponytail showed me around the apartment, and then it came time to give him a check. She had deposited the money into my account and I wrote it out for him and handed it over. He looked at it.

MmI'm sor*ree*, Christophe mumbled. But don't you 'ave to…sign?

I snatched it out of his hands and then handed it back, embarrassed that in my excitement and fatigue I had forgotten to sign my name. He smiled now and handed me the keys and turned to leave, but I caught him just before he did. I asked about the internet, was it working? I had her laptop with me so we could be in touch while apart. I wanted to write her right away.

Oh yes. Let me geeve you zee *code*, he said, and wrote it down.

He left then, and I walked over and opened one of the windows in the living room. There was the street down there. And there was Notre Dame. I leaned my elbows on the metal railing outside the window, looking at the church. My God, where was I? How did this happen?

*

After the first night, when I sat numbly having coffee on the quai at St. Michel, looking at Notre Dame and the strangers passing on the street, who in turn were looking back at me as I sat writing in my notebook, writing a little note about how I felt being here in Paris after six years, a little sad prayer of a note, and on their faces were curious looks as if I were some oddity observed as they passed, a curiosity from the past they caught sight of (and that still happens now as I've been writing, as if to see a man writing with pen and notebook in a café or at the bar of a brasserie is such an anachronism it is to elicit stares and smiles)—after this night when I sat lonely and heartsick and alone, the following days broke open and each day I was more in love with my surroundings and thrilled to walk the streets. And I walked and I walked and I looked and I ate and I drank and I remember standing on the crest of Pont Royal, leaning against the stone railing and looking about at the incredible beauty before me, the colorful autumn trees along the Seine and the green waters of the Seine itself, the big dark gray clouds in the sky and the patches of clear blue among them allowing warm light to escape and caress the curling stone of the Louvre just on the other side of the bridge, I stood there and looked at all this magnificence and knew in my bones I was standing in one of the most beautiful spots on earth, and wept for the beauty I saw, wondering why in the world it had taken so long to stand there. And soon she would be here, and she'd been to Paris many times before, seeing the city I'm sure in ways I have not and will never, but I would show her the city now with me, and we would walk the streets together and see the same things together and it would be our experience. It would be our time in Paris.

At night sometimes I'd amuse myself with the camera. There was a small mirror on the wall in the living room. The glass was round and the frame gold in the shape of wiggly sun rays. I positioned my face in the glass, so that mine was the face of Apollo, and took the shot.

The night before she came I sat with my notebook and a bottle of wine at the window looking at the moon and at the cross on the roof of the tiny church of St. Julien le Pauvre across the street, and they inspired lyrics.

The cross upon the roof of the church
Reminds me of the place where it hurts
She traced a promise with her finger across
*   her heart*
Placed it there like a candle and we watched
The flame dance for a while till she blew it out

I didn't know how prophetic those words were to become, but somewhere a part of me deep inside knew. Another verse came.

The moon is staring into my room
Like it's looking for something it can do
But the shadow of the pane that it makes
Falls like a cross like it's taking aim
Right on my heart to shoot it out

When I got done working on the song I went outside and sat on the empty plaza in front of Notre Dame, breathing in the solitude of the moment, reveling in it, bundled against the chill autumn starry night.

Then she came.

My phone rang in the morning and it was her downstairs. I went down and let her in, kissing her and holding her tightly to me. Then, just like Christophe did, I took her bag and I led her up the winding stairs, excited for her to see. At the top of the stairs was Christophe grinning wildly, hands clasped in anticipation of receiving her. I briefly introduced them, but as I did she wandered off as if in a trance into the apartment, leaving Christophe standing there without having said a word. I smiled and shrugged an apology at him, then followed her inside and closed the door. I set her bag in the bedroom and joined her in the living room. It was strange. We were awkward with each other. She sat on the couch, not speaking, and the only thing I could think to do was take her picture as she sat there, to document her arrival. She had just had her hair done again, I could tell. It was darker, and very straight. It was always very straight when she came from having it done. She looked beautiful, but I don't remember telling her that. Most likely I didn't. She certainly did not look like she'd just taken an 11 hour plane trip, that's for sure. Then she took a couple pictures of me, standing at the window.

I asked if she was tired, did she want to rest, did she want breakfast, what did she want to do?

She wanted to go out, she said, to walk, to yes have breakfast, and then walk. We put our jackets on. What was this she was wearing? This pretty wool coat, I'd never seen it before...I did not ask. I had an idea. You go down on the street first, I told her, and I'll take a picture of you from here, from the window. She did and there she was, smiling up at me with her big smile and movie star sunglasses and scattered yellow leaves at her feet. Oh my God, beautiful. How beautiful. I went down the stairs and into the anteroom and saw her through the glass of the door outside looking in, looking at her reflection. I had to take that picture. Beautiful...

I took her down rue Galande to Lagrange and then St. Germain, to the café there for breakfast. It was mediocre but wonderful just the same. She said she wanted to go to the Rodin Museum. Great, I'd never been. We walked and walked and then there we were, in the 7th arrondissement. We just followed our noses. Rather, I followed hers. She'd been to the museum before and had a general idea where it was without knowing exactly, but we stumbled upon it with no difficulty. Numerous pictures taken inside, but then there she was standing in front of a sculpture entitled *The Poet and His Muse*, and I took the shot.

There was a mirror at the back of the sculpture, and so I am also visible, reflected in the glass behind her holding the camera at chest level. A double portrait, of the sculpture and of the sculpture made flesh.

The next morning the first eruption occurred. We went to breakfast at a little restaurant I had noticed while alone. It caught my eye and I thought she might like it. It was nestled just off the quai, slightly east of Notre Dame and just a few blocks from the apartment. The place was very small and most the seats inside were filled, so we took a table outside up against the building. From where we sat you could see the backend of Notre Dame, the flying buttresses along the side were visible in the distance, but my back was to it. After we'd ordered, I'd turned around in my seat to look at the church and heard *Oh, Roman!* I turned back around. What was the matter?

There was a couple who happened to be seated at a table further out from us, behind me and in direct line of vision of the church. She thought I'd turned around to blatantly look at the woman seated back there.

I was looking at the *church!*

She would not believe me. To her mind, what normal man would be turned around in his seat looking at a church when there was a pretty woman behind him?

Now I became angry. The joy I'd felt while wandering Paris in the days before her arrival, anticipating her, longing for her while doing the best I could to enjoy the city on my own, seemed to evaporate. It had all been spoiled by that one ridiculous fit of mischaracterization. As usual I looked worse in her eyes than the actual truth of the reality.

Similarly, one night while at the apartment, I was sitting in the living room reading when suddenly she came out to me from the bedroom. *Craigslist*, Roman? You're looking at women on *Craigslist?*

It was true. The nights I was alone, at times I had perused the casual encounters section of Craigslist: w4m, mw4w, mw4m...

During my time in the wasteland I had gotten into the habit of doing this as a cheap thrill, because some of the photos women post of themselves there can be quite sexy, dirty even. That habit had carried over from the wasteland into my lonely nights while she was gone. When she was away from me, oversexed as I was now, the spirit of sexuality was felt all around me and I'd need it even more than I did when I was single and not getting it as regularly. So while alone in Paris this continued, and she saw it in my history trail I guess when she pulled up Craigslist. But she read it differently than it actually was. She thought I was looking to *meet* women in Paris, when in fact I was just looking out of curiosity, to see what kind of photos they may post in Paris—as entertainment. There was never any intention whatsoever of contact. I didn't do that in San Francisco I certainly wouldn't do it in Paris. But I realized how it looked, and again I looked way guiltier than the reality. I was just getting off to some photos, so what?

She would not accept whatever I had to say, and anger spun and spun inside her until finally it spun itself out and dissipated on its own, as it usually did, or at least transformed quietly into something else, and we resumed as we were before.

But the question may arise: what was she doing looking on Craigslist?

To answer this I must go back to the month of July.

She was still at the Shrader apartment, upstairs. There was a weekend where one of her sisters visited from Chicago, one she didn't care for very much it seemed because they tended to fight a lot when they were together, she told me. A friend of her sister's from Los Angeles also came up that weekend to join them. They both stayed with her at Shrader. I did not get to meet her sister because she would not allow me to, for my own protection she said. She said her sister was awful and she was doing me a favor keeping me away from her. I of course felt she was keeping me away for other reasons, to protect *herself*. Regard-less, I did not meet her sister, but I did meet her sister's friend, who she had met before and was friendly with, but after that weekend they forged their own friendship independent of her sister.

One night they ditched the sister and the three of us went out. Over the course of the night we became friendlier. At one point there was again an eruption, again a misperception. There was a woman I recognized. She was a bartender. I'd encountered her behind the bar at a couple different places in my time, she'd served me many a drink over the years, but this was the first time I could remember ever seeing her out from behind a bar enjoying herself as a customer. I was looking at this off-duty bartender, thinking this exact thought with a smile on my face because I was pleased to see her out enjoying herself instead of serving drinks, and bammo that's all it took.

She rushed out of the bar and I went after her, again having to mop up a ridiculous misunderstanding. Seeing me look in an-other woman's direction with a smile on my face meant I must surely be thinking impure thoughts. We were out on the street hashing it out for a long while, then I reminded her of her friend. She was in there alone, a stranger to the city, and when we walked out a creep was hitting on her. I said we should get back to her. She came to her senses, the tempest wound down, and we went back inside. Her friend was alright, but from then on for the rest of the night I was referred to by her friend as *the private eye*, because I was looking out for her. She seemed to appreciate it.

The friend knew a guy in town, had gone to school with him. They'd once had a little fling. They'd been in contact, and she'd slept with him the night before. The friend left us now to go meet this guy.

An hour later the friend called and wanted to join us again. We had just gotten over to my apartment. Shrader was out because the sister was there. Her friend came over and we were all in my room, and she told us what had happened. The guy was a jerk. When she arrived he was talking to another girl, big-headed and full of himself. She didn't understand it. What had happened to the sweet guy from the night before? She wasn't just some random chick he'd picked up and slept with, she said, they were friends, known each other for years, why would he do that? She was asking advice. As a male did I have some insight I could share?

I was stretched out on my bed, listening. The two of them were standing in the room. Suddenly the friend joined me on the bed, sitting down along my legs and looking into my face. She wanted to know what I had to say. I talked, but as I did I saw my girl's eyes as she watched from her place in the room. There was something in them, some secret fire. I saw it burning as she watched her friend with me on the bed. It wasn't anger, I didn't think, it was something else.

Soon she took her friend home to Shrader, and I went to sleep.

The next day, when she and I were alone, she asked: Did you think something was gonna happen when she sat with you on the bed? Did you think we were gonna have a threesome?

I admitted for a split second it did cross my mind. I mean, there was a silent undercurrent in that moment that seemed to conjure it. I didn't think it was actually going to happen, no, but the thought was there, sure.

Me too, she said.

She said when she saw her friend come to me on the bed that way she got very excited, and from that moment on she was consumed by the idea of having another woman join us. Our lovemaking sessions were flavored now with descriptions of what she wanted to do with her, our imaginary girl, and what she wanted me to do to them both. She'd lick and purr the words into my ear, and always her friend was the top choice to be the one; it was her face we held in the projection rooms of our minds as she spoke those words. But until that could be arranged, *if* that could be arranged, she often went to Craigslist for options. That's what she'd been doing—looking for a girl for us in Paris.

It was a strange turn because early on she'd said that she believed women only did that sort of thing to please their men, that no woman ever desired that of her own accord and free will. I did not agree, because I had personal experience here, but I didn't argue the point. Now she was proving my point for me.

As excited by the idea as I was, I was also wary. Destruction can steal in through these kinds of things. The one time this happened with my previous girlfriend led ultimately to our downfall. Once she got a taste of it, it seemed, she couldn't get enough.

It was at a New Year's Eve party, at a friend's apartment. We were on ecstasy. She and I were sitting in the kitchen alone, talking at the table. A girl came in. We had taken our hits a half hour ago and had just started feeling the warm fuzz invading our brains. The girl was on round two, I believe. Her eyes were black buttons, her dirty-blonde hair sweaty and plastered back along her head. Kneeling down before us at the table, this girl began caressing our hands and thighs. She wanted us to join her in the coat room, which was our friend's bedroom, to come lie with her on the bed piled with coats because it felt a*maz*ing. Sounded like an excellent idea to us, so we did.

The girl secretly led the way to the bedroom. We were like children sneaking off to play. We closed the door and lay on the bed in the dark, my girl on my left and the new girl on my right. It seemed obvious what was going to happen, but we needed a leader.

I took off my clothes, and there I was naked lying on a bunch of coats in the dark on the bed with two fully clothed girls, feeling great. What was their problem? Why did they still have their clothes on? Why was I the only one naked? I asked.

The girl took the cue and clothes started coming off. I decided to help. Now her sweater and jeans were off we needed to get that pesky bra out of the way, but unclasping it seemed way too much trouble. Rolling it up and over her head seemed best at the moment, so that's what I did. I started there with her boobs. They were big and the nipples fat. The girl took her panties off and I slid lower.

I'm glad I remembered to shave today, the girl said.

Though she seemed to have been enjoying it, my tongue was leather. I just didn't have any saliva. Nor was there any fluid flowing anywhere else I needed it. Ecstasy is not conducive to erections, at least not in this male. But I was doing my best to please. Suddenly though I remembered her beside me, watching, and how she'd been craving this exact opportunity. I knew she was attracted to women, she'd made that clear to me many times, but was still anxiously awaiting her first experience. So like a cat making room for another at the milk bowl I moved aside to let her in. Her clothes were off now as well, and she dove at her chance.

Oh, you're really good at that too, the girl said. Where'd you learn to do that?

There was a string of white Christmas lights in the room, which provided just enough visibility. I was watching perched behind her, the long red banner of her hair rippled in a smooth wave down her back, and muffled beneath it I heard her thin voice quaver through the darkness. Roman, she answered, and resumed between the split open thighs.

I felt flattered and proud. I remembered she did tell me once that no one had ever made her come that way before me. I was so happy for her now; her first time getting to try it herself...

Two nights later she decided to repeat the experience solo with a friend's wife, and then it became something else. Now it was a lurking danger to us. I didn't want to feel that again. Not again with this one. But she'd promised she was not a lesbian in waiting, she just wanted to experience this with me. She wanted this just with me. So until she could make it happen it was a nagging fantasy she carried and took out at night to let play with us.

Given time, she cooled off over the Craigslist thing and we resumed our love again, until the next time, which was when I took too long in the bathroom before coming to bed. I was flossing my teeth, and she got angry.

That's just not *sexy!* she said.

Because I was flossing my teeth?

Yeah. It's just not *sexy!*

I guess because we were in Paris I was supposed to want to come home and ravish her every night. But some nights I was just too tired. We walked all day long, and some nights I just wanted to hold her and go to sleep. I'd take care of her in the morning no problem, I'd promise, but can't we just hold each other some nights and go to sleep? I used to get criticism from other girlfriends for always needing to have so much sex, now here I was trying to be more loving with this one, because we needed to be able to do that too, and was being criticized for not fucking *enough!* I had begun getting the impression that she was only interested in the heights, and when things dipped below them she'd panic, sensing interest waning within herself, as if it signaled the end of passion. The night she got angry with me I just went to sleep. Moments later I woke to the bed shaking, but could not gather the energy to turn over and assist her. And what's more, this time I didn't want to.

The only other serious eruption I can remember happening was at the Musee d'Orsay.

We had planned our trip around a visit to the d'Orsay, to the James Ensor exhibit there. Like with the Picasso and Blake shows in New York, I'd read about this one too. A few months earlier the Metropolitan had hosted an exhibit on the Belgian painter, and I'd desperately wanted to go. But from New York the exhibit would be traveling to Paris in October, so we chose to skip the show at the Met and compose our trip to coincide with it in Paris. It was perfect. Finally the day came when we went.

But coming out of the Ensor show I somehow lost her, couldn't find her anywhere. I continued walking, exploring more of the museum, figuring I'd catch up with her just around the next bay. She must be just ahead of me around the next bay... Eventually, after looking in most of the rooms on my own, I doubled back, and finally there she was. I was so relieved. She looked particularly sexy that day, wearing a highnecked (almost like a turntleneck) rich purple, tight-fitting dress. It was short on her thighs, and she wore high leather boots. I took a picture of her shortly after I found her. She had just turned from looking at a painting, thick gold frame vertical along her face and dress, with the olive-green wall visible behind her too. Mixed with the purple of her dress and the green, the gold was striking against her, but her expression said it all. A gnarled thicket of prickly contempt sprouted in her eyes as their chill penetrated the camera lens. She was seething, as if I had purposely deserted her, and nothing I said made a difference.

Did she really think I wanted to wander that museum alone without her? Did she really think I wouldn't have preferred that to be a shared experience? How terribly mistaken she was. We walked together silently now. Or rather, obsequiously I followed the mistress.

Having already seen the wing we were walking, I occupied myself with taking photos of works that struck me as I trailed along. There was one particular sculpture ahead I wanted her to see, and it was coming up. I was hit as if by a velvet hammer when I discovered it. Meanwhile, we passed a painting I simply had to capture. Not for the greatness of the piece, but because what it evoked pierced my heart.

It was of a peasant woman standing with her back toward us waving farewell to a hot air balloon rising in the sky. The balloon was small in the background and ascending just off the woman's left open hand, as if she had released it herself. It reminded me of the candlelit lanterns she'd described floating away into the Thai night sky. I took a shot of that, a close-up on the hand and balloon. I brought her over and showed her, told her what it reminded me of. We hadn't spoken of it since that night, but it was there with us, silently, palpably pres-ent. A few days before when we'd walked through the Tuileries Gardens we stopped at a café in the middle of the park. It was too chilly to sit outside, so we had our wine and coffee at a table inside the round building. There was a family seated near us, a couple with two little girls, one of which was quite young—4 or 5. She was very cute, this little girl, with brown hair in a bushy ponytail spilling around her shoulders. She was playing at the entrance to the café, opening and closing the glass door to peek at us inside. I watched that little girl as she took her picture, and I started to cry. She took a picture of me then too, in close-up—my eyes only and the tears filling them. We did not speak.

We lit candles in nearly every church we went into, and there were many. The first candles we lit were at Notre Dame. She lit one and then I lit one while tears streamed down our cheeks. At Chartres Cathedral we lit two more, one in a red glass holder and one in blue, and she took a photo of them with the image of Christ in a red and blue stained glass window behind them, casting off Satan. Each time we lit candles we held each other but did not speak.

And here too standing at this painting, after I told her what it reminded me of we did not speak. A moment silently passed between us, and we walked on.

Then we came upon it, the sculpture I wanted her to see. It was carved from gray stone and lay low on a pedestal—a head of a woman with snakes for hair. It faced upward and lay with eyes closed, mouth slightly agape showing large teeth, the jaw lax with death, but the expression was almost ecstatic—and it was her. It was her face that lay there carved in stone, as if she had modeled for the piece two centuries earlier. It was her head lying there before us, a nest of snakes sprouting from her scalp and coiling about her, and even she thought so. I watched her stand there looking down at herself as if reflected in a cold gray pool and the resemblance was astonishing, absolute and undeniable, but I was insulted by the snakes. That was not her, I thought. That part was a mistake. And now I know it was not a mistake but a presentiment, prophesy right there before me. The snakes at the time simply had not hatched, but they soon came, and grew into their nastiness quickly. It was her face in stone lying there, forecasting my future, as I, ignorant to the portent, relished its meaning as benediction. It was ominous for sure, and I felt something turning over deep inside me at the sight of it, but I blindly chose to interpret it as a good sign. There before my eyes was the severed head of Medusa in the spitting image of my girlfriend, and it was a *good* sign?

We left the museum and had coffee at a café across the street, her temper eventually cooling as usual, and we recovered again soon enough after that. And aside from these few incidences we enjoyed the majority of our time in Paris—or so I believed. But maybe she never fully recovered from any of it after all, judging by what she'd said regarding that book of photos. Maybe she had simply held it all in and chose to ignore it, to make me believe otherwise, for my sake. Perhaps her letter would have provided some insight here had I gotten to read it.

When it was time to return to San Francisco I was very sad and did not want to go. In the cab on our way to the airport she saw how unhappy I was, how longingly I looked at Paris through the windows of the taxi as we left the city, and she took my hand.

We'll be back, she said. I promise.

We had one day to recover from our flight, Sunday, then right back to work. I was very depressed to be back. I felt my time in San Francisco had run its course and I was ready for something new, somewhere else. I loved San Francisco, but it was time for a change. I wanted that change to have something to do with Paris. She flew off to Florida to her company's other office and was gone for a few days. I didn't see her again until the weekend.

By the end of the week exhaustion set into my very marrow. Jet lag had caught up with me on top of the physically taxing workdays, and when Friday night came I wanted nothing but sleep. But as soon as I stepped through her door at Noe Street she was a whirlwind of action.

Come on, she said, get in the car.

For what?

It's a surprise. Come on, I've got us all packed. Get in the car.

No. I don't want to go anywhere.

Yeah ya do, come on. We're going.

Where we going?

I told you, it's a surprise.

I got in the car. She threw a carry-on in the trunk and we drove off. It was only about 5:30, but it was pitch black. I had no energy. *None.* My body had gone limp and my eyes sag-ged. I wasn't happy to be sitting in a car driving through Friday night traffic going anywhere. A bed! I just wanted a bed to crawl into. I sat there silent as she drove. Once we crossed the Golden Gate Bridge I figured it out, and now that I had I was twice as unhappy. An hour and a half of silence later and we were pulling into a parking spot in the little town of Sonoma—wine country. It was my birthday in five days and this was meant to be my surprise present apparently, a weekend in Napa Valley. She'd rented us a room in a bed and breakfast downtown Sonoma, across from the town square. We got out of the car and I followed her inside as she wheeled the bag. After settling in the room we went out to find somewhere to have dinner. There was a Mexican restaurant and we decided on that. I merely shrugged. Once seated I looked around the place, and my silence broke.

Why the *fuck* would you think I'd want to come here?

I looked at the faces crowding the surrounding tables. These people stank of self-righteous indulgence and unworthy self-entitlement, and I was frankly insulted she didn't know me better than to think I'd want to mingle among the likes of these fatuous, money-bloated fucks. Just because she could amply afford coming to places like this didn't mean I had to be dragged along.

It was the exhaustion talking, and I couldn't slap any reins on it.

Dinner passed miserably, and we went back to our room and straight to bed. It was densely black and very quiet in that over-stuffed room and I promptly fell into a long, hard sleep.

In the morning I woke refreshed, a new man ready to greet the day, then the memory of the night before hit and I was horri-fied at the things I'd said. I turned to her with profuse apologies. She wanted to leave.

I forgot, she said. You don't like surprises. I'll never do this again.

Eventually I convinced her to let us stay, explaining that I had badly needed sleep and now felt better, and since we were there let's enjoy it. We got up and dressed and left to find breakfast. It was a beautiful sunny day, and as soon as we walked outside and I saw where we were in the daylight I hugged her to me and apologized again. She was still very much upset.

In all my years in San Francisco I'd only been to Napa twice before, in the summer when it's terribly hot and the sun scorches the rolling hills sere yellow. I'd never really enjoyed it. But now, on this wonderful autumn day, the air was cool and the sun was warm and bright and balanced the temperature perfectly. The trees of the square were blazing with inferno reds and oranges, and the grass was topped with leaves curled into crunchy brown arthritic claws. I'd never actually been to the town of Sonoma before, and it was small and quaint and I liked the looks of it right off. I felt so bad about having thrown a fit the night before, but if I'd had some warning, just a little bit of information beforehand, a small hint, I know it would have gone much better. It was the abruptness of it, counter to my needs in the moment, and her stubborn reluctance to communicate that made my fatigued sensibilities react. I didn't even realize it was a birthday gift until that morning. I thought she was taking us because she simply wanted to go. Now I was ashamed and sorry, and had again put a strain unnecessarily upon us. Maybe I really *didn't* like surprises. Maybe I do need communication in advance when it comes to things like this. Was I that inflexible?

After breakfast we got in the car. Outside of town the vineyards were luminous with sunlight and the autumn change, and I'd never seen anything more beautiful than this. I loved driving through that scenery, the trees and the vines and the hills, it was an explosion of pure color all around us. After stopping at a couple wineries we were getting hungry for lunch. She drove to a barbeque place she knew outside of Calistoga, a ribshack roadhouse, and we decided to have a picnic. There was a plot of land down the road; I'd noticed it on the way to the barbeque place. I directed her back there after we got our food and she pulled the car over just beyond the red barn along the road. There was a house behind it, but to the left was a wide-open meadow with a view of mountainous hills way out in the distance. That's our spot, I'd said. We were on other people's property, but what was the harm? We got out and spread a blanket and had our feast, ribs and chicken and brisket and wine—we'd picked up a bottle or two at one of our stops. She had packed my brown herringbone hat from Paris and I sat wearing it as we ate. There was a shaggy white dog that wandered out to us, with rust spots around its eyes and speckles down its back. It liked us and the smell of the food and it lay beside our blanket with its tongue lolling out the side of its mouth.

There was way too much. The dog got a little, then she made a plate from the leftovers and walked up to the house to offer it to our unsuspecting hosts, to thank them for allowing us to squat unaccosted on their property. I played with the dog while she was gone. It took a little longer than it seemed it should, I began to worry. Then finally she was back.

What took so long?

Oh, they were so nice. It was an older couple, and when I came up they wanted to introduce me to their son. They said hold on, we want you to meet our son. So I had to talk to him. They were trying to fix us up, she laughed.

I only shook my head. Seemed the world was hellbent to take her from me.

From there we went to more wineries. She bought bottle after bottle. By the end of the day we had boxes of good wine to bring back with us to Noe, with more on order to be picked up in the spring when the new batches were ready. I was now very much looking forward to coming back with her to pick those up; I had such a great time with her there. We had discovered a hidden ranch that let out guest rooms. As we drove she noticed a sign along the road advertising freshly butchered meat. That piqued her interest. We turned around and pulled onto the long narrow gravel drive leading up to the white house in the distance. When we reached it we parked and got out of the car. There was no one in sight. The house was large and wonderfully old but in excellent shape and well maintained. We wandered around looking for someone. Finally we came upon a Mexican woman cleaning the rooms. She said the proprietors were not presently in, but feel free to wander about and look at the rooms and grounds. We did. We loved it. We sat on the porch swing and looked out onto the colorful hillside beyond the highway, languishing in the warm sunshine pouring down like honey upon the hills and us alike, and it was decided. This was where we'd stay on our next visit, when we came back for the wine on order. This was going to be our new place. But I wasn't to see it again.

A few days later on the morning of my birthday, upon waking

beside her in bed she handed me something. It was white and slender, about one foot by one foot in size. What was this? I slid the white cardboard slipcover off and there it was—the Paris book. There was the photo of us squatting beside the Seine with Notre Dame behind us on the cover. We'd taken that our last day by timer before we crossed Pont l'Archeveche into the Marias. I leafed through it and was overcome. When had she done this? While in Florida. She'd been staying up nights in her hotel room selecting images on her computer from our vast amount of pictures, assembling them into some kind of order. It wasn't perfect, she'd said, she'd wished she'd had more time to choose and juxtapose the images better, but she had to do it quickly if it was going to be ready by my birthday. Then she sent it off to get printed, hoping it would arrive in time. Luckily it came the day before, and she hid it under the bed to surprise me with this morning. I was amazed. I couldn't stop looking at it. And then she handed me something else, another smaller book. Paperback this time, thin, but also something she'd made. Something else I can no longer bear to look at. It was entitled *Our Own Paris: a delicious production*, and had her picture on the cover stretching across it in a sexy pink nightie. She was on the couch from the living room of the rue St. Julien apartment, I recognized it. Now what was this? I flipped through it. They were pictures of her, taken herself in the bedroom on the bed. Pin-up style photos. She was wearing pink and black corset-like lingerie, with garters and stockings and no panties. She posed with her legs scissored up in the air on the bed. She posed kneeling on the bed. She posed spread and crouching on the bed. She posed lying across the bed, on her side, and on her bottom, with her legs stretched out and crossed. She posed sitting and standing on the bed. She posed standing up beside the bed. And it was all for me, all while staring straight into the camera as if looking right at me with that fuck me face she wore. She had done that, secretly taken those pictures of herself in Paris for me, before I came in to her. And I went to her now as she lay beside me, made love to her fiercely. Oh how I loved her. There was a card along with what she gave me. The back of the envelope simply read, *My Man*. The card said: *I consider myself lucky to be able to spend this special day with you. I send you luck and love for your 44th year to be filled with bliss.*

I didn't leave the apartment until early evening after the night with Christophe. Eventually I decided to take a walk. I wandered the backside of the islands, then crossed over again to the Marais. I headed for the church Christophe and I had stopped in the night before—St. Gervais St. Protais it was called I learned. I wanted to see it in the daylight.

I entered, and again there was a service in progress. The smell of thick incense permeated the air. Gold and lavender light projected through the stained glass high above angling down in broad piers of color over the heads of the congregation. I took a seat in a chair to the back and to the left of the alter. The alter faced away from the entrance, I'd never seen that before in any church, and the priest was up there speaking to those seated in chairs facing him. It was Friday evening, and about half the chairs in front of the alter were filled, but the ones on the side where I sat were empty. I listened. The priest's voice echoed through the church and I liked the sound of it, and unable to understand a word he was saying that's all it was to me of course, sound. Something about that voice though brought it on. It was comforting in some way; permission for sadness rang through it. I sat doubled over in my chair listening, hiding my face in my hands as heavy splashes and strings of snot hit the cold stone at my feet. All day I couldn't get the thought of that letter out of my head. It burrowed into me and ate at my brain. What had she said in that letter? Why would she never tell me what she had written? Emptiness set inside me with disgusting, unbearable anguish.

When the priest finished speaking a pipe organ played, and there was singing. It was very beautiful and I sat up to listen, and the melt ran savage now down the clear fall of my face. Those in attendance sang. They were mostly women, and their voices were lovely and resonant, wringing my heart to hear. There were many nuns out there, sisters of whatever order that church represents, wound in thin white cotton from their hair all the way down to their sandaled feet. They stood before their chairs as they sang and I hung my head with sad pleasure listening. When they finished they sat down and the priest spoke again. I looked at them through blurred swampy eyes as they sat listening attentively. I listened too, to the wonderful sound that priest's voice was making, until my eyes dried some and I felt ready to leave. I knew what was coming next and I didn't want to stay for it.

At the part of the mass where people shake hands and wish one another peace, I got up and slowly made my way out. On my way, I paused at the rear of the church where there was a niche alter to Mary. Two women prayed there. One stood motionless, swaying slightly as if inwardly transported. The other was on her knees, bent all the way over with her face and hands in front of her touching the floor, completely prostrate before the alter and the statue poised upon it. I stood there looking at this woman, thinking that's how I should be praying, with all my being, praying with all myself for this pain inside me to go away. And as I was looking at this woman thinking this, feeling the pain twisting, grinding in my guts, just then a sister came walking up and took my hands. She was thin and about my height, swaddled completely in white, neither young nor old as she stood before me, eyes gentle, radiant with exquisite sympathy. Taking both my hands, sheltering them in her warm, tender palms, she gazed oh so softly into my face while quietly extending French offerings of peace.

Had she seen me crying in my chair, I wondered, and left her seat to walk all the way back here, to offer me her hand? I felt the sadness brimming as I looked into her face, thinking of her doing that, the compassion and kindness of that, and the dam almost broke again.

As if yanked from my tonsils the words tumbled out in a soft jagged choke, and stupidly I spoke them in English, or attempted to anyway.

'*An*—ankqu, I stammered, but the sentiment couldn't have been more genuine. I wanted to kiss her feet.

She gave my hands a gentle, final little bounce while still holding me in the steady charity of her gaze, then released them finally to greet the other supplicants inside the niche. I watched her slowly approach first one woman, then the other, but seeing how involved each was in their own prayers left them both undisturbed in the end and turned again for her seat. I left the church then.

On my way back across the river I passed my café on the island and stopped to drink there for two hours. There was a girl working I'd never seen before, her first night. She had tattoos and a silver hoop through her thick lower lip. Her lips were full and lush as overripe fruit and I wanted to suck them. She wore a black tank top and her skin looked so smooth, pure as glass, I wanted to glide my tongue along it in search of any flaw, seek out any small imperfection it might be hiding. I wanted to sink my teeth into it, leave my mark upon it, to feel between my jaws the spring of flesh incased within it. She was brunette with deep smoldering brown eyes and she wore dark-rimmed glasses and let her hair hang loose along the sides of her face down to the dull shine of her bare shoulders and I had a crush on her instantly. Her name was Sarah. Another Sarah. As expected the one from the river was never heard from again, and now with three days left in Paris it doesn't matter anyway. This was the first French girl in Paris I'd seen with tattoos and piercings. It's been so pleasant that way, so refreshing to see the bodies of women unadorned like that. It's not a style I'm particularly attracted to, but to see it on this girl now it caught my eye and reminded me of San Francisco, where ink is rampant on skin like contagion. Not that I wanted to be reminded of San Francisco, but I found it didn't bother me to be. I stood there at the bar getting drunk and flirting with this girl as she filled and refilled my glass, and though I knew better I thought she was flirting back. When I asked if she'd like to join me when she got off work she said no. She was going to drink with her friends.

There's a flower shop on 18th Street halfway between my place and where she stayed on Noe. She made a comment once while at Shrader: she felt I didn't bring her flowers often enough. Now I had no excuse. I wasn't going to let a little thing like buying flowers shake my relationship. If my baby wanted flowers, flowers she shall get. I had them for her now each time she returned to San Francisco. Since moving onto Noe Street I'd probably given her six or seven batches of fresh flowers. I enjoyed choosing them, trying to get something different each time. I'd smile with them in my hand while walking down the street to her place. If she was already there I'd present them to her directly when she greeted me at the door, or carry them inside to her. If she wasn't I'd have them waiting for her in the vase we kept in the kitchen on the granite bar.

Sometimes the flowers would overlap. Sometimes I'd bring more while the ones already in the vase still had life to them. Another vase was found for these, which sat in the center of the big round table, so we could enjoy what was left of their remaining days. At any given time, chances were two bouquets brightened that kitchen.

As good as it made me feel I was casual about it, played it cool. Oh these ol' weeds? Just something I picked up along the way. My smile would betray me though, and the way I'd try to arrange them so they worked best in the vase. I loved bringing her flowers, loved having someone to bring flowers to.

My new year started out promising. Thanksgiving came the week following my birthday and we cooked dinner together in her kitchen, the two of us. There was another card from her. I'd never gotten a card on Thanksgiving. A lot had happened all at once—returning from Paris, and everything that preceded that trip, then Sonoma, my birthday, now Thanksgiving. We had been celebrating a lot during the two weeks since our return. She referenced that in her card, that we'd been celebrating Thanksgiving almost every night after my birthday, drinking the good wine we'd brought back from Napa, making dinners. But still she couldn't help wanting to be with me on the actual day, her card said.

Let's face it, I simply can't help wanting to be with you any night of the year. Thank you for being such a wonderful part of my life. Thank you for showing me a part of life that I had forgotten existed.   *All my love, ...*

Did your letter come from Paris?

It was the second time she'd asked now.

No, I said. I've been looking for it but it hasn't come. What did you write me?

I told you, she said, I'm not gonna tell you. You'll have to wait till it comes to find out.

Then it was December. The letter still had not come and she stopped asking, and I'd given it up for lost. By the end of December everything changed. Still though, it began well enough.

December marked one year that we'd been together. The anniversary of our first date was coming up, in the middle of the month. Before that, though, her friend came to visit from LA and stayed with us at Noe.

I hadn't seen her friend since July, but she had spent Labor Day weekend in Los Angeles and stayed with her friend down there then. That's when I'd gone back to Illinois to visit my family, that weekend. I remember she picked me up from the airport when I got back. It was Monday, the actual holiday, and the weather was gorgeous. We decided to have a picnic. She had a blanket in the trunk of the Prius. We picked up some food and drove across the Golden Gate. I knew a spot I hadn't been to in a long time just on the other side of the bridge on a cliff overlooking the bay. We spread the blanket, ate the food. We were all alone, and the water beyond the cliff was deep blue. As I stretched back on the blanket looking out at the water, she took my cock out and started having her way with it. Then some people passed and she made it look good, shielding my exposure with her hair and head as she lay across my abdomen. The people took their time looking at the view. We lay there waiting. When we were alone again she lifted her skirt and squatted over me backwards. I looked at the beautiful blue of the water surrounding her while she feverishly bounced.

She came back from LA with even greater desire for her friend to enter our bed. The plan had been for her to subtly raise the question while in LA, to flush out whatever sense she could about it, how receptive her friend might be to the idea. But this type of thing can be a delicate matter, and in the end she didn't know how to go about it. She returned to San Francisco though with determined vigor and I reaped the benefits of that.

And now her friend was coming to San Francisco, to us. She was very excited.

Her friend arrived Friday evening. When I got to Noe after work, after having stopped at my place to shower and change, all the lights in the apartment were on but she wasn't home. I poured myself a glass of wine and waited. Finally she came in rolling a carry-on. She and her friend were at Twin Peaks, a bar around the corner on Castro and 17th. They had met at the train station, which is across the street from the bar, and decided to stop there first. She brought her friend's bag over to get it out of the way while her friend sat with their drinks. From there we were all going to dinner. I walked back to the bar with her.

They already had a couple rounds in them. I ordered one now myself, my usual beer and tequila, and tried to bring my energy up to meet theirs. It was the end of the workweek, which meant fatigue for me. The job had been slowly ramping in intensity, and we'd been at the reinstallation now nine months. I was coming home to her at the end of each day beat, with energy for very little after dinner and a shower. I spent most nights drinking wine in front of the TV.

I have a problem with TV. If one's around I'll watch it. That's why I don't own one, haven't for years, because I've recognized this in myself. I get sucked in to full distraction if I don't have anything else to do. I'd been living with very little inspiration and creative activity, except for the odd song I'd write now and then. With her in my life, that had been happening a little more. I wrote a number of songs over the year we'd been together, but presently I had nothing, and no energy to muster toward it. I let myself drift into the flat screen at night. Soon I was aware of the times and channels of certain favorite shows and rerun episodes. It'd become somewhat of an issue. One night when I finally shut the thing off and headed to bed she was sitting up under the covers and glared at me as I entered. She'd been doing her own thing all evening elsewhere in the apartment and I'd given her space to do that, allowing her time at home apart from me without expecting inclusion. But it was too much space for her. She'd taken a bath, I was aware of that because I'd heard the tub water running, but then I didn't see or hear from her again until I was turning in; she hadn't come out to say good-night.

When your girlfriend takes a bath, she said, and is waiting for you to come to bed, you should shut the fucking *TV* off and come to *bed!*

I didn't know you were waiting for me!

You knew I was taking a *bath!* was her answer, as if that should've been clue enough.

I do *not* want to become comfortable that way, she said, with you sitting out there watching TV and me in here. I do *not* want that.

I said I was sorry and climbed in then and tried to touch her, but it'd been ruined.

So far now my energy was fine. The girls were laughing and chatting and having fun. Her friend had a sultry, natural sexiness with coloring I like: brown hair brown eyes. I was attracted to her right away the first time we met, and I liked her, she was open and nice—but I loved my girl. Her friend certainly turned me on well enough to want to do this if she did, but the difference between them was vast. I didn't want anything to happen here if it was going to hurt us in any way. I knew how she felt about it, but it was not as important to me, not enough to hurt us over. I felt like I'd made that clear to her.

Soon we were all hungry, so we left for dinner. Over the hill on Castro Street in Noe Valley, just past 24th Street, was a very good Spanish tapas place we'd discovered a few months earlier. It was just a short cab ride away and we took her friend there now.

The restaurant was busy, had to wait for a table, and while we stood waiting we finished a bottle of red wine between us. Finally our table opened and we sat. With dinner we had another bottle of wine, topped off with a glass each of cava.

Now we were very high and the energy flowed. After dinner the night was still young and we wanted more drinks. We got in another cab and headed back over the big hill to Lucky 13, just two blocks from her place on Noe. Two more rounds here, which meant two more beers and shots of tequila for me, I didn't think it'd be a problem, and now things began to get interesting.

We were all having fun together, but there was still no clear indication if what we had in mind may come about or not, though the more we drank the closer I think we all felt we were getting to it.

At Lucky 13 we were sitting at the far end of the long bar, me between the girls—she on my right and her friend on the left. For some reason we, me and the friend, were both looking at her. She was sitting there looking sexy in the red and white reflected light shining on her. We both commented on her beauty. She was wearing a soft white sweater. It was thin and high around her throat and clung closely to her form, absorbing the red light. Her breasts hung prominently through it, though thoroughly covered behind it. They looked as if inviting hands to caress them in the soft cloth, and now her friend was inspired to do so. But just as her friend began reaching across me, reaching with both hands for her, a guy approached, and the reaching stopped.

This was the jerk the friend left us for last time. In between visits they'd made amends. He was aware she was in town, they'd been texting while at dinner, and he'd asked our plans afterwards. She told him, but had not invited him. To everyone's surprise he came in now looking for her. Seeing him brought everything to a screeching end. The reaching hands drew suddenly back.

He sat down on a stool and they talked. She and I made faces at each other. So close, we thought. We were encouraged now though—now we knew. But this guy...we hated him. So arrogant, so smarmy, just showing up here all on his own...We felt the night was over now, that her friend would leave with him and our chance had been spoiled.

But wait. Suddenly the guy was getting up and walking out. Was he leaving or going to the restroom? He was leaving, her friend said. He had asked her to come home with him but she refused. She was coming home with us.

We finished our drinks and walked up to Noe.

We opened a bottle of sparkling wine, one of the two we'd brought back from Napa.

Let's get in the hot tub! she suggested.

What a great idea! the friend and I responded.

I went down and got the tub ready. It was cold and drizzling, but the gazebo was just a few steps from the bottom of the stairs and the tub was enclosed. I folded back the padded lid and pushed the buttons. The jets churned the water and the lights embedded in the blue walls of the tub went on. The water quickly began heating up. Steam rose in the light. I went back upstairs and poured more wine. It churned in my glass like the water in the hot tub. I brought it down. The girls were getting ready. In the darkness beside the tub I took off my clothes. I saw no reason for any at all. I sat on the edge of the tub. I was excited but you couldn't tell. All the alcohol in my blood was getting in the way. I gave myself some pumps. I worked frantically at it in the dark on the edge of the tub. Nothing was happening. It was a noodle. I heard the girls coming and got in the water. They had their glasses and the bottle with them. They were wearing bikinis and carrying towels. Why were they wearing bikinis? I wondered. The girls stepped into the tub and she and I moved close together. Under the water I held her round her thin waist and pressed into her. Still nothing, no life at all. We drank the wine and laughed. Then she and I started get-ting a little serious, grinding in the bubbling water. Suddenly though, her friend coming into awareness, we restrained ourselves.

It's OK, her friend said. You guys do your thing.

We continued, kissing and rocking in the water as her friend soaked watching. She turned her back to me and I pushed into her, holding myself tightly against her. Her top untied now, and I cupped her breasts in my hands. Still I felt nothing. I was getting worried. She sensed something was wrong. We separated a little and drank from our glasses, and relaxed in the hot jetting water.

Finally we got out of the tub, it was getting late and the wine was gone. I came out first, and now my nakedness was apparent. It was a snail between my legs. Her top had been tied back on, and the girls climbed out. They collected our glasses and the bottle and wrapped themselves in the towels they'd brought and went upstairs while I turned off the tub and closed the lid. I gathered my clothes and, wet and naked and shivering in the cold rain, climbed the stairs and went through the open sliding glass into the kitchen, sliding the door closed behind me.

The door to the bathroom was open and the light was on. I saw it was free. Quickly but careful so my wet feet would not slip as I stepped across on the hardwood floor I went in to take a shower. Soaped and twisting in the warm water I thought of the girls, and the anxiety built. I thought of them some more, two beautiful girls out there. We still didn't know what was going to happen, but it looked good, I wanted to be ready. I pumped myself again, flailing and flailing in the water's spray, hoping the warmth would get the blood moving. But the more I worked the more anxious I became with lack of success.

I got out and dried off, put on my robe. Then the girls took turns showering.

It still wasn't clear what to do from here. The bedside lamp was on but I went into the living room and curled up in the dark on the big curved sofa. I must've drifted off a little because the next thing I knew she was coming out to get me.

That's silly, she said. We can all sleep in here together.

The light was out in the bedroom now and I climbed onto the

bed after her. She was in the middle and her friend was to her left. We all lay spooned together on our left sides, one little family. I still had my robe on, so did she. My arm was draped over her and I could feel the fuzzy cloth. The three of us lay still and quiet that way for a moment until tolerance for that left me. Someone had to make a move, we were all waiting. Like last time, a leader was required. I reached over then and rubbed the ass in front of her. It was round and full and clad in flannel.

With a giggle her friend asked her if she was touching her butt. That giggle told everything.

In the darkness I answered.

Yes, I said, she is.

And that's all it took. Her friend spun round and they embraced and pajamas and robes were coming off and covers were being thrown back. The friend was the aggressor, had her on her back, clearly no stranger to this. I knelt in the darkness and watched from the top of the bed, from the pillows, listening to the familiar yelps and squeals I knew so well, only this time it was not me causing those yelps, those squeals, it was not my tongue and fingers working them out of her but those of another, and that is an odd sensation, listening to your lover emit the same sounds with someone else that she does while with you. In that moment you realize almost anyone can be your lover's lover, make her feel the way you make her feel, and you are not irreplaceable or special after all but hinge upon a decision, her decision, as to who will be the one she will allow to make her feel that way. And here it was, her moment, and I watched the best I could in the darkness but could see only dark wiggling shapes. For me then it was only an auditory experience, and that wasn't good enough. The pleasure of this was in seeing, but I could not see.

I got up and twisted open the slats of the mini blinds, but it was a dark night. Very little light came in. I still couldn't see in detail, but I'd have to make do with this.

The friend was propped on her knees with her head buried low, that much I could make out, hoisting the plump furrow high toward me in the darkness. Sliding headfirst on my back I crept in now between the splayed thighs, like shimmying under a car. My palms formed themselves to the wide sensuous curves smothering my head and snoutwise I prowled upward to the scented treasure. Again, like last time, it was all I could offer. There was some slight shifting of positions, but I got a little lost in them and mainly remained where I began. I ached to contribute more, but it was no use.

It wasn't transpiring exactly as she'd fantasized, the things she'd been purring into my ear over the past months weren't happening as she described them, but I hoped she was finding her pleasure all the same.

There was a break, and then another round, but not like before. Now I did have some power, half a charge maybe but some juice was moving through me, and I was able to slip inside her while simultaneously touching her friend. I sprawled behind her while she lay on her belly and tongued the breasts that lay near her head. But this didn't last, and it didn't seem too thrilling to either of them. We gave it up and lay still on the bed. I sensed something in her, in maybe both of them, but particularly in her. I was a little afraid and embarrassed then.

Suddenly the friend got up and left the room. We heard her go into the bathroom, and when she came back she gathered something from the floor and left the room again without speaking. When we heard the living room door quietly close, I turned to her.

Don't touch me, she said.

What?

I'm your girlfriend. You should have been paying more attention to *me*.

I knew it, I said. I knew we shouldn't have done this. I told you I didn't want to do this if it was gonna cause a problem.

Did you fuck her?

No, I didn't. But you seemed to be pretty well occupied. I was just finding room where I could. I thought you wanted to be mostly with her anyway.

We lay arguing this way until the iron light of dawn slid through the blinds, then we made love with our usual fervor. And I hoped the sound of it went though the wall into the living room to revoke any question remaining in the mind of her friend, as it created this one in mine: why could this not have happened just an hour earlier?

We slept late into the morning, and then I left. As I passed the living room the door was ajar and I could see her friend lying on the couch with something over her eyes, a piece of clothing. I hoped there was not going to be any strangeness now, between any of us, but especially between them.

Christmas was coming, and later that afternoon while at home I began thinking about a gift for her. I remembered Cirque du Soleil was in town. I thought she'd like that. I was online looking at seats and pricing when she called.

Would you like to go to Cirque du Soleil? she asked.

I was just about to buy tickets, I told her. I'm online now. How'd you know?

Turned out she wanted to go that weekend, the following night while her friend was with us, and she bought the tickets. Great, but that still left me with the problem of what to get her for Christmas. And her birthday was coming, the beginning of January. I had to come up with something for that, too. She'd already reserved the cabin in Big Sur for that weekend, as well as for Valentine's Day. I thought going twice in two months was overdoing it; I didn't want to wear the place out. I mean, I was glad she loved it enough to want to do that, but I felt it was a little much. Still though, that was her present to herself. I had to come up with my own present to her.

I saw her later that night at Noe. We stayed in, just the two of us. Her friend decided to stay with her guy friend that night.

Was there anything wrong? I'd asked. Was her friend upset about anything? Why did she leave the bedroom like that?

She had just wanted to sleep, she'd said, and thought it would be more restful out in the living room. She was not upset or uncomfortable, but very hungover. She just wanted to be with her friend that night, and would join us tomorrow.

The following day the three of us went to brunch, and then to Cirque du Soleil, and dinner afterwards, and we all had a good time. The girls laughed and carried on as I'd seen before and it was as if nothing had ever happened, we had not had our fingers and tongues in each others' orifices and elsewhere on our bodies two nights before and made sounds of pleasure from it in the dark, and I marveled to see in them the ability of women to seemingly do this so easily, the ability to forget and pretend, to move between sexes and back again, to give and receive and let go as if it did not happen but in their minds and hearts know it did…After her friend left she said to me: Maybe you *should* carry condoms in your bag…

A week and a half later was what we called our anniversary. And here is where all detail of memory drops away. Only the framework and sensation of things that night remain in my mind.

Although she maintained that the first time we went to dinner at the German restaurant was not a date, that our actual first date happened a couple nights later, she allowed the date of our first dinner together to be deemed our anniversary. We planned to return to the same restaurant for the occasion.

I arrived after work, to Noe. Maybe I brought flowers, per-haps I didn't. I don't recall. I remember being very excited and happy though to come home to her on this special night.

There was a card. As soon as I saw it I recognized my blun-der. *Shit.* I should've gotten a card!

I just didn't think that way. I'd been alone for so long the concept of cards just didn't enter into my mind, and I'd never received so many cards from anyone since I was very young. I'm sure she was disappointed I didn't have one for her.

It was on the dresser when I entered the bedroom. I opened it. Writing covered both inner sides. *Can you still crumble*, it began, *after the world's turned you to slate?*

She was quoting me, from a song I'd written while she was living at the Ashbury Heights apartment. I remember the Saturday morning when I came up with that line. There was a light rain outside, and we were relaxing together into the afternoon inside. I was at the small table in the window with my notebook, going over some lyrics I'd been working on. I don't know why I still did this, try to write songs. I had no band, or prospects of creating one, but I still desired to make music. Writing lyrics had been the way my creativity manifested for years, and although I longed to get back to work on other things, writing prose again, I even wanted to try a screenplay, my words were still coming out as lyrics and melody. When I stumbled upon that line I was stuck with adding to this one:

Sympathetic as I am to the blade
The question remains, can true love come too late?
Can what you've been waiting for arrive past its date?

Then it came to me.

Can you still crumble after the world's turned you to slate?

I was very excited when I came up with that, and I read it back to her. It said so much, I thought, about myself, about growing older, heartbroken and jaded in the wasteland, longing for real love again but wondering if I'd suffered too much to really give over to it when, *if* it arrived, and now it had. It was about her having come into my life.

The words had apparently struck a chord with her, too. In the card she went on to say that she found herself crumbling more each day. That the walls she'd built around herself were turning to dust, and she wondered how I'd done it. How had I taken everything that had seemed fine before and showed her how empty it was? She thanked Fate, *or um Jari* (she'd written that in parentheses and drawn a line through it as a joke) for bringing us together. I can't remember it all, but it was a very beautiful card. That we both had walls fallen before the other was a sweet revelation…

After cleaning up and changing we took a cab to the restaurant in Hayes Valley. It was our special night, and I held her close. I opened the door for her, and then I saw the squirming crowd inside.

It was usually busy, but tonight it was unusually so, more than I'd seen it. Instinct told me we should leave, go somewhere else, but here was where we wanted to relive our night a year ago, so we stayed. The restaurant does not take reservations for parties under six; we put our name on the list with the hostess and moved toward our usual spot.

We liked to sit at the open window at the backside of the bar, in the dark nook. It was like being in a candlelit cabin, and if you didn't sit at the bar it was too dark, too secluded, like eating dinner under punishment with your nose in the corner. But if you sat at the bar it was intimate, removed from the main room crowd while still facing it. They were the best seats in the house as far as we were concerned, but those seats were taken and people stood jamming the space, leaving no room at all back there.

The noise in the restaurant was deafening, and maybe it had something to do with my time in the band but my ears are sensitive to loud sound. You might think it would work the opposite way, that my ears would've become used to volume, but it's not the case for me.

It was three deep around the remaining sides of the bar, with hands and arms reaching and bodies blocking and shifting and voices rising ever higher to be heard over the increasing noise. My nerves were shattering, exacerbated by hunger, and anger mounted. This place was a favorite of mine, and it's always been popular, but lately, along with many other favored places in San Francisco, I saw this one too steadily being overtaken and ruined by a new and wrong crowd. The post-collegiate professionals had recently found it. Word had gone out on the good German beer selection, and they'd discovered you could get a two liter glass boot of beer, something meant to be shared amongst a group, but they wanted to drink it all to themselves individually because nowhere else could you get that much beer all at once, and their eyes and drunken appetites popped for it. These were the people surrounding us now, glutting and exploiting our restaurant.

Over the months we'd been in many times together, mostly for Sunday brunch. It was busy then too, but much less frantic than dinner. I preferred it then. I started going regularly during the wasteland years, alone. Then I brought her and it became a favorite place for both of us. When she was out of town I'd still go on my own, and sit lonely beneath the mass of tin swallows suspended overhead like toy gliders. They hang decorously on wire from the ceiling in ever-shifting whimsical configurations, rearranged differently with each changing season, and under their static, playful flights I'd watch the Sunday lovers come straggling in fresh from bed. God, you could almost smell it on them. I had told her about that, how I'd sit there and watch the young lovers come in, how jealous and sad I'd be watching them alone without her.

She saw what was happening; she knew I didn't do well in the kind of energy we were now snared in. We stood waiting in the swirl of it for seats to open, struggling to order beers over the backs in front of us. Finally I got them, but I was becoming unglued.

We began trying to talk through the din. I remember nothing of what was said, no words whatsoever, I only remember the contrariness. You could fill it in yourself. Whatever I said she said the opposite. Down. Up. Red. Green. Out. In. No matter what I said my words were met with rejection and condescension, as if she were doing it willfully. It started to build in me, everything. The noise and chaos of that restaurant was drawing it all up like a big festering blackhead, all the things that worked at me below the surface of my mind. Her annoying way of always having to be right and you were the idiot to ever think otherwise, that was implied in the big smile she'd shine at you, which was part of her way of controlling you, along with her overgenerosity, it was her way of staying on top, having the power, expressing superiority, and the resentment of this was emerging without my even knowing what it was that was emerging. And the frustration with her constant absence, that was coming out too, all the loneliness I still felt while with her while at the same time feeling like her dirty little secret, knowing that no one close to her knew I even breathed and moved upon the earth, no one in her family, her sisters with whom she was so close, the sisters I'd heard so much so regularly of I felt I'd met personally, knew intimately, *they* didn't know, no friends, other than the one in LA and Jari of course, but no others in Chicago had ever heard of me. And then, on the deepest level of all, so deep it dare not come out of the shadow-depths it inhabited for the grotesque disfigurement it was, hidden but impossible to ignore was the loss, the insurmountable loss we had caused but never again spoke of, and the horrible pain and guilt of it so deep and so profound I hardly knew it was there, yet it was felt every day, lurking in me like some monster thing…All this was coming forward now by the time we climbed into our usual seats at the bar, she had somehow maneuvered us there, but it was too late. Our night, our special night and the life of it was about to die; it was being killed and we both knew it. We couldn't talk without disagreeing so we stopped trying all together and silently sat chewing over our plates, swallowed up in the roar lifting all about us.

I loved her. I knew I did. But a dark burrowing crested the surface that night and was demanding to be seen, to be heard, and I couldn't explain it. Was any of this real? The question was unformed, I could not hear the words, they were not yet distinct, but I knew they were there, just like the other monster thing, I could feel them somehow, as if inflating into me, these words, this question, it came from the blackest depths and wanted to know—was any of this life with her really real?

We left the restaurant in crushing silence. As we walked, a tentative suggestion was made by someone—odds are it was me but it might've been her—that we stop for a glass of wine on our way home. Over our wine there was more silence, and the damage of what just occurred was beginning to sink in. As much as I wanted to I could not explain what had happened. I'd open my mouth to speak but nothing would come, so I'd close it again. I felt horrible, like it was all my fault, but I knew there was so much that went into it, that created and fed the beast that'd just consumed us, so much I couldn't begin to explain, and it was useless even to try.

Yet when we got home I begged her forgiveness. It was just a bad night. The crowd. The noise. It drove me out of my mind. And my empty stomach. Low blood sugar. You know how I get.

She was quiet but forgave me, said we'd try again, and I was so grateful. I loved her even more for that. That wasn't our real anniversary anyway, she said. Two nights later we'd made reservations at the French bistro we liked, a few blocks down Noe Street. It was Saturday, and we had spent the day together shopping, wandering. We got back to Noe a little late. She said it was going to take a while to get ready. I sat with a glass of wine in the living room waiting, watching TV. She came in. It was getting later. She had not begun to get ready. I stood up and held her. She wanted me to go ahead to the restaurant so we wouldn't lose our reservation. I preferred to wait at home for her, but she wanted me to go, and bring a bottle of wine with me. I chose one of the old growth zinfandels that we had left from Napa. The store of bottles we'd brought back was almost depleted now, thanks mostly to me. She came into my arms again in the living room.

Don't hurt me, she said.

I kissed her and looked into her eyes. I saw the vulnerability in her face, heard it in her voice, and it pained me, but I didn't understand. I heard her say those words, but it was obvious that I was the one here who was going to be hurt if anyone. I'd known it all along.

I won't hurt you baby, I said, and held her to me. I took the bottle and walked down to the restaurant.

The last time we had eaten at the bistro we sat at a table, and we had said that the next time we come we were going to try it at the bar instead. Seemed a little less stuffy there, more relaxed. That's where we'd reserved to sit and that's where I sat now.

The waiter uncorked the bottle, filled my glass to half, and set the wine in front of me. The wine glass was large. I sipped from it and waited. My seat was right in front of the kitchen window. I watched the plates come out and transported to tables. The waiter swung by me constantly carrying them, and nearly each time he came back he'd pour a little more wine into my glass. I was only sipping, and slowly, but she was taking a long time, 30 minutes, 45 maybe, and now the bottle was getting low. The waiter came and tried to pour a little more.

Hey hold on! I said, capping the glass with my hand. Leave some for my girl.

The bottle was more than half gone, and I was on an empty stomach. By the time she arrived I was accidentally drunk. She saw it and got angry. The waiter, I explained, he wouldn't stop pouring. It wasn't my fault, I protested. I didn't mean to drink so much.

That's their *job* Roman. They're *trained* to pour like that. The ratio you take out of the glass matches what they put in. You realize that, right?

There it was again, that condescending tone.

But no, I continued to explain, I was only *sipping*. Every time he walked by he poured more in, even when the glass was here...

I showed her with my finger on the glass.

...and there didn't need to be anymore poured in. And you took so *long*, I said. I was by myself with nothing to do. I kept sipping.

She would not be dissuaded or appeased, and that superior tone kept coming, it set off something inside me, and now my anger began rising to hers, and I had done it again. She had given me a second chance and I had blown it. And again I couldn't explain it. What had happened? How could I have lost sight of the importance of that night and *let* it happen? I was given a second chance, and there are only so many chances you are allowed, and I knew that while again we silently left the restaurant and walked back to the apartment. We sat in the darkened living room. The anger would not fade in her.

It was an accident, an *accident*, I pleaded. *Please!*

She was leaving for Florida the next day, for the rest of the workweek, and from there she was flying to Chicago to spend Christmas with her family. Originally she said she'd come back Christmas Day, but she didn't know now. She'd let me know. And I was going to be alone again, alone on Christmas again, though this year I had someone, I was going to be on my own yet again. She left, quiet, distant, changed.

I knew I had to do something, something extra special to

make it up to her, if I could. I wracked my brain for what to get her as a Christmas gift. It had to be something great. But there was nothing I could afford to get her that she couldn't get 10 times better for herself. Then I had it—I hoped.

The set list! The Leonard Cohen set list!

We had intended to get it framed, but over the months it'd been sitting in my room collecting dust. Because she moved so frequently, in order to keep it safe, I took it home with me, where it sat, not forgotten, but patiently waiting out of harm's way.

The day she left I took it to a frame shop. There were only five days before Christmas, and I didn't know if there was enough time. I worked with the clerk choosing the matting and molding for the frame. The molding would have to be special ordered, but he said he thought it would come in time. I spared no expense. I chose a wine red matte beneath a dusky blue one, a double matte. There was a symbol floating in the white of the list, to the side of the printed titles of the songs—an open hand in a circle—and it was in these colors, red and blue. I pulled on them to surround the rest of the white sheet. The frame was simple but elegant, to reflect the elegance of Leonard Cohen's music and what we saw in him during his performances. It was black, about two inches wide, with an arabesque design raised in it. There was a thin red line that ran along the inner lip, which tied in with the red of the matting. I thought it worked really well. Last was the glass, museum quality plexi that showed no glare and was almost invisible. It was the premium choice. In all it came to nearly $300, but I didn't care. That was only little more than the price of just *one* of those tickets she'd bought for me.

Thursday morning, Christmas Eve, I got a call while at work saying that it was ready. I only worked a half day that day and picked it up on my way home. Later I bought a big gold bow the size of a peony, and gold gauzy ribbon two inches wide. I had paper already—green, with little red pine trees dotted in it. Leaving the cardboard the frame shop had folded around the piece for protection in place, I dressed it with the paper and ribbon and put the bow at the intersection where the ribbon crossed. Then I headed for Noe. On the way I passed the flower shop. I was going to buy flowers anyway, but I saw they were also selling holly branches and pine tree clippings from a table on the sidewalk in front of the shop. I was going to have to come back. I brought my present to Noe and set it on the dining table, then headed back to the shop. I chose a bouquet, big bright yellow flowers, and bought a holly branch and some pine clippings. Again I went to Noe. The flowers went into the vase on the island, and the rest in the vase at the center of the table. I got a text from her, telling me to go grocery shopping. She was coming back Christmas Day after all, and wanted to cook dinner. I bought a 12 pound turkey and everything else to go with it, and back to Noe I went.

I relaxed then.

Later I went to a movie, then to Lucky 13 and drank Christmas Eve away, trying to pretend I didn't care I was alone.

It was around 6 o'clock the next night when she came in. The turkey was nearly done. I'd been having wine but taking it easy, snacking on cheese and salami—what we'd brought back from Paris. I was in the kitchen slicing more when I heard the door.

We had not been in communication much since she'd left. I didn't know how she may be feeling, but I suspected, although she did fly on Christmas to be with me. Still though, I felt awful about what happened, and I was taking it slow, trying to gauge her, my tail hiked firm and curling between my legs.

I let her walk in instead of rushing to the door. When she came through the hall into the kitchen and I saw that she saw me standing there at the counter bar, at the cutting board, I went to her then. We were slow and quiet with each other. I held her, kissed her and welcomed her back, gesturing slightly with my palm to the flowers at the end of the bar. She smiled at them, and at the holly and pine sprigs on the table, but it was a bemused, vacant smile. And she didn't speak.

In the end these things went on the list, too. The flowers meant nothing because my small gesture toward them somehow to her rang insincere, as if I were merely saying look here they are, your flowers as usual. Like I bought them out of some rote conditioning. And what she saw when she came in was that I preferred to stand there and slice my salami than to hurry to greet her, as if I couldn't care less that she flew from Chicago on Christmas Day for me. That's how deathly comfortable she believed I'd become in our relationship. She was keeping a mental tally.

Then she went to the big green present on the table laid before the vase.

Merry Christmas, baby, I said.

Look at that bow! It's huge!

I only smiled, hoping.

Open it, I said.

Once the cardboard wrapping was off and she saw what it was, only then did she seem to come back to me.

We finished cooking dinner together as she told me about Christmas Eve with her family. Her brother-in-law dressed as Santa every year for her nieces and nephews. It sounded really fun. That's mainly why she wanted to be there, to see the kids with Santa.

She cleared the table of her present's wrappings to get ready for dinner. The wide vase with the tree clippings was left as our center piece. She'd tied the gold gauze I'd used to bind her gift around it.

We had elaborate plans to celebrate New Year's Eve, made them weeks before. She wanted to take a trip somewhere. We decided New Orleans sounded good. And like she did with Paris she found a place online to rent, a house in the Garden District. She sent a deposit. Our tickets were booked with her free mileage. We would be there four days.

But she'd arrived from Chicago with a bug, which didn't attack until later that night. While I slept, she'd been up vomiting for hours in the bathroom. I was not aware of this until early in the morning, when she had come into bed and I was awakened. She told me then. She was cold and sweating and weak, and it lasted through the rest of the weekend.

Monday came and she was better, but when I got home to her from work I crawled into bed. All at once I felt like I was dying.

Blood coursed cold through me. Even the electric blanket she loved so much and was a permanent fixture on our bed couldn't give me warmth. My body had no strength, and suddenly, as I lay buried under the covers, there was a swelling in my stomach, a sudden expansion that wanted out. I sat up to rest a moment on the side of the bed, hoping that would do the trick, quiet things, but it never does. I ran like hell out of the room but didn't quite make it. Some came through my fingers onto the hallway floor. By the time I left the bathroom she had it cleaned up. I crawled back into bed, apologizing for her seeing me that way, then got up and ran again, and this time I did make it. When I came back she had a trash can ready bedside lined with a plastic bag. This erased the danger of having to get up to run, but whatever it was lasted two days, and our New Orleans plans were canceled.

I was at a bistro on rue Des Ecoles, another place I discovered with wifi service. You have to order something to sit there of course, but it's cheaper than Café Contrescarpe, and the connection is more reliable. I've been going to Contrescarpe ever since arriving in Paris, by default, because it's so close to the rafters. But since I started trying this place, L'Authre it's called,

I've been coming here more frequently. It's like a diner, and along with its other assets I just like the atmosphere better. When I haven't wanted to walk all the way down to the café on the island, which is my first choice, and felt like skipping Contrescarpe, which is more upscale modern, I've come here. It's about midway between, and retains that simple, old school charm I prefer.

I had the laptop, writing emails and catching up on some current events. I've let the world slide by while in Paris without caring much. Here and there while at a brasserie or bar I've caught some things on TV, and ascertained enough through the images to vaguely understand, but for the most part I've been very isolated. During my first week here there was a major art heist, for instance, and I didn't know a thing about it until an email came from Jari implying I had something to do with it. I said of course, how else was I to finance this trip?

Matice called while I was at the bistro. She was in the area, and did I want to get together? I haven't heard from her since we parted on St. Germain, when she caught that bus home. She's been sick the last couple days, that's why, she said.

It was the middle of the afternoon on a very hot day, one of the hottest so far. The apartment was sweltering. I had to get out of there but wanted to stay out of the sun. That's why I was at the bistro, refuge from the heat. I told Matice it would be nice to go to the river later, for sunset.

OKee, she said, I meet you.

I wasn't ready to meet her then I wanted to wait for later, but when she asked where I was I told her.

She either did not hear me properly or was operating on assumption when she heard the word café, because she went to Contrescarpe looking for me. She'd met me there before, and because she was in the Mouffetard closer to my apartment that's where she thought she'd find me now. She called again when she couldn't.

I gave her the location of L'Authre again, the names of the streets, then texted them to her as well. A moment later my phone buzzed.

Just give me number of place, she said. I don't know those streets. Just give me number.

I went outside into the hot sun and looked at the building for the address, and then the other buildings, but couldn't see any numbers. I repeated the streets to her.

It's right on the corner, I said.

She didn't understand. She wanted an address so she could punch it into her phone and bring up a map. Matice didn't carry *Plan de Paris* like me, and although she's been living in Paris six months the names of the streets still elude her. I gave her directions from Contrescarpe. Just walk straight down the hill, I told her. But she'd already left there and was somewhere else. She hung up very frustrated.

Finally, while seated at my table, through the windows facing rue Des Ecoles I saw Matice walking down the hill. I shut down the machine and started gathering my things. Matice walked in and I saw it on her face but she waited till we got outside. I slung my bag around me weighted with the computer, and we stepped out into the heat.

I told you I needed *number!* she said. You give me names. Such and such. What does *that* mean! I don't know names of streets here. I needed *number*, to find in my *phone! Ahhch…*

Alright, I'm sorry, I said. I came out looking for numbers but I didn't see any. Let's forget it. What do you wanna do?

She made a face like she couldn't believe I just asked that.

You said you wanted to go to river.

Later. I meant *later*, in the evening, when it cools down. It's too *hot* now.

Ahhch…

We started walking back up the slope to the Mouffetard. I wanted to drop off the computer and lighten my load, and it gave us a starting point.

The heat was at its peak. Matice hates hot weather as much as I do.

It's hhhawwt. I don't like *hawt*, she said.

We got as far as St. Etienne, two blocks up rue de la Montagne St. Genevieve, and sought refuge in the shade of the church. We sat on the side steps facing down the street we just came up, not the wide shallow steps of the front entrance. Those steps face the Pantheon, which itself has steps too, big stone block bleacher-like steps, also facing the direction from which we just came. I've sat on those Pantheon steps many nights over the last couple weeks with only cans of Kronenbourg to keep me company, and looked at the beautiful face of St. Etienne in the moonlight. But Matice and I sat around the corner of the church, not looking at the Pantheon, in the very narrow lane running along St. Etienne's side, a spot where I imagine young Hemingway and his wife Hadley may have sat (they had lived only a few blocks from here) as they paused to discuss something on their way home perhaps, as I and a testy Turkish girl were doing now, talking over a plan of action.

Let's go to a park, I said.

OKee.

Do you know any near here?

No.

We sat in the shade and thought some more. Finally Matice said, Let's just get some white wine and go sit in a park.

OK, we'll find a place, I said. First I want to get rid of this laptop.

We got up then and continued walking toward my apartment.

Matice waited on the street while I went upstairs. I didn't blame her. I wouldn't have made that climb either if I didn't have to.

I opened the door to the rafters and it was an oven. I took the laptop out of my bag while it still hung around me and plopped the thing on the futon. I hated even to touch it, to look at it. Then I went over to the cabinet by the sink to get the wine opener. While I was there it occurred to me that if we were going to drink wine we'd need cups. I rooted around in the cabinet, thinking it was a good bet, and there they were—a sleeve of small plastic cups someone'd left. I took out two and tucked them in my bag. Locking the door behind me, I headed back down the winding stairs to Matice.

We set off in the direction of rue Monge. I tossed off a few ideas, but Matice did not want to walk or take the Metro anywhere. It was too hot, she said. We kept slowly meandering. I thought now of Jardin des Plantes. It was close enough so we didn't have to walk far, and there were trees and shade. I began leading us there.

There was a little store and we went in. I thought we were going to buy wine, but now Matice changed her mind and wanted beer instead. I bought two tall cans of Kronenbourg and we kept walking. The sun tore into us. We stayed tight to the buildings in the shade when we could.

We were walking a different way than before when I came, and entered the gardens at another place. There were large exposed grounds here of tan dirt and gravel, and the sun baked down. We might as well have been in the desert. It was miserable, and Matice was not pretending otherwise. We wandered a path away from there and then we were in the cool of the trees finally, where I'd walked before. But when I had come it was a workday and rather quiet. It was the weekend now and people crawled the place. We walked drinking from our cans, enjoying the shade, trying to ignore them—the tourists, the baby strollers, the loud groups.

Slowly we came down the hill of the path out of the trees to a familiar spot. This was where I'd entered last time. There were benches and we sat down. People passed as we drank our beer. Some looked at us, most didn't. Matice's mood was foul now.

I know why I am still single, Matice said, a revelation having apparently come to her in the time between our meeting last. You too, she said. Want me to tell you? *You*, I mean, not about me.

No thanks.

I was sick to death of the thought of the many flaws I carry and sick of others informing me of them. I tried to change the subject by discreetly bringing her attention to a man turtling by, each step made with great effort and, judging by his expression, much pain. I'd been watching him shuffle up the path toward us from the minute we sat down.

So? Matice said as we watched the man, the rasp of his soles amplifying now with our focus as they raked over the path's fine, sparse gravel. It's life, she said.

We watched the man struggle on toward the trees and after a minute, when he'd only gotten a few feet further and our eyes were still on him, Matice added: And they say God is fair...I don't like God. He takes everythink away. Everythink I love.

Disgust twisting ugly on her face then she looked away and was quiet, seemed to be thinking about something. I loved someone, she said, still looking off away from me. I loved very much. And God took heem away. What for I need God? He does nothink for me. *Nothink!*

She took a long pull from her can.

Nothink, she said again, and fell quiet once more with finality. And as we sat there together in that harsh quiet, Matice looking absently down the path to the left, I felt she'd found a way to finish telling me after all what I said I didn't want to hear.

Suddenly then she was standing up and throwing a leg over my lap like a feisty child mounting the high back of a large mellow dog. Straddling me that way, facing me, Matice rested her wrists over my shoulders, still holding the beer can, dangling it behind me, and with a little smile playing about her lips now she focused the piercing darkness of her eyes into mine and said:

Sex.

Kissing me lightly on the lips and bouncing a little with her legs spread across my lap, she stared smilingly into my eyes as people moved all around us. I kissed her back, but I was not interested in sex with her, not then anyway. I knew now though that this was the only reason she'd wanted to get together. But it was way too hot, and I was not very attracted to her right then.

Saying nothing, I avoided her eyes by watching the people pass behind her over her shoulder, drinking my beer. She got up off my lap and sat again on the bench beside me.

I don't like sex in the summer, she said. It's too hawt. I don't want it.

We finished our cans of beer and left the gardens, walking in the direction of my place but not sure where we were actually headed now from here. On the way she made a phone call and had a conversation in Turkish. When she hung up we were at rue Monge.

Who was that, I asked, your limo driver?

I have to go, Matice said. I need to talk to somebody. I'm going to meet my friend in Marais, have coffee. I can't walk anymore. Maybe I call you later.

She turned to walk off, then stopped and turned back around.

It's not you, she said. It's me. I need to go. Don't hate me.

And with that she turned and went down rue Monge, and stunned I stood there watching her, walking away when she said she couldn't walk anymore. I'm sure that's the last I'll see of her. I leave in two days. I turned and walked up the street and into the brasserie across from Place Monge and ordered a beer, standing in the coolness inside drinking it at the bar.

Left again. Why do I make everyone leave me?

I went home to the rafters, took off all my clothes and left them in a puddled twist on the floor, switched on the fan perched in the corner of the loft as I climbed up the ladder, crawled onto the mattress and flipped on my back, and naked lay there staring at the beams above. The air from the fan cooled the sweat on my body and the wretchedness wetting my face.

D o you ever think of moving in together? she asked.
Whatever it was that hit us had just passed. We were lying in bed after waking. The truthful answer to that question was yes, and it was something I very much wanted, but I was afraid of that thought. As soon as she asked, my mind filled with the haunting image of that living room piled with my ex-girlfriend's boxes. It all came rushing back.

I can't think of a quicker way to ruin a relationship, I said.

I was trying to be glib and it came out wrong. What she heard was no—and it was the furthest thing from the truth. But I was afraid of somehow injuring our relationship, like last time, afraid of being in that place again. And what if it did fail? What would I do then?

I need to start looking for a place, she said. The guys upstairs are letting me stay through January, but then I need to be out. I wanted to know if I should include you when I start looking.

Well, can we just see how it goes? I mean, you get a place, and after a couple months, if it feels right, I'll move in then. How 'bout that?

She gave a weak smile, and lay quiet in the soft morning light.

A few days later, after a choice round of email exchanges with my roommate, hesitance dropped away and I decided to go for it. Fuck it. I wanted it, I knew I wanted it.

Let's do it, I told her.

And as the new year began we started looking at our first apartments, but this shot up straight toward the top of the list. I only wanted to live with her after a row with my roommate, that's what she saw, when in actuality it only gave me the courage to follow my heart and nudge me out of the messy nest my life had become.

We made due with a local New Year's Eve, nothing exciting. I tried, but there wasn't enough time to come up with much after our plans fell through.

The next night we went to a movie. I see a lot of films during the holiday season, something I began doing during my lonely years in San Francisco when finding myself on my own at Christmas. It's become a kind of personal tradition now. Every Christmas Eve and usually Christmas night, and sometimes New Year's too, I go see whatever films of any merit that may be playing. A few good ones are usually released then, thankfully. I rely upon that. So we went to see a film together now, about a man whose lover had died, and after living without his lover for some time he decided there was no longer any point and planned to kill himself. He ended up changing his mind in the end, choosing to live after all, and just when he did he was hit with a heart attack and died. It was a beautiful film.

Afterwards we stood outside the theater in each other's arms.

I don't know what I'd do without you, we told one another.

I really don't, I said. I love you, baby.

I love you too, she said.

Our heads were bowed, foreheads touching, whispering into each other. And there was never anything truer that has ever come out of my mouth. I could not imagine life without her now. Could not imagine ever going back to the wasteland.

We walked the downtown streets from the theater, just to walk. It had rained earlier, and the black streets glistened with smeared, streaking light. We wound up by the Bank of America building at California and Kearny. Right across the street is the building where I had worked at that law firm ten years earlier. In front of the B of A building was a huge Christmas tree dressed in red light. We went to it and stood looking up the tree's skirt at the complicated weave of branches, standing in the red glow. We took our pictures standing there bathed in it, that glow.

We walked up the hill of California Street to the Mark Hopkins Hotel and rode the elevator to the lounge at the top. This was a place I'd never been because it's so swanky. She wanted to show me something. She'd gone here with her sister for lunch one afternoon during her visit in July. The hotel sits high on top of California Street and there's a great view of the bay from the east windows up there. These windows in the lounge were where women came to watch their men go off to war in ships. They call this spot the Widows' Room. She'd learned this when she was here with her sister, she'd told me about it then, but wanted to show me.

We got cocktails and sat at a table against the windows facing west. We could see Grace Cathedral down there from our seats, and it was the first time I realized that Grace Cathedral is a miniature modern version of Notre Dame. For a flash of a moment we were back in Paris together again.

Her birthday was a week away. It wasn't premeditated, but during a break while at work I'd made a little drawing—my version of a Capricorn. It had the head of a ram with coiling horns and the blubbery body of what looked like a walrus. I didn't put any legs on it because they seemed out of place, that's why it ended up looking more like the body of a walrus, but it was in a kind of art nouveau style and I liked it. I decided to do something with it. I'd make her a birthday card, I thought, and put it on the cover.

There was a light-table in the office and I used it to trace the drawing onto a nice piece of yellow paper I'd found—a remnant from something used for exhibit labels, no doubt. I traced it with a black ink pen, and in each corner I'd drawn angles echoing the edges of the paper, elongating the vertical lines which began breaking up into ever shortening dashes, and the dashes into disappearing dots. Inside the join of the angles I added curls, evoking sprouting flora. Not bad, I thought. It continued the art nouveau style, but there was something still missing. I thought about it and came back to it later. A circle, I decided. It needed a circle at the back of the image, like a big sun rising behind it. Using a waffle from a light fixture for a template to ensure a perfectly round line, I added the circle, and that did it. It seemed finished now. I glued it to a piece of thick white paper, trimmed the excess white away and carefully folded it, and there it was. I was pleased with it. I thought it was more special than buying something. I thought she'd think so, too. But it wasn't done. I still needed to write something inside. This required thought. I sat on it until the next day. The whole process of making the card stretched out over a few days, working on it only at my breaks.

I tend to always need to write something poetic inside cards. Can't seem to just write straightforward sentiment or a direct message, has to be poetic. Just the way I'm wired.

I'd written something months ago, thought I'd slip it into lyrics for a song. I decided to use it for the card.

> *The curtains of a dream*
> *Parted on your face*
> *Still can't believe I'm awake*

It said it all to me—that's how I felt about her. I finished it with *Happy Birthday my love*.

I thought of adding I love you, but it seemed redundant, and I wanted to keep the economy of what I'd written pure. I was being way too literary about it, I know, but that was exactly my thought process.

I found a goldlined envelope in the stationary closet in the front office that fit, just barely, it was tight, but it worked. I was proud of it, my little card, and I really hoped she'd like it. It made me feel good to have made something for her.

Since we were leaving for the cabin Friday night after work (Friday was her birthday) I had to pick up the gift I had in mind Thursday night. I left work a little early in order to pull off what I planned. I wanted to pick up her gift, take it home and wrap it, and bring it over to Noe and stash it under the bed to have ready for her Friday morning when we woke first thing, like she did for me. I thought that a beautiful gesture, to have a gift ready upon waking, and I wanted to do the same for her. It was close, she was due home any minute, but I'd made it. Then I left and came back later after she'd been home a while.

Friday morning came and I was very excited. I popped her present out as soon as we opened our eyes. It came off as I'd wanted. She was surprised at my having been able to sneak this big box in and hide it without her knowing.

She opened the envelope and worked out the card and looked at it.

I made it, I said.

She opened it and read what was inside, smiling, but it was similar to that smile when she walked in Christmas night and looked at the flowers and didn't say anything. She didn't say anything now, either, just set the card down on the bed covers and unwrapped the big square box, opened it and lifted out the first thing—there were two. Out of the tissue paper nest she'd found the pitcher in the shape of a cock, a rooster. That was another inside joke. We were always joking about cocks, and I'd send her pictures on my phone when she was away of images of roosters I'd see around town, on signs or little statues in store windows, to make her laugh, as she laughed now. But it was also a nice pitcher—Italian ceramic. Then the next thing came out. A copper olive oil can with a long spout. We had been in a culinary store the weekend before and I noticed her eyeing it. She'd always wanted one, she'd said. That's when I'd also seen the pitcher, and I knew what I was going to come back for. We got up and ready for work. She placed the card standing up on the top of the tall dresser, the one to the right of the door, beneath the Leonard Cohen set list on the wall where I'd hung it for her.

While she was in the shower I went over to look at the card again, picked it up and read it, then set it back down. I noticed another card laying flat on the dresser, on top of that book Jari's friend had written and given to her when he was in town that time. *Take This Book, Please!* it was called. Bugged me to see that book around; it'd been on her bedside table for months. I never said anything though, didn't really think it meant anything. I picked up the card and saw his face staring up at me from the black and white author's photo on the back cover. The card was one I'd given her many months before, sometime in May or June when we were having a spat. I opened it and read what I'd written. Oh no…

Among something else I wrote in there I'd also included the same poem fragment I'd written in her birthday card.

How could I have forgotten that? I knew it felt familiar, something nagged me about it, but I thought that was because I'd been carrying it around inside me for so long. Those words captured so succinctly how I felt they were so often in my head, but to her now they'd been rendered meaningless. That's why that smile and no words when she read it. I'd blown it again, and added to the list.

We left for the cabin moments after I arrived from work. Same drive, same pit stop for groceries in Carmel, same twisting climb up to the cabin through massive redwoods, only now all done in the dark. The only difference was we did not stop at the house but drove directly down the path to the cabin. It was too late to bother settling up with the owners; that could wait till morning.

We got settled and opened a bottle of wine. She put on her dark blue nightie, the one she bought in Chartres, and we made love standing up against the tall bed in the candlelight glowing within the cabin while void black darkness and silence engulfed us without.

The following day we simply relaxed, puttering about the cabin until it was time to make dinner, and then after dinner we climbed into the tub on the deck. In the warmth of the water and the suds she lay back against me as I rested against the high wall of the tub. Staring up at the stars we listened to the stream down there in the darkness.

Sing to me, she said.

I did, and looking back I could've chosen from any number of songs, there are hundreds, millions to pick from, and I wish now I had. I wish I'd simply sung Happy fucking Birthday to her for godsake and left it at that. But no, what I did was sing some of my songs, a couple I'd written shortly before we met, and a couple written while we'd been together. I just felt like singing these for a change—my songs, new ones. I was feeling like I wanted to make music again, and though these songs did not yet have music set to them I could hear it, to a large extent anyway, in my head. I'd been enjoying singing these songs to myself over the months we'd been together and now I wanted her to hear me sing them, because it was her who was bringing this feeling out in me.

She was quiet while I sang, did not speak or stir, but somewhere into the fourth one she bolted suddenly upright in the water and ran out of the tub.

Slowly I climbed out then too, and followed her through the sliding door. I closed it behind me and joined her by the heat of the fireplace, wrapped in the thick tan terry cloth robe provided by the cabin.

What's wrong?

I ask you to sing to me, and you sing about other *women?*

Baby…They're my songs…I was just singing my songs…

The first two were inspired by other people, that was true,

although she didn't know that directly. But the association to those who inspired them had long passed and they existed simply as songs. The other two had no biographical associations whatsoever, and in fact contained images or sentiment inspired by her. Regardless, they were just songs, songs I'd written and was singing to her, and I never dreamed she would react this way. But nearly everything I did now fed the secret list in her head, as well as what I did not do. The apparent fact that the words *I love you* were not heard from me that weekend, heard from my lips, ranked among the top as subsidiary evidence against me. And the songs I chose to sing that night found their own special place on the list, too.

In the morning we seemed to be back to normal. We made breakfast as we did the morning before. She'd brought the pitcher along that I'd given her and filled it again with fresh-squeezed orange juice. We relaxed and read, sometimes together sometimes separately, either in the cabin or out on the deck, as we sipped wine and snacked on the rest of the food we'd brought. I remember sitting out on the deck with her in the lounge chairs in the last moments before we left the cabin. She was wearing a dark mustard-colored sweater with a cow-collared neck and flared long sleeves, and blue jeans. Her hair was loose and wild like I liked it. We sat quietly out there, just looking up the branches of the redwoods that surrounded the deck, listening to the sounds of nature. She was smiling.

When we finally left late that afternoon, we drove a short ways down the coast toward Big Sur proper. We pulled over at a turnout along the highway on the cliff to enjoy the view. She propped the camera on a rock and set the timer, then joined me where I was sitting—on a larger rock at the edge of the cliff, my back to the ocean.

She quickly came and squatted beside me, hooking her palm at my shoulder and tilting her head to mine so that her hair spilled a woolly curtain behind me.

Hey we already did this one, I said joking. In Paris

She had positioned the camera on an old metal rope tie poking up through the cobbles and set the timer then too, joining me in the same way as I squatted near the edge of the wall of the river. I felt the weight of her dark hair cascade across the back of my neck as she leaned down close to me, huddling there in my black scarf and black Dickies jacket. She smiled big into the camera with the river Seine, and Notre Dame across the river, behind us. That was one of the shots she used on the cover of the book and was one of the very best out of the entire trip.

She giggled, and we stared at the red flashing light on the camera until it stopped. In this shot now, her same big smile, same unevenly posed squatting couple, but with the light blue and white of the Pacific Ocean crashing behind them into the rocky shoreline. It was my favorite new shot of us. It was our last portrait together.

The night of my birthday, before we went to dinner (she was taking me to a fancy Greek restaurant downtown in the financial district I'd never heard of), as I waited for her in the living room flipping through the Paris book she came out and handed me something else—an envelope.

What's this?

I set the book aside and opened it. Inside was a one-sided card announcing French lessons.

You got me a French class?

For both of us, she said. It starts in January. It's an emersion class. Supposed to be the best way to learn. And this place is supposed to be very good. I've done research.

It seemed she meant it. We were going back to Paris. And in order to really do it right we had to learn to speak French.

Sitting in a classroom to learn a new language was going to be new to me. I'd never taken a foreign language class, not even in high school. And *French?* It was the language I most wanted to learn, and I was excited to try, this was another great gift from her, but would I actually be able to do it?

As our apartment search went on—we'd looked at a number of them already, two-bedroom flats in Cole Valley and the Haight, Noe Valley, Hayes Valley, Castro and the Mission—French class began. It was one night a week downtown. We sat in a small room with four other students at one big table as the instructor addressed us in French. The first thing we had to do was introduce ourselves to the class, stating in French our names, occupations, where we lived, and nationality. Then we each had to introduce another student in the class, all in French, remembering their information the best we could. And it went on from there as we followed along in the class booklet. She was nice, the instructor, young, and pretty too I thought, and it was a beginning class of course, but it still seemed a little over our heads. What bothered me was that the instructor spoke only French in class, and I understand that's the emersion method, but at times I was lost and needed explanation to help clear things up. When questions were asked in English the instructor's response came in French, with gesticulations toward the whiteboard where she'd written out words with a marker, which produced very little clarification for me.

She and I talked about it afterwards and agreed. It was a little much, sitting there struggling linguistically for three hours after a tiring day of work. She phoned the school and we joined an even more basic class the following week. This class only lasted an hour and a half, but it started later than the other, which was good because it allowed us to grab a bite to eat before.

The same instructor stood before us, in a different room but the same size, with the same kind of big table and four other different students. The instructor seemed overworked, too harried for a woman of her young age, which I guessed was about 28. She seemed tired, a little sweaty. She looked like she could use a shower. I wondered how many of these classes she taught.

She employed the same method, spoke no English, but it was more basic, that was true. We students greeted each other. We asked how one another were. We counted. Those kinds of things. It felt silly. I didn't like it, sitting in that little room at a table with her and four strangers struggling to speak French baby talk. I remembered while sitting there just how much I hated being in school. This was much less formal than school, but it was still sitting in a classroom with a bunch of other people and I never was comfortable with that. She'd spent a lot of money, though, and I couldn't say any of this.

I carried the booklets with me daily in my bag (there were two, one from the present class and one from the prior) and practiced every day with them, mostly during my breaks at work. I enjoyed it. I much preferred that to class. I felt like some things were getting through, but I didn't like the thought of sitting in that room again to prove it. She on the other hand didn't seem to practice at all. I noticed her booklets never left where they lay in the apartment, and I silently questioned her sincerity in trying to learn.

Class was on Tuesday night. It was our third session coming up out of the scheduled eight. Sunday she got word from her family that her father was ill, but the seriousness of his condition was not yet known. More tests were needed. She left the next day for Chicago and was gone through the week. I chose not to go to class without her. She came back for the weekend, but left again the following Monday and so missed that week too. I did the same. We never went back. I was sorry for the money she spent, but I preferred to study on my own if she wasn't joining me. I continued with my booklets.

Her concerns of course were elsewhere. She was very worried. A whole new strain pulled at us now. She felt I wasn't being supportive. The first week while she was back in Chicago she called while I was having dinner at the Mexican restaurant on Valencia, after work. She said she wished she was there with me, and I said I wished she was too. I *always* wished she was, I thought that was understood, and I was honestly tired of wishing it. But because she'd said it first and I in response meant I only said it *in* response, again she felt from some rote, meaningless place. I'd been guilty of this other times (guilty would be the word *she'd* use) responding in the same way to the same wish, but in this instance I felt I was being supportive by *not* saying it first because she was gone due to tragic circumstances, and to say that I missed her then would've been a selfish and needy thing to do. That's how I saw it anyway. Needy was something I was trying desperately to avoid being. I'd been accused of that by the last one, and it killed me. I was trying to learn from my mistakes. But just like with the issue surrounding sexual frequency, I was seen now as not being needy *enough*. Of course I missed her. I'd told her that many times, how lonely I was without her. I wasn't saying it often enough for her liking, though, and couldn't seem to beat her to say it first. And as her father's diagnosis worsened and the process quickly proceeded accordingly, and the more she was gone, more stress tugged at our seams.

Still though, the days she was in town our search for an apartment continued. Near the end of the month we found it—that Victorian flat on 23rd Street. The man let us in and immediately it felt good. He and his wife and little girl lived there, but only part-time. They also lived in Ohio, that's where the man's wife and little girl were now. He was there alone. He and his wife owned the flat but they were going to be gone a year, beginning in February, and after that there was good a possibility, the man said, they'd be moving to Seattle. He and his wife had decided to rent the place at least through the year of their absence. We moved through it and it kept getting better. It seemed to extend the further we went into it, down the winding hallway, which emptied onto a large dining room, and then a large kitchen, and then a sun room, and outside onto a patio in back. The living room was the first room in front to the right as you entered, which connected to the bedroom. Then down the hall curving to the right was the bathroom, and a little further down off the hall to the left was the little girl's room. It was painted a dusky blue with white trim and that was to be my room, my workroom. I loved it. And we both loved the apartment. She took it, giving the man a deposit.

She'd hired a mover. We went shopping and bought things for the apartment. Everything was set, it was going to happen. She went back to Chicago. Then the man called and said that he and his wife had changed their minds, they were not renting the flat after all. That was two days before the end of the month, before she was to move her things. She called to tell me as I was leaving that café in Cole Valley, and somehow again I revealed to her my unsupportive qualities. An extension was granted at Noe, and she came back.

She'd begun having trouble sleeping. When I asked why she wouldn't try to explain. She was easily set off now, and there was a lot of tension between us. I could never say the right thing regarding her father. When she spoke of his condition it sounded grave. He'd been a heavy smoker most his life and it attacked his bladder. It had to be removed. But it had spread through much of his body as well, his lymph nodes. They hoped chemo therapy would help. I didn't know what to say, how to comfort her other than, oh baby…and, I'm sorry…and, I love you…and to ask how things were when she was gone with her family in Chicago. She painted such a grim picture I could only respond from what I was told. Comforting others in times like these is not something I'm good at. The words elude me. My heart hurts with the news and I listen sympathetically, but putting a positive spin on things to make someone feel better is difficult for me, especially when what I'm told seems so factually, clinically dire. Yet, although I didn't know how to express it, somehow I was silently optimistic and believed things would turn out for the best.

Most of our communication during this time was over the phone. I wished I could have been with her, by her side with her family, I wished that most of all, but of course that was impossible. So it was the phone. Texts mainly. A conversation now and then, but mostly texts, and a few emails. There were some where she was ferociously responding to my perceived ineptness or insensitivity, astounded by what she took to be absolute lack of support, but most were not like this. Most were loving and sweet. I still have them in my phone. The first in the beginning of February took me off guard. It was probably generated by watching her father fight for his life. It got her thinking about living.

I would like to start planning a major trip, she wrote. This week I will pull some country ideas together and maybe we can talk it over next weekend. Ok? I'd like to fly first class on my miles so would need to book something a few months in advance if possible.

Next day: Hi love. How you doing today?

Later the same day: Missing you. Harder without you to wrap myself in physically so I will settle for mentally.

And the next successive days were: Miss you.

Love you.

I thought about you once or twice today...

Hi sexy.

Had a dream with you in it.

Dreams are special to me, and when I asked her about the dream she'd had she wrote: A life dream. We were sitting together just talking. It went on & on. I feel like it lasted about an hour. I think it is because I miss just being with you.

Then she came back, shortly before Valentine's Day. We made love as if it'd been ages since we'd seen each other. Once. Twice. Then a third time. But on the third time when I could not finish, but after having satisfied her, she asked: Why couldn't you come, too much porn? Or are you just old?

We just fucked three times in a row, does that sound like I'm old?

Why couldn't you come then?

Jesus, I don't know. It was three times in a *row!* It doesn't matter, I said, and rolled over on my side away from her in the dark.

After a moment she apologized.

That was mean, she said. I'm sorry.

I didn't understand her at times. She took things like that so personally when it had nothing to do with her. Male physiology is different than a woman's. Didn't she know that by now, at the age of 35? Back in June we'd went to the North Beach street fair. At one point we went into the Italian-American Club across from Washington Square and had a look around, wound up on the top floor. I needed to pee desperately. We found a bathroom down a hallway, and when I went in she followed with other ideas.

Although having sex at that moment was the last thing on my mind, I remembered months earlier when we'd gone back to that wine bar on Rose Street, the one we'd gone to in the beginning. She had wanted to have sex in the bathroom then, but there is only one bathroom in there, in the backroom where we sat our first night, by that leather couch we kissed and drank champagne on. But now we were sitting in the front, and the backroom was full of people. It's an intimate space back there, we'd be noticed going in together, I thought, and as the line amassed outside the bathroom door it would've been too obvious what we were up to. I didn't want to walk back out to that. I had too much respect for her and our relationship to want to do that, so I refused. She was furious.

I could walk up to any guy in here, she'd said, and not have any trouble getting him to go into the bathroom with me.

I'm sure that's true, I'd responded. And if that's what you

wanna do, do it. But I won't be here when you come out.

She was angry the rest of the night. I wanted to avoid that anger now in North Beach. We fucked, but because I had to pee so bad, and because the voices outside the door waiting in the hallway were distracting me, I couldn't come—though she did.

I didn't care. As long as she was satisfied I didn't care, I just wanted to pee.

I unlocked the door finally and we quickly walked out, avoiding the eyes of those waiting in the hall as we blew by them. Down the hall and the two flights of stairs we went, she right behind at my heels. Back out on the sundrenched street her fury unleashed.

It's because you're not attracted to me, isn't it! That's why you couldn't come!

Of course not, I just had to *pee*. A guy can't come if he has to *pee*.

But there was no calming or persuading her otherwise. She'd been slighted by my mistaken lack of excitement for her, and the assault continued as we moved together up the street. She would not believe me, and I *still* had to pee.

One morning during this time as we lay together in bed, she said: I want to help you get your book published. I think I can. But we need to get it in digital format. I want to send it out to be retyped. I'll send it to India, to my old team out there. You'll get it back in a week.

No, if it's going to be retyped I want to do it myself, I said. There'll be some things I'll wanna rework, I'm sure.

With the idea planted in my mind now, I occupied myself at night transferring the manuscript into her laptop at Noe Street. It was going along slowly but I was making progress, though it did feel strange to be revisiting the work after so long. As much as I remembered it being a part of me, part of my life, I was not the same guy now who'd written it. I questioned my motives. It felt like I was reaching back instead of forward, but now I'd begun I was determined to finish. I believed she *could* help me do something with it. And after that I'd do something else, write something else. With her beside me I felt I could. So during her new frequent absence I did my best to fill it this way, while missing her. I was always very happy when she came back, and had flowers ready for her when she did.

Valentine's Day fell on a Saturday, and though we were supposed to go back to the cabin our reservations were canceled. With all the traveling she'd been doing it was too much for her, so it was postponed. Like our New Orleans trip was postponed. But deposits had been made and these things were not refundable, so I've wondered: did she just absorb the loss, or were these things used with someone else? In the case of New Orleans, that was unfortunate. I would've loved to have gone. But the cabin? That cabin was my wonderful, special place of retreat I'd planned to return to for years to come. Now it could never be the same place to me and I shall never see it again…

Even though our plans changed, she still wanted to do something special for the weekend. She rented a hotel room downtown using her accrued points, which meant it was free. This gave us the illusion anyway of being on a trip.

I brought her flowers and a card. I was slowly cluing in to cards finally. In fact, I had three for her. While she was gone I had stopped one day at the little gallery at Market and Sanchez. I passed there often but never stopped. This day, the work I saw through the windows as I passed drew me inside. They had a card rack and I started browsing. I found several I liked. I bought four or five. I used three of these for her that weekend. One with flowers Friday night. One on Saturday, actual V day, with the small gift I'd gotten her. And one the next morning; I put it on the hotel bed for her to find when she came out of the shower. She didn't know what hit her. She looked at me with a suspicious smile, like she wasn't sure who she was with. I only smiled nonchalantly back. What?

She wore a new jacket that weekend, a very red jacket. I'd never seen it before. And with her tall black boots and long dark hair it was electrifying on her. The hotel was very close to North Beach, so Saturday we went there for dinner, and Sunday we went for brunch. We bought a bottle of champagne afterwards and walked slowly back to the hotel that afternoon, drank the champagne on the balcony overlooking Battery Street. Then we checked out and went back home to Noe. It was a very pleasant weekend. A few days later I was woken abruptly by her.

She called! she said, bursting through the bedroom door with quick determined steps, handing my cell phone at me as I lay under the covers.

I had been in a deep sleep, and the strange thing was I had just been dreaming about her. The instant my girl came in bellowing about the call tore me from a dream where I had just been speaking with her. It confused me. At first I thought this was still part of the dream, but the rage in the eyes before me quickly told me it wasn't. I looked at the phone. There was her name in recent calls, but no message. She must've called sometime during the night after we'd gone to bed. How *she* had known that call had come was obvious, I needn't ask. The real mystery lay in the liberty at which she felt to go through my phone when I wouldn't dare even think of touching hers.

Why she calling you?

I don't know, I said, still groggy with sleep. I haven't been talking to her, I added, fresh from the dreamwords we'd just been exchanging. That made me feel strange like I was lying, but I wasn't.

She walked out of the room steaming. I got up and ready for work.

After work, I'm not sure why, I had a strong compulsion to go to that German restaurant for dinner. I just had a craving. It was early and the place was near empty, just how I'd hoped it'd be. I was sitting alone at one of the bar seats when a small group of people came in. They stood behind me in the nook and talked excitedly. I recognized them but apparently they did not recognize me. They were three women and a man. The three women used to work with my ex-girlfriend, and the man was the husband of one of them. His wife had since retired, I was aware of this, but the other two still worked at the same place as far as I knew. It'd been five years or so since I'd seen any of them. My girlfriend quit the office where they all worked a year after leaving me. When I saw them, after having a dream about her that very morning, and that missed call on my phone, I knew something was happening here.

The group walked past behind me and crossed the restaurant without seeming to notice that I was there, and walked into the backroom, usually used for reserved parties. A moment later I was looking directly at the door when she and her person came in. As if instinctively she looked toward the bar, and when she saw me the right corner of her mouth raised ever so slightly. She held my gaze and walked right for me while her girlfriend continued into the backroom.

I knew I'd see you, she said.

There was no reason she should've felt that way. We didn't go there frequently enough together for her to suspect she'd see me there now, and she didn't know how often I currently went to that restaurant since she and I broke up.

As soon as I saw your old coworkers I knew too, I said. I knew something was up, anyway.

I asked her why she had called, and she said no reason. It was just random. I had crossed her mind and she just thought she'd give me a call, no more than that.

I see, I said. All that drama this morning for nothing, I thought.

She left me then to join her friends in the back.

Later at Noe I told her about it as we were getting ready for bed. It seemed harmless. I wanted her to see that strange coincidence thing that tended to happen between me and her, whatever it was. I mean, I wasn't crazy enough to tell her I'd been dreaming about her when she'd busted into the room with my phone in her hand, but since she *had* come up that morning I thought it might be interesting to talk about. She did not reciprocate the feeling.

What, you wanted to show me just how connected you and your ex-girlfriend are? I don't need to know that! she said.

She was right, I guessed. What a mistake that was. I just thought I'd be honest with her, that it might be interesting to talk about. I pick the wrong things to talk too much about at times. That's one lesson I seem destined to keep relearning. It was that way last time, too.

Then I made another mistake, of sorts. I referred to my ex-girlfriend's girlfriend as her person instead of her girlfriend.

It's her *girl*friend, Roman! She's a *LESbian!* Say it!

She could really be ugly at times. I was seeing it more and more. I tried to ignore it and go to sleep. No chance.

Say she's a lesbian, Roman.

It wasn't as simple as that. I'd known her for a long time. I knew she liked sex with men. I knew she was still attracted to men as well as women. In the year after she left, and I was hopelessly trying to reconcile with her, after her first lesbian fling ended, the one with her ex-roommate, she'd met a guy. He was younger, a kid really it sounded like to me. They'd met at a bus stop. She was smoking and he bummed one. That's how it started. Simple as that. She told me about it, said they'd been hanging out, that they'd made a connection. Said he turned her on. They hadn't slept together yet, but she planned to. After she told me this I gave it up. I knew I'd never win, she'd never come back to me. Then somehow she took up with the person she was with now. But what she was doing was by choice. She was living as a lesbian by choice. Her partner was not. Her partner was lesbian by birth, had no option but to be. But my ex was choosing that life. There was a difference to me. I couldn't say it.

Say she's a lesbian, Roman. Say it or leave.

Slowly I rose in the darkness and left the bed. I walked into the living room where my pants and boots were and started putting them on, but stretched out on the couch instead. I was drifting off when she came into the room.

You're not gonna sleep on the couch, she said. You got your own bed to sleep in, go sleep in it.

It was late now. I didn't like the thought of having to walk home, but I got up and shuffled into the bedroom and slowly finished dressing in the dark, sitting on the edge of the bed. I didn't want to leave. There'd been other times this kind of thing had happened in the last couple months. I'd gotten dressed and gone home. By the time I'd gotten there she'd called or emailed me to come back. She didn't want me to leave now either, but she was angry. She kept at it.

Say she's a lesbian, Roman.

She's a lesbian, I said in a deadened voice, and lay down curled onto my left side.

What did I care? She still was important to me, as someone who'd *been* important to me, because I loved her, and that doesn't leave me, but I no longer was held by her in any way. I was in the hold of another, and that one meant everything to me now. But why did she have to do these things?

I was not in her good graces for days. Then one night we were to meet for dinner at the Mexican place on Valencia. I had some time beforehand after work, so I got off the train downtown and walked to North Beach to relax over a couple beers. While walking Grant Street in North Beach I remembered the night of Valentine's Day, when we'd walked Grant together. A store window caught her eye in passing and we'd stopped. There were umbrellas dangling open over headless mannequins. One umbrella was dark gray and one dark orange, and they each had a single white swallow printed on them, wings outspread in a swoop. It was just a quiet pause at a window, but I could see she admired those umbrellas. I went to that store. The umbrellas were still in the window. I went inside and found the shelf. There were other colors, but I thought gray was the one. *Forty-five dollars?* Oh well, I didn't care. I bought it.

I met her at the restaurant in the Mission. She was already seated at the bar when I arrived.

I have something for you, I said.

You do?

Yeah.

I took the umbrella out of my bag and put it on the bar. She looked at it. There was an odd expression on her face.

What's the matter?

I just called that store today, she said, to see if they had anymore of those umbrellas. I told them to hold one for me, I was gonna go back and pick it up. A gray one, I told them. I wanted a gray one.

And with those words an image flicked through me, a purple flash of a surprise I brought home once, to someone I once loved, and a smiling sigh of linkage lifted in me and told again the truth of what I already knew.

We seemed back on track after that, for a while. She went back to Chicago. We hadn't had much time to look at any new apartments, it was a very busy month for her and it went by quickly. But she had to vacate Noe. She decided she'd just get another vacation rental for March. Before she went back to Chicago she'd made arrangements with the mover she'd hired previously to move her stuff to storage. When she told me this I thought she'd gotten a rental unit somewhere, but as it turned out she got permission from the landlords at Noe to store things down in the garage. I didn't learn this though until the night before the mover came. I was confused by the whole thing.

There was a week left to the month, but she was clearing and cleaning the apartment now. She was going to be in Chicago for that last week, but since the stuff was only going downstairs after all, and not in storage off site, couldn't I box some things for her as needed and take them down while she was gone? That's what I assumed I'd do, but I never said it. I was also confused why a mover even had to be hired if things were only going downstairs. She and I could do that, couldn't we? Again that's what I thought.

I'm afraid I wasn't much help. I mostly stayed out of the way, relaxing in front of the TV at night while she was busy boxing things in the kitchen. If she'd have asked me I certainly would have helped, but it didn't seem like that much, and I'd never helped her pack before. The night the mover came I again stayed out of the way, having a drink up the street at Lucky 13. I'd go by later, I thought. I'd texted her from the bar to ask if she wanted me to help. No we got it, was the response.

When I arrived they were still busy at it. I saw a tall handsome young guy in the kitchen, dressed like a hipster in tight black pants and snug pea coat, carrying boxes on his back through the sliding door and down the stairs. I introduced myself. He had an Irish brogue. I walked into the bedroom to her. She was boxing clothes from the closet—my clothes as well as hers. I didn't realize those needed to go then too. Like I said, I thought I could do that while she was gone. I could tell she was upset. I asked if I should help carry boxes down; I once worked as a mover, and I always appreciated when the client lent a hand.

No, she said. I'm paying him to do it.

That doesn't matter, I told her. I could still help.

No.

I stood there not knowing what to do, confusion plastered across my face as I watched her, and it angered her to see. What's so confusing? she wanted to know.

Well, hiring a mover. If things were just going downstairs,

why couldn't we have moved them ourselves?

Because I didn't feel comfortable asking you, she said. I don't feel comfortable asking you to do things. You always seem so put out.

What? Why?

I don't know, she said, you just do. That's why I asked Jari to help me move my stuff over here from Shrader.

I didn't understand it, and my protests fell on deaf ears. Deaf and angry ears. I was embarrassed I hadn't been more help, that I'd been drinking. I just had it pictured all different. We separated again under stress. It all went on the list.

While she was in Chicago, though, our communication was sweet and loving. More text messages.

Good night sweetie, she wrote. Hope everything is good where you are.

And at the end of the month this one: I am so very lonely without you. Being away from you just makes me realize how my life is no longer whole without you next to me.

Me too, I responded. I feel the same way.

Then she wrote: Well, I hope you know I am always thinking of you. Good night and sweet dreams to you. I hope you are in my dreams tonight.

She'd found another vacation rental for March through the service she'd used before, for Shrader and the others, and as before she asked what I thought. It was in Noe Valley, 26th Street off of Church. I went and looked and told her it seemed fine, so she took it. What I didn't mention, however, was that I actually knew the area quite well. The studio apartment my former girl-friend rented after leaving me was just three blocks further up Church Street. She was no longer there of course; she'd begun living with her person from there years ago. But I had visited frequently during the year she *had* lived there, when I was still hopelessly floundering in a polluted reconciliatory sea, gasping and treading while waiting for her return. We'd even slept together a number of times during this period. But each time, after the passion of the moment had past, she was just as resolute in her position as the day she left, if not more so. She was a lesbian, she'd realized, and seemed giddy with the heady freedom the realization brought her. But just when the billowy sediment of this began to finally sift down through me she told me about the kid she'd met at the bus stop and her determination to become lovers with him. I remember walking down Church Street from her place the night she told me, making the final decision in the dark to give it up. I remember thinking as I walked that street I'd never forget that moment, how thoroughly off-balanced and unwanted and rejected I felt. These memories were what this neighborhood returned to me, and it seemed there was no escape, but I was willing to silently ignore them.

She asked me to pick up the keys to the apartment. I did, and then went over there with a bouquet of lavender roses. I wasn't sure there'd be a vase, so I bought one of those too while at the flower shop. I used one of the cards from the batch I'd bought at that gallery and wrote: *Welcome to your new temporary home! I love you*

I put the roses in the vase with water and set them on the round end table in the living room so she'd see them first thing when she entered, propped the card, and left.

As she'd asked, I'd dropped the keys to her new place in my mailbox when I left for work on the morning she was due back in San Francisco. She came by during the day and got them, and I met her there later that night.

Thanks for the roses, she said. You never bought me roses before.

I thought they were nice. A change of pace. Hope you like 'em.

Yes. I do.

And the card? I fished.

Welcome to your new temporary home. Loved it. Thank you.

You're welcome baby.

It was a simple place. One big room—living room and kitchen connected—and then a bedroom. It was crammed with clumsy overstuffed furniture. The kitchen space was clogged with a gigantic table and six wide royal-style wooden chairs with padded seats. That was way over the top. But we did a little rearranging, turned the table parallel to the wall and shoved it over, and it was fine. Besides, it was temporary.

It was strange making love there the first time—our first time in yet another new place. The wrought iron headboard knocked against the wall until she brilliantly jammed two pillows behind it.

Our apartment search picked up. One night we looked at four in a row, all in the Mission.

She still wasn't sleeping well, and still wouldn't talk about it. I didn't know, but I was beginning to get the feeling it might have something to do with us. It was wearing on her, the lack of sleep. Maybe that's what brought on her migraine one night.

I came over and found her lying in the bedroom in the dark. I sat with her on the bed. She whispered at me. To speak louder was painful. She couldn't see, her vision had gone black. I went to the bathroom and wet a washcloth with warm water and brought it in to her, placed it over her high, broad forehead. I lightly stroked her hair, and her face contorted with revulsion, as if my touch added to her pain, as if I should know better. But I didn't know better. I was only trying to soothe her. I stopped, went into the living room and watched TV with the sound down very low. After a while I refreshed her cloth and left her again in the dark on the bed. I did that one more time before she eventually emerged feeling somewhat better. Better enough to confront light anyway, to speak a bit louder. I saw the pain on her face. Her features seemed scrambled. I left her so she could rest more peacefully.

Not long after this, while I was at work she saw two apartments. One was in Cole Valley and one was in the Mission. She liked them both. She called and told me she was going to choose one of these. She described each to me. At first it seemed she was going for the Cole Valley place. Later in the evening she drove me by. It was right off Cole Street, in a nice spot. She was excited. It seemed like the one. But I couldn't see it that night, it wasn't available to be shown, we'd have to come back. She thought about it over night. She went to see the one in the Mission again. It was newly remodeled, had a lot of features she liked. At the Cole Street place there were some things she'd have to change; that lowered its standing in her eyes. She talked to the landlord in the Mission apartment for over an hour, she said. She liked him. He was an artist, she was told. (I've thought about this ever since she told me outside the BART station, that she's seeing someone, it's chased round and round my head, and this landlord—and that hipster Irish mover too, they seemed to be trying so hard not to interact that night at Noe when I arrived, he was also a dj she'd told me later, said he'd invited her to one of his gigs in Berkeley—they've both become prime suspects. But no, I'm fairly certain who it is.) The landlord sweetened the deal for her, dropped the price slightly. Said a new deck was to be built soon off the back. It was on the top floor, three stories. She wanted a deck. It was a two-bedroom, as was the place on Cole. There was a room in front facing 14th Street I could use. That would be my room, she said. I wasn't crazy about the location. She'd only seen it during the day; I wanted her to get a feel for it at night. We went down there and walked by the building, walked the block. It used to be a very bad neighborhood but in the last few years it'd cleaned up. Still though, for me it wasn't great. There was a lingering creepiness in the air surrounding it at night. She decided to take it, instead of the one in Cole Valley.

She hired the mover again that weekend to bring the things

over from Noe Street to the new temporary place on 26th. Seeing it here now showed me there was more than I thought. It amassed in the living room in heaps. It took over, from the front windows spilling halfway to the kitchen. It was outside in the hall, too. The apartment was on the first floor. Right outside the door was the staircase to the two upper floors. There was room beneath the stairs and along the side. The rest of the stuff went there. It was cramped and claustrophobic, but it was temporary.

That weekend we also went shopping again, for things to fill the new apartment. I'd never known anyone to buy all new things when moving into an apartment; I'd never known anyone who could afford to do that. She did.

We went to furniture shops. At one we picked out a new brown leather sofa with white stitching. While at the same shop I'd described a brown leather bed frame with a tall padded headboard I'd once seen and liked. We looked in the store's catalog and they had one similar and she bought that too. We went to numerous bed stores. We laid down on this mattress and that mattress. We discussed what we liked. Finally she found one. At that store she also found a table, a dark wood kitchen table, and added it. She wanted a rug. The place had dark brown hardwood floors, she said. She wanted to warm it up with a large room rug. We went to a store South of Market (most of our shopping was done in SOMA, some in the Mission, and a little on Van Ness, that's where she'd found the mattress and table) and looked at several that hung from large racks. There were two or three we liked but nothing perfect so she decided to wait on that. We went to another store, in the Mission, just to check things out. Here she picked up two large gray ceramic pigeons, for bookends, or accent decoration, she said. It wouldn't occur to me to get those, I thought, but I liked them. There were some lights we thought were cool too in the shape of pussy willow branches. She got those to use as ambient room light, or nightlights.

It was a lot to do in one weekend, and before it was over we made one more stop.

Everything you need is at Costco, it's consumers' heaven, from groceries to flat screen TVs. That's mainly why we were there—for a TV. She picked one out, then filled the cart with more things. I just followed, pushing it all behind her. The only thing I suggested was a roast chicken for dinner. I went and got a nice fat one in its plastic bubble container and put it in the cart. Then we left, and it seemed like we were finally finished for the day. It was almost dinner time and I was hungry. We headed to the apartment, but as we got close she decided she wanted to go one more place, down in San Bruno. I didn't need to go, she'd said, if I was too tired. I told her I'd had enough for one day, and so she drove by the apartment and we unloaded the car and she went alone. I went inside and rested, waiting for her to come back so we could have dinner together. It shouldn't be long, she'd said.

I waited among the piles of boxes and bags in the living room. I waited and waited. Then a text came.

I picked up Jari on the way. Going to dinner with him and a girl friend of his.

I felt ditched. Like she couldn't wait for the chance to call Jari, like she'd planned it once she'd gotten rid of me. What did Jari need to go down to San Bruno with her for? We were going to have dinner together, I thought. I'd been waiting for her. OK change of plans, but why not ask if I wanted to go to dinner with them? At least she could've asked. After doing all that shopping with her, she'd *ditched* me!

I went home angry. We argued that night on the phone. She didn't see the big deal. She'd called Jari after she dropped me off just to see if he wanted to go with her, to keep her company, because he likes to go shopping like that and I don't, she said.

That wasn't true, I told her. I liked to shop with her. I liked to do almost anything with her, and she knew that, but I was worn out then and needed a break. And the friend? I asked.

371

On the way back to town Jari said he was going to have dinner with a girl friend of his, and she decided to join them. So?

Nothing, other than I was home waiting for her, and she knew that too.

I stayed home that night and let her sleep alone, instead of going back like she'd wanted.

By the next night I'd cooled off and we resumed. At the end of the week she was going back to Chicago. More procedures regarding her father. She was leaving Friday and was going to be gone for a week, then back the following weekend to move into her new place. That was the plan.

Friday morning, as we were leaving the apartment, I hugged her in the living room amidst the pile. She was going to drop me off at the 24th Street BART station, and then drive to the airport. We were saying good-bye properly now.

She looked around at the room as I held her in my arms.

It feels like we're breaking up, she whispered.

Immediately my mind flooded with the picture of that living room years before, stacked and piled with my girlfriend's things; it came at me all at once with that whisper, standing there in this packed room now, came at me like a deadly wave.

I pulled back and looked at her.

Don't say that! I said and held her close again, trying to squeeze the memory away by holding her body tightly to mine. She giggled.

She pulled the car over along Mission Street in front of the train station.

Thanks baby, I said, and kissed her. I love you, I said.

She smiled silently back. Then I got out and she drove away.

She'd had a cold a few days before and lost her voice. She could barely speak that morning, nothing above a whisper, now I felt like I was coming down with it. As usual we texted heavily while she was gone, especially the first couple days.

We need to have more sex when I come back, she wrote that

afternoon, the day she left.

I reminded her that she'd been sick, and that's why we hadn't done it much. I didn't want to catch it too, though I did anyway.

How is your cold? she asked. Are you kicking its arse?

That was a reference to Jari. He said words like arse.

No, I told her. But you were cute as a mute. Still not talking?

Getting better, but no.

I told her I was going to dinner in North Beach, at a new favorite pizza place of ours.

I really wish I was home going to North Beach with you tonight, she wrote.

Me too, I wrote back.

The next day I asked how she was.

I'm doing ok. How about you? How is your cold?

Pretty bad now. Stayed at your place.

That's good. I'm glad you stayed there. Hope you feel better. Miss you, she wrote.

Thanks honey, miss you too.

Then Monday she wrote to tell me she was going to do something she was sure I was not going to like. She was not coming back Friday as planned. Instead she was joining Jari and his friend, the one with the three-lettered verb of a name, in Scottsdale, Arizona, for baseball spring training.

I don't understand, I wrote. What happened to moving? I didn't know you were such a big baseball fan that you need to do that instead.

It's more of my need to take a short break from all my family stress. I have always wanted to see the cubs at spring training but have never gone. I will still move in on sunday afternoon instead of saturday afternoon.

She was right, I didn't like it. Felt like she was choosing Jari over me again, ditching me again. Her voice was back, we spoke on the phone. I reminded her of how Jari's friend tried to court her under my nose, told her I didn't like her spending the week-end around him.

That was all blown out of proportion, she said.

I didn't believe that to be the case. I didn't like it and again told her so. I couldn't hide my disappointment, and the pressing feeling of disrespect would not lift. Yet through the rest of the week she continued to send loving messages, as though no cleft had opened between us.

Hi babe, she wrote. What are you up to?

Going to bed soon, she said. Hope I get to talk to you tonight.

Hi love. How was your day? she asked. How's your cold?

Thursday, the day before she was to leave Chicago, she simply sent: New Pink toes!

Aside from not caring much about that, that message seemed frivolously out of place, dismissive, which I felt only served to push the distance drifting us apart, so I didn't respond to that one. But, shielded by the curve of fate, blind are we to the size some small things grow into given time. Only now do I see the significance tucked away in that text, the synchronistic sym-metry that apparently rules to taunt my life. Our last intimacy, as our first, in the seemingly innocuous image of her toes…

Then Friday came and she wrote to tell me she'd landed in Scottsdale. Great, I mumbled…but I didn't write back that time either.

The more I thought about it the more I hated she chose to do that, chose to be with them rather than wanting to come back to me. I fought it, tried to be big about it. She *had* been under a lot of stress lately. That was true. She deserved to blow some steam. I tried telling myself things like this but it was no good. I was hurt and angry. It didn't feel right. It felt like something else was going on. She was so excited to move into her new place and now she's postponing, going to the trouble to reschedule the mover on top of it—*to see the Cubs?* I couldn't remember ever hearing her even mention baseball before. My mind just couldn't get around this...

I stayed at her place in Noe Valley over the weekend. When she called Saturday morning I was still in bed. She sounded chipper, but the pauses in my speech were long, and my tone was heavy. I tried not to say it, but finally it came blurting out.

I just wish you would've come *back!*

Another pause, hers this time.

Roman, I had a really great time yesterday, she said finally. We went to the game. Then we played cricket. I really had fun.

That's great, I said. Good for you.

I asked if the Cubs were playing again that day, and she said no, they're done. Then why wasn't she coming back? I asked. Why was she waiting till Sunday to come? I want to hang out more with Jari and his friend, she answered. We're going to other games. Then we're gonna play more cricket.

I just didn't understand. It felt wrong. What cricket had to do with baseball I didn't know, other than the obvious Jari/Australian Culture connection. We ended the conversation.

Later that afternoon I walked down to the Mission Branch library on 24th Street, only a few blocks from the apartment. I wanted to get a travel book on Europe. I remembered my promise to myself, started thinking about a trip in May after the museum reopened. I was hoping to take a month off. I phoned her and asked if we could plan a trip together then. That text she'd sent about planning a trip, I'd said, we'd never talked about it when she got back to San Francisco. Would that be a good time then?

I can't go anywhere right now, she said, alluding to her father I supposed, about being available for her family. But why then had she sent that text wanting to plan a major trip at the beginning of his illness?

I was resolved to go myself.

When I left her place the following day, I looked at the roses in their vase on the kitchen table. They were dead now, hanging brittle and shrunken like desiccated hearts. I thought of throwing them away, but I left them right where they were for her to come home to. I took one last look around and knew I'd never see the place again.

Later that afternoon she called. She was home now. My voice was hard and refused to soften, and suddenly she shifted from the one she'd been using and said: How about asking how my father is, you *asshole!*

Then it came, as I felt it would. The moment I'd feared from the beginning.

I don't want this anymore!

When it finally came I went still. I could not respond. Something in me wanted said but I didn't know what. The words fluttered and swooped around inside like elusive moths, like the swallows outside the rafters' window. I did not want to lose her, but this couldn't go on, she'd made it so we couldn't go on, not like this. And she knew that when she didn't come home. She knew we'd have nowhere to go from here now, at the beginning of our life together.

Moments later she was picking me up because we needed to talk, she'd said. I got in the car and by now faint hope was feebly growing that somehow we would be able to work through this. I closed the car door behind me and reached over to her at the wheel and grabbed gently the neck of her hooded sweatshirt. She was wearing her darkblue ILLINOIS sweatshirt. I hadn't seen it in a long time. I took the material in my fist and leaned over to try to kiss her, to try to shift the icy flow of the situation, but she would not allow it, made her lips hard and turned her head and drove on.

We went to Dolores Park and sat on the grass in the sun. Echoes of the past boomed crazy in me. I remembered sitting there in that park shortly after my ex-girlfriend and I split too, talking about things like she and I were doing now, the park just over the hill from where her new apartment was on Church Street and from where this one was about to leave. It was March, the same month she'd left, too. The stuff piled in that living room, and the fact that she chose not to come home, these things sent shocks through me—and now this. Even some things she said were the same, like feeling she was losing herself to me, feeling like she had to change who she was to be with me—the other one said that, too. She hid herself in her hood as she spoke. She wouldn't look at me or let me kiss her when I tried, as if she no longer recognized me as the same man to whom she, until just a couple of days prior, had been sending loving messages, and because of this she was unrecognizable to me as well. She was altogether different now and I didn't know her. Her face remained lost in her hood and behind her sunglasses. But then her hood did come down. She threw it back as if dropping a disguise. How do you like my hair? she asked. I hadn't noticed in the car when she picked me up. It was red now. She'd colored it red while in Chicago, probably the same day when she wrote about her new pink toes. It was red and writhing alive in the wind, and the commingling was complete. An engulfing fusion passed darkly then, two coalescing into one deep dangerous hidden lake.

Then the list unreeled. On and on my mistakes and faults real or perceived first dripped then rolled a torrent off her tongue, her new decision-sharpened tongue, all the things she'd been secretly holding onto over the months.

You didn't even say I love you on my *birthday!* she said.

I heard that one many times.

On my *birthday!*

You didn't even want to move in together until you had a fight with your roommate.

Heard that one a lot, too. She kept coming back to that one among the others.

You left me at the *clinic* that day.

I had not known she felt like this, given the card she gave me that night. Though I felt guilty myself for leaving, out of obligetion, she'd never accepted that I'd left and that that alone was the reason.

My obvious confusion that night with the mover at Noe Street, that came back as well. I can't be with someone, she said, who doesn't have *com*mon *sense!...And*, she added, you clogged my *toilet!*

The toilet across from the bedroom at Noe had stopped up one day after my use. We'd gone for months without it, using only the one in the full bath instead because, as she put it, *you plugged it up!*—as if I'd perpetrated a calculated act against her comfort.

What am I *doing* in this re*la*tionship! she cried. While away in Chicago she'd suddenly taken stock of all the items ganged-up in her and asked herself that. What was she *doing* in this re*la*tionship!

Out of the long list of things she recounted, ultimately it was that I didn't tell her I loved her enough that seemed to sit so ingloriously atop, and on and on the list came. It was like a heavy chain that kept unrolling, one complaint locked to another and another and another until it reached the end finally, and when it did ground back and forth, reverse and forward, up then down again. And it was heavy and strong and though I tried there was no breaking it. The chain rolled on, crushing me, burying me beneath its weight...

A few hours later, a feeling of loneliness overwhelming me, I climbed down from the rafters and dressed again. It had cooled off some now, and the light was softening. I wanted to get out and walk, be around people.

I headed for the river. There was one place I needed to go before I left Paris. I crossed the river at Pont au Double and entered

Notre Dame. It was Saturday night and as expected the church swarmed with the usual tourist traffic, but there were more people in there than I thought I'd encounter. I quickly understood why.

The seats were filled, and those who couldn't find a seat stood crowding around. I spotted a chair open way in the back beside a pillar and made my way to it. I felt very lucky to have come at the right time. I'd never encountered a mass at Notre Dame before. The church was dark and cool and it felt very good to be in there; it felt good to be a part of this temporary community comprised of so many from around the world. Suddenly, if only for a moment, I no longer felt lonely. A perspective came into focus, that I belonged to something greater, that I was still a member of something larger.

The service went through its paces. We stood we sat then stood again, and I watched the people around me as the voice wafting through the PA system spoke, the source of which I could barely see I was so far back, and like at the other church couldn't understand anyway. But here, this time, it was the people about me that held my attention most. I was curious to see how those from different parts of the world expressed their reverence, and I watched them. One man particularly gripped my attention. He was a number of chairs wide of me and a couple rows behind, and when my eyes found him in the crowd they would not leave him. This man held his hands continually aloft. Sitting or standing his palms were raised above his head, up toward the ceiling as if in surrender—to the priest and his words, to his concept of God, to life itself perhaps, I didn't know, to all these maybe, but his hands never dropped and I couldn't take my eyes from him.

After a while, as the mass continued, I left my seat and wandered the sides of the church, having one last look at its beautiful interior. There were stations of candles burning, and here now was the circle of candles where we stood together and lit one a piece last time. Here now I knew was why I came tonight. I went to those candles and stood looking down into their light and felt their glowing warmth against my face. I picked up a lighting stick and borrowed the flame from the fire of one and carried it to another, lighting one for myself. It was June now, and the math was simple, and as I did last time I let the tears flow as I ignited the candle, and didn't care who saw them. I stared down at the flame of the candle I just lit and let the tears roll out of my eyes, because they needed to, because they should. I lit that candle for the life that would have entered the world, I lit it for me, for her, for us, and I watched it burn…

A man next to me at the bar in the brasserie when I was writing this, in the Marais, asked if I was writing for my job. I said no, it's just something I like to do. That I thought of it as my job, but it's not. He smiled and shrugged. Later when I put the notebook away he smiled again and asked: Enough writing for today? I said there could never be enough writing, but yes, enough for today, for now anyway. Well, he said, I hope you spend good time, that's what matters. I've tried, I said. What a fucking liar. It's been a waste from the start. There's been no healing, no living, only a despairing attempt to tourniquet the wound. Perhaps at some point I'll see it differently, look back and see some service from my time here, this record. Perhaps I'll realize it has helped the healing to come in the end, that it's all been necessary and never to be otherwise. All of it…Yet, I *have* tried, in my way, the only way I knew. The only way I could… Parish, if you waste this…I keep hearing Pike's words. I've heard them in my head the whole trip.

I've added that last paragraph while sitting at Place de l'Hotel de Ville. It's now 8:30 PM. I've watched the light change on the beautifully ornate Hotel de Ville from glaring white to warm yellow now. It's nearing sunset. There are the towers of Notre Dame across the river off to my left and behind me. Matice called a few minutes ago to apologize, said she'd like to see me tomorrow night, my last night here. I watch Hotel de Ville grow more golden. Girls pass, as they constantly do. Some beautiful, some not. Parish, if you waste this…

Sent her an email earlier. Shouldn't have done that, just gave her even more power. She's gone forever and has been for weeks. And now she's with someone else, and I am as if I was nothing. But I remember when I wasn't, what was said, what was done between us. I remember how she seemed to love me. How does it just go away? How do you willfully forget what has happened with someone you've loved? I can hear her voice as we went to bed at Noe Street. Ohhh babayyy…she'd say, turning breathlessly into my arms with relief under the covers, as if it was the best thing in the world, the thing she'd been waiting for all day. I hear her voice right now so clearly saying that. How does that go away? How can she not remember that?...The golden light has disappeared now and Hotel de Ville is a flat beige tone. Still grand, still beautiful, but a lifeless façade. Parish if you waste this if you waste this if you waste this…Too late, it's nearly gone. I've done what I came to do—sit in Paris, to be and write in Paris, to feel what it's like, and I was right after all. She did help return my words to me, as I felt she would. But these have not been the words I've wished for; these words are not the words I want…People pass on the sidewalk, some ride bikes, most walk by. The ornate streetlamp before me is beautiful. Behind me is the Seine. People cross the bridge to Ile de la Cité. Two girls stand at the short wall overlooking the river, leaning into the sunlight and breeze that blows back their long hair and skirts. The red awning of Bistro Marguerite across the street looks majestic, if streaked with caked-on dust. One of the most beautiful girls I've ever seen just passed taking a picture of Hotel de Ville—she looked Italian—with her boyfriend, of course. That's something that's happened a lot here, beautiful women passing with their boyfriends. Hotel de Ville is licked again by golden light. I raise my hands now palms up to the sky, raise them high and empty and open to this hide and seek sun.

Made in the USA
Las Vegas, NV
30 March 2021

20460825R00216